Absolute Truth

by

Chuck Radda

Acknowledgment

Every novel begins with an idea, a few sentences, and if the author is having a particularly good day, an actual paragraph. Everything after that is a bonus. For guiding me through those first tentative steps I am grateful to the Chimney Crest Writers: David Fortier, Dawn Leger, Frank DeFrancesco, Judy Giguerre, Linda Lynch, Don Paglia, Ira Morrison, and a host of others who have been part of our writing group. These are the people who saw Absolute Truth in its inchoate stages and encouraged me to continue. Dawn actually did double duty (sorry for the overmuch alliteration) examining the alleged final draft and informing me that it wasn't really that final. There were many others: Mary Galiette, who would rather have read historical fiction, asked significant and incisive questions that needed to be addressed; Jennifer Radda improved my geography, my nomenclature, and the Boston-area characters' vernacular; Tom Ward read Absolute Truth in a day, after which we shared a ninety-minute phone call's worth of suggestions and observations; and Jim Radda presented me with a new list of typos to sort through—after I was sure I'd already found every one. John Brookhouse and Cindy Satagaj offered some important guidance on cover design, John Galiette verified my color choice, and Chris Radda helped me maintain meteorological accuracy. The act of writing may be solitary, but everything afterward is not. And to all those who have read my previous novel Dark Time and offered so many kind words, I hope you enjoy this new effort as much. Finally—thanks to my wife Deanie who has read Absolute Truth in all its mutations and permutations at least a half-dozen times. Whenever there were holes in the narrative, she found them; whenever there was a breakdown in logic or consistency, there was a Post-it note to show me what and where and sometimes why. She has been meticulous, thorough, and patient—and always encouraging. Note: my use of "inchoate" in the first paragraph is an homage to my former English students who complained that even I would never use those vocabulary words they were forced to learn every week. It may have taken a while, but at least I used one of them.

For Deanie

ABBY

Abigail Bennett wondered if, just maybe, her cursing was becoming a problem. She could explain it, having been raised in a sanitized home with quasi-puritanical strictures informally placed on what was spoken, watched, even read. So she was compensating; that wasn't the problem. The problem was that her six-year-old Nicholas had already heard a few too many indelicate phrases and her subsequent admonitions about using them himself. Eventually the child was bound to slip up—no doubt in the most embarrassing situation—and tell some teacher or parent of a friend that it's okay because I heard Mommy say that. Then again, years from now the no-longer-six-year-old would learn how perfect the vernacular was for a situation like this—trying to get past Boston on 93 the Friday evening before Christmas with snow in the forecast and construction signs warning of trouble ahead. Nobody could endure that shit without filling the air, at least the air inside the car, with an f-bomb or two, especially since she had slipped out of work early to avoid these sorts of muddles. Worse still, she had yet to reach the Mass Pike and the Drayton Mall exit, where even without the Christmas insanity, traffic invariably backed up well onto the turnpike and a skein of last-second lane changes with their resultant accidents and near-misses frazzled everyone. But here she was stopped dead on 93 with orange construction cones squeezing her into a different lane. She reached for her cell and called home.

"Honey I know you're not there yet...Nicholas has a play date at the Tremonts' and you can pick him up or call them and see if he's staying for dinner. I was supposed to get him by five"—her voice grew shrill as she squeezed the cell tighter—"and they're saying snow so I'm not going out with my friends after all...not that I could anyway...'cause I'm stuck in fucking traffic because some MassDOT assholes decided road construction was a good idea on a Friday afternoon. Fucking morons!"

She exhaled loudly, then took a breath. Calmed herself.

"Sorry, hon, you're just the messenger. Don't play this if Nicholas is around. Love you."

She clicked off, then realized with some embarrassed amusement that, actually, she was the messenger. She thought about calling back to clarify—God knows she had the time—but Andrew would understand and probably have a good laugh while she…well now she was being squeezed left again. What if, she thought, what if the lanes kept disappearing until finally there were none and everyone came to a complete and permanent standstill. Maybe that's how the world would end—merging traffic winding up at a DOT barrier. Wouldn't that make a good story—mankind erased not by a zombie apocalypse or a rogue asteroid but a massive traffic jam. She would have to share that thought with Andrew when she got home. It would be even funnier after a glass or two of wine and after this particular annoyance was a slightly more distant memory.

She flipped on her signal light and immediately some holiday-spirited soul in a cobalt-blue pickup allowed her into the lane, offering a perfunctory wave. But when she waved a thank you in return, he didn't acknowledge. "He didn't see me wave," she thought. "Now he's pissed off that he let me in but I didn't thank him…even though I did. Asshole!" she screamed at the rearview mirror, but moved her lips only slightly. People these days could read lips, and too many drivers casually tossed guns into their glove compartments, waiting to shoot ingrates like Abigail Bennett who willingly accepted little kindnesses and offered nothing in return.

She lost track of the blue pickup long before arriving at the construction site—not a site at all but merely an orange dump truck with a flashing arrow and more cones. No heavy machinery. No workers. Just orange cones and an idling dump truck, idling with the gasoline she paid for with her fucking taxes. She drifted to the left a bit and felt the thump of thick rubber under her tire—that was one cone they'd have to refurbish. She entertained the thought of knocking over a few more, but if a cop saw her—well, one errant maneuver might be a mistake, but the second would look like a DUI. She pulled to the right and moments later, once again traveling at highway speed, noticed the first traces of snow begin to slant past her low beams.

A white Christmas. Or white-ish, at least. Nicholas's skepticism about Santa Claus had not taken hold just yet, and if the old guy was going to show up somehow, a covering of snow would lend credibility to the arrival.

For Abigail herself, snow meant a virtual lockdown. She didn't drive in the stuff—didn't even consider it. In college she had spun out on a slippery road and wound up facing the wrong way on a street devoid of traffic. She had hit nothing or no one, but as for her mental state when she finally spun to a stop, she might just as well have forced a busload of children off a bridge. She called her father. He called AAA. A tow truck arrived. The driver, accommodating to a fault, turned her car around for her so that it faced the right direction, but he could not tow a non-disabled vehicle without police authorization (often the upshot of a DUI arrest) and finally convinced her to drive home, promised to follow and make sure she arrived safely. Abigail was sure he'd been laughing all the way, but she didn't care. The decade since that incident had not emboldened her at all: at the first mention of snow in the forecast, she had abandoned plans to meet friends for drinks after work.

The cancellation bothered her. Such occasions seemed to present themselves less and less often, and the friends with whom she had grown up—many of them still single—had stopped calling, perhaps having heard enough excuses about a husband working late, or a child with the sniffles, or some studies and recommendations that needed to be examined by morning. At times she missed those occasions with "the girls," but as the focus of her life centered more and more on her expanded family and thoughts of having another child began to play on her mind—and Andrew's—she had trouble summoning any real regret. Now she had some new friends, career- if not family-oriented, and they understood that a night spent sloshing Margaritas at some trendy bar meant a bad day of work ahead.

Friends like Brianna Cooper from the paper. Not much of a paper—the *Courier*—a weekly that often wound up going directly from people's driveways to their trash cans, but it had been a local custom for so long that some read it almost out of respect. And Brianna herself was pleasant enough company. Maybe she talked a bit too much about her fucked-up family life, but people's conversations always gravitated toward what upset them the most. The woman had no real interest in being set up with anybody, male or female—though if even a small portion of Brianna Cooper's confessed Friday-night exploits bore any truth—it wasn't females she was interested in.

At any rate, canceling had been a good decision. By the time Abby reached her driveway—several miles from the warm and well-traveled pavement of the Interstate—she could discern specks of white on mailboxes and bushes. She reached up, touching a button that sent the double garage door on its upward motion, and drove inside. No car in the adjoining space—despite the bottleneck, she was home first. She picked up her laptop from off the passenger side floor, then popped the trunk to retrieve the abundance of financial detritus she had volunteered to wade through over the weekend. The paperless society had not reached her.

Standing in the garage with the door still raised, she could actually hear the snow. All those poems about silent flakes—they weren't true, especially when they struck the scattering of oak leaves that had stubbornly survived a spate of November windstorms. She slammed the trunk closed and turned to retrieve the day's mail. Several feet away a large figure stood.

"You're Abigail Bennett."

She gasped.

"Jesus Christ! What the hell?"

"I had some questions for you."

"You can't be here—you can't come to my home."

"You turned me down. I made a convincing presentation, a logical request, and you turned me down."

"I...listen, the bank has rules. You can't just bop over here..."

"...And you bend them. I know that. I've seen it plenty of times."

"I don't have that authority. If you'd like to set up another appointment with a bank officer, maybe Monday...."

"You could have fixed this hours ago. You chose not to. You were the deciding vote."

"I know that. I didn't think the request was appropriate, given all the factors."

"You don't know the factors," he said, his voice nearly a shriek. "You don't know a goddamn thing. You sit behind that desk all day and ruin people's lives. You don't even know my name."

That much was true. She'd been called in to help with the decision, had scanned everything briefly, had seen enough red flags to engender a denial. No, she didn't remember his name, but she made her decisions based on data, not emotion.

"I'm sorry," she said. "I looked at the papers."

"Well you should have looked at me," he said, then took a step closer.

She reached into her purse to find her cell, to end this, but he grabbed her arm.

"Leave it alone."

She pulled away, began rummaging again.

And then she was on the ground, sheets of paper surrounding her, the phone from her purse several feet away. He stood over her.

"I didn't want much, did I? Couple hundred thou? I know your assets—that's a small loan for you people. It would have been like just another mortgage."

"Your previous loan," she said the details returning. There had been a default, or a delay, or something that made him a bit too much of a risk. Reminding him of those considerations would only make things worse.

"I was paying it off."

"Yes, that's true," she said. She searched for his name, couldn't remember. Maybe if he had been more demanding or angry when he was denied that loan— but he had been docile, polite, had thanked them for their time, wished them a happy holiday, and left.

"Listen," she said, "let me bring it up again on Monday."

She pushed herself to her feet and took a step toward the cell, now dampened by melting snow..

He held her arm again.

"I didn't come here to hurt you. I just wanted to know why."

"Perhaps another lending institution could help?"

"Tried them all. Begged them all. What's next, a loan shark? Thirty-five percent interest. Is that my option, because I already have that option."

"As I said, I can try...."

"No you won't."

He let go of her arm, looked defeated. So he had threatened her and intimidated her but she had held fast. Now he was ready to give up, go home, leave her.

"I shouldn't have come," he said. "I didn't think this through."

"Sometimes we make mistakes," she said, sounding conciliatory, utilizing her workplace demeanor. Finally it was about to end. This was the way he had been in the office—just a quiet supplicant being turned down. It was never pleasant, but it did happen.

Then, without warning, he struck her full across the face. Her right hand went to her ear where an earring seemed to drive itself into her brain. She yelled in pain. He struck her again in the same spot.

"If I had thought this through," he said, then stopped, struck her again, this time catching the tip of her nose as she pulled back. She could taste blood.

"I'm bleeding."

"Shut up. Just shut up. Don't say anything else. Nothing. I have to think."

The pain radiated out from the side of her head, the metallic taste sickened her. Instinctively she darted toward the open garage—but only a step or two before he caught her, wrapped an arm around her neck, pulled her back. She stumbled, fell again.

"I told you," he said. "I told you."

She sat in silence, sat in the wet and cold. He would leave soon enough—then a hot shower and a trip to the dry cleaners would fix everything. But now her head ached—the dull pain coming on suddenly—and she began to feel nauseated, her eyes were losing focus.

"Can you call my husband at work," she said to him. Apparently she had misplaced her cell. "Andrew Bennett. His extension…."

All those numbers she could repeat in her sleep now sounded strange and jumbled. She tried again, produced nothing intelligible, like a roll of the dice, or a spin of a roulette wheel, or a draw from a card deck—nothing but random digits that she could not fit into their proper order. What good was this guy's cell phone? What good was hers? And *where* was hers?

The scene around her raced ahead, frame after frame in rapid succession like some old black and white movie speeded up to amuse the audience. With all the effort she could, she slowed the stream, tried to focus on individual panels, turned the movie into a leisurely slide show clicking from frame to frame.

Andrew behind the wheel. (Click)

Andrew turning into their street. (Click)

The car in the driveway. (Click)

Headlights off. (Click)

Door opening. (Click)

Walking toward the house. (Click)

She paused the pictures—held them right there and, under control again, waved furiously.

So her husband had seen her after all—maybe he'd been there all the time. Had the other man left? Run off? Been frightened by the approaching headlights?

Just to be sure she tried to move to the next slide, the next frame, but the mechanism no longer worked. Her husband seemed locked and frozen into that last slide somewhere. He was probably taking in the scene for a while, smiling at the minor misfortune—that had to be it. Soon he'd help her into the house and open that new Cabernet they'd been meaning to try. They'd laugh at the stupidity of it all—slipping and falling in the driveway—a child's accident. Maybe they would even make love—Nicholas would not be home for a while and they'd have the house to themselves...and the wine...and that snow falling outside. Perfect.

But on top of everything else, Jesus, she had wet herself like some old lady in a rest home. The urge took her by complete surprise, but she felt the urine spreading, soaking through her underwear, her skirt, even her coat. No one wants to make love to a woman who pees her pants. She'd have to get in there first, clean up.

Then there were no more slides. There was no Andrew. No fireplace. No wine. Her head had become a slow-motion muddle of snow and phone numbers and stinging pain and embarrassment and the smell of urine permeating everything. She lay back—her legs splayed weirdly like a discarded doll's. She forced open her eyes and saw a shadow and a movement, saw another assault but felt nothing. Asleep but restless, she yelled dreamcurses at the driver of that flashing DOT truck on the highway—the one that made her late—the one that made her so tired that she needed to rest. Dreamcurses. Were they becoming a problem too?

And in that chaotic and disjointed muddle, she remembered his name.

At some distant reaches of her senses she felt another blow to her neck, and when yet another opened her skull, exposing the unprotected thoughts to the winter sky—all conscious and unconscious thought, curses and dreamcurses, numbers and cell phones, husbands and sons and familiar voices—ended together in a place where nobody moved anymore...with barricades, flashing lights, nothing.

Chapter 1

When I was twenty—far too young to be evaluating my life—I made a list of things I didn't like about myself. I avoided the superficial—my nose was a bit crooked, my voice had people offering me lozenges, my hair was pretty much brown but not as auburn as I would have liked, I was small-breasted and short-necked, I had two slightly over-prominent front teeth. There was probably more, but I'd have to go back to my old journals and check...which I can't do while I'm driving to work.

The point is I ignored those superficial weaknesses, concentrating instead on my over-sensitivity to criticism, my tendency to go my own way and ignore advice, my antagonism toward my family, and my willingness to size up people before they had a chance to prove themselves. That last weakness does, however, frequently turn out to be less bothersome than the rest.

That was seven years ago. In the interim no nose job, or speech therapy, one or two expensive (but ultimately useless) colorists, no breast implants, or major dental work. And if there's such a thing as neck elongation, I haven't had that either. I'm the same. Just older. But in those other areas, the non-superficial ones, unfortunately I'm also the same. And what worries me is that when I'm forty, fifty, however long life expectancies are supposed to be for a 27-year-old single woman with a college degree and a full-time job and a second-hand Subaru—what worries me is the list won't change—neither the "to-do" side nor the "completed" side. For all the talk about taking charge of our lives, I'm afraid our lives take charge of us. And though we may look for and talk about and genuinely seek growth, change, development, etc., I wonder if any of those items is attainable. I wonder if there'll be a Saturday morning in 2040 when I'm driving to work and, for instance, finally give up and decide to have my teeth fixed.

•••••

Most of Friday night's meager snowfall has melted by morning. Maybe because I'm from Maine where the roads are slippery from October to May, I don't pay that much attention to bullshit weather warnings. But others do, and so the prospects of some pre-holiday bitching and moaning with friends dissolved into an evening at home alone sending out résumés. It's what I do.

The traffic on Rte. 9 is unusually light—just the usual coffee crowd spilling out of the Dunkin' drive-thrus every half mile or so. And things will stay that way until the weekend shoppers remember they've got four days to settle Christmas and race off in a new panic. In an hour or so this road will look a lot less appealing.

Saturdays are pretty light days at the *Courier* and I don't mind working weekends. Besides, I used to waste Saturdays gulping down aspirin at 6:00 a.m. while trying to convince some naked guy in my bed that just because I was willing to fool around drunk at midnight didn't mean I was ready for a sober, morning-after encore—though he usually got one anyway, especially if the original performance had been satisfactory. But since I began working Saturdays, I'm a little more careful about my Friday night encounters—in several ways. As a result, only once in the past year have I fallen asleep at my desk.

That "date" wasn't worth it either, but never do you want to fall asleep at my desk. The joke is, and it's not much of a joke, that the desk once belonged to a Steven Resnick, a reporter who spent most of his adult life laboring obscurely for this weekly before slumping over and dying one afternoon at the age of sixty. Aside from a few poofs of Lysol after the "event," I doubt if anyone made an effort to remove the stigma, imaginary or otherwise.

Steven Resnick had been somewhat of an institution at the *Courier*. I'm not sure exactly what that means, but the title probably isn't as prestigious as it sounds. People here in Drayton, like everyone else in the Northeast, read the *Globe* if they can pry themselves away from their tablets and smartphones long enough to read any newsprint at all. Faneuil Hall, Fenway, the Common—they're all less than a half hour from here, and when I'm traveling somewhere outside Massachusetts, I tell people I'm from Boston. It's only when I'm actually here that I differentiate, you know, like "I had dinner in the North End then drove over to Jamaica Plain to meet some friends from Allston." My point is—and it took me too long to get there, something which Grumman, my boss, is always harping about—if you want the news and you don't want to gather it wirelessly or have it diluted or candy-coated by some pretty young thing on television, you're not going to race out for a *Courier*, not if there's a *Globe* nearby.

Even up in Maine where we had the *Press Herald* delivered daily like everyone else in Portland, my Dad would pick up a *Globe* on the way to work. I'm not sucking up for a job there—they have my résumé just like every other paper in the western hemisphere—they don't need me, not when they can lure the grads who've excelled at Northwestern and Syracuse while I was eking out decent grades at best from various community colleges in southern Maine before finally finding enough ambition to achieve an actual degree. My type of underachiever winds up on the *Drayton Courier* covering scout meetings, interviewing octogenarians, and navigating corn mazes every fall.

But I'm still better off than I was two years ago when I spent my twenty-fifth birthday clerking at an outlet in Kittery, Maine, having lost my seasonal job at a Chamber of Commerce kiosk in Kennebunk a few miles north. Nobody was better than I at directing people to the spot where George Bush One spends his summers, while never letting on that the Secret Service allows no one to come within a mile of it anyway.

I'm also better off because I like to write. I must have been ten when I told my Aunt Christine I had written a story and she replied without the least uncertainty, "Wonderful, now you can be an English teacher or a newspaper reporter." In retrospect I'd have been happier if she had said, "Can I read it?" I'd also have been happier if I had checked the authenticity of her suggestion or even paid a modicum of attention to career counseling sessions. But she was my favorite aunt, and that statement of hers stuck—English teacher or newspaper reporter. Now I sure as hell wasn't going to stand up in front of thirty students immersed in various stages of passivity, hostility, lust, or simple ennui: left with but one option, I took it. Aunt Christine is probably more pleased than I am.

Obviously, bitching about one's job has supplanted baseball as the great American pastime, so let me list the good stuff about this one. First off, the *Courier* doesn't have a police reporter, a social reporter, an education, political, or national reporter. There's me. And I live fifteen minutes from the office and eighty miles from my mother. It's the perfect amalgam of proximity and distance, especially with the holidays approaching.

And Grumman, the guy I mentioned before, that's Dan Grumman. He's a good man, but like my predecessor he's going to die here. He won't collapse in his chair in mid-afternoon—it won't be that dramatic. He has lung cancer—was diagnosed about a year ago—and I don't see how he can stay on that much longer. Even worse, if there's an even worse after some doctor tells you you're going to die, he's watching the paper die with him. Despite his condition, he comes in early and leaves late. Usually, though, he's sequestered in his office, the only proof of his existence the occasional coughing spasm. This morning I walk in and find him leaning against a jamb in his office doorway. His eyes are grim—those the-doctor-says-I-have-lung-cancer eyes that haven't brightened much since the diagnosis. I glance around to find my only two colleagues transfixed by their computer screens. Something else is wrong—no story can be that riveting.

I position my stainless steel travel mug on the desk and unwrap my scarf, but before I can get out a good morning, Grumman motions me into his office.

"Come on," he says, "you can bring your tea."

"What's going on?"

He doesn't answer. I grab the mug and follow him. Inside his office he stands near the only natural light source, a narrow four-paned window practically opaque from the dust and exhaust from the adjoining parking lot. His body says nonchalance; his face says otherwise. I take a sip of the tea—it's still boiling hot.

"Not much of a snowstorm after all, huh?"

I shake my head—Dan Grumman doesn't do small talk. He doesn't chat. Instead of trying more of it and failing further, he motions me into a chair before sinking behind his desk. Dan Grumman isn't a big man, well under six feet, and his hours and his smoking kept him thin until the cancer accelerated the process. Now he looks frail at times, even more so in the poorly lit and shadowy office.

"Sir, you wanted to see me...about something?"

"Yeah, Bree, I did."

With Grumman it's usually Coop when he's casual and Bree when he's avuncular, though he varies. Brianna is a difficult name to shorten, though I had once been seeing a guy who liked to call me Anna. One night I told him I preferred Brianna or Bree and an argument, all out of proportion to the subject, began and carried on sporadically for days. When it was over—when we were over—I wondered why I had endured the jerk for so long, and he probably wondered pretty much the same thing about me.

Grumman stretches his hands. I hear a knuckle crack.

"I wasn't sure you'd be in," he says.

"I was supposed to go out with friends last night, but that fell through. You knew I was coming in, didn't you?"

"I thought...have you heard any news this morning?"

"I usually listen to music in the car…probably not a good idea for a reporter, but I…."

He holds up a hand to stop me, exhales loudly, picks up a pencil as if he's going to write something, then lays it down.

"Look, Bree, there's no easy way to say this."

Someone's dead. My first thought is my folks. They're still pretty young, but who knows? And accidents never discriminate by age. But no, no matter how strained my family relationships are, I'd have found out before some news service picked up the story. So it's the paper. Dailies are shutting down everywhere, and the *Courier*—hell, we're just a weekly. That's it then—we're out of business and I'm out of work. But when I ask him, he shakes his head.

"Abigail Bennett. She's your friend, right?"

"Abby? We were supposed to go out last night but we canceled. Why?"

He keeps hesitating and my mind keeps racing. Like a lot of people in the western suburbs, Abby commutes every day to the North Shore, always on the highways, roads filled with accidents. Factor in the lunacy of a Friday evening, add a little snow, maybe some drunk driver careening home from a holiday party. We were worried about slippery roads and now….

"No easy way to say this," Grumman says...again. "Her husband found her dead last night."

People gasp at times like that—if I did I don't remember it. He gets up and closes the office door as I stare at that filthy window and let the words slowly take shape. Found her dead. Found? Jesus, she's my age. Found her dead? Not an accident? My mouth feels dusty but I try to choke out a syllable or two.

"How? Where?"

Grumman goes to the water cooler, fills a small cup, brings it to me, and puts it down. I don't want water.

"They think she was murdered," he says. "They don't know for sure."

"They *think* she was murdered? How does that happen, I mean someone is murdered or she isn't. You don't think it."

He waits. My last comment has undoubtedly been heard out in the main office. If they were uncomfortable before, I haven't ameliorated the situation. Still he waits—he wants me to calm myself before I say anything else, but I can't.

"Where did they—where did Andrew find her?"

"That's her husband, right? Andrew? In their driveway, last night about 7:00. The police think when she got home from work that maybe someone was waiting for her. It might have been a robbery. It's early on—they don't know."

Those stages of grief everyone talks about—I walk right up and grab the first one.

"It has to be a mistake."

He shakes his head.

"Was she shot?"

"No, it was pretty bad I guess."

Pretty bad? Jesus, shot is pretty bad. This was somehow worse? My hands start to move toward my stomach which has seemingly come loose somehow, moving about on its own. Grumman looks lost: he may be the voice of maturity and experience, but he's run out of hard information and doesn't know what to do next.

"Was she raped?"

"No," he says. "She was stabbed, cut with something."

"Something?"

"A knife, most likely. They don't know for sure."

"God!" I can't tell if I'm more sad or angry. Any loser can kill someone with a gun, but a knife takes force, intent, hatred. Then I wonder if there's more.

"What about her son?"

"No one else was hurt."

"I don't mean that. I mean, was he there? Did he have to see it?"

"Her husband found the body when he got home. She'd been dead awhile. I don't know about their son."

"And nobody called me? I had to wait to come in to work to find out?"

"I didn't know," he says. "I doubt if other friends knew. Police just started releasing information. There were even neighbors who didn't know what was going on. The cops needed to make a positive ID, notify next of kin, that sort of thing."

"What kind of bullshit is that? She was found by her next of kin."

"I'm only telling you what I heard."

"And it's bullshit. This is on the cops for holding back."

"Bree, listen. They wanted to notify her parents too."

"They live on the North Shore. Cops could have walked there."

"I don't know the details."

"Okay. Okay." Some sort of inertia is stifling my movements. Then somehow I send a signal to my legs and they manage to receive it. I'm standing.

"I should get over there, do some interviews. I mean to the *Globe*, well it's, you know, it's just another murder, and the services and the Internet, it's...we should be there."

"Sit down."

"The cops will be...."

"Sit. Now."

I lean on the chair and he realizes that's the best he's going to get.

"It's Saturday. There's not much to do here, not really. Go home, get yourself together. Her family might want you to be there later but not as a reporter. You were good friends, right?"

"You met her once."

"I remember," he says. "She came to pick you up one day. You were going to lunch or something. She was pretty. She seemed nice."

"She is nice!"

He looks apologetic and I feel stupid...as if changing the tense is going to alter the truth. Besides he's been handed a death sentence—if anyone is past all the theoretical aspects of living and dying, it's Grumman.

"Listen, Bree, are you all right to drive. I can have Arlene...."

"I'm not driving, I'm working. Could they have mistaken Abby for someone else?"

"You mean the murderer? Sure, anything is possible. Could have been a burglary gone bad. Like I said...listen, you know the cops. You know what they'll ask. Was there anything going on that...maybe would have put her in danger?"

"Such as?"

"Something secret in her life."

I'm still struggling between anger and sorrow, and for the moment, the anger wins out.

"What the hell kind of question is that?"

"The kind any good cop will ask...and any good reporter."

"There was nothing."

"A drug problem? Alcohol? Gambling? An affair? Some one-night stand gone sour?"

"You don't know her. That's not Abby."

"That's not anybody until it is. Cops will ask," he says, "and they'll ask her friends, too. Be prepared."

What's equally true—and he knows it—is that I would not have been privy to anything a friend wanted to keep from me. The last time I had a good friend I told "everything" to, I was in seventh grade and she stole my boyfriend. We all become a little more secretive as we get older—Abby's personal life seldom intersected with mine. It's not unusual among friends.

"Anyway," he says, "why don't you call your Mom and have her come down. When she hears it on the news...."

"She has my cell number. Driving all the way down here will just screw up her Saturday morning."

Grumman frowns. "Maybe at a time like this...."

I tell him no, that my mother is not interested in what happens to my friends when they're alive, let alone after they're dead. He isn't comfortable with the irreverence, but he's grown accustomed to it when it regards my family. *At a time like this*—it's of absolutely no consequence.

I pick up the mug and he walks towards the door with me.

"I'm not sending you out there as a reporter," he says.

"I know, but I think I need to be one."

My laptop and purse are on the desk where I left them. Nobody else in the outer office says anything. I know they're sad for me and there's always that palpable discomfort being around grieving people. I try not to dwell on the fact that they're lucky: they get to carry on with their lives, their work, their holiday plans. I have other responsibilities on this shitty December morning. Abby Bennett is dead.

I make a quiet departure and drive maybe a mile before I find myself weeping, shaking. I pull off the road into a convenience store parking lot and wait for the outburst to pass...for my eyes to clear and my focus to return. When did Abby and I last speak? A week ago? Longer? Of course she called a few nights before and I saw her name on the readout, but I was involved in something and let it go to voice mail, certain I'd get back to her. I never did. And our plans to meet for a drink last night—just a couple of texts back and forth. There were other girls going with us—I don't even have their names or their cells. By now they probably know about the murder and, even if they wanted to, couldn't reach me. Friends of a friend—nothing more. And for that matter, Abby and I weren't that close, though there was a connection that would have grown over time. Sometimes you can tell.

I pound on the steering wheel, as if such a display of muted violence will somehow assuage my frustration, then I turn the key and continue on. An all-news station in Boston has picked up the story and some commentator who has to fill an hour with five minutes of facts drivels on about the lack of suspects and the tragedy of it. There aren't enough events out there to keep an all-news station on the air, so after the initial summary, the human interest bullshit begins. And with a child left behind there'll be enough psychologists to keep the story current for days, especially with Christmas so near. I resent it, of course, though I'm in the same crummy business and I've done the same crummy thing.

Grumman asked about gambling, drugs, lovers. Abby and I may not have been close, but I knew her well enough: if there were skeletons in her closet, they were pale and powdery. He didn't ask the more obvious question: would Andrew Bennett have murdered his wife? We've read enough homicide reports to know the validity of the question, and some cop who wants a quick commendation will zero in on the easiest target and hope for that big payoff, the splashy headline, maybe a promotion. I need to talk with Andrew. I need to do it before someone like Karl Brandt does.

Most of the Drayton cops are good people. Then there's Brandt. A case like this will end up on his desk and he'll tend to it in his usual ham-handed manner—one that doesn't interfere too much with his drinking and whoring. Grumman once joked that Karl Brandt represents law enforcement the same way Dr. Frankenstein represents the medical profession; but even so, the thought of a creep like that interrogating a friend makes me drive a little faster. I can't rescue Andrew from his misery—it's too late for a heroine—but at least I can warn him that, as awful as this day is, it can get even worse.

Chapter 2

Standish Road is choked with police cars. At the makeshift blockade I show my press pass and some cop I don't know waves me through, but I wave back and drive away: I have no idea what I'm going to say to Andrew Bennett. When I return moments later, the same uniform gives me a curious look, then waves me through a second time. In my rearview mirror I can see him eyeballing me all the way, and then more new cops—unfamiliar faces. The locals are probably stretched well past their limits, so I'm probably looking at crews from other towns. At the front walk I actually have to show my press pass to a female officer. I check her uniform—she's from Lynn.

"You came a long way," I say to her.

"Half hour. I'm allowed to speed."

"At least you got your name on your uniform, huh?"

"Haven't heard that one before," she says without the disdain my lame comment deserves. "Bad deal here. What paper you from?"

"The *Courier*. We're a local weekly." The words sputter like an excuse.

Crime tape blocks the driveway and a young cop does sentry duty near the front door. He probably figures if I got that close I'm legit, so he pushes open the door to let me pass. And I see the carpet—before anything else. It's beige—or it was before it was trampled by mud-caked and snow-encrusted shoes. And there are other stains too, brownish but tending toward red. Dried blood perhaps, maybe tracked in by Andrew himself. I don't know what I imagined but already this is much worse.

Andrew Bennett himself slumps on an oversized couch, the collar on his crumpled white shirt unbuttoned and his pale blue tie hanging loosely about his neck. It doesn't take a reporter's eye to figure out he hasn't slept or changed. Alone like that he looks as though he's contracted some virulent and contagious disease and needs to be quarantined. The reality of it isn't that much different.

He sees me and starts to rise but I stop him with a gesture. He doesn't know who I am, not immediately. We've met three or four times, probably uttered a hello and goodbye with little in between, enough so that he associates me with Abby and now he's trying to retrieve a name from the sudden disarray of his life.

"Bree," I tell him. "Abby's friend...from the paper."

"Yes, Bree," he says. "I'm really glad you came."

He sounds almost drunk—complete exhaustion probably has that effect.

"This is so sad," I say, as if he somehow didn't know that. But I've come to hate the overly comfortable "sorry for your loss," though you know, goddamn it, sometimes it fits. I was sorry for his loss, and his son's, and mine.

He holds up his cell phone and opens it. The screen emits some lurid gray shading.

"I called all the relatives first," he says. "This thing has to be charged. All the cops are in there…."

He motions toward the kitchen. At first I don't know why I need any of that information, but then I get it: he's apologizing for not calling me. Of course I'd be on Abby's call list—not his—but I slough it off and make my own apology for being late. Then I ask him if there's a charger handy because I'm going to be all over that task—I can't bring his wife back or even express my sorrow in any appropriate manner, but that fucking cell phone is going to get charged really good.

In the kitchen there's a group of law enforcement people—some uniforms, some plainclothes, no Karl Brandt—and they treat me like a mourner as I pass by. There's a charger coiled on a counter near the microwave. "Just gonna grab this," I tell them, and I leave with my little trophy as if I had located a lost diamond, then waste another minute or two finding an outlet and plugging it in. I'm doing a fine job of avoiding the issue and Andrew is a perfect accomplice. One of the uniforms takes a few steps into the room from the kitchen and he and I make brief eye contact before he leaves again. I can't remember his name but he's a local. I grip Andrew's wrist loosely and ask about their son.

"He was at a friend's when it happened," he says. "He's with my mother now."

"It's good that he can be away from the house," I tell him. "All this…the police, everything…it would just scare him more."

"There was a phone message from Abby when I got home," he says, and I realize he's more interested in retelling the story than addressing my meaningless observations. Maybe it's cathartic, I don't know. "She was so pissed off. Traffic. Construction. You know how impatient she can be."

He smiles a little, but his face clouds over again immediately, his eyes half-closed as he trudges along.

"By the time I picked up the message she was already...home. The car was in the garage. I thought maybe she'd gone down the street to pick up Nicholas. You know, I must have walked right past her. All I had to do was look around. I was home for an hour before...before I started calling people at her job. I thought with the holidays coming up, you know, an impromptu party...."

"There was probably nothing you could have done."

"You don't know that," he says, his voice swelling in anger, as mine did with Grumman. Others have probably said the same thing and he's tired of hearing it. No doubt he will go to his grave believing he could have prevented Abby's murder or somehow saved her life after she had been attacked if he had left work early, driven faster, checked the yard for crime, etc. My disputing the issue will serve no purpose.

"You called the police?"

"I dialed 9-1-1 as soon as I found her. I tried some CPR, at least what I remembered how to do. It was too late."

"And nobody saw anything? Neighbors? Anyone?"

"Nothing. There was so much blood."

I avoid the temptation to look at the carpet.

"I guess with the darkness and all...."

"Well of course the cops think I did it," he says, forcing a laugh. "As soon as they know it wasn't me, they'll get on with it, maybe find out who's really responsible."

"Did Detective Brandt talk to you?"

"Who's he?"

"He usually takes the lead. He wouldn't have been wearing a uniform."

"Some hot shot in a sport coat and work boots came by an hour ago. Asked a lot of insulting questions."

"Probably him. He can be a little overbearing."

"I don't think he cared one way or the other. He just paced around like he had someplace to be."

"Then he probably knows he's wasting his time questioning you. That's probably a good sign—he's a pretty smart cop."

And that much is true. My aversion to the guy as a human being shouldn't reflect upon his work as a professional. He's put a lot of bad guys away, inasmuch as we have legitimate bad guys in Drayton. But Andrew Bennett seems unmoved by my analysis, and I don't much blame him. I take out a small note pad while his attention is focused on someone else. I know I told Grumman I was going as a friend, but there's something instinctive that makes me more comfortable as a reporter.

"Andrew, don't be afraid to say no, but can I ask you some questions on the record?"

"Sure," he says. "Phone calls at odd hours, unexplained late nights, that sort of thing. I told Brandt there was none of that. I'm sure every cheating husband denies those things, or every husband with a cheating wife, but as far as I know nothing was going on. Of course I could be lying to you; she might have been lying to me."

"Well I believe you both."

Even a first-year journalism student would know that's a self-damning statement for any reporter to make, yet it slips out with incredible ease. To gain some credibility for myself I ask him about enemies at work, ill will over a promotion, maybe something trivial like a sick day or a coffee-room argument. She worked at a bank on the North Shore, HR mostly but other functions too— lots of opportunities for interpersonal relationships to go south. She probably saw a lot of new faces every week—maybe one of them didn't like hers. But no, nothing.

"Her wallet was inside her purse," he says. "Nothing seemed out of place. They say it wasn't a rape."

He stands up, as if the seat has suddenly become excruciatingly uncomfortable, and walks over to the fireplace where he lifts a poker out of the stand and drags it back and forth through some of the ashes. "I think Brandt thought this was the murder weapon—I could tell by the way he picked it up."

"All the forensics people will be outside. If that's still by the fireplace and untagged, he's ruled it out. And if you're allowed to touch it, then nobody's concerned with it."

"They told me there was no sign of sexual assault as if that were some sort of good thing. When someone's dead, what difference does it make what happened before?"

His voice has grown louder, angrier. I have never seen him that way and, maybe because I don't know him very well, I feel better when he puts the poker back into the stand. The eye-contact officer peeks around the corner.

"Everything all right in here?" He asks me, but he's staring at Andrew.

No, nothing's all right and we all know it. It's then that I notice the Christmas tree, fully decorated, unlit. I stopped romanticizing Christmas many years ago—a family tragedy when I was ten ruined it that year, and my family has prevented me from overcoming that memory by making an annual mess of it. But there's a child in this house who hasn't reached my level of cynicism yet, and the thought of Abby's son forever associating Christmas with the murder of his mother is more than I can stand. I slide the pad back into a pocket and head for the bathroom just as my eyes begin to moisten, but I don't get more than a few steps when a woman in a charcoal-grey suit stops me. Her hair is pulled way back and her white blouse is buttoned to the throat like a nun. It's one of Abby's sisters—I just can't remember the name.

Andrew stands up and I force myself to stop sniffling, though my eyes are already wet.

"You know Shelley, right?" Andrew says. "She and I are going to the funeral home. Why don't you come with us?"

"That would be good," the sister says, but she looks apologetic. She thinks I'd rather not and she's fine either way. "Sorry," she says, "I think I stopped you on your way to freshen up?"

"Yes, thanks," I tell her and leave them both. She's absolutely right—I'd rather not accompany anyone anywhere—but I agree to come along. I hope it's not the reporter in me looking for some angle, but I'm never sure.

I have nothing to say in the ten-minute drive, and once we sit down with the funeral director, I'm totally superfluous. Shelley is better at this than I'll ever be—making decisions with a businesslike acuity and an air of detachment while still including Andrew in the conversation. The casket, the grave liner, the vault—it all goes way beyond simple wood/metal/color choices—and she treats the process as if she were buying a car—accepting the occasional accessory and turning down another. She must be hurting, I mean Jesus, she's lost a sister; but she knows what needs to be done and she does it.

By the time I get back to the office everyone is gone but Grumman.

"That cop friend of yours called before. Brandt."

"He's not my friend."

"He said he saw you at the Bennetts' but you looked pretty bad. Anyway, give him a call if you get a chance."

"He said I looked bad? Who the hell is he to say...?"

"Maybe I misunderstood. Maybe he said sad. Or mad. Anyway, call him. I wrote down his cell."

"Why?"

"Why did I write it down? I didn't think I'd remember it."

"You know what I mean."

"You're the reporter—maybe he has a statement. I'm leaving. The wife wants to go to dinner and she needs someone to eat with. And listen, Bree, you get out of here at a reasonable time—before dark if you can."

"It's like the shortest day of the year. That gives me ten minutes."

"Use the ten wisely. I really am sorry about your friend. Just...you know...let the police do their job too."

"Of course."

"We should go at this quietly."

"We? Or me?"

"We, but especially you."

"You mean because it's personal?"

His face seems stern, rigid, and he narrows his eyes a little. He's sleepy and sick and he wants to say more—I can tell—but he's too worn out to deliver a sermon, though he and I both know what the subject would be. Last summer, I broke a story that wasn't a story. Or maybe it was one until I broke it. As convoluted as that all sounds, it does occasionally happen in this business, and it's worse these days with the Internet where mistakes never die and there's so much anonymous bullshit out there that respectable news outlets need to be even more respectable, more cautious, more certain.

My particular gaffe involved a large parcel of land north and west of Drayton out toward I-495. There was some buzz about an industrial complex—a kind of techy sprawl—but then the rumors shifted toward a large subdivision of moderate-income housing with a small shopping area or two. We're talking upwards of two thousand acres, about the size of a small town where I come from. I only mention that because it would have meant more than merely another convenience store or glorified coffee shop: it would have been important for the community.

Would have been, until I took a ride to Portland one Friday night, back where I used to live. I was at a bar in the Old Port celebrating a friend's birthday when I met up with Tommy Dixon, a guy I went to high school with. As kids we had been no more than passing acquaintances, but we fell into an easy pattern of conversation, progressing through the usual litany of post-graduation achievements. Unlike me, he already had some—he was an engineer for a New Hampshire firm and had already been involved in numerous projects throughout New England. He named a few that meant nothing to me, but I'm sure I looked suitably impressed, mostly because I was. To be fair to the guy, I can't say he was crowing, just filling in the space between mouthfuls of beer. When I told him where I was working, he said the firm had just bid on some wind turbine project in Massachusetts and expected to win it. Maybe, he said, we could get together in Boston sometime.

"It's more or less still on the drawing board," he added. "It's all very hush-hush, so...."

He knew I was a reporter, and he probably knew right away he shouldn't have said anything. But he talked openly about other wind farms on the drawing board and how they were the hope for our energy future. He was sounding very green, but since young people are supposed to be socially conscious, he might have been adopting that pose just to impress me. And it was working. A few times he repeated that everything was still on the drawing board, even the land acquisition which was crucial, and that nobody wanted a lot of publicity. Then again, the noise level in that bar was so high he practically had to yell every syllable: it didn't seem like sensitive material at all. I remember laughing and saying something like, secret wind turbines? Who's gonna care? But when he gave me the proposed site—it was very local—for me it became a story. I'd like to pretend I didn't hear the hush-hush part; of course I'd also like to pretend he didn't have expectations of hooking up later—expectations which might have loosened his lips in the first place.

His expectations of intimacy (and to be honest, mine too) were fulfilled, and when I finally rolled out of his bed at one in the morning, gathered my clothes and drove myself home, the secrecy of the wind turbines was low on his list of significant events. I doubt if he ever thought of our conversation again, not until I filed my story. Shortly thereafter the project—well, I'd like to say it was scrapped, but it was never officially announced. You won't see any wind turbines on the Drayton horizon, figuratively or literally.

I looked bad, the *Courier* looked bad, and worst of all Grumman looked bad. Maybe he looked the worst because he had final approval of my so-called scoop, but he had been undergoing one of his treatments that week; and though he was physically present, offered little more than a shadow at an editor's desk. Even so he had asked the usual questions about my sources, and when I told him there was only one, sent me out to get someone to speak on the record. I asked around a little—there was a selectman I'd met a few times but he seemed unaware of any such project. I realize now that *seemed* may have been the operative word—everyone seemed unaware but there must have been a lot of secrecy at the time, probably engendered by a fear that something would go wrong. After a few similar dead ends and a few more closed-mouthed local leaders, I called my engineering friend. I should say I called his company, because he was not the one I wanted to speak to. I needed another source, preferably one I hadn't slept with.

This is probably a good time to confess that I had never done anything like this before and I don't think I was very good at it. I can't remember if I had any pangs of conscience at the time—in a way I hope I didn't—I guess I'd rather be amoral than immoral: people with no concept of right and wrong might learn it over time; those who already know it and choose to ignore it aren't going to get any better. Or maybe that's just a line I feed myself to justify having sex with men I'm not interested in or for skirting the ethics of my profession. I'm better in both areas now, though being more particular hasn't improved my sex life at all. I guess that's what being particular means.

At any rate, I didn't want to talk to Tommy Dixon again, and when he didn't answer—when I got a female voice—I dragged out my best Down East folksy accent. I told the woman who I was, said I was a classmate of Dixon's—friend seemed a bit of a stretch and lover just inappropriate—and most important identified myself as a reporter—real name, real paper. I said I was following up on a conversation Tommy and I had had a few weeks before and I wanted to make sure I got the facts straight. She didn't hang up and didn't tell me she didn't know what I was talking about, so I pulled one isolated trivial fact from that barroom conversation: I asked her to verify the location as Drayton Massachusetts. Near Drayton, she said. I had my second source.

So I wrote my story, and it was a good one, balanced and filled with documentation on wind turbines and their environmental and economic impact. I talked about sight lines and bird migration patterns and the ambient noise they produce. I learned a lot myself. And 2500 words to a man like Grumman, who hates pulling features off the wire, provided reason enough to continue cutting me a paycheck every two weeks.

I told him I had two really good sources and I was ready to name another engineer at the same firm, a name I'd pulled off the website. He was sick and medicated, true, but I think he wanted to give me a chance to break a story, to become less anonymous. Even so, he told me to run it by Arlene—she's next in seniority—but that he was happy with it.

Arlene, whose talents lean more toward design than reporting, read it through, found a typo or two, then handed it back to me.

"Grumman says it's okay?" she asked.

"Yes."

"Then it's okay."

I "ran with it"—as they like to say in newspaper circles, or they did when I watched *The Wire*. Then I spent the next month running *from* it.

The denials were quick—quick and often accompanied by personal assessments of me. The selectman who had assured me he knew of no such project came to the office and blasted me in front of everybody. At one point Grumman told him to control himself, but that was the only attempt anyone made to curb that man's anger. Then I got a call from my engineering friend, Dixon. He didn't seem interested in doubling our one-night stand, but neither did he seem particularly concerned about the project having been quashed. He and his company had plenty of irons in the fire, he said, enough to keep him far too busy to be in Boston anytime in the next hundred years or so. He also let slip that he was engaged—just in case I had any ideas about a repeat bedroom performance. We wouldn't be "getting together" any time soon.

It wasn't a good month.

.....

Every once in a while Grumman tosses a knowing look my way, a little remembrance of times past when, as he is wont to say, we were suckered good. He doesn't want it happening again.

By *we* he again means *me*. I'm the one who lied, cut corners, whatever I feel like calling it at different times—the one who, by all rights, should have been fired.

Dan Grumman has a little framed quote on his office wall, something from a journalist named Hunter Thompson. I've heard of him, though in most of the courses I took he was never held up as a paragon. I guess he was bigger in Grumman's time—a reporter who drank constantly and did acid and in many ways defined Grumman's generation. I don't know why he would be Grumman's hero or role model—the boss seems a little too staid for that. Maybe Hunter Thompson is no more than a cautionary tale, but Grumman quotes him once in a while. As for the plaque on the wall, it reads:

"If I'd written all the truth I knew for the past ten years, about 600 people— including me —would be rotting in prison cells from Rio to Seattle today. Absolute truth is a very rare and dangerous commodity in the context of professional journalism."
Hunter S. Thompson

I told him once that it seems as if the absolute truth is something we should avoid. He told me I should hone my skills and learn irony. Also I should check my sources.

So yes, I'll be going at this quietly, but not today. Grumman wanted me to leave at a reasonable time, and it's already dark.

Chapter 3

I have this foible: I refuse to call Brandt's cell. My reasoning will sound prudish now that we're well into the twenty-first century, but sometimes I'm at home, just step out of the shower, my cell rings, and there I am naked on the phone. I don't want to envision him having done the same thing, probably because I can imagine him imagining me that way all the time, and it's a little too weird. But he wants me to call so I do—at the police station where I'm sure he's fully clothed—from my desk where I am also. And though voice mail can sometimes be frustrating, this time leaving him a message is the perfect solution.

Grumman is right about domestic crime: invariably the assailant is a boyfriend, a husband, or most likely, an estranged one of the above. Nearly every incident is a crime of passion, but those passions run the gamut: anger, jealousy, revenge, even avarice and envy. And few victims go quietly. Most have scratched, bruised, stabbed, even shot their attackers. Maybe Abby did some damage in return. Of course if I know that, the police would have considered it long before, and maybe Andrew's looking basically unscathed made him less of a suspect. On the other hand, why would she have fought him off initially? He was, after all, her husband.

I can't erase Grumman's words from my mind. Could Abby have tried to end an affair? And could the jilted lover, in desperation, have made one final plea? Maybe the man had planned a reasonable conversation, not realizing or choosing not to realize that emotion and reason share little common ground. Maybe at some point a line was crossed and everything went sideways; and once it started bending, well, how far is it from a rebuff to an argument to a shove or slap or punch, and from there to God knows what? Couples can scream at each other and say the most horrible things, but it all seems okay until it becomes physical, or one of the combatants remembers there's a loaded gun in the end table.

Still, that's not Abby.

I drive back toward the Bennetts' and find the street more serene. Only two patrol cars remain, their flashers off, but the other houses are illuminated by strings of tiny bulbs tracing roof lines and shrubs and wire-form deer. It's Christmas, and Standish Drive is just another New England neighborhood prepping for the holidays, except in one house—and that's the only one that counts.

Inside I interact uncomfortably with some of the relatives—invariably I have to identify myself. I'm not sure how long I'm there—ten minutes maybe—before someone innocently asks what I do. After I tell him, the mood changes: nobody seems quite so eager to talk about Abby anymore, and since she's the only reason I'm there, I start charting my path to the door. Andrew and I acknowledge each other across the room, then Shelley stops me and asks if I want something before I go.

"I want to know what happened," I tell her. "I want to know who would do something like this."

She takes my hand. She's angry too. At that moment we're not good for one another, so when I tell her I have to go, she doesn't try to stop me.

Back in the car I call Grumman's office phone and begin to leave a message when he picks up.

"I'm here. What's up?"

"You're supposed to be home. You left an hour ago."

"Forgot some things."

"And you wanted to make sure I left."

"It's a safety issue. Are you home?"

"I just dropped by the Bennetts'. Things have calmed down. A few patrol cars—probably canvassing. Crime tape everywhere."

"Listen, I meant to tell you before," he says, "take Monday off."

"I can be in after noon."

"I'm not going to discuss it. By the way, someone saw Abigail driving home—some guy from her building, name's Connelly—I've got it right here—saw her, let her into his lane I guess."

"The guy remembers?"

"Only because he knew her. Said he waved to her but she didn't wave back. He's pretty sure she didn't recognize him. I guess he just started working a few offices down from hers."

"Do the cops know?"

"That's how I know."

"Is he a suspect?"

"He and his family were at a Christmas party with about twenty witnesses, but at least we know she was alone in the car, for what that's worth."

"You think she didn't wave back because someone was with her?"

"You mean lying in the back seat pointing a gun and warning her not to wave at drivers? Or lying across the front seat performing oral sex?"

Grumman doesn't pull punches, and people like that can often sound inappropriate, but I don't call him on it: he's my boss and he's ill. As for his suggestion, I've done it and been done to—vehicular oral sex. VOS I used to call it until I learned there was a Veterinary Orthopedic Society using the initials and making the act seem a lot more beastly. Feigning shock or outrage would be hypocritical so, in this case, I agree that she was probably alone.

"This Connelly," he says, "it's important that he saw her at a given point at a given time. At least the cops can work from certain premises."

"Such as."

"This was a normal day and she was driving home from work. No one was impeding her. She was alone. She was on schedule."

"As opposed to a lover's tryst."

"Tryst? Don't use that word," he says. "No one will know what you're talking about."

"I wasn't planning to use any word."

"But what if you found out it's true? Could you report it?"

"Of course."

"Just checking. I'm not asking you to be callous, but don't be hypersensitive about everything that's said. This is still a murder. A really bad person commits murders, and now your friend's name is tied up with a really bad person. If her life is clean, we should do everything possible to keep it that way."

"But you don't think it is."

"That her life was clean? You know more than I do. I'm just letting you know that everything was normal up until the time she arrived home. To the police that's important."

"How'd you find out about this semi-witness?"

"Brandt. I called him and told him you were under the weather."

"So it was legit—he really had something to tell me."

"He may have had an ulterior motive—the information is already on the wire—but yes, I guess he had something to tell you."

"Better you than me. Thanks boss. I do appreciate it."

He laughs softly. "Yeah, I can tell."

At home—eventually I have to wind up there—I pace the apartment, moving odd belongings a few inches from their original position. I should be hungry, but my stomach feels more hollow than empty—if there's a difference. A bite of an overripe banana doesn't really do the trick and the rest of it slides easily down the disposal, spun into oblivion with the flick of a switch. Then I'm back on the laptop, dredging up all the correspondence between Abby and me. Sometimes I go months without deleting emails, but just last Sunday I cleaned house. Then it occurs to me that maybe I didn't actually trash the files permanently, but, of course, I did that too. If I really thought there was a clue in there, I'd bring the laptop to a techie I know up at Chalmers College, but I learned a long time ago that emails have the same privacy value as a postcard. I would never put anything the slightest bit incriminating in one, and neither would Abby. It won't be worth it to undelete some innocuous exchanges about work and family. Even our complaints about the uncertainties and inequities of life were good natured and benign, and I doubt if they carried any clues.

I'm searching around inside the sent folder when the phone rings. At first I think it's my mother—she's heard about the murder and wants to make sure I'm okay. It's a long shot, but it's possible. Or it's Grumman with some new information. Or it's Brandt naked somewhere. I'm wrong on all three counts: It's Teddy McClendon from the office.

Teddy covers sports, or they cover him, so much so that he seems ill at ease in other areas, often hiding behind that black Bruins cap he pulls down low over his eyes the way most people would pull a shade.

"Actually I hate the Bruins," he told me shortly after he came to the *Courier*, having recently relocated from New Rochelle, just outside New York City. "Down there we lived and died with the Rangers, but this hat gains me a little more access to fans' hearts and souls."

When I joked that he was being dishonest, he shrugged.

"Honesty is for you news people," he said, in his typical ingenuous manner. "I just do sports."

Teddy is a little too obvious to be a mystery, but sometimes he can be baffling. We hardly ever speak, then a couple of weeks back he asked me how old I was, and when I told him, he followed up the first moderately indiscreet question by asking why I wasn't married yet. I used to say "I still haven't asked the right guy," because it always got a laugh. But even a clever reply becomes wearisome after a while, so I dredged up my old bullshit answer about many career and social opportunities available for single people. He agreed—why not? He's single himself—then provided another example of a twenty-seven-year-old girl he knew who was also unmarried.

"She's gay," he said, rattling the ice in an oversized Coke he had brought in from the luncheonette across the street. Then, apparently feeling the need to explain, added, "A lesbian."

"Oh, that kind of gay?"

"It's pretty common."

I guess he was trying to make me feel better about my lack of appeal to the male populace, but rather than tell him I'm not gay, I just let him go on.

"Yep, got a girlfriend and all. How about you?"

"Nope," I said. "No girlfriend."

I thought my answer was pretty clever in a cryptic sort of way, but Teddy just nodded and went back to one of the myriad of sports websites and Twitter feeds where he spends most of his office hours between junkets to area high school gymnasiums.

"Don't ask don't tell," he said passively, his mind already elsewhere. "Of course there is gay marriage so she could get married if she wanted to. I don't really, you know, keep up."

I allowed a few minutes to pass before I told him I wasn't gay: being clever in a cryptic sort of way had not left things with their proper conclusion. His response—neither am I—didn't quite wrap it up either, but sometimes a conversation should simply die from its own futility.

Teddy McClendon is a little younger than I am (23? 24?) and I suppose I could have played the big sister, maybe mentioned that guys don't go around asking women their ages or their sexual preference. I didn't though because I think I was a little annoyed. I'm not unattractive, and even a bit athletic though I've become increasingly sedentary over the past year or so. Doesn't this guy have some wild fantasies—forever to be unrealized, of course—in which I'm the featured performer? Wouldn't it be normal for a guy like Teddy to have a libido?

To be at least curious? Isn't that how guys are?

But then, this is Teddy: I'm pretty sure if I were standing naked next to a large flat-screen with a basketball game on it, I'd be a little chilly until I found a robe…or the game ended.

And tonight the young man on whose seismic scale I barely register a murmur calls me?

"Coop," he says, "I just wanted to see…you know…how you were doing."

He sounds so hesitant I can hardly understand him. Undoubtedly he has spent a good deal of time weighing the wisdom of a phone call on this particular evening and an equal amount planning what to say. Even so, he sounds almost pathologically nervous: we hardly speak in the office, let alone outside it.

"I'm okay, Teddy. Thank you for asking."

"Awful thing," he says, "I'd be a mess if that happened to me, losing a best friend like that."

His words cause me once again to consider the dearth of regular communication between Abby and me. Just to be accurate, I qualify that relationship.

"She was a really good friend."

Teddy goes silent, either having exhausted his script or unable to adjust to my correction. He clears his throat once or twice before paraphrasing his previous statement about losing a friend. It's excruciating, his awkwardness, but he's gone above and beyond and I can't let him hang there.

"Who's your best friend, Teddy?"

My question, intended to break the ice, engenders yet another pause. I envision him trying to catalogue his friends like some hockey standings, listing them by *point totals, wins* and *losses, penalty minutes*—all terms he uses regularly in his columns which I often glance at and mostly don't understand.

"I never thought about it much," he says. "You, I guess."

Laughter is the wrong response, but it's out before I can stop it.

"Me? Are you serious?"

"Well, around here I see you more than anyone else—except my Mom and Dad. And they live upstairs."

"But I meant guys, guy friends."

"I don't have any really close ones around here. Had a few back in New

York. 'Round here I have some people to watch a game with once in a while, but they aren't really friends I can talk to about, you know, important things."

"Like what?"

Silence again. In his mind there must be topics he considers more significant than last night's scoreboard—I wonder what they are.

After a few seconds pass he laughs nervously. "I guess I'd feel uncomfortable telling those guys I don't have a really close friend, but I don't mind telling you, so you must be it."

"Process of elimination."

"Yeah, I suppose." He seems pleased with the solution. "Anyway, I just wanted to know if you were all right, that's all."

"I guess I looked pretty bad this morning."

"I've seen worse."

"That's reassuring, my friend. You certainly know the right thing to say."

This time he gets the jab. "I only meant, you know…."

"Teddy, I was kidding. Believe me, I know how I looked."

He clears his throat a few more times, and when he speaks again he sounds a little more relaxed.

"I knew I'd say something stupid for sure. I even wrote stuff down. Of course I didn't know what you were gonna say so it was hard."

This time I stifle the laugh before I hurt his feelings, but my lack of response leads to another uncomfortable silence, and though I don't want to kiss off my new best friend, I can't think of where to go next except back to the crime scene.

"Grumman called me, said that Abby was in her car at the right time after work. She, you know, didn't go anywhere between."

"So she wasn't drunk or anything."

"No."

"'Cause you know those happy hour places."

"She was probably sober."

"So that's good then," he says, bringing that topic to its conclusion. I allow one more silence before I mercifully put an end to his struggling.

"I really am glad you called, Teddy. So I'll see you on Monday?"

"Yeah, okay good. Monday."

"I'll be in late. Funeral and all."

He hangs up without saying goodbye and I have this image of a sweaty young man tearing up a script which has failed him utterly, then recovering quickly, cracking open a beer, and settling down to watch a game.

Seconds later he calls back.

"Hey I forgot, I know you're probably not in the mood for anything, but I had a dinner engagement kind of fall through. Do you feel like eating? You probably don't, right?"

"You had an engagement fall through?"

"Yeah, someone online set it up but the girl went back with her old boyfriend or husband or something—I wasn't really paying attention. Anyway, I canceled the reservation."

"Husband?"

"I'm not sure—people fix you up and you never know—but I still have to eat. Would you want to join me? Probably not, right?"

I have no confidence that my knotted-up stomach is going to tolerate any food, but the temptation to get out of the apartment for a time wins out.

"I can do that."

"Really? How about 7:00 o'clock. Mattera's. That Italian place near you."

"On a Saturday night? It's going to be hard to get in if you canceled a reservation."

"I know the guy. I'm kind of a regular. Is 7:00 okay?"

"I can be ready by 6:30."

"Uh, yeah, listen Coop, could you drive?"

"Car trouble?"

"The usual."

"Six-thirty," I tell him. "I'll be there...."

At the *Courier* we all know "the usual." It means Teddy, who generally uses one of his parents' cars, has failed to top off the gas tank or leave the driver's seat in its proper position or readjust the rearview mirror or retune the radio to the correct station—any one of which misdemeanors would be a reason for his folks to withdraw his driving privileges for a day or two. Arlene, my other colleague in the office, has no end of fun with the situation; ordinarily I do too, but not this time. I have only about an hour to fix myself: I don't want Teddy to say about me twice in the same day, "I've seen worse." Besides, spending an evening with

Teddy McClendon is about as stress-free as it gets, and since we've talked in person a few times, conversation should be less elusive than it was on the phone. Most of all, I don't need some guy fawning over me with hopes he can lure me into his bed—or mine. No worries with Teddy.

Speaking of which, Brandt hasn't called back. Perhaps he's found someone else to lie across the front seat of his SUV, or maybe bed down in back. I don't have an acronym for that yet, and if it involves Brandt, I don't want one.

I lay out a clean pair of jeans and a cinnamon-brown sweater, allow myself a few more tears, then steam up the bathroom with the nearly scalding needle spray. If I'm going out to dinner with my best friend, then I shouldn't look too much of a mess.

Tonight would be an awful time to spend alone.

MELANIE

Melanie Johns wasn't sure how to react. She had known Abigail Bennett—had actually been out for drinks with her a week or so before. Even though Abigail—she preferred Abby—had been her student for only one session before moving on, they were practically the same age and had established some measure of friendship during the fall semester—a few chance meetings, a truncated conversation here and there. Abby was pleasant enough—a working mother who could carry on a conversation that didn't center on the rigors of being a working mother, but who left no doubt that her world revolved around her husband and their son. Sometimes you just knew. But now, in the blink of an eye, she was dead, the unlikely victim of violent crime on her own street, in her own driveway. How does anyone react?

From the other room a television continued to blare the details of the murder while Melanie, only half-listening, hurriedly sorted layers of clothing for a late afternoon run. It wasn't that she was heedless of the story's significance, and it wasn't that an awareness of her own vulnerability didn't occasionally creep into her thoughts. She was to have picked up Abby just last night—the very night she was killed—but then the weather interfered, and the get-together with her and a few other girls wound up being canceled. Frightening to be that close to a tragic event, but Melanie could either dwell on it in some sort of paralysis or squeeze in the normality of a late-day run. She chose the latter.

Besides, though she considered herself fortunate, she had never subscribed to the "outcome bias." Knowing the result of a sequence of events then plugging in a different factor was all well and good, but it made no sense. Had she been there with Abby, every factor would have been different, or none would have been different. And since there was no way of knowing, it wasn't so much a close call as it was a tragic event. Maybe she could not merely slough it off, but Melanie Johns, at this juncture, was not anywhere near ready to die or to consider how close to death she might have come.

She flicked off the TV, double knotted her shoes, zipped up an outer shell, and headed off into the late afternoon shadows.

Melanie had begun running three years earlier, the day before her twenty-fifth birthday, when she considered the possibility that one day she might want to be naked with someone other than Stewart Rohmer, the scumbag (her father's assessment had been correct after all) she allowed to fuck her on the night of her high school prom and wound up marrying the following October, four months pregnant. When she lost the baby in November, she felt worse than she could have imagined, considering her pregnancy was, to use the nomenclature of the time, unwanted. By then her friends had traipsed off to college and she had begun to accumulate the "fat clothes" she knew she would need soon. As for Stewart, he was just as happy not to be a father and excused himself from her life a few weeks later, legally and permanently.

She fought that first winter of near-despondency, then started college in the spring. Any feared "year-behind" syndrome never materialized and, over time, the trauma of the final days of her high school experience dissolved into a smoother adulthood. But getting to be twenty-five—that bothered her a little. Her own mother had been well into childbearing at twenty-seven, and Melanie was not unaware of the math. Still, if she could meet someone, maybe marry at twenty-six, start a family at twenty-seven, she would be more or less on track. Sure it was a different time and a different generation—to admit openly that she wanted to have a child went against the grain of the modern twenty-something, or at least the ones she had encountered. Not only that, but women in their forties gave birth and nobody even blinked anymore. Even so, the traditional numbers stuck in her brain.

Another number that stuck, or stuck out, was forty. Stewart Rohmer had groped and fumbled his way around and under the pretty prom dress of a 115-pound teenager. Carrying 150 pounds after her pregnancy and the malaise that followed had made Melanie feel bulky, unwieldy, and ugly. She needed to lose ten or fifteen…for starters. Stewart had never actually seen her naked that night—poor lighting—but her next lover might not settle for being straddled on the passenger seat of a '95 Corolla by a woman who outweighed him. Prompted by that realization, Melanie made that first slow, ponderous jog around her block, celebrating her twenty-fifth birthday later that day by being too sore to walk. That was four pairs of shoes and thirty pounds ago.

As for her social timetable, she discovered Marcus Johns halfway through that twenty-fifth year on a humid Fourth of July evening amidst noisy pyrotechnic bursts and the blinding flashes of pinwheels and rockets on the

Charles River. She had not planned to attend, but had confessed in work the previous week that, though she had lived in the Boston area all her life, she had never been to "the fireworks." A young woman, a secretary in the insurance company where Melanie held an executive position, looked horrified.

"Then you come with us," the young girl said—Christy something, "and join our group."

But groups became amorphous in the mob scene of the Esplanade, and at the end of the evening Melanie hitched a ride home with Marcus Johns, a transplanted Midwesterner who lived in Drayton. Then they met again—a movie, and then more times—dinner, the swan boats, a game at Fenway. She weighed 128 the first time they made love. Afterwards all she could think about was her inability to hold off for another three pounds—but fighting him and herself made no sense. They were married before her next birthday, and a year later all that was missing in her timetable was the baby. Maybe she could enjoy her figure for another year or two—what could it possibly matter?

And she continued to run. That first tentative foray had given way to longer jaunts through Silvermine Pond, the state forest which practically abutted their house. Silvermine provided the best of all possible worlds for a runner—she could tack trail unto trail and run as long or as far as she wanted with very little overlap or repetition. Even better, she could hurtle along unencumbered by some partner with whom small talk would be a requirement. It was just the runner and the trail, a trail that—though at times treacherous in the winter—for nine months of the year, provided a respite from work. On days when an associate called in sick or a technical glitch shut down the online claims service, or some new federal legislation upset the order of things, Silvermine restored some semblance of order. And though she disliked admitting it, even to herself, when Marcus buckled under his own pressures and took out his frustrations on her, Silvermine became her sanctuary. Several times her husband had struck her, and each time had apologized profusely and swore never to do it again. Maybe the last apology stuck, for their life together had become calmer. Still she didn't know, and wouldn't until there wasn't a next time. As absurd as that sounded, she knew no other way to approach it.

She pulled on her wool mitts and checked the remaining daylight. December meant early sunsets, but she refused to become a seasonal runner. Irrespective of weather, she was out there. Tonight she began on the sidewalk, slowly gathering pace and avoiding the occasional icy patch, then turned into Silvermine, into the wind. She hadn't noticed it before, but that's what it meant to run in the winter—to work up a sweat running in one direction, then be met with a cold blast that chilled you through all the layers. It wasn't bad yet—she had just begun and still felt comfortable.

She thought of Chalmers College, another source of normality and escape that had recently been taken from her. She signed on to teach economics, then when another instructor moved away, added a computer course. She threw herself into her work and the students recognized it. Then without warning a letter in her mailbox: regrets—good job—a valuable member of our community—you're fired.

Maybe it had been, in fact, cutbacks. Or maybe it had been the ongoing complaints that seemed to crystallize among the students in Melanie's classroom. They were never about her, centering instead on unwonted tuition increases, larger class sizes, an influx of unmotivated and worrisome, even menacing students. She provided a forum for her classes to vent and she frequently agreed with the comments. Maybe she'd agreed too much, but after all, she was teaching economics—discussions like this, at the heart of which was always money, provided hands-on experience for her students. But if her complicity had been heard by the administration, maybe she became too expendable. No doubt there was all kinds of shit going on up at that school, and she was just getting a handle on some of it. She'd even been to see the big man himself, but Joe Lawrence—King Joseph—had cajoled her at first, then stonewalled her. The firing came soon after.

Melanie Johns had never been a crusader. She was more likely to write a polite letter of disapproval than rouse a protest march. And since a recently terminated fling impugned her own morality, holding a college president accountable for some shady dealings seemed, at best, hypocritical. She was still pissed—she'd been fired for Christ's sake!—but there was little recourse.

She had only taken the teaching job on a whim—just a way to fill time, earn a few extra bucks. It became a refuge more by happenstance than choice. In the previous eight months her grandfather had been diagnosed with advanced-stage colon cancer, her older sister had endured more psychological setbacks, and

Melanie herself had had that fling. Fling—such a delightful and genteel word for an affair with a married man. Then again it was a word she could tolerate whenever her conscience rose up before her and labeled her something worse, something more abhorrent. And so it remained for her a fling, one that had begun with too much to drink with friends one night, the offer of a ride home, and a few tentative kisses. That could have been the end of it. But then he called again to see if she was bothered by what had almost happened, and she wasn't wise enough to know that the concern would go away if she let it. Then came "just a cup of coffee" at the mall—a public place, after all, no big deal—and she marveled at how quickly she went from gazing at the mall walkers to staring at the chipped ceiling of the Centurion Motor Court's Room 117, her exercise-slimmed legs wrapped tightly around her new lover's waist. They met three more times to settle just where they stood on all this—there was always an earnest reason—and then, as haphazardly as it began, it ended with a perfunctory meeting in the post office parking lot.

Just a fling.

Sometimes she wrote it all off as new and improved Melanie trying to show her less appealing predecessor that things had changed, that her period of unattractiveness had been vanquished, that she could get whatever man she wanted—tall or short, smart or stupid, single or married, Stewart Rohmer or not. And more than one at the same time if she chose. For those few weeks she dwelt in a world of clandestine meetings and outlandish promises and gathering guilt that occasionally broke the surface. Only when it was over would she comprehend the dreariness of it, the commonness, and worst of all, the immorality. But Marcus had not found out, and she could spend the rest of her life making it up to him in ways he wouldn't know. If someday he struck her again, it would merely be condign punishment. There was something almost equitable about that. Almost. And though she took little notice of religion, she even thought the upheaval in her extended family was, just possibly, some divine payback.

Her grandfather, wasted from the disease and its requisite treatments, and having, at best, months left to live, grew sullen. Melanie could hardly blame him, but she still resented his behavior toward his family. There had always been an unspoken bond between Melanie and him, and its loss was difficult to endure.

Her sister Jill presented different issues. Smart, maybe even brilliant, she had been in and out of counseling for most of her life; and though she had been declared no danger to herself or anyone else, day-to-day living often became an insurmountable obstacle. In the past year she had spent six months at a home in Worcester "resting," (and exacerbating the stress on their mother) then another two weeks at a facility in western Massachusetts. Only recently had she seen fit to return to work and pick up the pieces of a real estate career that had grown as fragmented and disjointed as she. The sisters talked almost daily, Jill continually feeding her information on properties in town, prodding her to move into something better. Melanie always listened patiently, but she wasn't moving.

Throughout, Silvermine remained a refuge. Heavily wooded and scored with serpentine paths and summer-silenced brooks, the park was crowded only on July weekends when families battled for the prime picnic areas. On winter weekdays though, especially evenings and early mornings, it practically belonged to Melanie.

But there was a price. Her parents, her siblings, her husband, even casual acquaintances at work had warned her countless times not to venture in there after dark, or before dawn, or at any time when the place was likely to be deserted. Her response had always been the same: never had there been an assault on a jogger or anyone else. Besides, she had learned how not to be a victim. In the warm months when the heat was sometimes oppressive, she knew what it meant to dress provocatively, and she knew enough not to. And she made it a point to remember faces, eventually coming to know, at least by sight, everyone who walked, hiked, or ran there, from the gate guard who waved her through in the summer, to the cross-country skiing club that used the trails when there was adequate snow cover.

Today would be dicey. The sun already lay just a few degrees above the horizon, and a seven-miler, even at her best pace, meant a return in darkness. Some mugger lying in wait would be the least of her problems on a dark trail laced with newly fallen limbs and leaf-obstructed boulders. But she needed the physical escape and she had a Christmas gift list to deal with. If she could mentally compose and check it off, she could then get home, shower, eat, relax, and later arrive at the mall when most of the shoppers were leaving and Marcus was watching some football game or other.

A half mile into Silvermine she passed the vehicle barricade, then came to the trailheads with their myriad of options. Even with the trees winter-bare, the sun was low and fading—the path looked gloomy, dim, tricky.

Five miles would do.

In an open area a runner passed her, an older man she had seen often. A rabbit—her nickname for anyone who could make her look slow. She was ready to mouth her typical "hi" when he surprised her with a "Merry Christmas." He was almost out of earshot by the time she hollered it back to him. He heard her and waved his hand in the air, then rounded a corner and was gone behind a thicket of leafless oaks and maples.

A rabbit—seven-minute miles, she thought. She ran eights. What would it take to lop a minute off her time?

Better muscularity, less body weight, more lung capacity, new shoes for Christmas!—there was something else to buy tonight.

She picked up her pace a little more, keeping it comfortable, when she saw a figure ahead, standing motionless.

"Melanie," he called out, and then he was running beside her, the man whose memory she was trying to escape. She hadn't seen him in weeks—that meeting in the parking lot was supposed to have added the note of finality—there was to be no postscript, no revival.

Underdressed, without socks, wearing what appeared to be high-top basketball sneakers—he looked as out of place as he must have felt. He was not a runner. He didn't live nearby. She had never met him there—had tried to keep him out of that particular refuge.

"Melanie," he said. "I won't bother you."

She didn't respond. This was her territory, and since they had dismissed each other from their lives, she was her territory also.

"I have to keep running. It's getting dark."

"I just thought maybe we could talk for a second," he said, his words halting, slipping out between labored breaths. It was the tone that had first seduced her and now, what, he missed her, wanted to start up again?

Against her better judgment she looked at his eyes—gray and luminous in the late light of a fading winter sun. She had felt something for him—still did, but she no longer trusted the genuineness of her feelings, present or past. If she could not trust herself, she could not trust those eyes anymore either.

"I have to keep moving. It's too cold when you stop."

"Sorry," he said. He was winded, out of shape, pathetically trying to keep up. Even in the open air she smelled cigarette smoke on his clothing. She slowed her pace.

"You shouldn't be here," she said, and then—some suppressed feeling struggling through—added, "I don't want you to get sick."

He struggled for breath.

"I know. I wouldn't have come...I just wanted to apologize."

"No reason to."

"I just wondered how you were. I didn't want to call."

She came to a full stop.

"You can't call. Don't, please. I'm fine, I am. Now, go get some warm clothes and a hot shower. You'll be shivering all night. Old guys like you have to be careful."

She gave what she could of a smile—it was not so difficult after all—and touched his arm before turning away. She had told him days before when they parted that it was time for the world to spin on a new axis—on its proper one. Maybe he didn't know it yet, but he would.

"You be careful," he yelled after her, still wheezing. "I'm not even twice your age."

She smiled—an old joke between them—then stopped her digital watch and left it off for a 20-count—she had lost about that much time on the conversation. It was obsessive, maybe, timing everything, but she had to chart progress. And she had to reorganize her thoughts—the Christmas list, the future, not the past.

Another runner passed her—an older woman. No words. A wave. The trail wound deeper into the woods, past a small pond on the right already crusted over with a thin layer of ice, though she knew that only from a previous run. It was already too shadowy to distinguish ice from water. And quiet—Jesus it was quiet. Silvermine was a veritable bird sanctuary, and even in the winter presented a cacophony of chickadees and finches and even robins, sheltering themselves deeper in the woods. But late in the day, aside from the occasional swooping whistle of a cardinal, there was nothing.

An approaching figure on the trail caught her eye—a bright yellow running outfit, top and bottom, and a ski mask to match. Melanie owned facial protection too, but reserved it for colder temperatures—she hated the way it trapped the perspiration and reduced her visibility, clouding her eyes with sweat. She swerved to avoid the oncoming runner, but just as they were passing, the other seemed to lose his balance—to wander into her path and catch her left shoulder, twisting her to the ground. She landed on her left knee, but the forest floor—not yet frozen and still cushioned with leaves—diminished the impact and she pushed herself up immediately. The person was still there, eyes wide. He was a big man—not built like any runner she'd seen in Silvermine. The body, the eyes, something seemed familiar.

In an instant an object flashed across Melanie's sightline and struck her throat.

Her mittened hand went to the spot and came away dark. In the shaded late afternoon light, color became a doleful spectrum of grays, but sometimes there was just enough light: the mitt was a glossy red. She looked up at the man in yellow just as an arc of pain tore through her leg. She had fallen harder than she thought.

She moved to all fours, as if mimicking some forest animal lumbering across the trail, then tried to push herself to her feet. She couldn't. She couldn't catch her breath. She would have to rest for a moment, wait until her wind returned and she could continue on. Strange, though, it was not like her to become so exhausted so fast.

On the ground below her the thin layer of snow darkened, the shading spread inexplicably fast. She struggled to a sitting position, her back against a thin-trunked tree just off the trail, and pressed her hand against her throat. Above her still was the man who had carelessly knocked her off balance. She lifted her head to speak to him, to ask him to help, when again an object caught her eye and struck her...somewhere. How odd to feel the concussion of a blow and not have any idea where it landed.

The darkness of course—it was hard to see anything other than the blackening snow.

"Can you help me up?" He wouldn't simply leave her there.

"This is your own fault," he said. Finally, words, the voice immediately recognizable.

In the instant she sought to raise objections or defenses, she saw the object that had struck her and opened up the fissure out of which her life was flowing. A blade. Gleaming. Sharp. So then....

So then...she was going to die right here in Silvermine on a Saturday evening when the pieces of her life had begun to coalesce into something whole, when the chaos had been sorted out, when she could envision a future without the interference of the past. Now, right now on the cold forest floor, it was all going away in meaningless silence. She should have felt angrier, should have fought against it a little harder. But here it was, and here she was. For a brief moment she saw her ex-lover returning to save her, but she had dismissed him—done it twice actually. And the Merry Christmas man—he was probably home already, his running clothes left in a pile, the cold a distant memory as the needle spray of a shower washed it away. He would not be rushing back with bandages and dressings. Nobody would.

She saw once more, in her mind's eye, the shopping list that she had planned to check off that very night.

Then she saw nothing.

Chapter 4

When I was still an English major and I thought I was actually going to do something with English... and I'm not sure anymore how much of journalism intersects English...I took a poetry course and read some poems by William Carlos Williams, Everyone knows the "Red Wheelbarrow," but I remember one called "Tract" even more distinctly. It's about a funeral and how we, the survivors, are supposed to be inconvenienced by death. Williams was a family physician and probably had a good understanding of death and dying before those words became a course in college catalogs.

Now here I am driving over to pick up Teddy so that we can enjoy an evening away from all of it, yet it's been less than twelve hours since I learned that Abby was murdered. Somehow I don't think I've been inconvenienced enough. Somehow "all this" should probably last longer.

*****

I've been to Mattera's before—been there with men who held my hand and ordered wine and said "the lady will have...." Teddy McClendon won't be playing that role, and that's fine with me, for whatever escape this might be, it's a brief interlude at best. In days to come there'll be a crush of mourners, disconsolate and perplexed, railing against the unfairness of life and the random idiocy of fate. Then eventually there'll come an arrest, and with it more anger and louder cries for vengeance—a segment of the cycle equally difficult to endure.

And of course I'll be part of the problem—scouring for angles like every other hack writer in the Northeast. A running story like this—even for a weekly—means not only hard news but all the features that give it a local bent. It can't be puff either—it's still a death, and a gruesome one at that. But while the *Globe* will back off until facts surface, we'll be relegated to "the victim's favorite pastime" or "what baseball team her son likes."

Given all the adversity ahead, I can do worse than spend an evening deflecting indiscreet but innocuous statements from a co-worker. In many ways being with Teddy is like chauffeuring a little brother and his friends...without the friends: he might embarrass you along the way, but in the end he's harmless.

And sometimes just baffling.

When I arrive to pick him up, he's sitting on the front step of his three-family FDR-era relic with a brown leather jacket across his lap. It's December. It's New England. It's not front porch weather.

"Waiting for the locksmith," he says before I can get close enough to ask. "She's on her way."

"She?"

"A cousin. Her father's the expert. She knows enough though."

"Why not get the father?"

"He's...he says he's done this enough."

"So you're locked out."

"Went to the car to get my jacket, the door closed behind me."

Which would all make sense if he were wearing the jacket. I remind him of that, but just as he rises to put it on, a car swerves into the driveway, sound system thumping. It jerks to a halt and a young lady with dyed-black hair and scattered piercings (I can only attest to the ones I can see—God knows how many others lie beneath that dark, monochromatic outfit) hurries past us, acknowledging us with a grunt. Five minutes later she's dropping some arcane tools into a small leather pouch, her job done.

"You're good to go, Uncle Teddy" she says, smiling. "You know some people hide keys outside...."

"I will, Suze," he says, then tells her to wait and hurries back inside. She shakes her head.

"He'll never learn. You're Brianna?"

"He didn't really introduce us. Yes, Brianna Cooper."

"The reporter. I'm Suzanne McClendon, student and lock-picker and cousin of the sportswriter. Teddy doesn't do introductions, I'm afraid, but he's mentioned you. Have a good date."

She looks toward the street and notices my car, then smiles.

"So he's grounded again, too. Oh well, as my folks always say, don't drink and drive."

Teddy comes back out and hands his niece a twenty.

"Uncle Teddy, you don't have to."

"Cheap for professional help," he says. "Save it up to pierce something."

She points to her left nostril. "This one'll be for you."

Seconds later she disappears down the street, the music barely keeping up.

"Good kid," Teddy said. "She'd make a good burglar if she wasn't going to college."

"She's very pretty...."

"But the piercings, I know—that's just her. Yes pretty and smart and handy with burglary tools. A hard combination to beat."

"Your jacket was in your car? I thought you weren't driving."

"I was today. Not tonight," he says, sliding into the passenger seat. "We had a little discussion and I lost."

"So you're grounded."

"I can ride with others. It kind of worked out."

"What did?"

"Locking myself out. My place is a mess. I wouldn't want you to see it."

"I've seen messes before."

"My folks would be pissed. It would be a poor reflection on...."

"Your folks are home? And you called your cousin?"

"I didn't want another lecture."

This is where one human being would implore a fellow human to straighten out this parental problem once and for all; then again my own family situation wholly precludes that lecture. For Teddy this is a glitch—he still has dinner with his folks, spends time with them, helps out in the yard with mowing and trimming and snow-blowing. He's a good son with whacked-out parents, but their moments of lunacy evolve out of some bizarre overprotectiveness. My situation differs; nobody is overprotecting me, so no lecture.

"How long were you sitting outside?"

"Five minutes, maybe ten."

"Without a jacket?"

"Didn't want to scrape it on the concrete. Listen, I might have told Suzanne you were my date, but that was just to make it sound like an emergency."

"I understand. I see you got dressed up."

He's wearing khakis instead of jeans—I don't think I've ever seen him so formally informal before—though he has not shelved the sneakers.

"I figured Mattera's was a little too classy for my usual outfit."

I look down and smooth the denim I carefully selected.

"Those?" he says. "I'll bet they're a hundred bucks a pair, mine are twenty."

I tell him I don't really remember what I paid for them. Actually I do, and his estimate is a bit conservative. "Is this what you were going to wear for your other date?"

"What other date?'

"The one that fell through."

He stares down at his feet.

"I made that up. I didn't want you to think I was stuck home on a Saturday night doing nothing."

"But now I know you were."

"But now I'm not."

Occasionally a conversation with Teddy can produce a mild case of vertigo, but at least I know why he's dressed up. It isn't so much a formal occasion as a solemn one. In some convoluted way, this is the way Teddy shows respect for my dead friend. It's a thoughtful gesture, so I tell him he looks nice—it's easier than some effusive speech of gratitude that would merely embarrass him.

As I've said, I don't know much about Teddy. I know he lives in the same multi-family house as his folks and works off most of his rent by keeping the place up. Because he lived in New York for a while, I tend to think of him as an outsider; but here he is with not only parents but uncles and cousins scattered about, maybe even some old girlfriends. I'm more an outsider than he is, a point that was gently and silently enunciated at the Bennetts'.

"I'm glad you got me out tonight," I say, clicking my seatbelt. "Aren't you missing games?"

"A few—no big deal."

"Because you're recording them, right?"

He sounds a little sheepish when he says yes. I almost wish he denied it— that I somehow had his full attention—but I'm not going to quibble. He wants to know how bad it was at the Bennetts' and I tell him it's hard to talk about it without weeping.

"Well listen," he says. "If you want to weep, you can weep. If you want to get roaring drunk, I'll drive you home and take a cab back. If you want to eat in silence, we can do that too. I eat in silence all the time. They say it's bad for you: I don't buy that."

I can tell by his tone of voice that he's okay with the drunkenness or the silence, but he's not going to do well with any weeping. I'm pretty sure I can hold it in.

At Mattera's, after I struggle to find a parking spot, we're greeted like visiting dignitaries; and though the place is packed to overflowing, the hostess hugs Teddy, finds us a booth, looks at me with an inquisitive smile, then nods to Teddy and walks away. I've won her grudging approval.

"That's Emily," he says, "some relation to the owner, engaged to a waiter here. The guy sometimes works on weekends but maybe not tonight."

He peers around the room but can't find him. I'm trying to figure out how much time Teddy actually spends here when our waitress approaches. Teddy knows her too.

"Maggie," he whispers to me. "She's good."

He asks me if beer is okay and orders a pitcher. Maggie doesn't see any need to ask what brand: what's the point of being a regular if the wait staff insist on asking superfluous questions? She's back in a few minutes with the tray and, while she's distributing glasses and napkins and pouring out of a dripping pitcher, I learn that her youngest—the one with the ear infection, is getting better. Of course I learn that only because I'm in the proximity—it's Teddy she's talking to. The whole situation reminds me of *Cheers*, a TV show I watched when I was a kid. One of the running gags centered on an oafish and indolent, but likable character named Norm, who never entered the bar without hearing everyone call his name—at which point he would offer some witty retort. It was predictably outlandish but always funny. In a way Teddy—neither oafish nor indolent, but likable—is the quieter Norm of Mattera's. They don't yell when he comes in; they jump.

Of course this restaurant isn't some raucous bar, not with their music service providing an endless skein of Frank Sinatra and Dean Martin over at least a half-dozen speakers. When I comment to Maggie that "Spanish Eyes" doesn't belong on the playlist, she tells me it's sung by Al Martino and so…. We all have a good laugh at my expense: it's a welcome glimpse into the world of normal people for whom the nearby murder is no more than a topic of conversation.

Teddy and I talk about work, mostly—Arlene's sarcasm and Grumman's illness. Teddy calls him a crusty old guy, though it's less a criticism than a term of admiration. We don't mention the cancer prognosis and the obvious question about the future of the *Courier* without him. For Teddy it seems more personal; professionally, there'll be other jobs. I don't have the same optimism—I need more time here to build up a résumé so that I can compete on the bigger publications someday...maybe. It sounds callous—as if I require Grumman's survival so that I can survive, but the whole publication business seems so tentative these days that one man's unwavering dedication—even someone as competent as Grumman—won't necessarily ensure a newspaper's future.

It seems the longer we sit there, the louder we have to speak to each other just to be heard. Mattera's is buzzing—I was right about the large Saturday night crowd—and I realize again how short a distance death's ripples actually travel. I mean here's a roomful of people trading bites of each other's Caesar salad and calamari and prosciutto and melon and maybe even a bottle of Chianti or Rosso here and there—and they might even be mentioning the murder. Some might know the victim's name and some, like me, might even know her personally. And yet here they are. And here I am.

"You're thinking you should be at Abby's," Teddy says.

"How'd you know?"

"Just a guess. We can leave," he says. "We don't have to order. The cops are probably gone and it's mostly family. Of course you don't want some third cousin five times removed to think you're meddling."

"I know."

"It's tricky, but you can drop me off and go over if you want. I can explain to Maggie."

"And Emily? And the rest of your entourage?"

"It's not a problem."

"You are flexible, aren't you?"

"I guess. What do you want to do?"

"I think I want to eat."

We bury ourselves in the oversized menu—one of those printed on thin paper but updated daily—and Teddy mentions some Mediterranean special that he's ordered a few times. If you can't trust Teddy on his own turf, there isn't much left to hang on to. Twenty minutes later the waitress arrives with a modest-sized pie piled high with God-knows-what. He shakes his head.

"I forgot to say 'no fish'," he says, lifting an anchovy and dangling it. I tell him they don't bother me. They don't.

In pretty quick fashion we manage to put away more than half of it and a lot of the beer, almost all of it in Teddy's glass since I'm driving. For a while Mattera's is a different planet—somewhere far from the miserable galaxy where Abigail Bennett has been murdered and her husband and child remain desolate in their suddenly blighted home. But then from a nearby table there's a fragment of conversation—murder, beaten to death, snow-covered, left a child—whatever people talk about at dinner, and we're back on earth. Teddy hears it too.

"Assholes," he says, looking around the dining room. He seems genuinely angry. "We can leave whenever you want."

"People are going to talk. You can't stop them."

He calls Maggie over again. She boxes what's left of the pizza and he hands her his credit card. I don't have to try hard convincing Teddy he should be the one to take home the leftovers. There are games to watch later and they'll require sustenance. And as for me, I already know I'm going back to Abby's. He drops a bunch of bills on the table for a tip and grabs the pizza box, then quickly we move past the tables and booths as I purposely try to block out all conversations. We're almost out the door when I hear a voice call my name from the bar. There's probably a split second when I can make believe I don't hear it, but that split second—well it comes and it's gone. I peer into the darkened room as if I'm as curious as hell, but I know it's Karl Brandt.

"Brianna," he says, meeting us halfway, "sorry about your friend."

I nod some token appreciation for his concern. "Detective, I tried to call you."

He flips open his cell and hits a few buttons. "No missed calls. You must have dialed the wrong number."

"I called your desk," I say, taking a few steps into the barroom.

"My desk seldom answers. I gave your boss my cell number."

"I like to keep things official."

"It's a phone," he says with a smile. "Are some more official than others?"

This isn't the time to explain my nakedness fetish, so I laugh and hope he doesn't realize I'm not answering the question. It works, but not because he's checking me out. I figure he's already done that from the dim lights of the bar. Instead he's distracted by my date.

"Who's your pal?"

Teddy steps forward. "You're Detective Brandt—we've met. Teddy McClendon from the *Courier*."

Brandt seems willing to accept Teddy's statement but doesn't respond. No one creates uneasy silences better than Karl Brandt and now it's incumbent on me to find something to say.

"So this is where a cop spends his off-duty hours?"

"Just grabbing a drink on the way home," he says, holding up a glass containing small ice cubes only. "Been on duty since Thanksgiving seems like."

"I don't suppose there's anything new on the murder."

"Which one?"

"That's not funny."

"It wasn't supposed to be. A jogger was assaulted in Silvermine tonight. They found the body a few hours ago. Two in two days."

Teddy steps in closer. "A woman?"

"A young woman, maybe your age give or take. Think you know her, sport?"

"I doubt it," he says, either missing or ignoring any innuendo. "Is this a serial killer?"

Brandt glares at him, then recomposes his features and looks back at me. "They found her with her throat cut. Bled out. I'm surprised they found her at all in the dark."

Teddy ignores the snub. "Different M.O. Think it's the same guy?"

"You sort of asked me that already," he says, still looking at me. Maybe he's waiting for my response, but I'm so stunned I can't think of anything to say. This is Drayton, where nothing happens; and now there's a murderer on the loose, someone out there killing young women? Brandt asks me if I'm all right—I guess I don't look it, but I tell him yes, I'm fine.

He nods. He knows I'm not fine.

"Anyway," he says, "going after women like that—same time of day twice. A serial killer is a possibility. You be careful. Women were really cautious before Deron Hillis was arrested; then they figured, well, it's safe now."

"Even Hillis never murdered anyone. And he's in prison."

"But he isn't the only creep out there," Brandt says. "I guess the vic lives near Silvermine—went for a jog like she always does...did. Young woman. Twenties. Pretty."

He draws a finger across his throat in case we missed his first indication that her throat was cut. His action seems vulgar and I figure he's probably drunk; but though Grumman would remind me he's also a source, I'd like to slap him.

"You said twenties?"

"Twenty-seven, eight. I think that's what they said. I don't know. Late twenties. Worked around here, insurance or something. She was running when he got her."

"Surprised she couldn't get away," Teddy says. "A runner? Why didn't she run?"

"You surprise someone like that, there's no time to escape."

"I'd still try," Teddy said, "unless I knew the person. Did they find a murder weapon? Was it a serrated blade?"

"We could go house to house, look for serrated blades. Do you have one? Should we consider you a suspect?"

"I just read how you can tell the difference...."

"You should be in detective school," Brandt says, any subtlety dissolving quickly. I feel I should step in before Brandt cuffs him.

"We'll leave that matter up to the people who know about it," I say, affecting a tone of near-jollity that makes me sound like an idiot. Brandt isn't giving anything I can use and I just want out of there.

"Nothing else then?"

"You're the reporter. Go and cover the story. Silvermine. Just follow the flashing lights."

Brandt is pissed at Teddy, and since Teddy is with me; he's pissed at me. God is he a pain in the ass. Now I have to coddle him so that when he does have something I can use, he'll be civil, if not forthcoming. That means using my interested-in-you voice, the voice I hate to waste on people I'm not interested in. I give it my best shot.

"It never ends, does it? Anything I should know before I get there?"

"We got a runner who saw her," he says, his tone more moderate, "but he's seen her a million times—didn't notice anyone else. You know how it is early on."

"What about, you know, my friend?"

"Vic number one. Nothing. Less than nothing. No weapon. No prints. Doubt if any DNA evidence is going to show up."

"Witnesses?"

"Nothing."

The admission lops off a bit of ego. He needs that, or I do. When he's not blustering, he's a good-looking man, five, maybe ten years older than I am. And he has these angular features you would expect to see on someone really skinny, though he's not. The anomaly works well for him. So does the backlight of the bar that turns his eyes a slate-gray, and every time his hair falls over his forehead, he can uncover one of them again, which, of course, means you have to look at them. Karl Brandt is accustomed to those interested-in-you voices: if hearsay is accurate, he gets them all the time, mostly from women, lots of different women—in bed. And yes, lots of different beds.

But not from me—no more looks tonight.

"I'll be busy with Abby's arrangements for a while, but maybe we can talk in a day or two?"

"Just call me...on the cell. Nobody has to play phone tag anymore for Christ's sake." He turns and walks back towards the bar.

Teddy waits until he's out of earshot.

"I guess it wasn't nice to meet me."

"What?"

"Well usually someone says it was nice to meet you when they're leaving. He didn't."

"Welcome to the wonderful, but limited, world of Karl Brandt."

"I don't think he liked me much."

"I don't think he likes suggestions from lay people."

"From what kind of people?"

"Amateurs. You know, non-detectives."

"But when you cut someone with a serrated knife, the surrounding flesh folds away differently."

"I'm sure it does."

"It's the first thing the ME would notice. I've seen photos…."

"Teddy, I really don't want to talk about that."

"Oh sure, yeah. It's funny, he said I should be in detective school. I didn't think that was the right time to tell him I am. I'm taking an Internet instructional course to be a PI."

"Why would you want to do that?"

"When I was young my dad and I used to watch reruns of *Mannix*, an old TV show my father liked."

"Never heard of it."

"I don't know anyone who has. Seventies. Even my faher was a kid. But this detective had it made—nice car, a beautiful receptionist—I thought that would be a great life."

Odd how we both thought of television characters: I had Teddy pegged as a lovable barfly, he sees himself as a hotshot detective.

"So you became a sports reporter."

"I like that too. I'm thinking maybe I can do both. Anyway, I'm just starting, but I thought my knife question was valid. I guess Brandt didn't agree."

"I have a serrated knife at home. Do you?"

"I guess."

"So that may not break open the case."

"Probably not. Of course he's got two homicides to deal with and he's drinking vodka at the bar."

"How'd you know it was vodka?"

"I couldn't smell anything. If he's too tired to dig up clues at fresh crime scenes, hc ought to be too tired to toss back a few, don't you think? You could tell he didn't like me, right?"

"He's territorial—you write about sports and he'll solve the crimes. With Brandt you have to stay in your own lane."

"If he has time to sit around while Ted Bundy is out cruising the streets, hey, who am I to judge?"

"Ted Bundy was executed."

"I was speaking metaphorically."

Seeing Teddy miffed is amusing enough; but hearing Teddy use words like *metaphorically* is bizarre, like listening to a couple of street punks arguing a girl's pulchritude. But typically, in an instant, he's past Brandt and the entire conversation. "I can drive to the Bennetts' if you'd like...if you feel woozy or anything."

"You mean drunk."

"No," he says, almost apologetically, "I meant woozy."

"I'm fine—really. Thanks for the offer. And listen, you don't have to go with me. I can drop you off."

"I said I'd go and I will. Just as long as you know—I really hate things like this."

"I'll have you home by ten, watching football and eating cold pizza."

He nods, but he doesn't smile. Teddy McClendon truly does hate things like this.

Chapter 5

The Bennetts' is a few miles from the restaurant, long enough for Teddy to revert to detective mode.

"Who's this Hillis guy—the one Brandt mentioned?"

"Deron Hillis. Never heard of him?"

"I don't think I was living here then."

"But your family was."

He shrugs. "We're not big on current events. So who is he?"

"We had a string of assaults a while back. Three women—one fought him off, but the other two were beaten badly."

"Were they rapes?"

"One victim claimed she was groped, but whether that was intentional or not, who knows. And in light of her other injuries, that seemed minor. Hillis seemed an unlikely candidate, but the cops arrested him."

"Why?"

"Deron Hillis was more likely to attack women from a distance. I mean, he'd scream at them, threaten them, say he was going to kill them. He was arrested plenty of times—disorderly, threatening."

"Sounds like more of a lunatic than a criminal," Teddy says. "And he never followed through?"

"He was too busy committing other crimes probably, none of which he was very good at. Botched burglaries, failed car thefts, he was more inept than dangerous, but you never know if a criminal mind is progressive—if it keeps getting worse and the crimes become more serious. Still you're right, he probably needed to be committed more than imprisoned. But once they arrested Hillis, the assaults ended. Maybe the real criminal took the warning and fled. There's been nothing since."

"And Hillis is in prison?"

"Supposed to get twelve to twenty, but the trial was a mess. Lots of circumstantial evidence, the attacker wore a mask and gloves, no prior record of violence...."

"Wait," Teddy said. "This guy who screamed at women wore a mask and gloves?"

"See what I mean? And the missing DNA. Not good. Of course a few months later there was an assault on a woman down in Fall River, same M.O. But the woman died. They made an arrest, put someone away for life. I always thought he was our guy, but regardless, the world is a more stable place with Deron Hillis in jail."

"Where he is now."

"Better be."

At the Bennetts' everything has quieted, and Teddy's prediction of an angry third cousin five times removed doesn't materialize. I almost wish it had. Andrew Bennett, practically catatonic with grief and confusion, careens from person to person—each, it seems, propping him up for short periods of time. There's eye contact—he even calls me by name when I arrive—but when he thanks Teddy for coming—Teddy whom he's never met in his life—I know that behind those eyes very little is registering. Their son, Nicholas, is upstairs with his grandfather, but so far I've seen neither of them, nor do I expect to.

After a while the living room, choked with visitors when we arrived, begins to thin out, and I tell Teddy I don't want to become the last remaining mourner. But when I try to leave, Andrew stops me and tries to remember the calling hours so that I can be there. He's already forgotten I was with him when we made the arrangements. His sister-in-law rescues him.

"It's 5:00 to 8:00 Sunday," Shelley says quietly, the words barely audible. Her eyes are shadowy and sunken and she leans unsteadily against a breakfront, the business-like perfection of the afternoon having given over to a smothering fatigue. Still, she knows we're leaving and takes my arm.

"Everything seems so rushed," she says, "but with the holidays coming. You never know the right thing to do."

"There's no right or wrong way, I'm sure."

"I hear there was another murder," she says, her voice quiet, as if sharing a scandalous secret, "over at Silvermine. To be murdered is bad enough, to be one of a list…and not just Abby."

She doesn't finish the thought, but I know what she means. Individual loss can too often be absorbed by the horror of a mass killing: Abby Bennett will no longer be that murder victim; now she'll be one of them.

"Another young woman," I tell her but she just nods: she already knows.

"I don't want to put you on the spot," she says, "but Andrew thinks it would be nice if you said a few words at the funeral." Her voice is full of apology, and she even gives me an escape: "He's asked lots of people and he'll never remember who, so don't be afraid to say no."

"If he wants me to, I'll do it."

My stomach is knotted again and I curse myself for this little drop-by. Shelley knows.

"That would be wonderful," she says and squeezes my hand. "We're not a large family...."

So I'm the replacement, I get it. And I don't mind that so much as speaking in front of a group who may have known her better. Longer.

"Everyone's biggest fear," Teddy says once we're outside. "But you're a writer. Write something and read it. You'll do fine."

"It's different. You can't write an essay and read it and call it a speech." My new assignment has me feeling stone sober but flustered. "Listen, why don't you drive, okay? And take a ride by Silvermine. I want to see what's going on there."

He looks at his watch.

"Don't worry, Teddy, the football game will wait." I'm joking, but it sounds malicious. "I didn't mean that the way it sounded."

"Oh it's not that," he says. "I just mean the chances are pretty good that the cops have set up a canvass of the area. I don't know if you want to be part of the investigation."

"I'm not a suspect."

"I didn't mean that. I'm just saying it might be better to stop by in your official capacity than to rubberneck like everybody else. Why let people think you generally drive by there and might have seen something, you know?"

"Did you learn that on *Mannix*?"

"*NYPD Blue*, I think."

He finds a parking spot but leaves the car running.

"I'll wait here for you," he says.

"You're the press, same as me."

"You're the reporter. I'm just a sports guy."

"You can be Ring Lardner."

"I actually know who that is. I read about him in a journalism course."

"History?"

"No, journalism."

"But I mean, what journalism course? History of journalism?"

"Just journalism—I think it was called Intro to Journalism."

"You took only one? Ever?"

"My high school didn't offer many electives."

I can usually tell when Teddy is joking—this time I don't think he is.

"The only journalism course you ever took was in high school?"

"Got a B+. I was a business major in college, remember?"

I do. He told me once before about his parents trying to direct him towards accounting, a stable field with a secure future. He could have paid off his entire college tuition in his first year on the job with what those entry level accountants get these days. But then came an opening for a "jock who can write" as it had been inelegantly phrased in the college paper, and Teddy had answered it.

"I admire your economy," I said. "You've parlayed one course into a full-time job. If kids get wind of this, college majors will disappear."

"And I have time enough to study something else too."

"So you'll leave the *Courier* when you become licensed?"

"As a private detective? Maybe."

"But you love all those sports of yours."

"Sports of mine? That's what my mother and father say—when you gonna do something instead of those sports of yours?"

"You know what I mean. You love all that stuff."

"I do, but writing about them tarnishes them a little—unless you really are Ring Lardner, or Red Smith. People like me, let's face it, we take beauty and grace, reduce it to clichés, and call it a column."

"It scares me when you become introspective."

"Don't worry," he said as we approach the cordoned off area, "I'm mostly thinking about the pizza in the trunk. Come on, I'll set a pick for you. Sorry, sports lingo."

As we draw closer to the activity, the first line of defense is an older policeman who seems extraordinarily unhappy to be stationary on a frigid Saturday night. Our credentials get us through, and once inside we see more familiar faces, among them, Karl Brandt.

"Decided I should be here after all," he says, "you know—keep things under control."

He seems sober enough, despite where he was earlier, but he shivers continuously. Maybe it's the alcohol. He pulls up the collar on his sport coat, then points to the darkened expanse of state forest behind him.

"I guess she was a regular in there."

Teddy peers into the same blackness. "You can't possibly run in there at night, can you?"

"Some people carry flashlights," Brandt says.

"Did she?"

"We didn't find one."

"So she was killed in the daylight."

Brandt smiles. "Maybe an owl did it. I understand they see well at night. Did you get to the O's in detective school?"

"Just thinking out loud," Teddy says. He seems unperturbed by Brandt's sarcasm, but I'm beginning to feel like a mediator.

"Detective Brandt has probably considered those things already."

"Not the owl," Brandt says, and I really want to slap him. But Teddy has already drifted off to where the greatest assemblage of police has gathered. For someone who was going to wait in the car, he has become involved quickly.

"Amateurs are always the same," Brandt says, lighting a cigarette. "They think it's cute to solve crimes, meanwhile this girl is dead."

"You don't have to give him such a hard time. Teddy's a good guy," I whisper. "He just watches a little too much television."

"How about you?"

"Not so much."

"So what do you do with your time?"

"Oh this and that, detective, same as you."

"I doubt that, otherwise our paths would cross more often."

A subtle come-on from Brandt—no surprise there. He's handsome and he knows it, clever and he knows it, married and everyone knows it. Worse, he's been loosened up by a few drinks, so subtlety should be the next casualty. This time he fools me.

"She was only 27," he says. "What kind of miserable son of a bitch goes and kills a young girl like that?"

"So you found out her age."

"Twenty-seven. A kid."

"Would it be different if she were older?"

His eyes narrow and he looks skyward, as if he genuinely expects an answer to drift down from among the multitude of visible stars. He's angry—an unusual emotion for Brandt to put on public display, especially if it might ruin his chances of getting some woman into bed. I've lost count of—and interest in—his rumored liaisons, but the commonly accepted belief is that marriage has had a minimal impact on his social life. Still, for him not to give me, or any woman, the right to first refusal is odd, so I try to answer the question he has probably forgotten he asked.

"Sick people in the world."

"And your friend, Abigail. Same thing. No robbery. No rape. Just senseless murder."

"Who found the body?"

"Her husband got a little panicky when she didn't show up, called 9-1-1. By that time another runner had found her and called it in. It was like a fucking execution. I don't get it."

"You're a cop. You have to get it."

"No, I don't. You seeing this guy, this Teddy?"

"I'm his best friend."

I could have said we were members of a sadomasochistic blood cult: Brandt isn't paying much attention.

"It's no secret," he says, pointing in a direction where apparently the body was found. "We've always worried about this area, and we patrol it. But some of those trails wind so deep into the woods, practically up to the Pike. I'm not crazy about having women in there alone, even in the daytime. You warn them, you hope they listen, what the hell else are we supposed to do?"

I pull a small notepad out of my purse. I have a recorder but the pad is less threatening. "Do you think the crimes are related?"

"For attribution?"

"For conversation."

"I don't *conversate* with reporters at a crime scene."

"We've already been doing that for five minutes, detective. Come on."

He looks back toward the park. "As an unnamed source...from a distance and without any real evidence gathering...."

"Jesus, Brandt!"

"All right, yes, I think they're connected. But it's just a gut."

"Who caught the case?"

"Who catches every case? Now you know why I was drinking. Once I enter that tunnel, that's it."

"What tunnel, detective?"

It's Teddy—he's wandered back from his short foray beyond the perimeter.

"The tunnel you enter when you become involved in a major crime—any case that involves human life. You go to sleep with it and wake up with it."

"But there's a light at the end of it, right?"

"If there is, you never see it. Then one day you're out, maybe. If you never get out, that's what they call early retirement. Trust me, you're better off being a sports reporter, Inspector Teddy." He glances around quickly. "I gotta go. I can't be in charge if I'm bullshitting with you people."

You people. Reporters.

"Have a name?"

"I do. You don't, not yet."

"Next of kin. Have they been notified?"

"In the process. One of them lives in the area—her folks are out on the Cape. They should be here soon."

"If you hear anything...." But I don't get to finish. Some disturbance has arisen maybe fifty feet away. Shouting. General movement. The mayhem of crime. At least three uniforms rush in that direction. Relatives must have arrived—maybe her parents. Brandt looks right at me—I did after all leave a question hanging—and I know he's about to tell me something—then he shrugs. "I'll let you know if there's a news conference," he says, then turns and walks away.

"What about the edge?" Teddy yells after him.

Brandt stops, stands motionless for a moment—I'm sure he's going to shoot Teddy right there.

"Serrated," he says without turning, then blends into the gathering of uniforms and bystanders.

"Hard to believe," Teddy says, "that he'd be in Mattera's with another victim lying here this way. He claims he catches every case—not this one?"

"Procrastination. Like he said, he knows what's ahead."

"Or he had a lead. And anyway why's he so pissed at me? It'll be years before I get a license. I won't be stepping on his toes."

"Competition, that's all."

"It'll be years...if ever."

Job competition wasn't what I meant. I'm Teddy's best friend, but Brandt probably wants me to be his best friend too. Of course their concepts of friendship probably don't coincide.

Chapter 6

Sunday morning dawns a little too dazzling and my curtains don't diffuse the sunlight much. I wish they would: last night, after I dropped off Teddy, I completed my evening of light drinking with a screwdriver. I don't even know why—I was thirsty, took out the orange juice, thought I'd drop in a little vodka—always a safe liquor—to help me sleep. I was obsessing over the eulogy and kept adding a little more vodka for good measure, until the proportion was probably one to one and the orange juice looked like faintly tinted water. It helped me get to sleep but not stay asleep. I saw various three-digit configurations on my alarm, the last one beginning with a four, I think.

At 10:30 my head is pounding but I drive to Deal's and bring home one of their breakfast sandwiches and a giant coffee. I'm a tea drinker but I figure maybe an extra infusion of caffeine will get me started, especially since I'm popping Excedrin laced with the same ingredient. By early afternoon the failure of my plan is becoming more evident. I've never had a vodka hangover in my life: goddamn orange juice must have done it, so I punish the remainder by dumping it down the disposal. The hours pass almost without my notice, and by late afternoon—the whole day having been trashed and the calling hours looming, I'm queasy from not eating and hyper-alert from too much caffeine. With few options remaining, I open a small can of tomato juice and measure out a shot of vodka—a desperate measure but it seems to work. A temporary fix at best, but it enables me to stand in line waiting to view the closed casket. Teddy volunteered to accompany me, but I gave him a pass on this particular event—I'll handle it alone.

And I really am alone. I know very few of the mourners: relatives from the area, colleagues from work. For some it's a kind of solemn reunion with pockets of high school and college buddies gathering in corners to catch up. But Abby Bennett and I don't go back very far—there's no catching up or reminiscing. For me it's just sad and lonely and I wind up not staying long. I'm worried too: what will these long-standing acquaintances feel tomorrow when some stranger gets up to give a eulogy? *Who the hell is she? Who asked her to say anything? What gives her the right?*

Again I'm obsessing, and this time I have no orange juice. I could always stop and get some of course, but on the short drive home a blinding squall blows in: by the time I get to my apartment the small amount of snow that fell has become airborne, making even the short walk through my parking lot miserable. Two more pain killers and a cup of tea and I'm back in bed with my laptop, working on tomorrow's memorial, having pretty much lost the entire day. I haven't given two thoughts to that second murder, haven't even touched base with Grumman. I'm not good at compartmentalizing, but in an attempt to get better, I call him.

"Do we have a name on last night's victim?"

"The woman in Silvermine?" he says. "Yes. Melanie Johns."

I'm stunned. I know her, or would have had it not snowed a few nights ago. She was a friend of Abby's and part of the group that was going to meet for drinks. My mind starts racing toward a raft of horrible possibilities and my early morning nausea returns with a vengeance. I hang up the phone and barely make it to the toilet. After a flush or two and some heavy-duty toothbrushing, I'm on the phone with Karl Brandt, sputtering about Abby and Melanie being friends and the possibility of my having been with her.

"They weren't close," he says.

"And that's supposed to make me feel better?"

He doesn't realize his job is to make me feel better—something I myself have failed to accomplish in the last twelve hours—so I rephrase the question I never asked. Should I be worried?

"Everyone needs to be careful," he says. "Lock your doors and such. Otherwise no, I don't think an acquaintance of a victim is necessarily in harm's way."

He doesn't want to talk about an ongoing investigation, and he doesn't even drift on to anything smarmy or suggestive. Instead he again tells me to lock my doors and hangs up. I double check: I have but one door. It's locked.

Sometime after midnight, still unmurdered and a little calmer, I awaken to a dead laptop and an unwritten speech, but physically I feel a lot better. I burrow through a bag of corn chips and brave another glass of tomato juice sans vodka (not a combination I would recommend as a regular snack), plug in the laptop, and finish writing. When I awaken at dawn the wind is rattling the windows and

Abby's sister calls: weather has canceled the graveside ceremony. It isn't much of a relief: my eulogy is planned for the funeral home.

I don't own one of those dull and dreary black dresses that fall just below the knees. But I have black slacks made of adequately somber wool, and I can wear a black sweater for a top—wool also, a modest v-neck—and I'll look as dismal as I feel. I'm probably still a little young for the really bleak outfits; then again, I'm not there to look nice. I'm there for an exercise in futility—capturing a life in a five-minute speech.

In my few non-head-pounding moments yesterday, I rewrote the piece several times, changing words here and there, but I haven't done what an old speech teacher insisted we do—say it aloud. So while I'm eating my first real food since Saturday, a piece of toast, I give it a try. It sounds pretty good, but at the end my eyes begin to tear—some combination of words or images or memories has set me off, so it's back to the laptop to de-emotionalize the ending. I understand it's all right to cry at a funeral, but I always fear losing control entirely, being unable to continue. I saw it happen once when my cousin gave a wedding toast. A wedding toast for God's sake! What chance do I have?

I go through it again. Everything centers on her devotion to her husband, to her son, to her friends—but even then Grumman's questions haunt me. What if that isn't true either? What if her unfaithfulness becomes public knowledge afterwards? Would people remember this eulogy and laugh at my naiveté? *See, she didn't really know her at all...some reporter she is.* All of the options are bad, but I decide I'd rather be wrong than cynical. And as I implied before, I doubt if the skeletons in her closet rattled very loudly, nor would they after.

The funeral home is packed and even though I arrive early, I'm forced to park in an auxiliary lot and then wrestle with the bitter winds. I'm shivering when I get to the viewing area—it gets worse when I realize the only people I know are Abby's husband, sister, and son and, not unexpectedly, Teddy. I have a brief word with Andrew before a minister arrives and the room quiets down. He's a young man in a blue blazer and an oxford shirt—I'm not sure how much more non-ministerial a clergyman could look, but then his homily is pretty much non-religious—an occasional mention of God but none of heaven, just an emphasis on the peace and comfort we will all achieve some day.

He doesn't realize it—and probably didn't plan it—but his calm and reflective talk is a good lead-in for me, certainly preferable to following a presentation on angels and paradise. My eulogy is fine—brief and, to my mind, accurate. My eyes are moist all the while, but I don't dissolve in front of everybody. Afterwards her sister takes me aside and thanks me, and in a heartbeat the façade of passivity dissolves. For the next few moments she and I hide out in a small office alone with bottles of water and a fresh box of Kleenex, having been guided there by a young man whom I'd never seen before but who apparently works at the funeral home and tries to keep crying jags from escalating into hysterical displays.

When a semblance of self-control returns, Shelley smiles and says if she owned a funeral home there'd be liquor in these sorrow rooms, and even though my latest hangover is fresh in my mind's eyes, I take her hand and nod. We agree to keep in touch. We won't, of course, but you say things like that at a funeral.

And then it's over, and as impossible as it seems, the world outside has continued to spin and I'm back in the office as if Saturday and Sunday and this morning had never even occurred....except for Teddy's constant reminders that he never could have given that eulogy in front of all those people. The compliment begins to wear thin and finally I tell him that if something happens to me, he'll have to do the same.

"Me?"

"You said I was your best friend."

"Shit, you're right. Oh, man."

He looks terrified. I don't want to tempt the fates, but I can't let him suffer.

"You shouldn't have to worry about it for a while. But if you want, I can write something out for you. Keep it on file—read it when the time comes."

As soon as I say that I remember my panicky call to Brandt and my vague connection to the victims.

"Or maybe," another voice says, "you two could talk about something else?"

It's Arlene. She's been quiet, but now has found her opening.

"Or do something else," she adds, "like—maybe some work? Boss wants a piece on keeping yourself safe," she says to me. "Gear it toward women."

All I can think of is Brandt's suggestion—lock your doors.

Arlene Holland's abruptness can be annoying, but today I'm grateful. She's not my boss, but she's twice my age and has been working here twenty years.

And if anyone belies the stereotype of the older person struggling to understand technology, it's Arlene. She flies through every bit of computerized assistance she can find. In an office where Dan Grumman would prefer Underwood portables and a mimeograph machine, Arlene is forever upgrading and Grumman is forever allowing it. She has bragged a few times that she could put the paper together on her smartphone, and I don't doubt she could. Whatever the truth, our product always looks good—layouts are crisp and headlines are catchy. And though it pains me to admit it, the quality of her work generally surpasses mine.

So yes, she's not my boss, but she's earned the right to bark a command now and then, and today she moved us away from an increasingly uncomfortable topic.

"Steal a list from the Internet," she says. "I won't tell. And you, Mr. Sports. Don't you have an interview at 3:00?"

"High school basketball coach, undefeated or something."

"Or something," Arlene says, checking an assignment list. "They haven't won a game in two seasons and their best player has just been suspended for dealing coke. That's coke without the capital C, Theodore—just so you don't look like an idiot when you get there."

"I knew it was something," Teddy says.

"Yes, something." She rolls her eyes. "In the journalism field we call it background. Did you study that in your high school course?"

Teddy has pretty much tuned her out. He's not being rude; he's just being Teddy.

"I'll put a positive spin on it," he mumbles.

Arlene shakes her head.

"And we wonder why the Internet is killing us," she says, her fingers flying over the keyboard.

She's right. The *Courier* may not be much, but it's still a little bastion of independent journalism in a world of electronic reporting. And even though I give in to Arlene's suggestion and cobble together an amalgam of articles from some websites, I head out immediately afterwards to cover a little local controversy. A Christian group has complained about the public display of a menorah near town hall, and an atheist has complained about the public display of anything Christmas- or Hanukkah-related. It happens every year in one town or another, but it's sure-fire for a reporter—a story with no legs that riles up everybody for no good reason. I figure I'll start with Public Works, but one of the receptionists there tells me that the sides have come to some agreement. I'm pretty sure I know why: the two murders have blunted their anger and produced more of a live-and-let-live attitude. Experts claim that after 9/11 there was a nationwide decrease in traffic accidents and conflicts in general. Statistics verify it. On a smaller scale it happened with the beltway sniper, and after the school killings in Newtown. Now it's happening here. Poison for a journalist; a benefit for the town.

But that can be my story—a town coming together behind a tragedy. Maybe I'm exploiting the situation, but it'll be a nice holiday lesson like all the other holiday lessons—trite but somewhat true. And discovering the story and the angle makes me feel something like a journalist—it's a feeling I don't get every day.

When I return to the office Arlene is just leaving.

"Weeks like this," I say, "I'm just as happy not to work for the *Globe*."

"I'm sure the *Globe* is equally grateful," she says. "Be sure to tell the boss you went home early."

It's after five and she knows it—just more of her lovable-fascist act—but I'm not buying.

"He doesn't want me here after dark, but if you have to tell him...." I shrug to prove how little it matters. "Anyway, have a good holiday, Arlene. I know you don't come in on Christmas Eve."

"But I worked through Hanukkah and never complained."

"Mazel Tov. You're quite a trouper."

But not a Jewish trouper, or one of any other denomination so far as anyone knows.

"Brianna," she says, her tone more serious. "Teddy says you did good today. He's not the best barometer of...well of anything...but assuming he's even half right half of the time, you should be proud. Now try to get past all this—enjoy the holiday with your folks."

"I will. Thanks."

Arlene seldom displays any warmth or kindness, and yet the one time she does, she's totally off target. You don't enjoy a holiday with my folks, you endure it, or tolerate it, or any number of other verbs not synonymous with enjoyment. Arlene doesn't need to know this, but as horrible as it was to lose a friend, spending Christmas with my family is not going to provide any solace.

Predictably Arlene is not there on Tuesday morning, and neither is Teddy. It's Grumman and I staying out of each other's way until 11:00 when he gives me an envelope and a poinsettia and wishes me a Merry Christmas. I return the favor with a holiday card and a tray of cookies from Leslie's Pastry Shoppe up the street—it would be nice if I had made them myself, but I know we're all better off this way. Besides, Leslie's is a real bakery—not a donut drive-thru; it's one of those small businesses that have somehow survived mergers and takeovers and everything else that has shut down America's Main Streets. My card, however, comes from CVS (not quite a local pharmacy) and features a cardinal perched in a snow-laden pine. It isn't necessarily Christmasy, but it's seasonal enough—the essence of the New England winter Frost would have poeticized had he worked for Hallmark.

An hour or so later I pull off I-93 to get gas and open Grumman's card: inside is a check for $500.00. I'm shocked and immediately call to thank him, but he sloughs it off, even though it's twice what I expected.

"Don't tell the others," he says.

"I won't."

Of course now I'll wonder if my bonus was larger than theirs and it's our little conspiracy, or it was smaller and the conspiracy lies elsewhere. That whole gift horse in the mouth idea never worked for me, but I should probably try it— last year I got $200.00 and was thrilled with that. There's the other matter too: his cancer. Maybe he thinks this is his last Christmas and wants to leave a pleasant memory for all of us. I hope that's not the case, but whatever his motive, the generosity will help pay for the carload of gifts I'm hauling northward like Santa in reverse—presents for cousins, aunts, and uncles—and yes, another tray of cookies from Leslie's. My mother doesn't mind cooking, but she won't bake; and as she incessantly repeats, if someone wants to honor the tradition of holiday cookies, then someone is just going to have to bring them. I can't pinpoint the exact Christmas Eve that particular pronouncement made its debut, but, as with the infallibility of the Pope, we don't argue it.

I'm just about to get back on the road when my cell phone beeps. It's my mother, for sure, checking to make sure her incompetent daughter has picked up the order for Angela Cooper and not some other lunatic from Maine. When I fish the cell out of my pocket, though, I don't recognize the readout. Instead of answering I yell at it—leave a message or leave me alone—and send the caller to another queue. It may not be "reporterly," but I'm already late and I'm not taking calls from unknowns. I'm off the clock.

At my parents' there's the usual pretense of happiness that I'm home for the holidays, but that act closes at sunset, and Christmas Eve is predictably awful. Talk of the two Drayton murders surfaces a number of times, and the guests— some relatives but mostly neighbors who have moved in since I moved out— seem certain that I possess inside information. I don't even know them and I keep trying to shift the conversation to other subjects, but that's like pointing out how pretty the moon is while an asteroid is hurtling toward earth. Luckily there's enough alcohol flowing to take the edge off, but I fear that a little too much imbibing might unleash my own assault on their ghoulishness, so I stop at two glasses of wine—some awful red my father has picked out. Fifty dollars a bottle, he says, adding that he had bought three. If the price is supposed to impress his guests, the first taste ends it for me. And who the fuck spends $150.00 on wine?

As soon as I consider that question, I think about Abby: she began practically every sentence with those same four words or some variation thereof. The thought of her flying off the handle over some real or imagined idiocy makes me smile, but it also tells me I've had enough wine. One more glass and I'll be pondering these great mysteries aloud—in front of children.

The evening isn't all bad. When I do manage to isolate some relatives— gather a few cousins together to relive some youthful silliness or corner a tipsy uncle and remind him of some ancient faux pas—my spirits improve. But always the shadow of my mother threatens to spoil these moments, to do so in subtle but nonetheless effective ways. *Oh don't embarrass Maureen, or you should really be nicer to Uncle John, or don't be mean at Christmas*—such little admonitions, always uttered with a smile, effectively dissolve the small splinter groups and re-assemble them into one large flock she can more easily lead. I may have implied that my colleague Arlene can be a bit of a fascist at times, but she's a poseur compared to Angela Cooper.

Christmas Day provides more of the same, albeit with fewer people. I manage to keep busy picking up wrapping and ribbons from the living room and trying to keep the tags with the gifts so we'll know who bought what for whom. Boxing Day may be big in Canada, but nowhere is it as honored as in the Cooper household—we repackage almost everything we've received and return it. Gift cards have slowed us down, but not that much.

All the essentials of the day are completed by noon, including the adherence to the Christmas morning temperance policy. My father has just begun brandying the eggnog for the first afternoon quaff when my cell phone beeps—same number as yesterday. The person left no message the first time—one indication it may not have been vitally important. So then why call on Christmas?

I excuse myself from my father, busy eyeballing the recipe, and take the call. I don't think there's any reason for a cordial hello.

"You called yesterday. Who is this?"

"Are you Brianna Cooper from the paper, the *Courier*?" A woman's voice, mature, not old, businesslike and oddly formal. She hasn't answered my question—damn if I'm going to answer hers.

"You called this number yesterday and didn't leave a message."

"You didn't pick up."

"I was driving. Who is this?"

"I never heard of a reporter screening calls. What if someone had something important to pass on?"

"I wasn't screening. I was...is this a joke?"

It has to be. It has to be Arlene, or a friend who's conspiring with her. She knows what a zoo my house is at Christmas and wants to make it just slightly more insane. Or maybe she wants to cheer me up, but I'll be damned if I'm going to ask who it is again.

So I wait.

"Okay listen," the voice says. "We're getting off to a bad start here. I'm Jill Dennison. We've met at some Chamber of Commerce events."

The name means nothing to me, but I've met my share of locals and admittedly I don't remember every one of them. But okay, I have a name. And it's not Arlene.

"I don't remember the name, but...why are you calling on Christmas?"

"Because Melanie Johns is dead. What are you doing about that?"

The question catches me off guard.

"Me?"

My father looks up—apparently I yelled that response a little louder than I had intended, so I signal to him that nothing's wrong.

"Hang on," I tell the caller and walk upstairs to my former bedroom to find some privacy. "I don't know what you mean. I'm not a cop."

"Melanie Johns, the jogger who was murdered in Silvermine. She was my sister."

That admission effectively puts me in my place, or at least in a different place. Now we're mourners together, and her loss of a family member overshadows mine.

"Miss Dennison, I'm sorry. I didn't know."

"She used to be Melanie Dennison—kind of a mouthful she used to say. Two three-syllable words together. Marriage took care of that. But she was a Dennison, like me."

"I'm very sorry."

"So you said. I am too. Now there's work to be done."

"I'm not sure I know what you mean."

And I don't. I remember the name, of course, but it's also true that I lost track of the specifics—I certainly didn't attend the wake if there was one, or the funeral. Nor would I be expected to—I'm not family, and I felt awkward enough at Abby's. I still don't know what this call is about, and if there's work to be done, then the police should be doing it. Not me.

"The reason I'm calling," she says, "I was wondering if you've heard anything about my sister's murder."

"No. It's early on…."

"Because I saw you talking to Karl Brandt Saturday near Silvermine and he seems to be in charge."

"It had just happened…."

"He's a friend?"

I'm not sure why that question annoys me, but it does. My tone changes and I'm no longer the commiserating mourner, just an employee of the local paper who's being interrupted on a holiday.

"He's a cop and as such I speak with him at times. He had nothing for me that night. Now if you want to call me back in a day or two, maybe it'll be different."

"And you'll tell me everything you know?"

"No, of course not."

"Why not?"

"Because that's not my job. Once we verify a story and confirm...."

"Okay listen, it's Christmas and you want to get back to your celebration and I don't need a crash course in journalism, so let's move on."

"To what?"

"I'm sure your friend's death will get great coverage in your paper. I hope you're fair to the other victim."

"We try to be fair to everyone," I tell her in tones as flat as I can make them. I'm annoyed and she knows it, but she's just lost a sister and has every right to be impatient, angry, even rude.

"Miss Dennison, let me find out what I can tomorrow. Maybe there'll be some news."

"I doubt if Brandt is working on Christmas. You should withhold the paper for a week."

"What?"

"Withhold the paper until you know something. Otherwise why bother publishing?"

"We're a weekly...."

I wait for her to interrupt me, but she doesn't, and I'm stuck with the usual disclaimer for our ineffectualness—we're a weekly. After she allows enough time for me to complete my thought—which I don't do—she asks when I'm working again. Unfortunately Boxing Day isn't a paid holiday and twenty-four hours from now I'll be at my desk—a fact that appears to fit nicely into her plans.

"Good, then you come and see me—I'm right across the street, second floor, Jay-Van Real Estate. Maybe I can help you make this right."

Jay-Van—I've seen the name around town. It's legit, but now I just want to get rid of her: even a Cooper family holiday debacle deserves not to be interrupted.

"I'll call you when I get in."

"Around 9:00 would be good," she says. "We can't all have a Merry

Christmas you know."

She clicks off.

It's a snotty little seventh-grade trick—get in the last zinger then hang up. I toss the phone on the unmade bed as my mother pokes her head in.

"Who was that, hon?"

"A subscriber. I guess I'm in circulation too."

"He shouldn't call you here."

"I gave him the circulation manager's number."

She nods, unaware that there is no circulation manager. But nothing is as certain as my mother's complete lack of interest in my job—my life in general—unless it has some direct impact on hers.

"Maybe you should just turn off that phone," she says, then continues on to wherever she was headed.

My mother is fifty-one and looks great. I don't mean she looks great for fifty-one; she just looks great. She takes care of herself, eats right, exercises, does all those things that middle-aged people are supposed to do to forestall the impending decrepitude that, according to the pharmaceutical ads on TV, lies just ahead. And she's pretty, always has been. In her college yearbook, despite the changes in hairstyle and clothing in those three decades, she's a knockout. It would have been nice if I could have inherited even a scintilla of those looks, but I have more of my father's features which, though they serve him well enough, don't do quite so much for me. I'm not hideous, not even grotesque or ugly, but no one has ever used the word knockout to describe me, and I doubt if anyone ever will.

I heard a journalism professor say one time that good-looking people constituted the most challenging interviews: we don't want them to dislike us, so we feed them softball questions. They smile we smile and everyone goes away happy—except the journalist who sits in front of the keyboard later and tries to figure out how he's going to pull together a story out of the crap he just accumulated. I don't think my mother has that power over me, but when she tells me to turn off my phone, I do—more or less. I put it on vibrate...and immediately it begins to vibrate. It's Teddy. I pause for a second and try to restore the tone of voice I use for normal people.

"Teddy, Merry Christmas."

"Merry Christmas," he says. "My folks went to the movies. Think I might drop by?"

"I'm at my parents' house. It's two hours."

"I know. No traffic on Christmas. What do you think? I'm fine either way."

"Numbers don't matter, it's Christmas. If you feel like driving that far, come on up."

"Cool," he says. "See you in a few."

In one respect that's the truth—numbers don't matter unless they comprise outsiders on what has been consecrated a family holiday, one on which—and I remember the quote—"friends don't count." Jimmy Castle can tell you that—wherever he is this Christmas. Jimmy was my first semi-serious boyfriend, a cute but somewhat shy young man from South Portland, a high school senior like me when we began dating around Halloween. We were at that awkward stage—far enough along for a presumed exclusivity and the occasional clothed sex, but not quite far enough for any real nakedness or, as the holidays approached, exchanging gifts. I'm making it sound as if nakedness and gift-giving are linked: they're not—in most cases—prostitutes excepted.

I think we went to the movies the night before Christmas Eve, then both figured we wouldn't see each other for a day or two. But on Christmas night he called. He had a gift he wanted to bring over.

I was eighteen: I'd have felt foolish asking my parents if my boyfriend could stop by. Besides, they had met him and seemed to like him well enough. So I said yes, then told my mother. By that time some of the relatives had left, but an aunt and two cousins remained —I like to refer to them now as *the witnesses*. Before that night I had always thought the expression "flew into a rage" was metaphorical; then I saw my mother do it. Her arms were actually flapping, as if she were trying to elevate somehow. The whole scene was cartoonish but not at all laughable; in short, I had committed sacrilege bringing an outsider into the Christmas House—it was probably akin to pissing on a church altar.

"Friends don't count on Christmas," she screamed. I don't know how many times she repeated it. If Ebenezer Scrooge had said such a thing, people would nod and say, that's Dickens all right. See why I remember the witnesses? Who would believe me otherwise?

It was during that tirade that I first heard that term, Christmas House, but the irony never gets old. Think about the term and everything implicit—a crackling fire, cut-crystal glasses of eggnog, jovial carol-singing, mistletoe, laughter—a panoply of images worthy of some elaborate woodcuts. Currier and Ives, right? Unfortunately our Christmas House is more Leopold and Loeb...without the laughs.

When poor Jimmy Castle arrived that night (he had no cell phone—I couldn't intercept him once he left his house) the vitriol had already been spilled and cleaned up, but the residue remained in the expressions of the survivors. My new boyfriend stayed less than a half hour in an atmosphere of silent tension, and he never came by again.

Friends don't count. Dwelling on a statement for ten years—dwelling on anything for ten years—probably isn't the best exercise in mental health. But I only become immersed in it when I'm actually home, and I'm not there very often. My obsession, or monomania, whatever a competent psychologist might call it, is seasonal, like sunlight deprivation. I can live with it.

But now Teddy, not even a boyfriend, more a colleague than any kind of friend, wants to visit the Christmas House and I've told him that numbers don't matter. There's still time to rescind the offer. He has the cell phone that Jimmy Castle didn't, and he hasn't clicked off yet.

"Teddy. Do you know someone named Jill Dennison?"

"No."

"Real estate."

"I live with my folks. Listen, I just ordered the Christmas special at Mattera's—red and green chilies."

Pizza on Christmas. That's Teddy. If I turn him away I'll feel like one of those innkeepers in Bethlehem denying a pregnant lady and her husband. The thought of a friend sitting alone with a pizza—even one festooned with holiday colors—is almost as distressing as the prospect of his being here. I can't uninvite him.

"Okay, see you at two."

Fuck it—it's my Christmas House too.

Except it isn't, and I pretty much know it.

Chapter 7

Teddy's room-temperature holiday food-in-a-box arrives in the early afternoon and immediately my young cousins haul it into the kitchen. Those kids, satiated of traditional Christmas specialties they can neither describe nor pronounce, leave no trace of the pizza other than a small pile of red and green chilies they feared were too hot for their young palates. So much for festive. Mom has taken the passive-aggressive approach, refusing to offer it to any of the adults or partake of it herself but not openly criticizing it. Whatever is raging underneath, I can only surmise; but if I can coax Teddy into sticking around until it's time for me to leave, the worst that will happen is maybe an angry phone call in a day or two or, preferably, the silent treatment for longer than that. The latter I'd hardly notice.

Throughout the afternoon I'm tempted to call Andrew Bennett, and when the murders once again come up in conversation, I mention the idea.

"Oh my God, no!" my mother says. She's just come from the kitchen with refills for various snack and candy dishes and a bottle of Crown Royal for my Uncle John who likes to have the bottle near him. Maybe it's for moments like this.

"Why not, Mom?"

"Well for one thing, you don't want to disturb someone's Christmas, hon."

Her response is so tastelessly inane that for a moment I think she's joking. Then it occurs to me that this is a cleverly composed slap at Teddy who has, obviously, disturbed her Christmas. I look around—nobody responds. Maybe within the general frivolity of the day, that non-reaction should have been my cue to shut up too, but some things shouldn't be allowed to pass without appropriate disapproval, if not outright revulsion.

"Mom, you're kidding, right?"

"It's a family holiday."

Slap number two. I could stop this now, but that wouldn't be me.

"You know Mom, it's hard to celebrate a family holiday when one of the family has been murdered. You do know what happened, don't you?"

"Of course I do," she says. "I watch television, but I don't think it's our place to dwell on it."

She picks up an empty dish and a beer glass; then, with the grace and austerity of an English butler, whisks them off to the kitchen. Of course I follow her. This is a palpable mistake and I can sense the apprehension in the others as I leave the room—they know her, they know me, they know us—but her comments indicate either a total separation from reality or the first installment of payback for inviting Teddy.

"Dwell on it, Mom? It only happened last weekend."

I keep my voice low—there's a doorway but no door into the kitchen and people in the living room can, if they so choose, casually eavesdrop on any conversation.

"Our guests don't want to hear that. And we don't ply them with pizza."

A few feet away at a small table in the den my eight-year-old cousin Dennis is forming some Legos into a building, but even at his age he senses a problem and leaves. I wink at him but he doesn't respond. I wait for him to get out of earshot.

"Ply them? What does that even mean?"

"What's next? Some Happy Meals for the kids?"

"Maybe they'd enjoy it more than that lamb concoction they hid under their plates. Lamb? Who the hell eats lamb?"

"Keep your voice down. Your aunt worked hard to make that."

"She bought it and tossed it in the oven. It's not that difficult. And nobody eats lamb anymore."

"We do. Maybe next Christmas we'll just order some subs and slice them up. Maybe that would suit this Teddy more."

"This Teddy? He was alone on Christmas. I thought it would be nice for him to have some company."

"Are his parents dead?"

"Shall I have him bring a note? But then who'd sign it?"

"That's uncalled for. I only meant that we already had guests.They're the ones...."

"Fuck the guests, Mom. Two women are dead. My friend is one of them."

For a moment there's a twinge of outrage at my language, but she knows better: I've heard her say worse at a greater volume.

"Aren't you nice, Brianna?" she says—a mild rebuke. "And on Christmas."

She looks away and busies herself with something she's just removed from the oven—the torte whose recipe she'd seen on the Food Network and was, she said during dinner, "just dying to try." She eyes it carefully, then says to me as if we've just bumped into each other in the kitchen. "Looks pretty good, doesn't it?"

She doesn't require an answer so I don't waste my time giving one. That would be tantamount to burying the whole problem, and I'm not ready to do that. Instead I find a strategic location between her and her latest masterpiece.

"Do you even understand what happened? I mean, what if it were Dad? Would you dwell on it for a few days or throw together some crème brûlée and light it up graveside?"

She waves off the question with a look of disgust. I deserved that.

"I understand you spoke at her funeral," she says. "Of course I had to hear it by the by. But no matter—I can only hope you used more appropriate language in church."

"It was at the funeral home."

"Lucky. I guess you could blaspheme to your heart's content."

"It was a nice eulogy."

"Good. Now it's Christmas, Brianna. Let the dead bury the dead."

"Don't go quoting fortune cookies, Mom. There are some topics they don't cover."

"It's from the Bible, dear."

"So is love thy neighbor. Same Bible."

"Brianna," she says, all cordiality and patience gone, "you're not going to ruin Christmas again as you did that other year."

That other year—Jimmy Castle and the Christmas night drop-by. It's not just me being obsessive.

"I'll tell Teddy to leave if you want, but I'm going with him."

"You're an adult, Brianna—you can do what you want. Now please move so I can get this tray into the dining room."

I look at it—while I've been seething she has been multitasking a pattern of cheeses and crackers and crudités and dips in perfect geometric configuration on a gleaming silver tray the size of a small patio. If this were some tragicomedy, I'd give it a good kick and send the contents to the ceiling. But it's not, and I won't. I can only refuse to move.

"You're in the way," she says.

"And if I don't move, are you gonna hit me with the hors d'oeuvres?"

"Brianna, don't overdramatize. I have never hit you."

"I want to know what that means, let the dead bury the dead. Do the dead grieve for them too? Because if that's the case, what do the living do? Oh, never mind, I know. The living exchange gifts and stuff their faces with store-bought cookies...."

And there it is—the first misstep and it's mine. She crows every year about her refusal to bake: it's more a running joke than a cause of embarrassment, and I've contributed to the gag by bringing those store-bought cookies myself. I can back off here and call it a defeat, but the battle has been engaged and I'm all in. And I do know a way to pierce the armor.

"Except some of those living," I say, my voice reduced to a whisper, "some are sent far away and forgotten. Is that what we do in your Christmas House?"

She purses her lips and stares at me, stunned. I've crossed the line, broached a topic that's off limits, one that even in our most rancorous moments is not to be mentioned.

I feel a hand on my shoulder. My father.

"Is there a problem, girls?"

I'm not sure how much he heard but he smiles, that vacuous smile he conjures up whenever his wife and daughter are renewing ancient hostilities but he wants it made clear that he still loves them both.

"Dad, what do you think? Should I call my friend's husband today—my friend who was murdered—and ask how the family is holding up?"

He doesn't respond. He can't. He doesn't know the answer until he gets a hint. This codependency has worked efficiently for thirty years: changing it now would be madness, but I press him anyway.

"Come on, Dad, I need an answer. Mom doesn't think I should spoil their Christmas."

My mother shakes her head. "Hon, I never said that. I said we shouldn't dwell on it."

She's right. Another misstep. It's a marvel how quickly you can lose an argument here—the technicalities always trip you up. In the ensuing silence my father starts kneading both my shoulders but I pull away. He looks stunned.

"You used to like having your shoulders massaged."

"Go spike the fucking eggnog, Dad."

I've never been crude with my father and immediately I feel awful; of course by now I feel awful for so many reasons that it's hard to find slots for them all. The tears will come next—that's a given—but since I don't want that to happen, I move quickly from the room and find Teddy talking baseball with my Uncle John, the die-hard Sox fan for whom every season is baseball season. I paste on my best artificial grin, one that I know I can't maintain for long, and fill my voice with what is supposed to sound like regret.

"We have to leave."

As little as I know of Teddy—I know he won't question me.

He stands up but I motion for him to sit, then rush upstairs and pack my small suitcase—dirty and clean clothes all forced in together. I hastily smooth out the bedspread and straighten the comforter (no sense being a slob on top of my other bad qualities), head back downstairs and casually make some apologies to the remaining relatives—early day tomorrow, long drive back, some other gibberish that doesn't require proof: everyone there knows why I'm leaving. My mother is already elsewhere when I walk out the door; my father remains impassive near the fireplace, then apparently remembers his role as peacemaker and follows me outside to see me off.

The turn to colder weather, begun on the day of Abby's funeral, has deepened in the days since and steaming breath fills the space between us.

"Go inside, Dad," I tell him. He's coatless and shivering. I'm still mortified from having cursed at him. I put my arms around his neck and kiss him, then back away quickly before my eyes well up.

"Calm down and drive slow, okay?" he says.

As I'm backing away he whispers.

"He's not forgotten."

"Who?"

He nods as if to say I don't need an answer—that I should know. He waits for some recognition on my part, and when he sees it, leaves me and shakes Teddy's hand.

"Merry Christmas, Teddy" he says, and he winks at me—his way of saying that he doesn't require an apology and this guy Teddy is all right after all. He walks away before the scene becomes any more awkward.

"Sorry, Dad," I yell after him. He turns and nods, then hurries into the house.

We watch him disappear. I'm crying, weeping, shaking from the confrontation more than the cold while Teddy—who again has dressed unwisely in a light windbreaker—stands near me, lost and uncertain of his part in the drama.

He's probably not a hugger, or maybe he thinks insanity is infectious and doesn't want to catch it. But he stands near me—I'll give him that—and when I've regained some control, he offers to drive me home, maybe return later in the week when I feel better and pick up the car. His folks, of course, very much alive, would murder him. At that point, though, I don't want anyone doing anything for me except staying the hell away.

"I'll just follow you," I tell him.

He walks to his parents' sedan, then stops and turns around.

"You have presents," he says, pulling the insubstantial collar around his neck. "I can go back and get them if you want."

"I don't want them. Some other time."

"Your relatives will feel bad if you don't take them, won't they?"

He's right—the kids especially still attach some significance to gifts. They haven't reached the stage where they have to buy things for people they don't even like and then spend Christmas exchanging them in an asylum like this one. It bothers me that Teddy insists on doing the right thing when I am perfectly willing to hurt everyone's feelings, but conscience is good, I suppose—keeps us from making a lot of bad choices. I agree that he's probably right, and after a few minutes he returns with a shopping bag and we start for home. After a half hour or so I pass him out and signal him off the Interstate and into a diner where I buy him a coffee, then apologize.

It's my second apology of the day—the only ones necessary.

*****

I have a brother, or had one. Daniel.

The name is never spoken in our house. Not at Christmas. Not ever.

I was ten and Daniel was thirteen when he got sick a few days after Thanksgiving. Everyone said it was the flu—chills, fever, terrible headache. Later that day he couldn't move his head—his neck was stiff. In the early nineties the Internet wasn't what it is today, but we could find stuff—it just took a little more effort. I found the word *meningitis*, but when I told my parents they said this whole Internet thing was getting out of hand. You listened to doctors, not the computer: Daniel, they said, would be better the following day.

He wasn't. The following morning he vomited constantly and lost consciousness on the way to the emergency room. We waited. An hour later a doctor told us it was, in fact, meningitis, the pneumococcal variety. My parents stared blankly—I started crying. Of all the different strains on that big long Internet list, this was the worst. Half the victims died.

Daniel wound up in the other half, what some might call the fortunate half. He stayed in the hospital while they fed him a continuing and varied diet of antibiotics. Some apparently worked, but only up to a point. Meanwhile I waited for him to come home and tried to be normal: I went to school, played with my friends, watched TV, even made two wish lists for the Santa I no longer believed in—one of them filled with things I thought my brother would like. One night Mom and Dad took me with them to buy a Christmas tree so that it would be decorated for Daniel's return.

For ten days our lives centered on hospital visitations as we watched him improve, but the improvements were so imperceptible that I couldn't see them. I just took my parents' word. Daniel never really got well. When he hobbled into the house and noticed the Christmas tree, there was no sign of recognition, appreciation, excitement. Nothing. He looked at me and around me and through me, then moved on to whatever else his eyes happened on.

"Danna," I said—I had called him that when I was first learning to talk and the name stuck—"Danna, how do you like the tree?"

He stood stock still in the middle of the living room, leaning on my father. We waited. Finally my father took his hand and led him to the den where his bed had been placed—climbing stairs was out of the question. My brother never spoke to me again, never smiled at me, never showed any indication of recognizing me. Sometime in January he went to what my folks called a "special school" up near Bangor. They impressed upon me what a long drive it was from

Portland, so we wouldn't be going up there very often. But that was okay with me—he didn't know who I was anymore and he never would again.

That Christmas tree stayed up until March. We never lit it, never moved it, just sat and listened to the needles dropping on the plastic sheeting below and tried to ignore the smell of desiccated pine. All through that first year Daniel was away, we would get updates on his so-called progress, but I was still getting my truth from the Internet. Progress might be measured in some learned motor skills, but never in anything that mattered to me. I had had a brother and now I didn't.

Some time after that a routine started: my parents would occasionally leave me with my grandmother while they "got away for a weekend." The first time I asked them where they were going and they just said up north. When you live in Maine, you don't go north without a purpose. It wasn't Bar Harbor or they'd have said that—it was one of those places we'd gone as a family. Just "north." And when they came back there was always some kind of gift for me, some junky souvenir you find at a turnpike gift shop, a memento that required little money and even less thought—a small teddy bear wearing a "Down East" sweatshirt, a plastic cup with a lighthouse and my name on it—my last name because Brianna wasn't available but Cooper was, and one time even a throw-pillow embroidered with a lobster—a frightening representation of a food I've always refused to eat. I kept my disappointment inside, convincing myself that Daniel had taken part in choosing the gift, though part of me knew that each purchase was a perfunctory effort to let me know I wasn't in their thoughts but should have been.

And now almost two decades later my father stood in the bitter chill on Christmas night and assured me Daniel Cooper wasn't forgotten. He still couldn't say the name, not Daniel or even Danna, but it was the first time in all those years that my brother was even mentioned. I doubt if it will happen again anytime soon.

I do love my father, but as I get older we connect on less and less. I don't know if that's a function of age or distance, but I know it's happening. When I was in my teens we used to watch classic movies together—some of which even he was too young to have seen the first time around: *The Graduate*, *On the Waterfront*, *Vertigo*, more whose plots I can remember but whose titles escape me. My mother liked movies too, but she denigrated the old ones as being primitive and amateurish. I realize now that her criticism was not directed at the movies (that would have been ludicrous) but at my father for liking them and, maybe a little bit, at me. But that's how Dad and I connected—mentioning my brother was never part of the equation. Coming right out and saying he's not forgotten was a gigantic step, but one that would undoubtedly be forgotten when the recent confrontation became just another bad memory.

I could have shared all this with Teddy when we found that diner, could have offered him some insights into just how fucked-up the Cooper family was. But as a sociology professor once told our class, "The term dysfunctional family is redundant." We laughed at the time, but the woman wasn't wrong.

"Bad as it is," Teddy says as we sit at the counter and watch a short-order cook scrape the griddle—are they done for the day? Waiting for us to leave? "Bad as it is, what would you do on Christmas if you couldn't go home?"

"I'd go to a Chinese restaurant and have duck."

"Like in that movie," he says, "but that was a family. How would it be to end up there alone?"

"You're not cheering me up."

"Did I ever tell you what my father does on Christmas?"

"You never talk about your father…or your mother."

"Well I'll tell you," Teddy says. "My father provides a gourmet meal for the birds. He buys the cheapest seed he can in fifty-pound bags and dispenses it all winter. But every Christmas he buys a small amount of top-quality seed—the best, you know, no waste, no shells, the filet mignon of bird seed."

"Do birds eat filet mignon?"

"My father's do, at least on Christmas. He figures that someday—not in his lifetime, but generations from now—all of birddom in this area will know it's Christmas because it's when they get the good stuff."

"Seriously?"

"Well, they'll know it's something. Pretty cool, huh?"

"Birds don't live that long."

"Neither do people. I'm supposed to carry on the tradition, and my children, and their children. Eventually it will become part of the genetic structure of birds and they'll know it's Christmas. Four days after the solstice—and that's something they can know—four days after the shortest day there's a feast. They won't call it Christmas, but they'll call it something."

"But only at the McClendons."

"Word will spread."

I'd like to think he's joking, but something tells me he's not.

"Is this supposed to make me feel better about my family?"

"No," he says, "but you feel bad because you and your dad connect on less and less. It's the same with me, but I do think about that—about whether I should stay in that house and continue this…this quest."

"To what end?"

He shrugs. "I don't know. I was hoping you would."

"All I know is I shouldn't have acted the way I did today. There's no excuse."

"That's why I told you about the birdseed. There's always an excuse."

Chapter 8

About halfway between my apartment and the center of Drayton is one of those houses you hear about at the end of holiday newscasts. It's owned by an Armenian family who came to this country a decade ago and decided to acculturate themselves by purchasing a billion holiday decorations. If that's an exaggeration, it's not by much. Strings of green lights stretch from the roof to the lawn in a fir tree-shaped triangle, while other lights, only white, frame the house and adjacent garage. Giant pinwheels in candycane colors line the walkway to the front door, and the lawn is covered with snowmen, reindeer, Christmas trees, elves, candles, and one gigantic inflatable Santa that shambles menacingly whenever the wind blows. It's all electrified, all glowing from dusk to midnight. There's more, but you get the point.

None of that is amazing—there are homes like this everywhere. But what is amazing is that by dawn on December 26, it's all gone. The family apparently hires a crew to come in on Christmas and return the house to normality. The sight of the suddenly unadorned house used to make me sad—I didn't like to see Christmas come to such a crashing halt. But I just drove by it a few minutes ago, and I'll have to admit—I felt nothing.

*****

Before I can even get my coat off in the *Courier* office, I see the note on my desk. It's Grumman's scrawl—Call Jill Dennison.

I don't even have time to get pissed before he sticks his head out of his office.

"Buying a house, Coop?"

"Me? Of course not."

"Jill Dennison," he says. "She's the Jay in Jay-Van. Real Estate. I figured maybe you were looking to move."

When I explain why she called, his tone changes. I don't always know what Grumman's unwritten rules are, but everyone sure as hell knows when someone breaks one of them.

"On Christmas! The hell with that. You're under no obligation to meet with her."

What he means, I'm pretty sure, is that there are plenty of assholes out there, that Jill Dennison may be one of them, and that I should meet with her anyway if I'd like to keep cashing paychecks. Coat on, out the door, cross the street.

Like a lot of small towns in New England, Drayton is an amalgam of old buildings that have outlived their useful lives and even older buildings that ought to have been razed decades before. Jay-Van occupies an office in one of the former, a three-story brick structure on North Main with a first-floor coffee shop where we were pretty much regulars until we got our own coffee maker, and an entryway a few yards down that presumably provided access to several upstairs offices. The building itself is seventy or eighty-years old, maybe more, and though it has undergone some modernization here and there, it still bears the look of an antiquity: undersized windows, elaborate masonry, a heavy wood-paneled outer door. I've heard that it was a WPA project during the Great Depression, but I don't know if that's true or just another way of saying it's old and ugly. The interior provides little solace with its darkened hallways, incandescent lighting, and even the occasional transom. And though heat in the winter is not exactly a modern convenience, there doesn't seem to be much of that either.

At least there's a directory on the main floor, and Jay-Van Real Estate on the second is easy enough to find. When I get there I utter a tentative hello, more a question than a greeting, and receive an immediate reply.

"Come in, Miss Cooper. We have no receptionist."

It's the voice from the phone, the one I'd like to blame for the previous day's fiasco but can't in good conscience. Her role was minuscule compared to that of the entire Cooper clan. Even so, I want this person to be grotesquely unattractive, some gnome rushing about ruining holidays with a cell phone. She's not—not a gnome, not unattractive. A little too much blush—no one's face glows like that in a New England December, and no human lips anywhere can be that red or that glossy. But with a little effort and better choices—including a haircut that didn't remind me of a monk from the Canterbury Tales—she could be really pretty.

"You're Brianna," she says, then looks down again, tapping away at a laptop. "Coop, that's what everyone calls you. I didn't think you'd come."

I don't even want to know how she learned my nickname.

"Miss Dennison?"

"It's Jill. So goddamn cold in here every morning. Vanessa's off somewhere—yes, I'm the Jay part of the name. Slow time of year. Why don't you sit down."

Without looking up she motions toward a straight-back chair. I decline.

"I only have a few minutes," I tell her, then unzip my jacket, move the chair a bit—proof that I'm in control—and sit anyway. She pulls her immeasurably thick tan sweater a little tighter around her neck.

"Thing must weigh ten pounds," she says, grabbing at the material. "You might want to leave that jacket on. I can smell the heat coming up but it'll be a while, you know, after being pretty much off yesterday."

I leave it unzipped—further proof of my mastery of the situation. I doubt if Dennison is buying any of this. I know I'm not.

"I understand how hard it is to just drop everything," she says, still typing. "I appreciate your rushing over here. Just let me get this done."

She races through a few more key strokes and, with a flourish, closes the cover. "Gotta return those emails. How was your Christmas?"

The question is so absurd it's like talking to my mother. There's a world of death and sorrow spinning around us—my friend, her sister, two victims of violent crime, two families bereaved, the bodies hardly even cold, and she wants to know how my Christmas was?

"It was quiet, of course." I'm not ready to share with strangers the parts that weren't so quiet. "I'm very sorry about your sister."

She nods. "Melanie was a good kid—not a good decision-maker—but a good kid. My folks are taking it hard."

"I know they live out on the Cape."

"Brewster. They're staying with me for a day or two. They are pretty tough in their own way. They didn't want me babysitting them so, here I am. You talk to the cops a lot, don't you?"

The change in topic jolts me. Then again that worn-out expression—*your meeting; your agenda*—probably still prevails. All I can do is follow along.

"Enough I guess."

"They tell you things?"

"Only when I ask."

"This Karl Brandt," she says, "how well do you know him?"

"As well as anyone else on the force."

"He was asking questions at my place on Christmas Eve," she says. "He was tight-lipped, but I had the feeling that if I'd offered to blow him, he'd have told me whatever I wanted to know. Is that about right?"

"I couldn't say."

"Come on, Coop, it's just an expression. I wasn't trying to be vulgar. Want some tea?"

"No, thank you. Karl Brandt is pretty good at what he does."

"Everyone knows what he *does*. Sure about that tea?"

"Maybe later."

"Melanie was a tea drinker too. A fanatic. No bags, just loose tea from some place in Watertown. And a timer. Are you finicky like that?"

"How do you know I even drink tea? Have I been under surveillance?"

"What? The tea? No, Chamber of Commerce luncheon. We all got our coffee while you had to wait for someone to bring you hot water. I'm one of those people who actually pay attention."

She re-opens her laptop, taps some keys, then waits a few seconds as the printer churns out copies which she picks out of the tray and lays in a basket on her desk.

"Vanessa will need these. Is Brandt as big a lecher as he seems?"

"Brandt? Like I said, I don't know him that well."

"Don't tell me you're interested in him too. He is a good looking man, but my God! You have to draw the line somewhere."

She gives me this knowing smile as if she and I are in this together somehow, old buddies vying for Karl Brandt's affections. I came here predisposed not to like Jill Dennison, and so far she's done little to persuade me I was wrong. I slough off each new innuendo, but it doesn't make any difference: as with most people who have their own agendas, I'm really not required to contribute anything to the conversation, just listen and observe. People like Jill make a reporter's job easy, but only when they provide something newsworthy.

"Don't worry," she says in response to my silence, "I'm not going to sleep with him. I have better taste than that, believe me. Melanie wasn't quite so selective. Sure about the tea?"

"Positive. What did you mean Melanie wasn't so selective?"

"She and Detective Brandt were going out. You know, I can use the hot water from the coffee maker and...."

"What do you mean going out?"

"Kind of a genteel way of putting it. You're the wordsmith—call it whatever you want."

"Your sister and Detective Brandt?"

"I don't think there were others involved. Poor Melanie was unwise, but not kinky."

"You know he's married, don't you?"

"I know she's married too. You read the obit, didn't you? Leaves a husband...."

"All right wait. Why are you telling me this?"

"Seems important to know what your friends are like."

"If you mean Brandt, he's not my friend. Are you sure about this?"

"Melanie was my sister," she says. "Do you have a sister?"

"I'm surprised you don't know."

"I do know. Only child. But sisters talk even when they don't have a lot in common. It's genetic. Melanie and I talked all the time. She listened because she didn't want to offend me or set me off: there've been some times in my life when I've gone...well, let's say askew. Anyway, she and Brandt were...is *dating* a better word?"

There's no sense feigning shock. Brandt's reputation runs more along the lines of capriciousness than lechery, so yes, something on the side seems well within reason. And to be hitting on me at the same time—absolutely in character. As for Jill's not knowing that I'm not really an only child, it's the only point during our conversation where I feel superior: I know at least one fact she doesn't...and won't. Of course if she's not just blowing smoke about her sister, then Brandt immediately ascends to the level of suspect. Despite my original intentions of blasting this woman for disrupting my Christmas, which I'm more than capable of doing alone, I have to sound reporterly, maybe start by announcing my integrity.

"I just want you to know, Miss Dennison, that the *Courier* doesn't play favorites or bend the truth."

"You make that sound like you're the only one," she says. "Isn't that the least we can expect from a paper? Look, I don't care about the *Courier*. This is about Karl Brandt. He and Melanie were together for a couple of months and now she's dead. What if he killed her?"

"You're talking to a reporter you know."

"Then do what you do. I don't care what gets out. And Mel doesn't care any more, that's for sure."

"What about your family?"

"You just said you're a reporter. Are you a grief counselor too? Maybe I'm just wasting my time."

I sit back and try to look comfortable, then resurrect Dennison's words from the previous day.

"We're off to a bad start here. I came over here pissed off...."

"Because I called on Christmas."

"And Christmas Eve."

"When you didn't answer. Why didn't you?"

"And why didn't you leave a message?"

"Saying what? 'Just got back from the services for my sister If you get a chance, Karl Brandt murdered her. Happy Holidays'? I don't think people leave that on an answering machine."

"Nobody said anything about him murdering anyone."

"I just did," she says, and starts tugging at that sweater. She was right—it has become warm in here. I lay my jacket across my lap and listen to Jill Dennison's account of her sister's affair, her decision to break it off, a skein of phone calls from Brandt.

"I should have asked," I tell her, "the services. Were they...?"

"They were nice. Sad. Tasteful I guess. What can I say? Someone that young dies, it's hard to put any positive spin on it. You know that."

For a moment there's a shared grief, but it doesn't last.

"The calls he made to your sister. Threatening?"

"Pathetic calls. *Take me back* calls."

"From Karl Brandt? That doesn't sound like him."

She shrugs—it's my prerogative not to believe her, but then I remember my talk with Grumman: the husband has to be the first suspect.

"Your brother-in-law," I say to her. "Have the police questioned him?"

"They're old buddies, the cops and Marcus. They've been to the house, mainly to subdue the guy."

"I don't understand."

"Sure you do, of course that was a while back. Maybe he's changed. At any rate he has an alibi."

As objectionable as I find Karl Brandt, I can't envision him killing a woman who lost interest in him. He'd be more likely to ask her if she knew of any available prospects in the immediate vicinity. Karl Brandt the undiscriminating lover is easy to envision; Karl Brandt in love? No.

"I've known him a long time…."

Dennison cuts me off.

"The cops aren't going to try to find the murderer if he's one of their own. Now do you see why I called you?"

"No. And what did you mean about your brother-in-law?"

"Forget my brother-in-law," she says, and without taking a breath launches into a biography of her sister, one replete with bad decisions and misplaced confidences and unwise choices, beginning with some pimply teenager named Stewart Rohmer and a prom night gone pregnant, continuing on to the floundering years and the fat years and the dieting years—a laundry list of missteps before settling down to marry this Johns character prior to one final misstep with Brandt.

"So," Jill says, "is that enough?"

"Enough?"

"For the story you're going to write."

"That's not a story."

"It's not a fantasy."

"The story is the murder, both murders, and the attempt to find the ones who did it. Involving Brandt doesn't further that."

"Unless he killed them."

"But you have no proof other than the fact that he and your sister were involved. Hearsay like that is not something I can bring to my editor."

She lets my response hang there for a moment, then wipes a sleeve across her forehead. "I was right about the heat, wasn't I?"

She pulls her sweater up over her head like a three-year-old, taking her blouse with it and giving me an adequate view of a desirably flat stomach and a lacy lavender bra. I don't spend my time trying to figure what kind of underwear women are wearing—I just like to assume they're wearing some—but there's something about that dismal building and that ancient office that seems to call for more utilitarian, less pretty clothing. I'm immediately jealous—not because I don't own nice underwear myself, but because whatever weight demons Melanie battled never spread to her sister: Jill Dennison has an amazing figure.

After she pulls her clothes back into position—the monastic hairdo survived the ordeal easily—she reaches down and takes a box from the floor. It's about a foot square and wrapped for the holidays with blue foil paper and silver ribbon. It bears a gift tag which Dennison rips off, then hands me the box.

"Since you already said no, this is not a bribe. For you. It's Hanukkah wrapping. You're Jewish, aren't you?"

"No."

"I thought you were, or someone said you were. Or maybe I thought Cooper was a Jewish name. Anyway wrapping is wrapping. Ignore the dreidels. Open it."

"Cooper is English."

"I'm okay with that. Open it."

"What is it?"

"It's a gift. If I'd wanted you to know what it was, I wouldn't have wrapped it. Twice."

"I can't accept a gift."

"I bought it for Melanie. She can't accept it either. I'm not going to return it and I'm not going to stare at it as a reminder of my dead sister. Open it. You can throw it away when you get home. How would I ever know the difference?"

Even delivering Abby's eulogy didn't make me this uncomfortable, but she's waiting and staring and I feel inexplicably threatened—open it or else. I struggle passively with the ribbon while Dennison stands and tosses her sweater into a cabinet, trading it for a navy blue jacket that's been hanging on a hook in the corner. Now the look is complete—a styleless suit that makes a pretty, young thirty-something look like an aging spinster. I doubt if there's a man in her life. Not that I should talk.

"Hope you like it," she says, as I expose the flimsy, brown, corrugated box under the wrapping and she applies another schmear of lipstick.

The flaps aren't taped and the packaging easily gives way to several layers of bubble wrap and, finally, the prize: a tea preparation kit— a brown ceramic pot, a stainless steel infuser, a black thermal mug with "tea time" tastefully etched on one side in faux-Japanese lettering, and a sack of loose tea—some variety I've never heard of and can't hope to pronounce.

"Everything but the water," Jill says. "Do you like it?"

"This is lovely, but I can't accept it."

"No worries," she says. "Take it, walk across to your office, go out the back door, and throw it in that dumpster. It'll be your little secret."

"I would never do that."

"Well, you're not leaving it here," Dennison says, her voice resonating with that same peremptory quality she used on the phone. Then she tones it down again, and though I'm still there, she isn't really talking to me.

"It's tough to lose a sister like that. Unless it's happened to you, there's no way to explain it."

She doesn't have to. I lost a brother.

"Those things I told you about Melanie," she says. "I just thought you should know."

"Even though I couldn't…I wouldn't use them."

"Yes. But I wanted you to know her a little, even if you refer to her as the woman with the crazy sister who gave me the teapot I threw away."

"I told you I wouldn't...."

"Sure you would. People toss away gifts all the time. Let me ask you something. What happens when there are people with stories and no one to tell them?"

"As a journalist I have to be more...more circumspect."

"But what happens? It worries me. Doesn't it worry you? Are we going to be responsible for telling our own stories because nobody else will? Who's going to tell yours?"

"I don't really have a story."

"Then you are indeed a *rara avis*."

"A what?"

"You can look it up. Now really I have to make some calls. Thanks for stopping by."

It's not the most elegant dismissal, but it works. Moments later I'm back at my desk, the cardboard box in front of me. Teddy's computer is barking some play-by-play from a recent sporting event, but he pauses it and looks up from his screen.

"What's that?"

"Teapot. And tea."

"Nice. Where'd you get it?"

"Across the street."

The answer, simple and direct, is all that Teddy needs, as if it makes perfect sense for me to leave the office for a few minutes and return with a teapot. Grumman, though, requires more. He ambles by, picks up the box, and shakes off some scraps of packing material.

"This is very nice. Those aren't real Japanese letters, of course, but very nice."

I try to sound nonchalant. "I didn't know you spoke Japanese."

"I didn't say that, but I can read some, and I can tell when someone is trying to change the subject. Where's you get it?"

"From that Dennison woman. A kind of late Christmas present."

He nods, then launches into a prolonged coughing spasm, my chance to escape any further teapot discussion.

"What do the doctors say about the cough?"

Grumman catches his breath and ignores my question.

"What did you buy her?"

"What?"

"This Dennison woman, what did you buy her? They call it *exchanging* gifts. If only one person…"

"Nothing."

He smiles and puts the cup back in the box. "So much for that tradition. You know you can't keep this."

"I didn't know what to do. She's bitter and angry."

"Am I missing something here? Because when I'm bitter and angry I don't usually buy gifts for strangers."

I explain as much as I can about a situation I don't fully understand myself. He gets it, but he doesn't like it.

"No way you can refuse, I guess. That's why she wanted to see you?"

"She said I was a *rara avis*. What is that?"

"Rare bird. Why did she call you that?"

"She said everyone has a story to tell, and I told her I didn't."

"She was right then. And that's why she was so hot to see you?"

"She wanted to know what I knew about the murders."

He frowns. "You don't ever want to become the story. Let the police do their job and you do yours. You can't very well be leaking stuff to a reader."

"But isn't that kind of what reporting is, leaking stuff?"

"In print, with confirmation, to everybody—not just some pest across the street."

"She just doesn't see anything happening with the investigation."

"It's only been a few days. And if she feels that way, she should take it up with the police. Or hire a private investigator. Sometimes people do that when they get frustrated with what they consider a stagnant investigation."

I look around to see if Teddy is listening and Grumman notices.

"You have something more?"

I motion toward his office.

He nods, then interrupts Teddy's viewing.

"Coop and I are going into my office and we're going to close the door because she has a secret to tell me. If Arlene comes back, don't tell her. And don't tell her about the tea set. We can count on you, right?"

Teddy shrugs. He couldn't possibly care any less.

"I don't know about that kid," he says, once we're inside the office.

"We spent Christmas together."

"Seriously?"

"He was alone—he came up to my folks' for a while."

"I thought you and your folks…."

He doesn't want to say we hate each other, so I finish his thought with the more moderate *don't always get along*.

"That was nice of you," he says.

"Needless to say it didn't go well. How was your Christmas?"

"Kids and grandkids. It was fine. You know I'm sixty years old and it seems as though I've lived through hundreds of Christmases, but it's only sixty. Ever think about stuff like that? You're not even thirty—you haven't even had thirty summers."

The answer is no—I never think about that, and I'll bet no one does until he's past what he knows is the midpoint in his life and some doctor has shown him an X-ray that puts an expiration date on it. I can understand why he's so philosophical. Then he shrugs to prove that everything he just said was insignificant.

"So tell me," he says, all business again. "What do you have?"

"Dennison claims that her sister and Detective Brandt were...involved...once."

"Involved, huh?" He smiles at my word choice. "Moral judgments aside, so what?"

"It could be important."

"Brandt would need a Rolodex to list all the women he's been involved with."

"People don't use a Rolodex anymore. Their phones do the same thing."

"Wherever this guy keeps his list—if he murdered all of these women afterwards, we'd need to hire another coroner. Brandt didn't murder anyone."

"Maybe not, but if the husband is always the first suspect, wouldn't a spurned lover be second?"

He motions me to a chair and leans on the edge of his desk

"Let's say *she* broke it off," he says, "and *he* got mad and went after her. Even if that explains the second murder, he probably wasn't sleeping with your friend. Besides, Brandt's too much of a philanderer to mourn the departure of one woman. How do you know Dennison didn't make the whole thing up?"

"Why would she?"

"Because she lost a sister and she's hurt and angry and needs a convenient scapegoat. Brandt is perfect."

"I don't think she was lying."

"Then ask him," he says. "You're the reporter. Report."

"I wouldn't know how to...."

"Were you having an affair with Melanie Johns?" he says, "that's all."

"You know I wouldn't do that."

"Tell you something, Coop, ten years from now I'll be long dead and just as sure as that's going to happen, you're not going to be a reporter anymore."

"You don't know that."

"I do. The whole turbine fiasco queered it for you, made you cautious. Caution's not a bad thing, but neither is taking the occasional leap. And if you believe Dennison, then what she said is evidence. You can't withhold it."

"It's hearsay."

"We're not in court," he says. "And that's what I mean, Coop. Another reporter would have jumped on that, gone right after Brandt, maybe find a picture of him and show it to Melanie's co-workers, people who might not know her husband and would assume it was Brandt."

"You think he picked her up at work?"

Grumman smiles. "That's the question I'd want you to ask."

"But crap like that—innuendo and sleaze—since when is that news?"

"You mean do we print it? No. Right now it's 'I know something you don't know.' That's not news. News is when we tell people something they don't know, but we know, and we're sure of, and it matters. It mat-ters. Does this matter?"

"It would make him a somewhat more likely suspect."

"Does it matter?"

"If he's a suspect, yes."

"Then get going. Ask him. Or find another source to at least confirm the relationship."

"And we'll run it?"

"I don't know," he says. He must feel like a high school journalism teacher trying to impart a feel for reporting to some eleventh-grader who gets all his news on YouTube. "But I do know this—go hide that goddamn teapot. Put it in your car or something."

Back at my desk I quietly put my new present on the floor.

"Chalmers College," Arlene says before I can even settle in, "what time is your meeting?"

"Noon."

"Don't be late."

"Or Joe Lawrence will lock his door?"

"*Joseph* Lawrence. Christ, don't call him Joe," Arlene says with an exaggerated frown. "He'll launch some new campaign to outlaw the abbreviation of names."

"Joseph Lawrence...I don't know why we bother with him as much as we do."

"Because," Arlene says, "in a small town a college president is a political force, and when he makes a sweeping indictment of secondary education—our town's secondary education—we have to pay attention."

"Even if he's full of shit?"

"Especially if. There's some clout left over from his term on the town council and we're a newspaper. Tip O'Neill said all politics is local, and since he was from around here, we have to live with it."

"Who's Tip O'Neill?"

Arlene shakes her head ruefully. "Are you sure you went to college?"

I actually do know who Tip O'Neill is, was, but I'm from Maine and if I can play the rube from Down East—a tack which invariably gets a rise from Arlene—I figure I won't have to talk about that gift or the closed-door meeting. The plan would work with most people, but Arlene isn't a rube from anywhere.

"So, Brianna, Greeks bearing gifts?"

She points to the area where I've secreted the tea set, and Teddy starts gasping for air.

"I didn't say anything!" he says, the sweat visible at his hairline.

"Theodore," Arlene says. "Please relax. We know you're not a rat. Rats aren't nearly that oblivious."

Her criticism doesn't register—he's too desolate to be harmed any further.

"I don't know if she's Greek," I tell her, "but I can find out."

"Think back," she says. "Maybe you actually attended class one day, if not college at least high school. Greeks bearing gifts? Troy?"

"Don't know him."

"Consider it deep background—maybe you can use it sometime."

Now she knows I'm feigning ignorance, but it gives me a moment to catch my breath and, even though I'm early, grab my Christmas gift and head off for the Lawrence interview. Usually I spend travel time formulating questions and responses and followups, but this time I find myself turning over Grumman's words—in ten years I won't be a reporter. It wasn't an insult—he probably didn't intend it to be. It just isn't the kind of thing you want your boss to say.

As for Arlene, maybe I'll tell her later that her Greeks bearing gifts line only applies if you're a Roman. Which I'm not. On the other hand, I'm not Jewish either, but I have a Hanukkah gift in the back seat.

Chapter 9

Chalmers College began as one of those discount stores that sprouted in the sixties, rose to prominence in the seventies, eviscerated the American Main Street in the eighties, and went belly up before the millennium. Most of those buildings either lie empty or have been resurrected as paintball war zones, but one of them became Chalmers College—a nice little kingdom on the outskirts of Drayton with Joseph Lawrence wearing the crown.

Every community has a Joseph Lawrence I suppose—a guy nobody likes but who winds up with a lot of money and more than his share of, if not prestige, at least notoriety. Like Richard Cory, maybe, in that poem we all read in high school—the local aristocrat who goes home one night and puts a bullet in his head. Such an ending for Joseph Lawrence, however, seems eminently implausible: self-reflection is not part of his daily routine. Still, in every election (if he isn't running himself) he's throwing his support behind somebody who will eventually win. He's at every victory celebration, every parade, every 5K or 10K or walk-a-thon or grand opening. His attendance alone is proof that the event is significant, but he can also provide an impromptu speech if you need it, and do so with a voice that probably came along a century too late: he'd have been superb on the radio or even in the early days of television when a speaking voice mattered. Nowadays you just have to look good, though admittedly that works for him also.

Occasionally a little untoward rumor circulates—some sort of run-in with another administrator or someone on the clerical staff or, because he can't keep his mouth shut, some local politico. There was a story not long ago about punches thrown and a threatened lawsuit, but there was never an arrest—at least not one that anyone heard of. Most people revel in his little setbacks, but the accusations and innuendo never stick; and as long as the college continues to turn a profit and provide jobs for a couple of hundred people, most of the town fathers are just as glad he comes out of everything unscathed.

He's fifty maybe, or thereabouts, but he's been in Drayton longer than I've been alive. We've all heard his routine: he came from the Midwest with nothing except a scholarship and suitcase, graduating with honors from BU, meeting the woman of his dreams, settling down, and never looking back. He's even tried to adopt a New England accent, the problem being he never knows what part of New England to mimic and ends up sounding like someone from a foreign country. But he reigns over Chalmers College while we remain compelled to listen whenever he chooses to make a pronouncement or, as is often the case, when Grumman thinks we need something collegiate in the paper.

Like this week.

I get to the school early for my appointment, and since my car is nice and warm from the trip over, I decide to sit there and call my folks. There's always a chance my father will answer—he's around the house during the holidays and uses that week to play homebody and perform little domestic tasks like answering the phone. But not this time. It's my mother who reads the caller ID and greets me with a frigid hello.

"Just wanted to say hi, Mom."

"Uh huh," she says. "We just saw you of course."

"Yesterday. Christmas."

The jab doesn't land, or if it does, it causes no reaction other than silence.

"What time did everyone clear out?"

"Do you mean our guests? Right after you and your pal left. Did he give you the presents? He said you sent him back to get them. That was true?"

"No, Mom, he drove all the way up there on the off chance I would run out of there without the gifts and he could go back and steal them."

Silence—it's her rebuke for my sarcasm. Just when I think she might have hung up, she clears her throat. "I didn't realize you were seeing someone."

"I'm not."

"This Teddy...."

"Teddy and I are not seeing each other. We work together."

"Do all your colleagues visit each other on Christmas?"

"Some do. (How the hell do I know?) Teddy has a small family and his folks don't celebrate Christmas."

"So they're Jewish?"

"Does McClendon sound Jewish?"

"I didn't know his last name."

"But I introduced him."

"Maybe I was out of the room. All I know is Christians celebrate Christmas."

"Maybe he's a Scottish Jew, I never asked. Would that be a problem?"

"You're free to associate with anyone you choose."

"But not on Christmas."

"It's a family holiday, Brianna. I'm surprised he didn't drop by for brunch so that he could watch us open gifts."

"He didn't just drop by. I invited him."

"That's what your father said. I said you would never do that without asking."

"Asking who?"

"Me," she says, her voice showing the exhaustion of having made the same speech too many times. "When you chose not to live with us any longer, you relinquished the right to use this place as your own. You can eat here and sleep here, of course, and you never have to ask. But isn't it logical to assume that you can't invite your friends to our house? I wouldn't visit you then ask some others to come along."

"If they wanted to, I wouldn't mind. And I think everybody liked Teddy."

"Not everybody."

"Aside from you, then."

"Yes, Brianna, aside from me who plans the days—both days—invites the guests and buys the food and cooks the meals and cleans and dusts and decorates and puts up the tree so that everything looks wonderful—aside from me, everyone liked him."

"I thought Dad put up the tree."

"Dad refuses to be a party to an artificial tree—says they're made from toxic waste—and I won't have a real one."

"I didn't know that."

"You didn't ask. Do you know how much an eight-foot tree weighs? No, you come along and expect everything to be in place so that you can put everything out of place."

I wish I had a witty reply—or any reply. Take away any familial prejudice and the woman is absolutely right—I don't live there and certainly can't invite guests to a place that isn't mine, not without risking some criticism. And she does do everything, no matter what her intentions may be. My father, and I love him, can be counted on for little more than spending a king's ransom on liquor and maybe answering the door when company arrives. I didn't know about his new artificial-tree phobia. Of course I could remind her that, even when I did live at home, violating the sanctity of the Christmas house had cost me that boyfriend: Jimmy Castle was just an earlier version of Teddy, though Jimmy had had his hands inside my sweater a few times and I'm pretty sure that kind of exploration isn't on Teddy's to-do list.

Here's where I could offer some semblance of an apology, but it would never be accepted anyway. Besides, it's not as if either one of us is going to change in the time between now and the next family celebration.

What comes next is as predictable as the seasons. My eyes moisten and my throat goes dry, and—maybe sensing weakness—she hauls out the heavy artillery. In short order she accuses me of hypocrisy—of exploiting the brother I've never tried to see; of cruelty—cursing my father who had nothing to do with the argument, who liked Teddy for God's sake and who is fine with anything; of ingratitude—letting my relatives think I placed no value on their gifts. When the woman gets me to the appropriate level of self-loathing, she tells me that she and my father are just on their way out of the house, spits out a perky gotta go, and hangs up. I in turn slip on my sunglasses, since anyone within a ten mile radius can see I'm a mess.

I carelessly toss my cell toward a tote bag; of course when I miss the target, the plastic case rattles off into the millimeter-wide opening between the seat and the passenger-side door. When I fish it out, I find all manner of once-edible detritus that has fallen into the same opening—some fries, a piece of a bagel, a tiny cream cheese container that should probably remain unopened. I slam the phone into the bag without checking to see if it still works.

"Let the damn thing break," I tell myself. "One less way my mother can annoy me."

Of course seconds later I check it (it seems all right) before laying it away more gently and walking into the administration building where Lawrence's secretary spots me immediately. My glasses fail as a disguise, but suffice as make-up.

"Brianna," she shouts. Marcie something or other, always shouting it seems, freckly and insanely cute. But I like her—she talks about Joe Lawrence as if she knows what a jerk-off he really is.

"Right on time," she says. "Mr. Lawrence will entertain you now."

"He's not having a nap, is he?"

"He's about to have his midday feeding so I can't promise civility. But you can go in—give it a shot."

I point to a restroom and ask if I can use it. She hands me an entry card and I'm able to get my appearance back in order enough to lose the sunglasses. Minutes later, looking like someone who hasn't just lost a bar fight, I return the card and thank her.

"Anytime," she says. "Hey, those murders last week—did you know the victims?"

"The first one, Abigail Bennett."

"That's what I thought. I thought someone said you gave a eulogy."

"Just a few words."

"Sorry you lost your friend. The other one, Melanie Johns? She taught here."

"I think I read somewhere she was a part-timer."

"Weird how your friend was in her class. Just one week. She left for a more advanced course."

"I didn't know."

It's true, I didn't, but Abby used to complain about having to take classes in order to advance her standing at work. I guess I assumed they were at Chalmers. It's more coincidence than surprise.

"She was an adjunct," Marcie says. "Couple nights a week. Economics and a watered-down tech course for older people who thought they should learn computers. I guess she was pretty good—always got good evaluations. I should know—I'm the only one who ever looks at them."

She motions towards Lawrence's office. I get the implication.

"Women around here are a little nervous now," she says. "Should we be? I mean my boss is talking serial killer and crime spree. What do you think?"

"I honestly don't know. It wouldn't hurt any of us to be a little more careful would it?"

"I guess not."

She seems anxious, so I flash her a smile—an everything-will-be-fine smile—and she waves me in. I find Joseph Lawrence, as advertised, awake, sitting at his beautifully appointed oak and leather desk whose thick plate-glass top is clear of everything save a paperweight—some flattened oval of clear glass or Lucite with streaks of red interspersed through it like the tendrils of a jellyfish— that and a white letter opener in the corner nearest the door. Nothing more.

"Nice to see you again, Ms. Cooper," he says. "Sorry to keep you waiting."

He's not sorry, nor is he happy to see me. I'm not exactly sure if I annoyed him or he's simply become a little less friendly recently. I used to hear that he was moody, but up until recently I hadn't seen that side of him. Of course I can be as big a pain as he, so I assure him I just arrived and haven't been waiting at all.

I sit opposite him, flip on the recorder, and lay it on the beautifully uncluttered surface. He looks at it as if I've just put a cockroach on his buffet table, but then, since it's only one cockroach, he pulls back and relaxes again.

"What can I do for you, although I think I know. People say I shot my mouth off about the local schools again, huh?"

I pull out some notes and riffle through them—it's only for effect. I know what he said. It's his usual diatribe against overpaid teachers, ineffectual administrators, and unprepared students—all of whom make his life of martyrdom as a college president that much more taxing, albeit a hell of a lot more profitable. That last fact he would just as soon suppress.

"Something like that. You said you won't support any local budget increase that pays teachers a higher salary until they have shown positive results. Is that accurate?"

"Support or defend, but you're close enough. I think I also said extending the school year would be valuable."

"And the school day."

"Right, well Ms. Cooper, I don't know why you're here—you have everything you need. I suppose you could write an editorial, agree or disagree, but you have the facts."

"I do, but I have some questions. Mr. Lawrence, as a college president...."

"Joseph, call me Joseph."

That won't happen. There's something a little too Biblical about Joseph, and if he won't accept Joe, then I'll avoid it altogether.

"Anyway, what I was getting at—isn't it important to create a good working relationship with local schools? I mean, that's where your clients come from."

"Clients? Yeah I guess that's what they are. You're right. I recant. That first woman that was killed. I heard you did some eulogy at her funeral. How did you know her?"

"We were friends."

"I figured that much, but I mean you're not from around here; she is. How did you meet?"

"A car repair shop. We just started talking, mostly about the horrible coffee and the dirty pot. We decided to get a real cup somewhere, and it just went from there. What do you mean you recant?"

"Lengthen the school year, shorten the school year. What's the difference? So just like that you became friends."

"That's how friends usually meet—just odd circumstances."

"You weren't there when the murder occurred though."

"Of course not."

He nods and moves his hands across the desk as if he were clearing it, even though there's nothing to clear.

"Makes you wonder, if she hadn't been alone, she might be alive. Or maybe whoever she was with might have died too."

He's taking some pleasure in my discomfort—that's obvious—and it's not completely out of character. He's always struck me as one of those time bombs, ready to explode, but who because of their position or status never do. Maybe this kind of semi-sadistic conversation satisfies his need to hurt people in a socially acceptable way: he wants me to admit that I'm glad to be alive because he can then imply that, to me, my life is more significant than Abby's. I won't do it. And again he's controlling the interview, which is no longer even an interview but more a casual but uncomfortable conversation. Grumman warned me about this at least three interviews ago, and I've gotten a little better at keeping things on track, basically of doing the job I'm paid to do.

Try again.

"When you say you recant, what does that entail—salaries? school year? school day?"

"Don't forget teacher evaluation," he says with a smile. He hasn't forgotten what got us to this point.

"That wasn't part of your original statement, was it?"

"That's a given."

It's not. I'm here to clarify statements he's made, not to be sidetracked by new ones. It's all about control and who gets to set the rules for this interview.

"How do salaries at the Drayton schools compare with the salaries you pay your teachers?"

"That's not really relevant," he says. He isn't comfortable with the question.

"Why not?"

"Well for one thing, the town teachers have a union to negotiate their salaries. I just follow some statewide community college guidelines. Not only that, but many of our teachers are part-timers, work maybe three, four hours a week. They get an hourly pay. Grocery money. Night-out money."

"How do Drayton salaries compare with, let's say Cambridge, Somerville, farther west maybe, Framingham?"

He glares at me. He doesn't know the answer, and since he's already declared one of my questions irrelevant, doing so again would make him look evasive, or worse, ignorant.

"I would assume they're comparable," he says. He has no idea. But I do. They're not comparable; in fact, Drayton's yearly salaries fall somewhere between five- and twelve thousand dollars lower than surrounding communities. When I tell him so, he gives me a condensed history of Drayton, concentrating on some recent factory closings and the drift of stores and shops away from town. I don't doubt the argument, but it's all too facile.

"And now with those murders..." he says, and we're back at it. "Cops sitting on their asses? They're up here enough."

"It's still early. You don't want to take on the police again, do you?"

"I've done it before. If I have to, I will. It's important to shake things up in a community. These murders. See how everyone is mobilized? Thinking about safety, being more careful? Sometimes it takes something like this to shock people out of their complacency."

I'm used to his railing about matters of which he's completely ignorant, but this assertion is so patently stupid that I'd like to take the beautiful paperweight and flatten his face with it. Of course I need my job and the income, and my tone proves equally effective, though not so satisfying.

Lawrence sits back. "Sounds like you don't agree."

"You're talking about a lot of suffering and pain, but if you'd like me to print that observation, I will."

"You know me," he says. "I'm always on the record. Just make sure you quote me correctly. You don't want to screw up...."

Again. I'm waiting for *again*, but it doesn't come. I guess he feels it isn't necessary.

"That Melanie Johns," he says instead, "she was one of ours. Damn shame. Good teacher. I didn't want to let her go, but we just couldn't use her anymore. Everything is money these days."

"I thought everything was education."

"Time to wake up, Ms. Cooper. I would think if anyone knew it was always the bottom line, it was somebody in the failing newspaper business."

I won't be sucked in to some other angle, so I shift the conversation to drop-out rates, college acceptances, graduation-to-job transitions. He's been bitching about high school prep for years, about how they keep sending him kids who need remediation. There's a certain disingenuousness about the complaint—these remedial students are the ones who fill the coffers with hefty, often state-subsidized, tuitions. And given the Chalmers open enrollment system and the PR juggernaut that continues to push college for all, the raw materials are endless, like an oil pipeline that can never dry up. Drayton is not a fashionable Boston suburb, but neither is it some forlorn outpost. Grumman insists that the middle class is disappearing, but if the term retains any functionality, then Drayton is a middle-class community. One high school, a few Ivy Leaguers in every graduating class, and lots of community college kids too. And though it may not be a "university town" like Chestnut Hill with BC or Medford with Tufts, Chalmers gives Drayton an academic feel—it's so much a part of life in this area that I can't believe it's suffering financially. I'm willing to talk more about money, but he quickly morphs from societal gadfly to concerned educator.

"What we do for these kids," he says, "is we give them a chance. Harvard isn't going to. Or B.U. Or Northeastern. Nobody up in Chestnut Hill is rounding up these castoffs and telling them *come on down—we'll take care of you.* Only we do that."

He seems ready to weep over his own magnanimity. I can't just let that go.

"But do all these kids belong in college? What about the trades?"

"That's an elitist approach."

"Could you expand on that a bit?"

"You're deciding who deserves a higher education," he says. "There's enough government intrusion without them telling us who can be educated and who can't."

"Would you say the kids decide based on their own actions?"

"Is this a debate or an interview? Listen, kids make mistakes all the time. We're here to rectify them."

This is the kind of asinine statement you don't call him on, not unless you want to be frozen out of the news-gathering process at Chalmers, or have him withdraw the weekly ad that helps pay our bills. He did that once when Grumman wrote an editorial critical of some proposed landscaping project: no ads for one month. Easier for me to just nod stupidly and suck it up.

"Marcie has some stats about our student body," he says. "Ask her for my P.R. folder."

"She keeps your files?"

"I don't like to clutter up my office. Look, hon, truth is nobody's gonna want to read an education interview with some Midwest bureaucrat like me when you got two murderers roaming about. As far as those high school teachers go, pay 'em whatever they want. It's not like they're getting rich. Now if you want some quotes about the Johns woman...."

"So just to clarify, you're claiming the high school teachers are not overpaid."

"Some of them maybe. But an evaluation process would separate out the bad ones."

"Do you do that here in Chalmers?"

"Absolutely. Marcie will give you our evaluation procedure."

"Melanie Johns. When you let her go...."

"That was money," he snaps. "I told you, she was good. We just couldn't keep her."

Before I can ask a follow-up, he picks up the phone. "Marcie, give Ms. Cooper a copy of my P.R. files and the eval protocols. And grab her a Chalmers tote—fill it up for her."

He puts down the phone and assures me he won't charge me for the tote bag.

I know I should thank him but I can't force out the words. I've already said this isn't my first rodeo with Joe Lawrence, but he looks different. Older. I've heard rumors that his wife is leaving him, but she's not the story so I don't think it's my place to verify them. It's only news if it affects his job, and aside from looking a little more worn out, he's the same windbag as he ever was. I suppose a better reporter—or at least a different reporter—would go after him, especially since colleges enjoy certain perks in a community—tax breaks and town services. And it's no secret what the cops think of the place. One of them said if they could stop answering calls at Chalmers, they could reduce the force by half. He was exaggerating, I know, but the only dorm houses some pretty bad actors for whom college is a dizzying sequence of drinking and fucking and fighting, not always, but usually in that order. The local citizenry ought to know that, since its tax dollars pay for those police. And when he said *two murderers*, someone a little more brazen might have asked if at least one of them was matriculating at Chalmers.

I'm not brazen, but I'm not unaware either. Crime on campus—mainly assaults on women—has garnered months of headlines, and though there's been nothing in the Boston area, we both know it's more a question of victims coming forward than a lack of victims.

"Campus rapes," I say, and catch him off guard. "Do you have a mechanism in place where a young lady—a victim—could report an assault?"

"We've had none here."

"You're sure?"

He gives me a derisive smile.

"Maybe you read the papers too much. Look around—this isn't some university with 30,000 students and a couple dozen dorms where anything can happen. We have a couple buildings and a thousand day-students. Where would you expect these assaults to take place?"

"You do have one dorm, and anyway, rapists don't have designated areas."

"Maybe not, but rape is a crime of opportunity and convenience. If kids meet up in class, become friends, lovers, and wind up at some motel on Route 9, that's outside my jurisdiction. And if they do hook up there, then that implies it's consensual, doesn't it?"

"Not always. Kids rent rooms to drink and do drugs. If a girl in that situation gets hit on and says no and the boy doesn't stop, that's hardly consensual."

"Route 9 is outside my jurisdiction."

"So you said. Do you counsel students on that sort of thing?"

"Do you mean do we get them all together in the football stadium and give them a talk on hygiene? Because I'm sure you've noticed we have no football stadium, or field house, or auditorium. We communicate by email, and yes, we do advise on proper behavior and respect."

"Anything beyond that?"

"Outside my jurisdiction. I have spoken."

He's still smiling, but the first hint of a darkening expression is visible and I know I'm about to lose him. When Joe Lawrence shuts you off, he's not the type to lose control and blurt out headlines. He's more likely to call security. Still, his statement about a rape-free campus flies in the face of every statistical study done in the last two decades. Rape on college campuses is rife; it's the reporting that lags.

"Well, anyway," I say, and make a big show of turning off the recorder, "the place seems busy, active."

"Gonna be busier if things fall into place. We're going to expand."

"You certainly have enough room."

"Not here. There's a plot on the market closer to the center, right off Route 9. Enough for two good-sized buildings, maybe more."

I haven't heard of this and I don't think the plan is out there yet. Again I remind him he's talking to a reporter and he seems undeterred by the fact—talks about the possibility of a dental program, culinary, automotive—he's all over the place but it seems like a done deal with only the specifics needing to be ironed out.

"Anyway," he says, "I know you didn't come here for that—maybe some other time, huh?"

I have sense that he wants me to pursue this, but I have enough to satisfy the requirements of this assignment and I don't want to muddle it with rumor or hearsay. I ask him if we might set up another time to pursue the topic of expansion, but he ignores me. That *another time* is now.

"Of course negotiating can always be tricky," he says. "Plus there's a building there already—gotta tear that down. Part of that was a machine shop so there have to be all these ground studies to see what's buried there. Zoning complications all over the place—hey, maybe I'll back out. I always wanted to run for Congress. People know my name. With the morons we have running this state now, I'd win easily. Who knows?"

Again he's wresting control from me. Jesus, this is a continuous battle.

"Thanks for your time," I say. "Can I call you if I need anything clarified?"

"Sure, or better still, how's about emailing a copy of the story my way before you publish?"

"You know we never do that."

He laughs. "'Course I know. Tell you the truth, hon, I don't read your paper. And listen, I'm sorry about that friend of yours. I know she had a son. Should we start a fund or something?"

"A fund?"

"You know, college for the kid. What's his name?"

"Nicholas. He's six."

"He's not going to stay six. I can throw in a thousand and just like that you've got a fund. Put some donation cans around campus—people like to think they're helping at times like this and you know the family. Let me know."

"He does have a father—you should contact him. What about the other victim? The one you fired?"

"It's not a firing; it's a reduction in force," he says. If I struck a nerve before, I found it again and he's struggling a bit more with his composure. "And if she had kids, we'll do the same."

"I don't know if she did."

"Then," he says, forcing a smile, "put in your notice at that rag and come work for me."

We've had this conversation before. He has no job in mind, though he has some nebulous idea about my doing his PR—maybe sending out a better newsletter or online report. He likes cute young girls—one look at Marcie and you know that—but there's no lechery in him and I doubt if that's the reason his wife left, if that rumor is even true. Or maybe the lechery works only when the women are vulnerable—when, for instance, he holds their livelihood in his hands. Maybe he came on to Melanie and she slapped his hand away and he sent her packing. Of course she was busy holding Brandt's hand at the time.

A nasty comment—the Joseph Lawrence effect.

"If you're firing good teachers," I ask him, "how can you hire me?"

"Different accounts. And now that we're expanding...."

"I don't have much medical experience and I can't cook."

"So you buy a book, read it, and teach it. How hard can that be? Think about it. You'll be able to walk to your new job from your current job."

He knows I won't, of course. And I won't check with Andrew Bennett about a college fund for his son, not because it isn't a good idea, but because Lawrence won't follow through and the fund will dry up soon after Lawrence's benevolence has been well publicized. So I retrieve the material from Marcie, mostly research from a clearinghouse of educational materials—a mishmash of unproven theories and outmoded ideas, gathered by someone with neither the time nor the desire to discern the difference. But I dump it out of the Chalmers College tote bag and carry it loose: I don't want to be beholden to Joe Lawrence.

Instead of heading back to the office, I call Arlene from the parking lot.

"Tell the boss I'm feeling lousy. I'm going home."

"The Joe Lawrence effect," she says. "The nausea will come later."

.....

I heard in an editing class once (from a somewhat dogmatic professor) that the word *suddenly* is the most unnecessary word in the language—that everything happens suddenly, from a lightning strike to the realization that someday we're going to die. "Don't use it," the woman said, "unless you suddenly realize you have to." But sometimes it just fits, like when you're leaving an interview—one that was heaped full of so much useless information that all you want to do is erase the memory and start again...and suddenly there it is—the one observation that escaped but shouldn't have: if Abby had not been alone that night, whoever she was with might have died too. *Whoever she was with.* Me.

Up until then I had not thought about it in those terms. But there were after all two murder victims, and one of them was a close friend. And that canceled evening I was supposed to spend with Abby—I know that others were involved. It seems more and more likely that Melanie Johns would have been one of them.

And if all that conjecture turned out to be true, there were two logical outcomes: the first is we all go out for drinks and Abby is no longer in the wrong place at the wrong time and she's at work now, waiting to come home and enjoy an evening with her family. The second is a lot darker, and at the end of it Abby and Melanie are both dead, and someone like me becomes what the military likes to call collateral damage.

It's a sickening feeling, and it comes about—I'll have to admit—pretty suddenly. I look around the huge parking area and see a small amount of pedestrian traffic—students and instructors going back and forth between classes—and I wonder which one of them wants to kill me. Which one would take a knife and cut my throat, then just walk away and grab lunch? Until now I guess I thought that somehow the two recent victims had made dangerous enemies, one of whom had come back and murdered them both. But now I'm wondering if we all have dangerous enemies, and life is more a matter of evading the fatal episode than it is going about your business or being a nice person. Abby was a nice person, a fact which did not protect her.

Arlene said the nausea would come later, but she wasn't privy to the way my thoughts lit out on their own. I sit there in silence for a few moments more; then, when I'm confident that I won't be cleaning vomit out of my car—or paying some detailer a couple hundred dollars to do it for me—I turn the key and drive home…where my first order of business is to toss my non-artificial Christmas tree off the deck and observe the one-story plummet to the frozen ground, a single somersault and a point-first landing. It has been undecorated since I got home from Maine on Christmas night and tore off the ornaments. Some of the less fragile ones survived—the vacuum took care of the rest. Since then it has stood like some hapless sentry, dropping needles and smelling more and more acrid with each new day. It was supposedly a "fresh" tree—I had it cut down at one of those Christmas tree farms near Concord—yet it died as fast as any chopped down in Quebec before Halloween. I did buy an oversized plastic bag for disposal, but the stairwell is quite a ways down the hall and dragging it down the steps and out to the dumpster is a pain in the ass, especially since my sliding glass door is so conveniently close. Besides, I know the couple on the first floor and they won't mind my retrieving it later and dragging it off into the adjacent woods. Both options are preferable to struggling with the shedding branches in the living room, then spending the next six months piercing my bare feet with pine needles that my vacuum never quite sucks out.

I don't like giving up on the holidays so soon. And even this year, as nightmarish as it's been, I keep waiting for that one incident that will reaffirm my faith in all those schmaltzy, weepy holiday specials on television. I'm waiting for proof that it's a wonderful life, but New Year's is coming and I have no prospects other than an invite to a party near Portland; and since that would involve a long drive and an expensive hotel room, I'm passing on it. That holiday spirit and I will probably spend the evening at home, and I don't need some dying tree to underscore the fact that I've trashed another Christmas.

As for Joe Lawrence's Chalmers College expansion news, I'll wait until I see the land transfer come out of town hall, or maybe see how it's progressing. Even then, I don't know if it's worth getting excited about.

YASMIN

Yasmin Maskhadova was the best Chechen painter in Eastern Massachusetts, or so it said on her Facebook page—the boast a facetious self-effacing stab at her own painfully slow advancement in the artistic community. It seemed that an appealing website filled with thumbnails, even those as compelling as hers, was doing very little to propel her forward in a profession so competitive and subjective. There had been progress, small steps: she had found a gallery owner willing to display a few of her pieces, she had latched on to a group of painters who had formed a kind of collective on Cape Ann—kindred spirits with whom to paint on the weekends (but an hour away), and just prior to that had sold her first $1,000 canvas, a 16x20 plein-air seascape she had done near Gloucester the previous summer. Then came the *Globe* article, which was picked off the wire by the local *Courier* also, and most recently an interview—if a five-minute segment of a generic morning TV show with three other young artists counted as such. The program had aired early on Sunday, and she couldn't imagine more than a dozen people watching it—most of them friends she had alerted and who undoubtedly slept while their DVRs awakened. Even so, for Yasmin the struggle to come to America, to pay for art school, to become established in the art community—everything was beginning to pay off, albeit in a frustratingly slow manner.

But now she had inveigled a meeting with a museum official. Yasmin understood full well that her work was not going to be hanging next to Eakins or Homer or Lane anytime soon; and she was aware also that she would be meeting not with someone from the MFA curatorial staff, but with a communications/PR person. Still, talking was good, and meeting people was good, and hell, even visiting the art museum was an afternoon well spent, especially during this Boston winter when she could paint only from photographs—a task she found tiresome.

She had worked hard at her art, but she had worked just as hard at being an American, acclimating herself to every aspect of American culture. Then the marathon bombings occurred, and *Chechen* became a word no longer associated with a struggling artist, but instead one synonymous with anarchy and murder. Yasmin was not even a Russian name but one more associated with Iran, not that

that fact would make her acceptance any easier. But she refused to hide, to cower, to let two miscreants or some national prejudice undo the strides she had made. Maybe, she thought at times, she could undo the damage these two brothers had effected. Today would be another step—she could be the artist and the ambassador, proclaiming that Tsarnaev was not the only Chechen name in the world. Convincing the world might be a different story.

As a rule she took the T from her apartment in Brighton, but she had other errands to run that day and so, accepting the risk of losing her spot in the parking-poor neighborhood, she started up the old Pontiac Firefly a friend's grandfather had sold her and headed down Huntington toward the museum. She hated the drive, short as it was, but she had grown accustomed to the lunacy of sharing the road with all manner of conveyance; in less than a half hour she had found a parking place on the street only a hundred yards from the museum entrance. She had barely begun relishing her good fortune when she saw the revolving blue and red lights next to her car.

"Ma'am, you can't park here. They got something going on and they need to clear this section of the street. Try the parking garage."

"I won't be in there long," Yasmin said. "I'm not visiting: I have an appointment. I'll be back in an hour."

"A half hour after it's towed. Sorry."

The cop was polite and understanding, but this was an argument Yasmin could not win. Her exotic look, those deep-set eyes—they might be effective in evading a speeding ticket, but they weren't going to keep her from retrieving her car from some impound lot and parting with money she didn't have. And the accent—these days that might have the opposite effect. The garage meant a few extra bucks, but this wasn't some whimsical visit—it was a building block in a career. Would Monet have balked at an outlay of $10 to park his car if it meant having his paintings hang in the Louvre? If he had a car. If he had $10. Okay, she thought smiling, bad example.

The decision to park legally bought her a pleasant half hour at the museum (she was a member—admission was free) and another half hour in the company of a personable (and yes, very good-looking) young man perhaps slightly older than she who seemed genuinely interested in her life in Chechnya, her experiences in the U.S., even her artistic philosophy—in short, everything that meant something to a struggling young artist. She showed him a picture of that first piece she sold, her usual semi-cursive and characteristic "YMask" emblazoned in the lower left. He'd liked it, congratulated her, but he was honest—she had a long way to go—and he made no elaborate promises. She'd have liked to dismiss his criticisms because he was "just a PR guy," but he spoke the language of composition and form and texture and color, and his critique was not far different from her own. Yasmin, who had attacked every obstacle in her life with a stoic determination, shook the man's hand, then left with the names of some "important" gallery owners and a vague feeling of accomplishment. She had been bullshitted by enough people to know the difference between a wasted visit and a meaningful conversation.

When she returned to the garage, still packed in mid-afternoon, someone stood beside her car, facing away.

Sequestered as she may have sometimes found herself in her Brighton walk-up, she was not unaware of the world outside her. That morning, in fact, there'd been an informal meeting at the coffee shop where she sometimes waitressed—just the owner and Yasmin along with one of the part-time cashiers and Marianne who ran the grill most mornings—a little impromptu gathering about the recent murders, keeping safe, being aware. It was difficult not to be aware of a large man standing next to her car. Still, she reasoned, this was broad daylight, even in a dimly lit structure, and she assured herself that she knew the difference between caution and paranoia. As she drew closer she noticed that the person wasn't standing near her car, but instead leaning on the car next to it.

"Damn thing won't start," the man said. "Just called for a tow truck."

Yasmin nodded in commiseration. "Anything I can do?"

"No. Good that you came along—when you move yours there'll be room to tow this piece of shit out of here."

His grey herringbone overcoat probably exaggerated his age, even more so with the collar up and obscuring some of his face. The sunglasses? They just looked foolish. He was an older man, yet he seemed big enough to hoist the car out of there on his shoulders. When he spoke though, his voice carried a false quality, like a ventriloquist playing with different speech patterns and timbres. She couldn't laugh or criticize, though: her own mastery of English was far from flawless: she still left her share of articles out of sentences—still went to the bank and said *may I please cash check?*, still asked the deli counter for *bagel and cream cheese*. Not more than fifteen minutes earlier she had told the young man in the museum what an honor it would be to "have painting in this museum," quickly correcting it to "a painting." She'd have to be a lot better before she dared criticize anyone.

There was little she could do for this man with the broken car, so she began to dig for her own keys just as a red sports car came skittering up the ramp, screeched around the corner nearest them. The rest unfolded like a disjointed event in some bizarre dream: the coupe smashed into a black SUV parked a few spaces over. It sounded as if a bomb had detonated. Shrapnel flew everywhere while she stood frozen, stunned by the booming explosion of metal on metal. She clutched her hands to her breasts; then, because she was by nature calm and methodical, began to balance her breathing, then steady herself on the car next to her, and then in control again, race toward the point of impact. The odor of gasoline was unmistakable, and she could not dismiss concerns of a fire. But there was a driver to worry about first.

Except he was already out of the car—a young man in ripped jeans and a bright-white shirt, his sunglasses askew—standing next to the crumpled SUV. His left hand shielded his forehead, his right pressed a cell phone to his ear. Yasmin stood and watched. And waited. Seconds later the young man dropped the phone into his shirt pocket, gingerly touched what used to be his left front fender, shook his head, then seemed to notice Yasmin no more than a few steps away.

"Sorry if I scared you," he said. "I thought this car could take a corner. It's supposed to handle well—I mean, look at those tires!"

She did. One of them was flat, a fact she chose not to point out. He was already more miserable than hurt—the machinery he trusted had betrayed him. It seemed he could tolerate anything else, but not this particular act of mechanical treachery. Then he pointed to her forehead.

"You're bleeding."

She touched the spot just above her left eye and her fingers came away wet. How? She didn't think she'd been hit by anything. She looked down: at her feet were some pieces of broken red glass.

"It doesn't look bad," the young man said, then took her hand and put her thumb on the injured spot. "Keep light pressure—I'll be right back."

He returned to his car, reached in through the sprung door, and somehow popped the trunk. As she watched him, the gasoline odor intensified.

"How about that trunk, huh?—gotta love a well-built car," he said, returning with a small white box. "Guess that's how I stay alive. I'm Ben."

"The gasoline," she said, less concerned with his name than a wet area near the wreck.

"Do you smoke?"

"No."

"Then it's fine. Trust me—I know my way around a wreck."

He opened the box—a first-aid kit it turned out—took a wipe and daubed at her forehead, then put a small bandage on the wound.

"Not a big cut," he said, taking out his cell phone again. This time he requested medical assistance for two. "Better to have someone check you out—I usually feel it the next day."

"Usually? This happens to you often?"

"Often enough."

She nodded. She could not stop the crash echoing in her head. Now that things appeared to be under control, she faltered a bit, leaning on her own car for support.

"You should sit," he said, and opened the door, guiding her toward the seat. "Jesus, you raced right over. You're pretty brave."

"I thought you were hurt."

"Your friend didn't. I scared the shit out of him."

"Who?"

"Your friend. He took off for the stairs."

"I'm alone," she said, and pointed to the car next to hers. "This one wouldn't start."

"Neither will mine...anymore. So you were alone after all?"

She nodded.

"At least I didn't waste the glance, huh?"

He walked back for another closer look at the crumpled mass, at both vehicles, then returned.

"A fair trade," he said, still smiling. "A pretty girl for a wrecked car."

It was the oddest compliment Yasmin had received on two continents. But his glances and words, flirtatious maybe, were not the least bit smarmy. There was something incredibly cute about him, and *cute* was probably the perfect word for someone who appeared several years younger than she.

The sound of sirens grew louder, fighting for dominance with the incessant humming in her skull.

"I'm kind of a regular with the Boston PD," he said, his tone sincere but rueful—he was in trouble but just needed a dollar amount attached. "I'll introduce you. What's your name?"

"Yasmin. I guess they will need tow truck?"

"Flatbed," the young man said. "Two. These former vehicles are beyond a tow truck. Remember, I'm the expert. And listen, when the cops come, just tell 'em the truth."

"Well, of course I...."

"Yasmin is a pretty name. Like the flower, right?"

"Yes."

"Your accent, Rhode Island?"

"No, I...."

"I'm joking," he said. "Where are you from?"

"Brighton. Now I am joking."

"One for you then," he said with a grin. "I deserved that. And listen. Don't let my good looks distract you. Or the fact that I'm a decent guy. I am, really, and rich, too—but I'm irresponsible. Totally irresponsible. And like I said, most of the cops know me anyway. So some story about how I was rushing to save your life, you know, from that seizure you were suffering from...well, like I say, they all know me."

"Chechnya."

"What?"

"That's where I am from."

"That's like Russia, right. You people are always fighting?"

"We struggle for independence. Like your people."

"Touché," he said, then glanced at his car. "I'm not winning many arguments today."

He was immediately, unavoidably likable, but Yasmin's temptation to extend the conversation was blunted by the glare of flashing lights. Along with the police came the EMTs who checked her and found that her injury was, indeed, superficial. The young man himself suffered nothing more than a few bruises. And as Yasmin would have done irrespective of the cute face nearby, she told the police her account of what had happened.

"And there was another witness," she added, pointing to the vehicle next to hers. "The owner of this car was waiting for tow truck…a tow truck."

The cop looked around. "Where is he?"

"He went."

"And the tow truck?"

She shrugged, then motioned to the young man talking to another cop. "He saw the man run. I did not notice."

Then a curious thing happened. With the broken glass swept away, and the accident scene no longer a hazard, a silver-haired woman walked up the ramp holding the hand of a small child, both of them well-bundled against the damp and cold of the garage interior. They stopped to take in the scene, their mouths wide in astonishment, and the woman briefly spoke to one of the cops. Minutes later she opened the door of the car that purportedly wouldn't start, belted the child into the back seat, and drove off.

"That woman," Yasmin said to the cop. "That wasn't the person…."

"It was her car," the cop said.

"But that man before," she said, beginning to doubt her own recollection, "Are you sure?"

"Yes ma'am. Matched her name with the tag. The other guy could have been a car thief, could have been most anything."

Yasmin, who had just become calm again, felt her heart racing. It amazed her how quickly the terror of the accident scene dissolved and the two murders in Drayton came rushing back at her.

"Those girls that were murdered," she said. "Do you think this guy…I mean…."

"Not likely. Probably wanted your purse, or that car, or your car, anything. Even in broad daylight, you never know."

"But it could have been worse?"

"Crime of opportunity—someone just happens upon an unlocked car or an unguarded item in a store or a nonchalant purse carrier. Anything. It's there and he takes it. That's my guess. If it hadn't been for the accident, you'd probably be reporting a purse-snatching."

He nodded, as if to verify his theory, and Yasmin reached out and shook his hand. She wanted desperately to believe him, but she didn't. Women in cities were assaulted, raped, murdered. Who in his right mind would steal a Pontiac Firefly?

As for the careless young man driving a car too fast in a garage too narrow, Yasmin learned his name when she read the *Globe* the next day. She bore him no ill will. She had been unhurt, taken responsibility, been a good citizen, left an open and honest statement. And this young man, this Ben Talbot, had absorbed the blame, been perfectly forthright, and conducted himself charmingly. It all seemed very American.

Yasmin Maskhadova, who had no current boyfriend, pictured herself that evening riding in the passenger seat of Ben Talbot's next car. But at the same moment she envisioned his next accident, then closed the paper and threw it in the wastebasket. She did, however, add his name to the database of potential invitees to her first exhibit. That show might be years away, but she was sure that the young man, possessing by then some new sports car, would race over to see it. She smiled at his fictional account of saving her life—wondered how many times he had used it—then returned to the business at hand. There were pieces to be completed if there really was ever going to be exhibit.

An exhibit.

Chapter 10

The report of the Talbot incident came across the wire last evening—the state senator's kid in the news again, this time for totaling his Mercedes coupe in a Boston parking garage. Teddy has the details. A CL-65, he says, a hundred-and-fifty grand. It sounds like an exaggeration so I look it up. It's not. I'm driving around in a late model Jetta which more than meets my needs, but I could have bought seven more of the same car for what Ben Talbot spent on his latest pile of now-scrap metal. That kid is in the news more than his father, and nobody pays much attention to the shenanigans other than the senator's political enemies who demand that he "rein in his son." Maybe they're right, but the younger Talbot has never been arrested—no drugs, no date-rape, no DUI—just a lot of irresponsible behavior that, so far at least, the old man has been able to contain.

This time there's mention of one minor injury, an artist from Brighton, Yasmin Maskhadova. I know her, sort of. I covered some exhibit a while back—new faces on the Boston art scene or some such—and a few of her pieces were in it. I guess during the collision she got hit with something—a piece of metal or glass. When I tell Grumman he's unimpressed—it's not much of a story, just another political gotcha involving a negligible politician and his even more insignificant enemies.

"Kid's an idiot anyway," Grumman says. "He's gonna kill someone sooner or later."

Teddy perks up. "Maybe he just wanted to meet her."

Grumman and I look at each other, then wait for an explanation.

"The Talbot kid—new girlfriend every week. Maybe he wanted to get a date with this Maskhadova and figured he'd do something dramatic."

"Dramatic," Grumman says. "Totaling a $100,000 sports car would qualify."

"More like $150,000. They'll probably be dating soon," Teddy insists.

"Really?" Grumman takes a few menacing steps toward Teddy. "What do you know about this?"

"Nothing else. She's an artist so she's probably cute."

Grumman nods. "Someday we'll look at some photos of Grandma Moses—we'll see how they fit into your theory."

Teddy concedes that he's never seen nor heard of Grandma Moses, but I have seen Maskhadova. Teddy's right. She is pretty, exotic looking. I don't know how the art world operates, but good looks can pry open doors in many areas. When I defend Teddy's theory, Grumman concedes the point and asks if I bought anything.

"I had some wine at the opening. That was free. I couldn't afford a painting."

Teddy seems surprised.

"What were they, like over a hundred?"

"There was an 8x12 for $300. Everything else was more. Five-hundred at least."

Teddy hesitates. "That's 8x12...inches...I suppose?"

Grumman sighs. "It's not an area rug, Teddy, it's a painting. Yes, inches."

"So she was a real artist. And you know her, Bree?"

"A friend was there and he insisted that I meet her. It was kind of embarrassing. I really didn't care for her work that much. I was dreading her asking me what I thought. She never did."

"Tell you what," Grumman says, "if you want to talk to her, play up the Russian angle—she sounds Russian anyway—it might make a good piece. But the Talbot thing...no."

I know what he means—it's a lede with no legs. I'm ready to drop it, but Teddy isn't. He thinks we should get her in here.

"Looking for a story or a date?"

"A story," Teddy says without the hint of a smile. "For you. Rumor is there was someone else in that garage with her. Bothering her."

"Rumor?"

If Grumman hadn't left the room, that word would not be bandied about. But it's just the two of us.

"Rumor," he says. "Some EMT was talking about it and somebody must have overheard it."

"What do you mean bothering her?"

"I don't know. Sometimes I just hear things," he says. "I told you I'm studying to be a detective. I'm not the only one. There's a cadre of us."

"Cadre?" Grumman yells from his office. "Both of you, get in here."

We don't get called to the principal's office much, but Grumman sounds annoyed. And he is. He's heard the same rumors; in fact, it's already on the wire that a prospective witness ran away.

"You and your cadre aren't the only ones who know."

"He wasn't a witness," Teddy says.

Grumman waits. So do I. Silence.

"All right," Teddy says. "My group—we keep our ears open. This potential witness made up some story about a car that wouldn't start. Turns out it wasn't even his car."

"So he was a car thief," Grumman says. "Big deal."

"Car thieves are in and out in under a minute. This guy was just waiting there. He wasn't planning to steal a car. The cadre...."

"Say *group*, please," Grumman says.

"Okay, my group—we like to talk about motives and connections. Bree here—she knew Abby and she knew the artist. In a roundabout way she even knew Melanie Johns—after the fact, because she knows her sister. If Bree has that connection, then it exists somewhere else also. Bree didn't want to do these people any harm, but someone else does."

"Listen, Teddy," Grumman says, "your theories are lots of fun I'm sure...."

'They're not really theories they're..."

"Stop. Just listen for a change. There's no connection here. There were two murders on successive nights and there was a car accident weeks later several miles away. Now if you and your cadre of wannabe detectives want to fuck around with that, go ahead. Don't make the *Courier* part of it."

"Sure," Teddy says. He doesn't seem chastened at all. "I'll just maybe keep the job I still have."

Grumman nods, our cue to leave.

At her desk by the window, Arlene is smiling.

"That seemed to go well. *Cadre*, Teddy, really?"

He grins and looks like the kid he really is...which makes me feel worse because he was reprimanded and embarrassed while I stood by and watched.

After a few minutes pass, I move my chair close to his desk.

"So, am I a suspect?"

He studies me for a moment. I don't see anything that resembles anger in his eyes.

"I don't think so."

"I was being facetious."

"About being a suspect, I know. And I don't want to date that artist. But listen," he whispers. "What do we know about her? Came to America a few years ago. Unmarried. Works part-time as a waitress. Lives alone, has some friends but mostly keeps to herself. It can be dangerous for someone like her."

"Unmarried. I guess that removes the husband as the runaway witness."

He nods. "You know, Melanie Johns had the cops there. It's on record. No arrest, but I'll tell you something: if you call the police and tell them your husband's beating you, and they arrive and find you basically unbruised, they can't do much unless you press charges. They can arrest you for filing a false report, but then what? You wind up punishing the victim."

I don't know much about the law, but I know some phrases. Probable cause, for one. Teddy shakes his head.

"If the case goes to trial the wife says she fell down the stairs. Or walked into a cabinet. Or fell on a newly waxed floor. And the husband agrees. They've already lied to the cops. Lying to a judge is a piece of cake."

"It's perjury."

"Prove it. Now this Marcus Johns works at Logan. He has no sheet. No on-the-job disciplinary record...."

"Sheet, Teddy?"

"Rap sheet," he says. "You know, a list of priors. And you should know this—the only one of the murders he could have physically committed was his wife's. Of course that's also the one he's most likely to have committed. Then again, if we like Marcus Johns for killing Melanie, then we're back to square one with your friend."

"If we *like* Marcus Johns? Is this more TV-cop language?"

"In a way."

"But that makes the crimes unrelated—which you don't think is true. What does your cadre think?"

"My cadre of wannabe detectives, as the boss might say, thinks there are more coming."

"More...what...murders?"

"Yeah. I really don't know. These connections and relationships—sometimes it's just coincidence. Take that artist, Maskhadova. Marcus Johns was at work when she was in that garage. He could have gotten from Logan to the museum in a half hour if it's not rush hour, which it wasn't."

"So he's a suspect?"

"No. Everyone remembers him hobbling around the airport because he hurt himself the day before—turned an ankle. He sure as shootin' couldn't have run out of that garage."

We've gone a little far afield of the original discussion, and I don't know what's worth pursuing here: everything seems related and, at the same time, nothing does. And despite Teddy's dire predictions, we've gone a month without another incident. That's not any unusual accomplishment in Drayton where we generally have very few major crimes, but folks have begun to relax. Now, though, I'm curious about Marcus Johns. I didn't really talk to Abby's husband— not as a reporter. But even a cynic like Karl Brandt knows that Andrew Bennett isn't a suspect. With Johns, whose house I haven't visited and whose son I haven't played with, maybe I can be more objective.

I drag Teddy back in to see Grumman, who looks up but says nothing.

"We've straightened out our differences," I tell him. "I'd like to interview Marcus Johns. He's the husband...."

"I know who he is," Grumman says. "What about Joe Lawrence yesterday? What happened with that?"

"The usual. He complained about teachers, then backed off. Talked about campus security. Future expansion."

"What kind of expansion? If he's putting another dorm up there, we'll have to double the police force."

"Doesn't sound like a dorm—doesn't sound like anything—and whatever it is won't be on campus. Lawrence says there's some land available nearby that he can convert or demolish or...I know I sound like I wasn't listening to him, but he's all over the place."

"We do have some old factory buildings over on the other end of Church St., but I haven't heard anything about converting or repurposing. Maybe I haven't been as attentive as I should be these days."

"Or maybe he's just dreaming out loud. Who knows with him?"

"How do you plan to handle this?"

"With tongs, from a distance. I've get plenty of info on Chalmers, on the

Lawrence philosophy, got a bunch of quotes. This expansion thing—it's for another time, or never."

I deliberately underplay the story because I don't trust it; besides, I'd rather concentrate on Marcus Johns—more interesting, more readable. Grumman agrees, then makes a few disparaging remarks about Joseph Lawrence—reminding me they're not for publication.

"Then set up something with this Johns," he says. "He's a sympathetic figure. Readers might want to know how he's bearing up under the loss of his wife—the one he murdered."

Teddy responds immediately. "He didn't do it."

"Well there's a trial the state won't have to pay for."

"He does have a history of violence," Teddy says.

"Not one that's ever been proven."

"There's always a first time," Teddy says.

Grumman shakes his head. "That must be one of those principles of journalism one learns in a Principles of Journalism class at the local high school. *All the News That's Fit to Print*—now that's a noteworthy slogan and philosophy. But you prefer *There's Always a First Time*. My God, Teddy, what happened to the dependable young sports fan who would go to a hockey game, have a few beers, then come home and write an amusing article?"

"Have you seen the price of beer at the Garden?"

"I'd almost be willing to expense it out for you."

"Can I get that in writing?"

"I said almost. Now go back and be sporting or fluffy. Brianna and I have something to discuss that doesn't concern you.

You don't need to tread lightly around Teddy. He just smiles and leaves, the same as he would if Grumman had told him to grab a broom and sweep the office. I admire that kind of restraint, self-confidence, nonchalance—whatever it is. I wish I had it, especially now, since the last time Grumman and I had a heart-to-heart, he told me Abigail Bennett was dead.

"Something wrong?"

"You two are dating?"

"What two?"

"You and Teddy."

He seems serious so I try not to smile. "Not at all."

"I don't want to get into semantics here. Is dating not the right word? Are you seeing each other? Are you FWBs?"

The abbreviation makes me laugh.

"Nobody really uses that anymore. But no benefits of any kind other than an occasional pizza and beer."

He leans back in his chair. "Listen. We aren't some big corporation. I don't have a policy on this because there's nobody here I'm interested in sleeping with. Same for Arlene. Same for you, probably, until I hired Teddy—unless you're gay, or he is. And that's fine. Anyway, I'm not trying to offend anyone or break any discrimination laws."

"Those past few sentences must have broken most of them."

"All I'm saying is I have no right to ask about your personal life, and there's no policy here about interoffice dating."

"Would it bother you if Teddy and I were dating?"

"Hell, no. Not as much as the fact that you might not have a boyfriend at all."

"I don't think you can ask me that."

Grumman frowns. "I have cancer—I can ask you whatever I want. Of course you don't have to answer."

I already had a pretty good idea where this was going; now I'm sure.

"This is about safety."

"Basically, yes."

"More than a lifelong fulfilling relationship."

I'm needling him, but he knows it.

"That would certainly be a pleasant bonus."

"And you can actually envision Teddy and me sharing a lifelong relationship?"

"Right now I see him as a deterrent, but he could grow into something more."

"Hey wait," I say, and slap my forehead as if I've just had a brilliant thought, "what if I date a bouncer, or a professional wrestler?"

"Now you're talking sense."

We're both smiling at this point, and I think we both realize we've taken the absurdity as far as it can go.

"Mr. Grumman, I appreciate your concern, but even if Teddy and I were married, he couldn't be with me every minute."

"I'm married," Grumman says. "Elise and I don't go out separately much at night."

"Yasmin Maskhadova was..."

"I know...it was the middle of the day. But we don't know what would have happened to her if that idiot hadn't wrecked his car. I just want you to be careful."

"You mean when I talk to this Johns guy?"

"When you talk to anyone, when you go anywhere. We've had two young women murdered. Teddy's cadre may very well be a bunch of idiots, but maybe they're right about these murders not being over. I just don't want you putting yourself in compromising situations."

"I'm pretty careful, sir."

"We're all pretty careful. I'm sure your friend Abigail considered herself pretty careful when she stepped out into a dark driveway because, hey, it was her own driveway. I want you to be more than that. Be cautious, suspicious. You want to talk to this Johns character, do it at a good time; know where you are, the surroundings, even the layout of the room. Like when you go to a movie and check the fire exits first."

"I don't do that."

"Cautious people do. You, however, are pretty careful. See the difference?"

He's right. I ignore fire exits the same way I ignore pre-flight instructions about escape hatches and seat cushions and lighting in the floor. Maybe there is a part of me—a part of many of us—that's primed to be a victim.

"Now this Johns," he says, "lives on the north side—Spring Street."

"Near the park. I know where it is."

"It's a decent neighborhood."

"Like Abigail's."

"Keep that in mind. And go easy on him. These abusive types...well, it's easy for them to transfer feelings, especially if his problem is with women, not just with his wife. Understand?"

"So I shouldn't make him mad."

"That might be a stretch."

"I'm not joking. Abuse victims often share the same story: *I don't know what happened—we were just talking and he snapped*. Or sometimes it's a she. Two days ago up in Revere a woman beat her own daughter to death. Six months old. Woman claims she actually witnessed herself doing it, like from the outside, and couldn't stop it. She had had some argument with a boyfriend on the phone and insisted that he come over and straighten things out. He refused."

"I read about it."

"We just misunderstand that while we're saying one thing, the other person may be hearing something different, or just seething."

"About what?"

"Who knows? Someone shortchanged him at a store? The boss was critical of some task? A stranger gave him a dirty look? The baby won't stop crying. I'm just saying, know the signs. You okay with that?"

I assure him that he's gotten through to me, and when I make the appointment with Johns, I try for a daylight meeting. It won't work for either of us, but seven o'clock does—after dark—unless I wait until June. I tell Grumman I have a late-afternoon meeting but spare him the details; otherwise he'll make me wear a miner's hat.

When I pass by Teddy, he's playing a bowling game on the computer.

"Research," he says. "Did you know Drayton High has a very good bowling team?" He doesn't wait for an answer. "Well they do, and I'm going to interview the coach and some of the star keglers in a few minutes. Right at the alleys. Don't ever tell me journalism isn't glamorous."

The air quotes around keglers is a sure indicator of his annoyance. He doesn't like bowling and doesn't like golf—he's told me but he can't tell Grumman. Sports are sports, and local sports fill the void left by the big-city papers and their national interests. Teddy doesn't have the right to pick and choose, but then since he's busy in the afternoon and I'm busy in the evening, I could easily ask him to accompany me to my interview. I know he'd agree, but I don't know how Johns would take to a double team, to borrow a phrase from Teddy's world, and I decide that a month without a murder, if not exactly an all-clear, is at least a positive sign that I can venture out solo after sunset.

Chapter 11

Just for the record, I can make myself look pretty decent when I want to. I get to the gym occasionally—maybe I should say sporadically—but keep pretty fit despite my somewhat unpredictable work schedule, one which I'll have to admit has been unpredictably predictable this past month: no late-night calls, no sudden rousting out of a deep sleep to cover some hit-and-run or convenience store stick-up. It's almost as if the major crimes have suppressed the day-to-day activities around Drayton and put us all on a more normal footing. I've been to the gym three times this week. I'm not one of those to go bragging about their dress sizes (or worse, bemoan the fact that I've gone *up* to a four), but I figure if I can keep it in the single digits, I'm doing okay.

It's in the single digits. So far.

The point of all this—aside from building my self-esteem when I've gone about six months without a boyfriend to convince me how pretty I am—is that I'm small-breasted enough to dress in a fairly unsexy way if I want to. And today I want to. After work I change out of my casually conservative reporter clothes, gray jeans and a gray wool sweater, into an even less provocative outfit—somewhat loose black trousers and a plaid flannel shirt, the latter fresh from the L.L. Bean catalogue where it appeared on a man with an axe held across his body with both hands and a wood pile at his feet. It truly is an ugly outfit, but to be doubly sure I throw a black fleece vest over it to disguise any residual femininity. I don't plan to spend the rest of my days traipsing around looking androgynous just to avoid questionable people, but for today it's the best course. I guess I'm a little spooked.

Marcus Johns has apparently done his part also. He's wearing his own flannel over a pair of unevenly faded jeans, and he ushers me into a room illuminated like a research lab. The glaring light accents his stubble and untended hair—it looks clean enough though each strand seems headed off in its own direction. But good-looking men are good-looking men, even in disguise, and he seems perfectly suited for a pretty girl like Melanie—at least the Melanie in the photos I've seen. He walks me into a sparsely furnished living room—a couch, a love seat, an undersized coffee table, and an abundance of cheap art prints in commensurately ugly frames.

"We were going to buy more stuff," he says. "A few end tables, a bigger TV."

"Bigger?" I look around: there's no TV at all.

"We have a little set in the bedroom," he says, then corrects himself. "I do. Can I get you something?"

He's holding a glass of something brown—bourbon? Scotch? but I politely refuse.

"Melanie had it tough for quite a while," he says, and immediately launches into her bio. He's very much at ease, talking about her various setbacks—the teen pregnancy, the former weight problems, self-esteem issues, bad relationships—it's a laundry list of misfortune and error leading to (fanfare please) the transformation—the running, their dating, the marriage. I guess I sound callous, but he does seem to tie himself to her salvation. Maybe it's true. Melanie doesn't seem to have kept anything from her husband, not according to what Jill has told me, and that kind of openness is more indicative of a healthy relationship than an abusive one. Of course if Jill is right about the affair with Brandt, then that's at least one tidbit she didn't share.

"She has a lot of siblings?"

"Three sisters and a brother."

"And she got along with all of them?"

He squints at me, as if the lights have finally become too bright, then he smiles.

"That's a weird question, unless you think they all got together and plotted her murder."

Actually it *was* a weird question. What's next? *Do you have a serrated knife?* Asking how they're bearing up under it would be far more appropriate, but even that would be the desperate query some vapid TV reporter might ask—a question everyone knows the answer to. I have little choice here but to come somewhat clean.

"My own family can be a little contentious."

"Do you worry about them murdering you?"

"Of course not."

Maybe time to come a little cleaner.

"The thing is, I got a call a while back...from Jill."

"My condolences. That's the scourge of the listed phone number. Sometimes people like that can reach you."

"She called my cell."

"If she knows that number, you're really screwed. No escape. Get used to it."

"Care to elaborate?"

"I'm not saying anything you can write in the paper. Why don't you give her a few weeks and come to your own conclusion? At least now I know why you're here."

I don't want to agree with him, but he's basically right: I came to find out why he killed his wife...as if the cops hadn't cleared him already.

"There are rumors of a strained relationship between you and Melanie."

"Rumors? Strained? That would be Jill talking. Don't worry—you won't have to divulge your source. What do you want to know?"

"Were the police called here once?"

"It's public record. Since you already know the answer, you must want my side."

"Maybe some clarification..."

"Let's say that things, at times, became...well let's use your word...*strained*. That probably happens in a lot of marriages, don't you think?"

"In some maybe, after a while. Did you ever see a marriage counselor?"

"Geez, Ms. Cooper, why not get right to the point?"

"I only meant..."

"We always worked things out. We didn't need a counselor. Are you married?"

"No."

"Then maybe you wouldn't know, but there are always adjustments and some of them take time. Things were smoothing out. Schedules. Working. Eating. Sleeping. They all require adjustments."

"And you fought over these?"

"At first. We were both used to living independently and neither of us would give in. It always blew over. Then my job was, well, let's say not the kind of thing she wanted her husband to be doing. She considered me a common laborer."

"I'm sure she never said that."

"Not in so many words, but her father had dressed for work in a shirt and tie each day and taken the T into Boston; her mother had taught school for a while. Neither of them was coming home at night with muscle strains and twisted ankles and the occasional cut and bruise. So no, Melanie was never happy with my chosen field, but that was really a small part of our lives. We talked about it, moved on, sometimes came back to it."

"How did you wind up in that job?"

"You mean how does a young man with a history degree from a prestigious university wind up slinging suitcases at Logan? Cutbacks. Retrenching. Call it whatever you want. I've never been fired for cause—the jobs just went out from under me. It was either move freight or starve."

"Did Melanie ever pressure you to quit?"

"Pressure? Yeah, I guess, a little. I mean she never held up some other guy as an example, but there was some pressure."

"When the police were here, was it an argument over work, or was it something else?"

"Something else? That sounds sinister. Tell you the truth, I don't know how it started. It just did."

"I heard the cops came here a few times."

"Once. Last fall."

I can't argue with him—my information came from a neophyte investigator working unofficially with some ragtag cluster of online amateurs. Oh sorry, *cadre*. I trust Teddy to be truthful, but not necessarily accurate. And according to Jill whose time frame is fuzzy at best, last fall would have been the time Melanie Johns was sleeping with Brandt. I don't think that's a direction I want to go, no matter how bright the room is. Besides, I still remember how to ask a follow-up.

"After being married for a while, were you still the same people?"

He takes a deep breath.

"Wow, that's a new one."

He seems neither upset nor pleased, and that's good. I wish I could take credit for the question, but it came out of a seminar when a visiting journalist told us to treat interviews like character analyses in a book review—think in terms of development and change. It was all very high-schoolish and we all dismissed him as daft and stodgy and made jokes that he should have been an English teacher instead of a journalist, but here I am stealing his material, and I'll bet the rest of his detractors are doing the same.

"I guess," he says—and he seemed more contemplative—"we became better at not being alone. Having to think about doing things with someone else all the time. Sometimes it was okay; sometimes not. But Melanie was patient with me. I think she understood, but I think I scared her at times."

"We all get a little out of control occasionally, I guess."

He puts both hands behind his neck, stretches his head backwards, smiles.

"I trashed the bedroom once...just threw things around."

"Did anyone get hurt?"

"That's why I'm smiling. Melanie wasn't there. I even had it all straightened by the time she got home. And I was smart enough to throw around things that didn't break...mostly."

"Mostly?"

"The fastener snapped on a bracelet. Afterward I told her it was a common problem with cheap plastic. I didn't tell her it was a problem only when cheap plastic was launched into a closet door."

"Why did you do it?"

"I don't know. It was just...a release?"

"Running is a release. Weightlifting. Sudoku. Yoga."

"And throwing things around, believe me. Try it sometime."

So I take the chance and tell him about last Christmas—the big blow up with my family—because as angry I was, what did I do before storming out? Straighten the room. I didn't know throwing things around was an option. He laughs, asks me if I'm sure about that drink. I tell him I am, that I'm working. He doesn't push it. As the minutes go by he becomes more introspective, less caricature and more character; but even so, I'm not sure who this guy is.

"Just a few more questions if I could?"

"Sure," he says. 'Whatever you need."

"You saw her a few hours before the murder, is that right?"

"The day she was killed. I went to work in the morning...."

"At Logan."

"I fly the big jets."

"I don't think so."

"I suppose you need a pilot's license for that, but I used to say that to Melanie when our arguments were winding down. I could always get her to laugh by assuring her that someday I'd 'fly the big jets.' But you obviously prepped for this interview. So you know I'm just another petty administrator with an office job who's never in his office. I'm always on the floor somewhere. I probably move as much freight during the day as FedEx."

"And on the day of the...of the murder, you saw your wife in the morning before work?"

"It happened often: we slept in the same bed."

"Dumb question. I mean you didn't leave before she awoke, or vice versa."

"No."

"What were your morning routines like? It can be a little hectic with two people rushing off to work."

"A little hectic, like you said. That was one of those adjustments."

"This is a pretty good-sized house, though. How long have you lived here?"

"Since we were married."

"No children?"

"We wanted to buy the end tables first."

"I guess they can be pretty important." Our conversation seems a lot more relaxed, but I try to keep Grumman's warning in the back of my mind.

"Seriously, we talked about kids," he says. "She wanted to keep her figure for a while before she gave it up again. I liked her figure, too. As I said, she used to be heavy. She was pregnant at eighteen. She wasn't quite ready to go back down that road."

"And you?"

He shakes his head. "I can't bear children. My body...."

"You know what I mean."

"It wasn't a priority. Straightening ourselves out was more important. You can't bring a child into a home where the parents are in turmoil. You said you aren't married. Ever been?"

"No, why?"

"Don't worry, I'm not trawling—Melanie was it for me. But sometimes couples are at each other's throats and then the situation passes. Our problems could have passed. They always had."

I'd like to tell him that he's right—that his dead wife's affair with Karl Brandt had ended and that maybe she was ready to settle into an honest life from there on in. But a man with a temper and that new knowledge, what would keep him from going after Brandt and what would keep Brandt from shooting him? So instead of reassuring him, all I can do is nod and look sad. I am sad. He's blaming himself for his inadequacies as a husband—and he may very well have had them—but if Melanie could have paid a modicum of attention to her wedding vows—to simple morality—she might be alive. Who the hell knows?

I like to avoid the ubiquitous but snarky *we're done here*, but we are.

He stands first and asks if there's anything else he can tell me. There isn't, but instead of leading me back to the front door, he walks into another room and flicks on the light.

"I want to show you something. Come on, it's safe."

Rather than run scared all the time, I follow him into a small study off the living room. Near the window is a tripod with a yellow telescope attached, and next to it are a chair and a number of books on astronomy. Aside from that, the room is bare. He nudges the telescope a quarter turn.

"Cost me a couple hundred last summer. I don't understand the thrill, but..."

"Did she use it a lot?"

He nods, then explains more about his former wife's interest. I can tell he doesn't get the whole planets-and-stars thing, the way most of us don't "get" others' hobbies, but now I have an angle, one that will focus my article more on Melanie's life than her death. It won't cause the same stir as the image of an enraged man alone running roughshod through his home, but then neither will Teddy's bowling piece.

We both mention some asteroid that's going to miss earth by 40,000 miles—it's the sum total of our knowledge in the field—and a few minutes later I'm at the front door.

"Thank you, Mr. Johns."

"Marcus. Gonna print that astronomy stuff?"

"That's up to my editor. Would that bother you?"

"There are perverts with telescopes trained on their neighbors' bedrooms. Make sure she doesn't come off as one. Or I don't."

He opens the front door, giving me plenty of room to get by. When I thank him again for his time, he smiles.

"I bought some big light bulbs today," he says, "upped the wattage a little. I read your article about women being safe, staying in well-lit areas. If I can't pay next month's electric bill, I'm sending it to you."

"Just send it to the *Courier*. We probably have an account for that."

"You be careful—lots of bad actors around. Melanie saw them every day up at Chalmers."

"At the college?"

"That place'll take anybody with a checkbook, or the means to steal one."

"Open admission. Was Melanie worried about it?"

"The kids who gave her the most trouble were the same ones who told her later how she'd got them on the right track. No student would have done this to her."

"Anyone else she had a conflict with?"

"Aside from the asshole that runs the place—don't print that."

"The *Courier* is a family paper."

"Just the same—the less said about her boss, the better."

"Joe Lawrence."

"I mean it—the less said...."

I get halfway between the front door and the car when he yells after me.

"Miss Cooper."

His head is cocked to one side. "Your outfit. Was that for my benefit?"

"I like to dress appropriately."

"And you're what, working the graveyard shift at the sawmill?"

"I don't make much as a reporter. Gotta do part-time."

I like the guy. Every instinct I have says he wouldn't have harmed his wife, though the image of him chucking objects around their bedroom is disturbing. It doesn't need to be part of what the public knows about him, but I'm always weighing Grumman's question—does it matter?—against that quote in his office about the absolute truth.

And Marcus's willingness to laugh at his own demons—is that some highly developed self-awareness or a complete lack of empathy for others—victims included? Knowing you're a lunatic doesn't necessarily excuse the lunacy—I saw *Silence of the Lambs* too. (Yes, one of those movies I watched with my

Dad—I watched; he squirmed.) Anyway, I have decent notes, the astronomy angle, and a somewhat clearer understanding of the person Jill Dennison had demonized.

Spring Street where Marcus Johns lives is, as advertised, a quiet area, but as I drive to the first stop sign, my headlights illuminate a figure on the corner. At first it appears to be someone walking a dog, but the figure is not moving, just leaning behind a small blue four-door parked facing the Johns house. And there's no dog. Instinctively I snap down the door locks. I'm about ready to tear through the intersection when I notice the jeans, the bulky sweater, the scarf. It's a woman—a woman I know. And she's waving as she walks toward the car.

Jill Dennison.

Before I can even ask her why she's hanging out on a darkened street corner, she signals me to roll down the window.

"I'm parked right there," she says. "Follow me. We'll talk."

Chapter 12

I follow her to Deal's. As good as that little dive is for breakfast, it's equivalently awful for anything else, dispensing a diverse but only marginally edible selection of items that travel direct from truck to freezer to deep fryer, with an occasional detour through the microwave.

Jill Dennison assures me—with a noticeable smirk—that we won't need a reservation.

Inside, a pair of middle-aged women occupies a booth near the door and a few forlorn looking men in knit caps turn coffee mugs alone at the counter. A desolate waiter watches them. There's a radio on somewhere, but the music is indiscernible—quiet and distant. Dennison leads me toward a booth near a window, though the view outside is obscured by a green plastic Christmas wreath that should have been taken down and stored weeks before...or never have been hung in the first place.

"Your boyfriend," Dennison says before we had even sat down. "He said you liked the tea set."

"I don't have a boyfriend, and if you mean Teddy, he doesn't even know you gave it to me."

"You didn't tell him? I'd have thought you might share everything with him. Truth is the foundation of a good relationship."

"And that's why you just made up a story?"

"We don't have a relationship. Did you like the set or not? I never really heard anything afterwards."

"You told me it would be our little secret. But yes, I liked it, but it's too expensive. I can't accept gifts like that from strangers."

"A crappy little present. It's not a big deal. Besides, I got it on sale."

She flags down a waiter who glances our way, then holds up his index finger to let us know he'll be by in a minute. He's doing nothing and doesn't need a minute—unless he's going to spend it laundering that hideous grease-stained orange apron he's wearing.

"And anyway," I tell her, "it's not a crappy little present. I checked online."

Or Teddy did—she doesn't need every detail. She's about to contradict me when index-finger-man drops two menus on the table and continues on by.

"Just coffee for me," Dennison says, stopping him in his tracks, "and tea for my pal."

He turns, straightens the brim of his red baseball hat, and pulls out a pad. "Got pies," he says, reading off a list. "Got apple and cherry, out of blueberry."

"Are they fresh?" Dennison asks.

"They're pies," he says, as if the question of freshness is complete nonsense, then adds, "they were baked this morning."

"Where?" she asks. It's a question he isn't prepared to answer, but to his credit he doesn't lie—just stands there.

"Apple," Dennison says, "one piece and two forks."

The waiter writes down nothing and turns to walk away when I stop him.

"And I'll have coffee."

He shrugs. "Up to you," he says and continues off.

"He's only going to fuck it up," Dennison says, then looks at my outfit. "Nice shirt—very flattering. Moonlighting at the sawmill?"

"Lumber mill."

"Didn't know there was a difference. Now what's this shit about coffee. You're just gonna show me who's boss, right?"

"What do you mean?"

"You're not good at this, Miss Cooper. You only want coffee because I said you wanted tea...because I gave you a tea set. Maybe I'll drop by the office tomorrow with a coffee maker for you. Then what are you going to order the next time we're here, hot chocolate?"

"I don't plan to come here again."

"With me," she says.

"With anybody. This is not one of my hangouts."

She's right, of course—I wanted tea. And she's probably right about another thing too—I'm not very good at establishing control. I probably proved that trying unsuccessfully to keep Joe Lawrence from using me as a promoter for his agenda. Or maybe Dennison's so good at it that I have no chance.

"I'll take you at your word," she says. "Besides, it's pretty much a crap shoot what that re-tard brings you. Speaking of re-tards, how's my brother-in-law bearing up in widowhood? Or is that widowerhood?"

"Were you following me?"

"No."

"Then how did you know I was there?"

"I didn't. I drive by his place once in a while, just to see if he's screwing anybody new. I saw your car parked in front—waited around."

"How do you know my car?"

"I have a surveillance camera set up in the parking lot behind the *Courier*. I know everyone's car. You should see the list in my office."

Dennison looks around, then pulls out her phone and turns it on.

"If I can get some bars in this dump," she says, tapping her cell as if it were some balky watch, "maybe I could show you your parking place right now on the parking-lot-cam I had installed."

"There's no camera in that parking lot."

"I'm joking. Jesus, you should be dating that re-tard of a waiter, not Teddy."

"You know that's really an offensive word."

"I thought Teddy was his name."

"You know what I mean."

"Yeah, yeah, I get it, Ms. P.C. journalist. What would you have me call him? He's not wearing a name tag and he didn't introduce himself and tell us he'd be taking care of us. How about Filthy or Witless—he could be one of Snow White's extra dwarfs—though he's kind of tall...."

"You've made your point. You just didn't answer my question."

"What, about your car? Christ, you drive to work and sometimes you park in front of the building. I've seen you. We're not talking about a lot of investigative work here. More like looking out a window once in a while. So how's my brother-in-law doing?"

"Why don't you ask him?"

"He and I don't speak much."

"You could put a surveillance camera on his house. It would save you time and gas."

Dennison leans far back in the booth and stretches her arms in front of her. "You're pissed off because I know what kind of car you drive? Jesus," she says, her voice rising to overwhelm the sparsely filled restaurant. "Put a fucking tarp over it from now on."

One of the men at the counter turns and looks our way. I lower my voice to a near whisper and tell her. Dennison looks at them.

"She wants to put a fucking tarp over her car," she says to them. "A fucking tarp."

The man shakes his head as if to agree I truly am nuts, then turns back to whatever processed delicacy sits on a dish in front of him.

"That was nice," I tell her, "making me look like an idiot."

"Right, he was the man of your dreams and now he won't ask you out. I've ruined your chances for a lifetime of magical evenings in Deal's."

"That's not the point."

"Then don't get all pissed off. What am I gonna do, lower this place's Yelp rating by cursing?"

"I'm not pissed off."

"Thank God for that. Look, all I'm saying is if my brother-in-law had something going on the side—with my sister out of the way and all—I'd want him to wait a suitable length of time before he dragged some new whore into his bed. 'Course that's just me."

"And I'm the whore?"

"Nice try—counterattack. I already told you I was watching him. You were just in my sightline."

"Well, now I feel better."

"Now you're deflecting."

"Is it possible that I might say something...anything...without some instant analysis? We all have ulterior motives for doing things—saying things—your awareness of that doesn't make you incisive...or different...or better. Now I followed along and met you here. Can you just get to the point, or was that it? You wanted to know if I was sleeping with Marcus Johns."

I'm never that peremptory unless my mother backs me into a corner, and Dennison, unlike my mother, actually backs off a little. It's not something I experience very often.

"Tell you the truth, I am a little curious about why you'd be there."

"I told you before. My boss gives me assignments—this one was go interview Marcus Johns."

There's enough truth in my explanation to get me through it with good eye contact—it makes the explanation seem credible. Of course Dennison immediately wants to know if her brother-in-law is a suspect, if I'm privy to some things she doesn't know. I remind her why human interest stories are so popular, especially ones that hit close to home. The interest in astronomy, in maybe having children someday. She listens politely enough and lets me finish before shaking her head.

"Bullshit. A guy's wife is murdered and you want to know how he's holding up? How do you think? If he's celebrating it won't be in front of you, and if he's mourning the loss, where's the surprise? You could have pretty much written the story before you got there."

"I wouldn't have known about the telescope."

"If I could be speechless, I would be now. Unfortunately that particular attribute is not part of my DNA."

I nod toward the men at the counter. "I think we all know that."

The waiter arrives, predictably, with two cups of hot water and a pair of tea bags.

"Sir," Dennison says—and even I have to smile at the pretended deference, "remember, we both said coffee?"

"It ain't bad tea," the man says, staring at the wreath. "It's Lipton."

"Lipton," Dennison says, shaking her head. "Gourmet." Then she glances up at the waiter who seems incapable of eye contact. "She'll take the tea. It's what she wanted anyway. But I need the caffeine."

"Tea's got plenty of caffeine."

Dennison glares at him until he quietly lifts the cup of hot water and walks away.

"Holler if you need anything," he says, and either that final command or the confluence of everything that had gone before elicits an actual smile from Jill Dennison. I said before that I wanted her to be ugly but she wasn't. She's actually pretty when she smiles.

"It's Tetley," she says. "Six letters in each name—no wonder he got confused. I'd like to use that word again—the one that doesn't have a place in our language."

"Sorry, it doesn't."

Obviously terms like that are a sore spot with me. I look at this young guy and see my brother who will never rise even to this fundamental level of social interaction, never be able to support himself with even this menial a job. And why? because he caught some germ and never recovered while this young man—and they're probably close to the same age—this young man remains content in his own narrow world where all six-letter words are the same and customer orders are merely suggestions. So no, re-tard does not have a place in the vernacular, but fuck if I'm sharing that story with Jill Dennison.

The pie arrives moments later. It appears to be apple. And there's coffee too.

"If you guys want to order food," the waiter says, dropping the check, "you got about ten minutes. Chef goes home at 8:00."

Dennison smiles at him. "Chef?"

"Goes home at eight. Want to order?"

"We'll let you know. How about that other fork?"

He pulls one out of his apron.

"It's clean," he says, as if it's some perk. "You got ten minutes on the food."

He steps away and looks at his digital watch. "Nine."

"Before that jerk-off comes back again..." Dennison says, "...I can call him a jerk-off, can't I? Is that better than re-tard? And while we're at it, I didn't say you were a whore."

"That was so many insults ago, I'd forgotten."

"When I fuck up, I apologize once. If the person doesn't accept it the first time, too bad."

"You mean once per insensitive remark or once per evening?"

She smiles again, then ignores the creamer and lifts the mug, holding it in the air. It steams ever so slightly.

"Not exactly hot. So what did Marcus have to say? Are you allowed to tell?"

"It'll be in the paper—he knew everything was on the record."

"Honestly, I don't always get a chance to read your paper. I suppose I'll have to apologize for that too."

"Not at all."

"I'm sure his *mea culpas* were coming fast and furious. He's good at that."

"He said there had been some incidents but they were working things out."

"Did you believe his so-called remorse."

"It's not my job to believe him."

"Of course it is! What do you think, nobody else ever took a journalism course? Remember that old saying about the grain of salt? You people don't carry that anymore?"

"We do."

"So, did you believe him?"

"I think he feels bad, yes. I think he misses your sister."

"Of course he does. What if it were you? Wouldn't you feel bad if you found out your spouse was cheating on you and killed her, then found that you kind of missed her after all?"

"Is that what you think happened here?"

"I don't know what happened here." For the first time she seems more frustrated than angry. She pushes the pie away slightly, then relents, picks up the fork again, breaks off a small section with her hands.

"Not as bad as it looks," she says. "Have some."

"No thanks. Do you mind telling me why I'm here?"

"I told you, I wanted to know about Marcus."

"You already have him convicted and executed. Of course the last time we spoke you had Brandt convicted and executed."

Dennison is silent for a moment or two. She's not the kind to be chastened, but her voice is quieter.

"You should drink your tea. It's Lipton."

"It's Tetley."

I've already let it steep too long and it looks like motor oil, but I dutifully take a few sips. Dennison slides the creamer in front of me.

"Swallow your pride and add a drop. Even I know enough about tea to know you can't drink that."

A few drops of cream turn it the color of wet sand, but they do take the edge off the over-brewed bitterness. She reaches behind her head and massages her neck briefly as she stares at the rickety-looking ceiling fan.

"You'd have liked my sister," she says. "She was very cool, very hip, very pretty. You wouldn't think we were sisters."

"You don't seem to be doing badly."

"You can dispense with the bullshit. I had an aunt who once told me I had classic good looks. I didn't need a thesaurus to know what that means."

"That doesn't sound like an insult."

"*Moby Dick* is a classic—anyone reading that these days? Anyone who doesn't have to? My aunt knew what I was. But Melanie—she was different. She could have done anything with her life."

"But she married Marcus Johns."

"The great micromanager. He did her clothes-shopping for Christ's sake. He had to oversee everything, comment on it, correct it."

"I don't want to seem disrespectful or flip, that's a motive for her to kill him, not the other way around."

"Unless he found out about Brandt."

"Did he?"

The question hangs in the air for a while. She obviously doesn't like the only possible answer.

"I don't think so."

"How long were they together, your sister and Brandt?"

"Six months? Three? A week or two? I don't know. Melanie didn't tell me about it until just before Thanksgiving. It may have been over by then."

"Whose idea was it to end things?"

"Melanie said it was hers, but she was concerned that Brandt wouldn't take it well."

"Brandt takes everything well. Is that why we're here? You want to tell Melanie's side?"

"I don't want her to be a victim. I don't want people saying 'poor Melanie.' She was a good person, smart, ambitious. People liked her, and believe me I know about being liked...or not. That astronomy stuff, the telescope, the teaching—all that's fine. But there was more to her than all those little parts. Can you write that? Add me to your story without mentioning my name? An informed source?"

"Family members," I tell her. "I can write that family members say that...etc."

"Really? Just like that?"

"Pretty much."

"I guess I want a eulogy for my sister like the one you did for your friend."

"But I didn't know Melanie."

"And now you do. Just, you know, make her special."

The yelling has been reduced to whispers and Dennison motions toward the counter again.

"We have company," she says. "Those two guys—they think we're together."

"We are together."

"I mean really together," she says. "Lovers. I always wanted to date a lumberjack. Of course I'd always thought it would be a man."

She stares back at the two as only she can and waves a finger at them.

"My partner and me—a little dispute."

They stare for a moment, then both shrug in unison like some sort of precision drill team.

"At least they'll have a story to tell," she says, "...There were these two lesbians arguing out at Deal's, then they made up...."

"You don't really care what you say, do you?"

"Sometimes I do. I try to pick my spots.

"Can I just ask you...what about your parents? How are they doing?"

"They're adjusting, reconfiguring. They never worried about Melanie. As many ups and downs as she had in her life, they were always confident that she'd make it. I was the one they fretted over, the one they called everyday to check on—to see if I was stable. Now they call every day to make sure I'm alive. I liked it better before. Now I'm afraid they expect me to take Melanie's place."

"And you won't?"

"I can't. We may share some DNA, but that's about as far as it goes. I do what I can. I'll call them when you and I finish arguing."

"We're not arguing anymore."

"Now there's something else to argue about."

I smile a little—I can certainly concede that much after what she and her family have been through. And there's something likable about her, but it's so deeply buried under layers of sarcasm and anger that it's suffocating most of the time.

"So maybe after all," she says, "the murderer is just some garden-variety lunatic prowling for female victims. Maybe one of those men at the counter."

"Or those two women near the door."

"It's a man thing, killing like that," she says. "Do you carry a gun?"

"Of course not."

"I have one," she says, "maybe I should start toting it around?"

"I can't tell you what to do."

"Took a safety course and all—got to be a good shot. Of course if I get attacked at work, the gun in my end table at home isn't going to help, is it?"

"Your office seems pretty remote, pretty secure."

"Yeah, and real estate agents don't get robbed much—nobody steals escrow, do they?"

Before I can answer, she picks up the check.

"I enjoyed our little chat. You owe $1.50 for that tea," she says. "I'll get the rest."

Chapter 13

There's a green Post-it note on my apartment door when I get home from my tryst (so I do like that word) with Jill Dennison—*Don't forget the tree. W.*

I know it means something, but it takes me a moment to figure out it's the Christmas tree—the one I tossed over the rail weeks before and which was then buried by snow but has now, through melting and the strengthening February sun, become a rust-colored eyesore.

I call the Willises and apologize. They know I've forgotten about it—out of sight out of mind. I offer to go out "right now" and move it but the husband, Peter, won't hear of it.

"You come down—we'll all move it."

He doesn't mean the three of us of course. His wife Betsy is about a hundred months pregnant and seemingly carrying octuplets. I'm not being insensitive, just quoting her own assessment of the current condition. In short she won't be helping us drag anything anywhere. And she won't be joining in the margarita frivolity that erupts when I arrive, at least not the tequila part of it. But we all have a laugh over a pregnant woman drinking a virgin anything, and her husband Peter keeps filling up the glasses until I'm too silly to remember why I'm there. Neither does Betsy, whose brain cells are not dying with anywhere near the rapidity of her husband's or mine.

Then I notice Peter, his eyes a little glassy, staring at my chest. It's not that impressive—the chest not the eyes—and in my current outfit, hardly even discernible. With the alcohol and all I feel this momentary rush of sexiness—Peter is a good-looking guy but he's never come on to me or made a comment in any way suggestive. Still, he's a guy so I figure I know what he wants and I sit up a little straighter so that whatever I do have makes some sort of impression—actually the opposite of an impression if you want to be literal. And then I realize he's not looking at my chest at all—he's looking at my stomach. It's kind of flat: Betsy's kind of isn't.

Maybe he'd like to see it. It's clean—I mean no piercings or tats—just smooth flesh with a small navel that he could touch if he wanted to, or lick, or kiss, or just gawk at to see what it was like—to see what it will be like again when his wife finally drops this kid. And where's the harm? I wouldn't show him anything important. I could always stop him before he got to the good stuff—though that plan has seldom worked with others in the past. But they're my neighbors so this would be different, or maybe those brain cells are dying off more rapidly than I thought. I try to remember what underwear I have on—I own some nice things that I keep for special occasions, but tonight I probably maintained my sexlessness right down to the utilitarian panties.

Betsy is laughing at something, but I was playing out her husband's fantasy (and maybe a few of my own) and missed the joke. She says she's never felt this high on no alcohol, and Peter says something about drunk by association and since I'm paying attention this time, I laugh too. But he's stopped gazing at my stomach—perhaps the flannel shirt told him there was nothing to see—and I finally remember why we're there. The tree. It'll be Peter and me, just the two of us outside walking toward the woods in the dark with nobody looking—a perfect time for sex…if we were in middle school. Then again, what if Betsy traipses off to bed? What if she says she's tired—pregnant ladies need their rest. She could be asleep while her husband and I made our way upstairs to my place and he could explore my stomach right above her. He's probably had enough of altering their sex positions to account for her pregnancy, or maybe they've stopped doing it altogether. No wonder I look so appealing.

I'm trying to fantasize an appropriate venue when he says let's do it and I practically jump off the chair.

"Did we awaken you?" Betsy says, still chuckling at something, probably me.

"I was spacing," I tell them, holding up another empty glass as an excuse and slouching a bit.

"Refill?" Peter says.

"I couldn't," I answer, and it's the truth. I'm about a salted rim away from really embarrassing myself.

"Look," he says, "we don't give a shit about the tree. We just thought you needed a good time, what with, you know, what happened with your friend and all. We wanted to give you some recovery time."

"Thanks," I tell him. "Now let's get at that tree while I'm still conscious."

"Too late for that," Peter says. "I told you, the tree was just a ploy. Do I need to walk you home or can you make it to the elevator?"

I force this drunken laugh—it sounds pretty authentic I think—and stand up, steadying myself on the arm of the chair. I do want him to walk me home, you know, just to see if I can still read signals. But then I'd have to face Betsy and, I suppose, myself. I've been pretty sanctimonious about shit like this. I want to be better than that, better than Karl Brandt at least.

I tell him I'm fine. Just as well—he's already cleaning up so that Betsy doesn't have to. So okay then, Peter's a good guy—but I can't be blamed for my harmless little drunken fantasy. As for the sex part of it, I can go upstairs, fill the tub with warm water, and take care of that on my own. Not giving in to temptation—that's what's important. If Melanie Johns could have…and I stop myself right there. That's the kind of moralizing I need to avoid, especially with my fairly extensive catalogue of undiscriminating Friday evenings in Boston-area bars. That threshold—the one Melanie crossed with Brandt and I would have crossed with Peter Willis in the winter woods if he'd even hinted he wanted me—that threshold is so blurry sometimes that it's a wonder more of us don't cross it. Or maybe we do but keep our secrets better, or don't run afoul of a murderer.

I'm reluctant to leave: I can't remember the last time I really enjoyed an evening, embarrassing fantasy aside. It must have been before Abigail's death and before these ongoing imbroglios with Jill Dennison and Brandt, before Grumman's illness and my continuing battle with my parents. I'm not sure how I'm going to feel in the morning, especially with tequila's reputation for deferred payments, but that worry seems distant and remote.

A hint of that headache arrives with the eleven o'clock news as I sit at the laptop with a cup of tea and try to convert my Marcus Johns notes into something coherent. I remember the telescope and type *she always had her eyes to the stars*, but it sounds almost amusing, as if it's a lead-in for some inappropriate punchline about a concussion or something equally tasteless. The woman is dead. She's fucking dead. You can't make jokes, but I want to laugh at everything anyway—it's the residue from that tequila. I close the laptop and continue berating myself in a manner befitting someone who has drunk too much.

The buzzer goes off—a visitor. I flip on the speaker.

"When you get three strikes in a row, they call it a turkey."

It's Teddy.

"What are you doing here?"

"In bowling, they call it a turkey. Four in a row is a four-bagger, like a home-run in baseball. I learned that today doing my job as a sportswriter. How'd your interview go?"

"Teddy, it's 11:30."

"I was just curious. I'll see you in the morning."

"Why didn't you just call now?"

"I didn't want to disturb you in case you were out somewhere."

"That's very thoughtful, but what if I were sleeping?"

He has no answer, but the fact is I'm not sleeping. I haven't even changed.

"Why don't you come up for a minute."

I expect a refusal—maybe an agreement that yes, it is too late. Then again, this is Teddy.

"Okay," he says, and I buzz him in.

I don't keep a lot of food in the house, but I find an opened bag of corn chips and get him a beer. I already have a bottle of water open, having used it to down the three preemptive Excedrin I've taken. The coming day is looking less and less productive.

Teddy's not one of those guys who like to vent, but I can tell that the bowling assignment has made him rethink his career. This probably isn't the time to remind him that he's done quite well with one course in journalism. Then I find him staring at me. Above the neck. Twice in one night I've been the object of men's gazes, though Teddy's looks less sensual than curious. When he speaks I know why.

"Are you drunk?"

"I had some wine before."

"At your interview?"

"I would never do that."

"Marcus Johns didn't kill his wife—you know that right? Spouses do kill their partners, but they do it at home. I mean it's a crime of passion and you're right there in the same room, you probably got a kitchen full of knives, a cellar full of tools, you know where all the blunt instruments are, maybe there's a chainsaw in the garage, or a pitchfork, or....."

"I get the picture."

"And if you own a gun it's handy. If you're really clever you'd even have access to the food if poisoning's your method."

"You know, Teddy, you've thought this through a little too well."

"It's theoretical—I'm not even married. Just studying. But seriously, if you're living in the same house, why wait?"

"Because it isn't passion."

"Then what is it?"

"Jealousy. Revenge."

"But those are passions, emotions."

"So the guy who takes his wife hiking, takes a break in their pleasant conversation, and pushes her off a cliff...?"

Teddy nods. "Possibly. But he's created that proximity based on earlier trust. She might not go near that cliff with a stranger."

"Then Jill's first accusation—that Brandt did it—makes more sense."

"It makes sense but it's wrong, and she's a nut case. It doesn't take a PI to figure that out. And it wasn't murder for money either. That only happens in old black and white movies. Melanie didn't have anything salted away. She earned a decent salary—so does her husband—but there's no real wealth in the Dennison family. By the way, I like your shirt."

"Oh God."

I take off the vest and the flannel and toss them toward my bedroom leaving just the black turtleneck. Teddy is unimpressed by my transformation to womanhood. He's not staring at anything. Maybe I'm more attractive drunk and sitting next to a pregnant woman in her fourth trimester.

"I'll burn that shirt in the morning. I only wore that because..." and I don't know what's dumber, my rationale or trying to explain it to Teddy. Finally I settle for logic. "...it was cold."

He nods. "If you're really going to burn it, I'll take it. I can always use..."

"I'll let you know. You said Jill was insane?"

"I found out a few things about her college experience."

"This was from your cabal?"

"Cadre," he says.

"You know, Teddy, that discussion we had about friends—how I was your best friend and you didn't hang around with a lot of guys—what about this group of yours, this cadre?"

"I wouldn't know them if I saw them. We talk online. We don't even Skype."

"So your information isn't necessarily local."

"Some is. But one woman is from Kansas, and there's a guy from Georgia who usually serves as the moderator. He gives us a case and we look for ways to approach it, exchange tactics, that sort of thing. Someone in the group knew Jill Dennison from college. It was not a pleasant time."

"For her?"

"For anyone. Apparently her roommate demanded a room change within a week, said she carried on conversations with herself but wouldn't communicate with anyone else. And she walked around in this frayed bathrobe all the time—you know, that towel material."

"Terrycloth."

"Yeah. Wore it everywhere. There were some hygiene problems too."

"College can be a tough adjustment. She must have a degree though."

"Probably got it evenings somewhere because by Thanksgiving of her freshman year she officially withdrew, and the rumor was she even got some tuition returned. Three months into the semester nobody gets a refund unless you're really bringing the place down—seems UMass was really eager to get rid of her and they cut some deal."

"Do you think Melanie knew that her sister was unbalanced?"

"Everyone did. There are five siblings in that family—four girls and a boy. Everyone knew from the outset that this third child was messed up somehow. Parents had two more after her, though, and they both seem all right. That genetics stuff, really confusing—the pool dries up, then gets refilled or something."

"Was she ever arrested?"

"You mean carted off to jail? Charged with something? No. Once they had to get security to remove her from a classroom at college. Some professor made the mistake of telling her she couldn't wear her robe to class so she removed it. Apparently she has a flower tattoo below her navel."

"She was naked?"

"She wore a necklace. Remember that trick if you ever need your tuition refunded. I'll tell you, that Melanie was a beautiful girl."

"Where'd that come from?"

"I was just saying."

"I never hear you talk about girls being pretty or not."

"You sound upset."

"About what? No, of course not. I'm just, you know, a little tired."

Tired, and buzzed and yes, upset. I don't have any interest in Teddy as a boyfriend, but it would be nice if he noticed something about me other than I looked drunk. Of course I could alleviate that problem by not actually looking drunk, but it's too late for that.

"Even Jill," he adds, "she's attractive and all, nice figure, but not beautiful like her sister—if we're being honest."

"Good to be honest."

He gives me a quizzical look, but it doesn't stop him.

"She may be nuts, but she is independent and very successful. I mean she has a job in real estate."

"Tell you what, Teddy, ask her business partner when Jill last showed a house."

"I don't know about that," he says. "Gonna tell Grumman I was here?"

It's an odd question. Does he not want the boss to get the wrong idea—he and I together at midnight—or does he want him to know? Remember that useless word, *suddenly*, the one we're never supposed to use. Well suddenly I realize.

"Grumman sent you, didn't he?"

"So you know then."

"Know what?"

"So you don't know."

"Teddy, please, could you finish a sentence? Or answer a question?"

"I'm not supposed to tell, but Grumman asked me to call. He didn't want to seem overprotective but he was worried."

"He asked you to call me?"

"And I did, earlier. No answer. I could have called your cell, but that wouldn't necessarily mean you were home."

"And so here you are."

He looks embarrassed, and that's good. He should be, and so should

Grumman.

"I've been out after dark several times in my life. So far so good."

"Sorry, I was just trying to do the right thing."

"I think Grumman is hoping you and I are dating."

"We're not."

And "rejection night" mercifully draws to a close.

"Getting late, Teddy."

"Your eyes still look a little...funny. You should get some rest."

The buzz, in truth, is gone, having evaporated in the smog of over-protectiveness and worthlessness. Downstairs Peter Willis has probably put his drunkenness to good use and had wild, sloppy, uninhibited sex above and below and around Betsy's oversized belly. I should have had the same; instead I learned from Teddy what a pretty girl Melanie Johns was. Less chance of an unwanted pregnancy, I suppose, but I'd like to get some mileage out of those birth control pills I spend thirty bucks a month to take every day. It's surprising what a high success rate you can achieve when you crawl into bed alone each night.

With Teddy gone, I head off to the bedroom where I catch a glimpse of myself in the mirror. If I can wear this ensemble every day, I'll never need to worry about those pills.

Chapter 14

Nothing exacerbates a hangover more than the glare of a sunny morning. Maybe it's psychological—the world is alive and I'm basically not. In that respect I'm lucky. I awaken and find the outdoors a uniform gray—some late-winter fog has settled over the Northeast. Or maybe it's mist, I can't tell, but something seems to be suspended in the air and making the world look as fuzzy as I feel. Several more Excedrin and a somewhat cautious drive to work later, my brief run of luck dissipates: Karl Brandt is waiting outside the *Courier* office, holding a covered paper cup and leaning against a well-marked Drayton police sedan. Just a regular sedan—maybe I was wrong about the SUV that night Abby was murdered. The mist, the shadowy figure—the scene resembles some hackneyed movie version of London...with coffee.

"I don't want to sound like a jilted lover," he says, "but you never call anymore. I had to check with Arlene to make sure I hadn't missed your retirement party."

"Or my funeral."

"Six of one," he says as he follows me inside. We both look at Arlene who appears unduly involved in some project—too involved for such an early hour when she's usually finishing a sudoku or accumulating recipes from some food website. Grumman isn't in yet, nor is Teddy. Grumman shouldn't be angry about that: it was his orders that kept the kid—and me—up so late.

"Anyway," Brandt says, acknowledging Arlene with a nod and putting his coffee on my desk, "I would have noticed the obit in the paper, eventually. So what's keeping you out of circulation—to use one of your terms?"

"The usual crap nobody cares about. Then of course there are those murders. Remember them?"

"Hmmh, murders, that sounds like something the police should deal with. Oh wait...were you being sarcastic?"

"January's come and gone and still nothing. What's going on?"

"You're the reporter. Maybe you should ask someone. Or should we do a newsletter at the house? Could you survive the competition?"

"There are police departments that do newsletters, that have Facebook pages and websites to keep the public informed."

"I'm told there are newspapers that do the same thing."

"We could if you ever gave us anything."

"I'm here now," he says.

But I'm not sure why he's here. The way it works, and Brandt and his colleagues have made a career of it, is that reporters beg for information and the police toss a few crumbs their way, or throw together a news conference and scatter larger crumbs to everyone at once. For Brandt to offer them willingly may very well signal the end of days. Of course I don't want to appear too eager, so I shuffle through some mail on my desk, just to verify how swamped we are with the day's requirements. He watches me for a moment, says nothing, then laughs.

"Okay," he says, "you're very busy. I thought you glossed over the Target circular a little too fast, but that's just me. Of course if you're thinking of a new toaster...."

"I'm not. I have to go through everything."

"No wonder you're too busy for any real reporting."

My polite-employee voice has hung on as long as could be expected, and I quickly revert to my interaction-with-Brandt tone. It's an easy switch, one that comes naturally.

"Why are you here, detective? You must have things to do."

Brandt doesn't react, but Arlene does.

"Who wants a coffee?" she says. "I'm going to run across the street."

Brandt glances at the coffeemaker in the corner, then back at Arlene who has already planned for the eventuality.

"Filtered water. They use filtered water over there. We get ours from the bathroom sink. Anybody? Coffee? Tea?"

Brandt holds up his full cup in response. I put forth my most placid and non-threatening look.

"You don't have to leave."

"I'm not going to Europe," she snaps, feeling for the door handle behind her. "Be right back."

"A little break never hurt," Brandt says as the door closes, "and you can't argue with filtered water."

"Not funny, detective. Now she's pissed off and I'll have to deal with it."

"I can arrest her if you'd like—let her cool off in jail."

"Look, really, I have work to do. If you have nothing for me...."

"...We've already been through this. You know, contrary to some mistaken belief you have, we don't drop by newspaper offices to provide updates on the progress of criminal investigations. But sometimes—and stop me if you've heard this—sometimes a newspaper will send something called a *re-por-ter* to find out what's happening. I've seen a few of those lately, but not from your paper. What are you covering—upcoming Presidents' Day celebrations?"

"This paper has one reporter and she has other assignments."

Brandt laughs. "I'm the biggest bullshitter I know. Are you really going to challenge me?"

"It's not bullshit. You know there are dailies with staffs this size—all computerized—all wire service crap. They're an embarrassment. Grumman wants to maintain some personal quality to the *Courier*, so we go weekly, but we do it honestly, and that means we talk to people...I talk to people."

"Funny, if I talk to people, all they want to talk about is those murders."

He's right, but I don't know a discreet way of telling him he's useless to me as a source of information or truth, not if he'd been sleeping with a victim. There's no way to say that without implicating Jill Dennison who, even though she has proven to be little more than a pain in the ass, may have some function as a source down the road. But Brandt is right about other things: ordinarily I'd be hounding someone at the department about the progress of the cases.

He rolls the chair closer to my desk.

"Look, just so you know what's out there, we're pretty sure Melanie Johns knew her attacker and your friend didn't. And we think someone may have seen Melanie Johns' murderer and not even have known it."

"I read that in the *Globe*."

"Then it must be true. There were a couple of other runners in Silvermine when she was killed. They both remember seeing her, and they remember seeing some people they didn't recognize. But in the winter, all bundled up like that, so-called strangers are hard to identify."

"Man? Woman? Black? White?"

"White male. Or a very tall light-skinned black woman. I'm not trying to be funny, it's just that people wear these ski masks...."

"You don't run, do you?"

The question slipped out almost as if it had escaped on its own. There's a momentary regret, but it passes quickly—surprisingly quickly.

"Do I look like a runner to you?"

"You look like you're in decent shape."

"Wow, a compliment, sort of. The smoking keeps my weight down and I make it a habit never to eat while I'm drinking. We do have a fitness area at the station—sometimes I'll take a spin on the stationary bike, maybe a step or two on the treadmill. What else do you want to know about me?"

"Maybe a little treadmill work can actually give you enough wind to run for real."

"For real?"

"Yeah, on the streets like runners."

"Like Melanie Johns," he says, and his face relaxes into what might pass for a smile. "So, you're a reporter after all, uncovering all the news we need to lead better lives. How'd you find out?"

"Find out what?"

"That I smoke. Come on, Coop. We can talk—we're friends."

"Of course we aren't."

"Okay then we're professionals in different fields. How'd you find out? It's damned certain you didn't uncover anything yourself, so somebody must have told you something."

"Is that the way you talk to friends? Insult the way they do their job?"

"When someone does their job for them, yes."

"You haven't told me what you think I found out."

He shakes his head. "You never seemed the type that would enjoy watching a person embarrass himself, but maybe I'm wrong. Anyway," he says, then stands and rolls the chair back where it came from, "I didn't come here to make small talk about my life. I came to ask you about your friend Abby."

"What about her?"

"She could be a screaming bitch at times, did you know that?"

"Why don't you define the term for me?"

"We have two incidents where she was abusive to people—once in a store at the mall; and again in a restaurant drive-thru. The second time involved the police and a hundred-dollar fine. Would you like me to quote her suggestion to the female employee?"

"No."

"So you were aware of this?"

"I heard her go off a few times. Just blowing off steam."

"Any chance one of the recipients of that steam came back let off some steam at her?"

"You don't kill people because they swore at you."

"Yes you do. I can cite you a hundred road rage incidents where people died. How about it? Did she ever mention anything about a threat?"

"No, and even if that were true, there's a second murder. Was Melanie Johns a screaming bitch too? Or just a regular bitch? And would you use the same term if she were a man?"

"No. I'd use son-of-a-bitch. More masculine."

"These days *bitch* can be...."

"I get it. You and coffee girl have yourselves a good day."

Brandt is not one of those people who threaten to leave for effect. He's pretty much out the door before I stop him.

"Okay wait, detective. Let's just say I know that there was...a relationship."

"What are we talking about here?"

"You."

"Relationship," he says, coming back inside. "That's a euphemism, isn't it?"

"I don't want to be vulgar."

"Vulgar? Jesus, can you be any more self-righteous? Melanie Johns and I had sex a few times. You want details? And with those details, do you want euphemisms—shall I clean it up for your readership?"

"I'm not writing this."

"Even though it's news? It is, you know. It would make me a suspect."

"I know you didn't kill her."

"You don't *know* anything. But let me lay this out plainly for you: I didn't kill her, I didn't hire someone to kill her, I didn't rejoice at her death or ever wish her dead. If this gets out it could make my divorce a little messier, but that's the price I pay."

"Your wife is divorcing you?"

"Why didn't you ask if I was divorcing my wife? How do you know she hasn't been having euphemisms with other guys?"

He's right. And as for impugning his morality, not even twelve hours earlier I was ready to slip my flat stomach into bed with my neighbor's husband. I can always blame my behavior on the alcohol, but Brandt was more accurate than he knew. Besides, divorce is the ultimate shitty experience; and as big a jerk as he is, I hate to think of him going through that and trying to do a job at the same time.

"I really didn't know about you and your wife."

"Well then maybe you misspoke. Maybe several of your assumptions are wrong."

"So you and…."

"Linda. My wife's name is Linda. You didn't know that?"

"I had no reason…."

"It's been a long time coming, but I figure by Valentine's Day it'll be over. One less card I'll have to buy."

"That's pretty grim."

"Ironic," he says. "Not grim. We're both fine with it...cordial...sometimes even happy it's over. We still live together like compatible roommates. We even do things together. Nothing physical—no euphemisms—we just don't love each other. You can quote me on that. Anything else?"

"That night Teddy and I saw you in Mattera's—you were in the bar. That's why, isn't it?"

"What's why?"

"That's why you weren't in Silvermine. You recused yourself."

"Judges recuse themselves; cops have a drink. I'm not a judge."

"But you went back to the crime scene."

"For the same reason I just gave you. For what it's worth, I had a club soda when you and Inspector Clousseau saw me."

"You remember what you had?"

"It's all I ever have. I stopped drinking a while back, apparently too soon. Anyway, print what you have to."

Brandt is still leaning on the same chair he's rolled all over the office. I'm not sure if he wants me to respond to what he said, he wants an assurance that I'll keep his secret, or he wants me to spew out some bullshit about running it past

Grumman to see what he thinks. Why doesn't Arlene come back? or Grumman arrive and call me into his office? or the phone ring?

"What did you do for the drinking, some kind of program?"

"I never thought I was addicted, so I used a one-step program: I finished all the liquor in the house, and when I eventually ran dry, that was it."

"Cold turkey?"

"I never drank that."

"You know what I mean."

"Sorry for the levity," he says, "but if you're gonna quit, you don't talk about it, you just quit. No other way."

"Now you're smoking a lot."

He laughs.

"I tell some people I've stopped drinking and they're all *congratulations* and *good job* and other little encouragements. Not you—you just find another vice."

"I didn't mean it that way."

"Look, Coop, you write what you want, or don't. I came to ask about your friend, that's it."

"Your secret is safe with me," I tell him, pretty much another formal admission that I'm in the wrong job.

"Like I said, your call," he says. "What are you doing for Valentine's Day?"

"Friday? Working."

"Have dinner with me."

He doesn't look surprised when I laugh.

"I'm serious," he says.

"I don't think it would be wise."

"If this Teddy really isn't your boyfriend and I'm not really married, where's the harm? Besides, you shouldn't be alone. It's a dangerous time for young women—and I have a gun."

The comment is in such bad taste that I'm tempted to end this little back-and-forth right there. Then again, he's a victim too—I let it pass, even try to extend the joke.

"Valentine's Day is more a bow-and-arrow holiday."

"I'm sure we have one in the evidence locker," he says. "What do you say?"

"But the time we spend at dinner you could be working on those cases. Are you going in early that day to make it up?"

"I can. I don't sleep much now that I'm sober," he says. His voice sounds almost pensive.

"How do you get by without sleep?"

"How do you?"

He's got me there. He knows a hangover when he's near one, so I confess to having had a bit too much the night before. He already knew that.

"Getting along without sleep is an acquired skill. You learn it. Keep drinking and you'll figure it out. It's not something you want to learn."

"Pills?"

"Tried those. Takes me all day to wake up. Once the divorce is final I think I'll be better—we both will—Linda too. Right now there's that tension where we don't know exactly what our relationship is. We used to sleep in the same bed, then in different rooms, now I find an excuse to fall asleep on the couch or work a third shift for someone."

He sounds vulnerable, and then, in an instant, he shuts down.

"Keep in touch, all right? I mean be a reporter. I'll be a cop. That'll probably work out better than...whatever I was planning."

"Wait. Can I ask you something personal?"

"How much more personal can we get?"

"It's about Melanie."

This time there's no witty comeback or smart retort. For the first time I can see lines in his forehead. It's strange, I always thought Brandt was too creepy for me—maybe too crude, or rough, or drunk—but I never really dismissed him because of any age difference. But at this moment, whether it's the inadequate light in the room or the general tenor of the conversation, he looks old.

"Ask away," he says.

"I wanted to ask if you missed Melanie."

"I don't have that right."

He moves toward the door again, a little less purposefully, and this time he stops of his own accord.

"But I do have the right to be a suspect. I just don't want to do that to her memory. Her husband is mourning the death of the woman he loved—she shouldn't become the woman who slept with her murderer."

At times like this I wonder what I'm hanging on to. I'm sitting behind a desk smothered with crap I don't care about. The previous day—Marcus, Dennison, too much alcohol, even Teddy—proved to be a nightmare. I'm estranged from my family and immersed in a job I'm not particularly good at—a job which itself may disappear soon enough. Grumman is dying and I'm a pink slip away from being a tour guide in Kennebunk...again.

"You know," I tell him, "I could do lunch."

"I can't today, I..."

"I mean whenever. Friday."

Lunch seems safer than dinner, especially on Valentine's Day when the marriage proposals will fill the air like ragweed in spring.

"I'll call you," he says. "We have a meeting with the attorneys this week and...I'll call you."

"If something goes wrong...."

"About Melanie," he says. "Sometimes people take a long time to find themselves, but the payoff is worth it. I think that's how it was—would have been—for Melanie. She was still making mistakes—probably married the wrong guy though he was coming around. Throwing in with me was no act of genius either—but even so, she was finding herself. You'd have liked her."

Jill said the same thing. It's troublesome to be discussing his ex-lover without condemning his immorality, and even more troublesome in light of my own willingness last night to "throw in" with anyone interested. So maybe, yes, I would have liked Melanie: maybe we had more in common than anyone knew.

Chapter 15

Teddy missed the Brandt conversation as well as Grumman's arrival and the boss's first few questions about his whereabouts. I know I've portrayed Teddy McClendon as the poster child of nonchalance where I'm concerned, but when it comes to showing up for his job on time, he's almost obsessive. He doesn't miss work and generally has to be reminded when his vacation days have piled up and he needs to, as Grumman likes to say, use 'em or lose 'em. I've never needed similar reminders.

But Grumman, though not a stickler for office protocol, insists that we call in if for any reason we're going to be late. By 10:00—a good two hours after Teddy should have been in the office—the boss is ready to explode.

"He had all day yesterday—that interview was supposed to be filed by now," he says, stalking between my desk and Arlene's. "I can't reach him at home or on his cell."

Arlene glances up. "Boss, please, it's a freakin' bowling article. And there's nothing on his schedule this morning."

Only someone like Arlene Holland can risk such insubordination. She doesn't need the job, doesn't need the money, doesn't need the aggravation. She's been pretty much alone since her husband died a few years back, and she needs a place to *be* more than she needs a place to earn money. Her independence makes her invaluable in that office, at least to me. But since sparring with her is useless, Grumman turns to me.

"What do you know about this?"

"You know as much as I do."

More actually, since it was his idea for Teddy to drop by for a visit when most people are going to sleep. I figure I'll let that slide.

"I don't care what's on his schedule, he should be here. It's one thing if he's sick..." Grumman says and rushes back into his office, slamming the door behind him. Once inside he completes the sentence but the words jumble together into an indecipherable amalgam of obscenities and curses of which only the stronger ones survive the journey.

Arlene smiles. "He knows a lot of adult words. How come you didn't defend your boyfriend?"

"He's not my boyfriend, Arlene."

The older woman nods. "Brandt thinks he is, probably the boss does too. So where is he, really?"

"He doesn't report to me."

"But he's your...well, whatever he is. Maybe his mom wouldn't drive him to work. Or maybe he got drunk last night. You know him and hockey games."

"He doesn't drink on the job."

"You keep saying you're not his girlfriend. Okay, then maybe he has a real one. Men have needs...and so does Teddy, I'd bet."

And so do I, but Arlene—fiftyish toward sixty, attractive, and probably getting more regular sex than I am—knows all that. I'm not having this conversation, and since I have some morning appointments myself, I grab my jacket and ask her to call me if he gets in. Of course Grumman is upset mainly because he wants a report on the previous evening when Teddy the spy was checking on my safety. He's probably sure Teddy divulged his reason for visiting me, and of course he's right.

When I get to my car all I can think of is Jill Dennison's annoying fiction about the surveillance camera in the parking lot. I don't see one, but I did read some article once that claimed the average American was surveilled without his knowledge about 75 times a day. One more set of eyes in the parking lot hardly matters; besides, I know damn well that crazy woman is not monitoring it.

Nothing at Teddy's except some mail piled up inside the mail slot, so I stop by Town Hall to talk to the comptroller about some new accounting system, then the water department manager about an increase in rates. This evening there'll be a zoning committee session where I can learn about a possible asbestos issue at the high school. No Pulitzers today, and when I return to the *Courier* after noon, no Teddy either. Grumman agrees to make some calls.

"I don't know what the relationship between you two actually is," he says, holding the phone in the air, "and I don't care—but to me, well, it could be typical irresponsible guy behavior."

"I don't think he's shacked up with someone, if that's what you mean."

"That's what I mean," he says. "If you two have some kind of understanding…."

"Seriously, Mr. Grumman, does that sound like Teddy?"

"Not really. Shit, I don't want to report the kid missing, then have him turn up naked in some girl's apartment."

"But you just said...."

"I know, that's not him. Or maybe this is a step toward—I don't know—something."

"Maturity?"

"Hardly. Unfortunately, some might call it that." He shrugs and picks up the desk phone. "Let me call around and see what I can find out."

"If you hear anything…"

"I'll have the little scamp call you."

He coughs again, a milder, less menacing spasm.

"Having a bad day," he says, "Aren't you supposed to be at some health food restaurant for a grand opening?"

"In an hour or so. Grand re-opening. Is that kind of coughing normal for that, you know…?

"Cancer? Is that the word you're fumbling for? Yes, it's normal, good days and bad days. I don't think about it. So listen, on the off chance that it really is a grand re-opening," he says, "which I doubt, get over there. I promised the owner—Gretchen something—some coverage. Tell her I said hello. Make it believable."

In other words, lie. I can do that. On the drive over I figure my angle will be the fact that natural-food restaurants—palaces of tofu and tempeh and lots of other things I don't want to eat—are becoming passé. But I'm wrong about this one. The parking lot is packed and I easily convince myself (1) there's no place to park and (2) it would be unfair to disturb Gretchen when she's being slammed like that.

So the new place is a success—I have a lede and I can always pick up the details after—after I stop by the police station where the Karl Brandt I agreed to have lunch with mutates as soon as I mention Teddy.

"Missing? Gee, who do you hire when a detective can't find himself?"

"He's not a detective."

"I think we've pretty much established that."

Maybe it's the surroundings that make him so disagreeable. The town needs a new, twentieth century police station, one that would leave it only one century behind the times, but every bond issue is voted down because it somehow ties any new building to the razing of this one, a decrepit heirloom that happens to reside on some historical register. About a year ago someone actually put up a sign reading "This Cite—Home of the New Drayton Police Department." The misused *cite* was the first indication that something was awry; the second was the sign's location—a raft about fifty yards from shore in Silvermine Lake. It was one of the few times I've ever heard Grumman laugh out loud, and he gave the whole incident way more column space than it deserved. The scuttlebutt was that some cops had erected the sign as a last desperate plea for modernization. It didn't work, and now I'm here with Brandt in this hell hole. It makes no sense to maintain a structure this antiquated, but who the hell votes on bond issues? Nobody, including me. So I pay for my fair-weather citizenship by squeezing myself into an undersized box making a hat-in-hand visit that only exacerbates my discomfort. And Brandt's.

Even so, it's surprising how I've changed from Brandt's confidant to his supplicant in so little time. He doesn't even ask me to sit down. A chair is filled with file folders, so I clean off a corner of his desk and lean there instead.

"So you won't help."

"Help do what?"

"I don't know why his wanting to be a detective bothers you. You should take it as a compliment—he wants to do what you do."

Brandt leans far back in the wooden chair and rolls it against the wall behind him.

"Remember what I said about bullshit? That still applies. Let's start again. You say he's missing—let's just deal with that. How long has he been missing?"

"I saw him briefly yesterday—he covered a hockey game. Then he came over to my place."

"Did he stay over?"

"Of course not."

"I forgot—he's not your boyfriend."

Brandt's just being pissy now, but I can't afford to attack the stupidity—or validity goddamn it—of his comment. I need him.

"So he went home. What time did he leave your place?"

"It was late. Grumman sent him and...."

Rather than metering out dribs and drabs of the story, I just rewind to the Margaritas, leaving out the salacious parts.

"Got it," Brandt says. "Now first off, his folks are in Florida."

"What? How do you know that?"

"We had a discussion. It came up. Why don't you sit in a chair? You're making me nervous."

Knowing he wants me off his desk is motivation to remain there. "What kind of discussion?"

"Mostly about detective work...who does what…that sort of thing."

"You threatened him?"

"I advised him."

"Now he's missing."

Brandt smiles. "Well you caught me, Coop. I told him to stay out of police business, he said no, so I murdered him and buried the body. Then I waited for you to drop by so that I could let slip a piece of incriminating information to make you think I'm involved. You're a far better detective than Teddy."

"So you really won't help."

"You already asked me that. Aside from going house to house looking for someone with a hangover, what would you like me to do?"

"He doesn't have a hangover. He was fine when he left."

"Well," he says with a knowing smile, "that makes you a suspect, doesn't it? Now if we could just deduce a motive…."

"Can't you just help me out here?"

Brandt moves the folders off the chair and points to it. I'm not going to get anywhere until I adopt a subservient position, so I sit.

"I don't want to be insulting here, but you must know the difference between being late for work and being missing. I understand with the murders and all, and I get that he's never late. But really, a doctor's appointment, a haircut, car trouble, a stomach ache."

"Then why didn't he call in?"

"You can ask him when he calls in He hasn't been gone long enough to be considered missing, and he's not a child, even though…forget it, he's not a child. We can always bend the rules—especially since you and I are pals—but aren't there a lot more reasonable explanations? What time did you say he left your place?”

"After midnight.”

"After midnight four in the morning or after midnight like 12:05?"

"Before one. Well before. He had a beer or two at my place. And just so you know, he was there only because my boss was afraid I couldn't conduct an interview without being assaulted. Don't ask me to explain.”

"Well I hate to say this about your not-boyfriend, but he could be uh, you know, slippin' it to somebody else.”

“As far as I know Teddy doesn't have a girlfriend.”

“I've heard lots of women say that over the years, usually just prior to divorcing their husbands…or killing them. Did you kill Teddy because he had another girlfriend?”

I refuse to give Brandt the satisfaction of a smile, though the absurdity of the comment deserves it. And I agreed to have lunch with this guy? Jesus!

“You've had your fun, detective, now what should I do next?”

“Confess.”

“I'm serious.”

“God, I know you are.” He leans forward, maybe to look more official, more professional. “I already know where he lives—get me some information I don't have—where he runs, where he hangs out, who his friends are, previous girlfriends or boyfriends. Is he gay?”

“I don't think so.”

“Okay then, girlfriends. What does he like to eat? And where? Give me his cell number too. You've tried it, right?”

“Straight to voice mail.”

“You know sometimes guys—even if they're not your boyfriend—like to disappear—find someone to disappear with.”

“After midnight?”

“There are parts of men's anatomies where they don't wear watches.”

The image is too funny and this time I have to smile. Maybe he's trying to help, in his own derisive way.

“I know this sounds naïve, Karl, but Teddy's not like that. He can be lackadaisical and casual, but he's pretty responsible.”

“He must get that from his parents,” Brandt says. “Not everyone notifies the police when they're going to be out of town for a while—asks us to keep an eye on the house—especially when the place isn't going to be vacant."

"That's how you knew?"

"Not that we could really do that, but we can drive by an extra time or two. I'll poke around a little. You call me when he runs out of condoms and shows up for work."

"Nice."

"Come on," Brandt says. "If he's responsible, like you said, he'll use condoms. Probably bought a package of three and now they're on their fourth go-round. True love...."

He stops himself in mid-sentence, as if the joke has grown thin even for him, and his tone becomes closer to the one he used in the *Courier* office—more cordial, even obliging.

"You call me when you hear from him," he says. And listen, don't worry—this is probably nothing."

I wait for some final barb but there is none, nor is there an indication that he'll be seeing me soon, though as far as I know we haven't canceled our lunch date. I find myself in my car hoping that Teddy really is screwing his brains out somewhere, though the possibility seems preposterous. And hoping is probably the wrong word—the thought of it pisses me off. It's a betrayal of sorts: even if he doesn't owe me the fidelity of a boyfriend, he owes me the explanation of a friend—purportedly his best friend.

I drive by his place once more and try to imagine him shacked up with some bimbo who'd been lying spread-eagle in his apartment waiting for him last night. It's an image I just can't draw, no matter how carefully I trace the lines. It's much easier to envision him back at the office watching hockey highlights; but rather than race back, I fit in that stop at Gretchen's and manage a perfunctory interview with the owner and a few customers while I snack on some of her famous homemade granola. It's like eating pebbles but without the piquancy of pebbles. There may very well be some really delicious food in the place, but I've never found any. Of course I can always focus on the enthusiastic turnout—we need her advertising more than we need integrity, at least in a fluff piece.

And of all people my pal Joseph Lawrence is in there, sitting at a corner table deep in conversation with a man in a navy blue suit and an "I gave blood" sticker on his lapel. Or at least it's a red cross—I'm assuming that's why he's wearing it. The man doesn't seem like a student, and I doubt if he's a staff member, most of whom Joe Lawrence wouldn't condescend to dine with—nor would they want him to. So it's got to be a business deal of some sort—maybe that expansion thing he was talking about. Yet there's something vaguely unpleasant about the scene—some indefinable aloofness between the two. At one point Lawrence looks like a child being castigated by a disappointed parent, and the other man seems to tower over him—odd, since Lawrence is a big man and they're both seated. But the real mystery—or comedy—is Joseph Lawrence inside a health food place, man's man that he thinks he is.

I wait for him to look up and I make eye contact, but he looks right through me without the slightest hint of recognition. Ordinarily I would consider that a blessing and leave, but the guy doesn't miss a chance to lord over reporters and similar drudges, and now he's what—making believe he doesn't know me? I sidestep a few customers who are waiting to be seated and get to Lawrence's table just as his suited friend stands up. He's a clean-shaven heavy-set man with eyes that are just a bit too small and glasses that are just a bit too large. I guess it's a perfect balance. By the time I yell out Lawrence's name, blue suit is already walking away and we brush past each other a few feet from the table. He smiles at me—an excuse-me smile you get when you almost bump into someone, and when I look toward Lawrence again, he's standing too.

"How was your lunch, Mr. Lawrence?" I ask him, although there's nothing on his table except a few mugs.

"Fine."

"I didn't know you were a natural food kind of person. Who was your friend?"

"Just a business associate."

"Oh. I didn't mean to ruin your lunch—he didn't have to leave."

"How do you know what he had to do?"

Now there's the nasty Joe Lawrence that resides just below the surface and shows itself whenever anyone challenges his superiority. Good to see that guy up and around.

"I only meant...."

"If you want to talk about something related to Chalmers, call Marcie.

Otherwise I'm really busy today."

He takes a few singles out of his wallet and leaves them under a mug—either he's the world's lousiest tipper or their total outlay came to nothing. I'd guess the latter. He walks past me, then turns around.

"If you're here as a reporter," he says, "I don't need to see my name listed among the local dignitaries at the opening of this...this place. Do you understand?"

"I had no intention of mentioning individual diners."

"Then make sure you don't or your editor over there will be scrounging for advertising again. Are we clear?"

We're clear. I'm just saying that because Lawrence himself didn't wait for an answer, assuming that I had been sufficiently cowed. The truth is I really didn't have any intention of naming anyone other than Gretchen herself and maybe someone at the counter or on the waitstaff, but now I think, why not mention a few local celebs. The problem is there aren't any that I can see or that I know. Of course I can always say something like *everyone from casual diners to college presidents* and let people guess. I can always check with Grumman—see what he thinks.

 As soon as I get to my car, the cell chirps. It's Teddy.

"Arlene said to call you. I'm back in the office."

"Just like that?"

He doesn't know what to answer and I hardly understand the question.

"I guess so," he says. "There's been an arrest in the murders."

"How do you know?"

"Brandt told me."

I just saw Brandt—it couldn't have been more than an hour ago."

"Well," Teddy says, "breaking news."

Chapter 16

"Some creep named Curwell—local—drifter—long record." Teddy has a sheet on the desk in front of him, but he's speaking from memory. We're all gathered around listening as if he's Socrates in that famous painting. All we need is the hemlock—which I would gladly feed him for scooping that story. Grumman keeps asking for more details and seemingly forgiven Teddy keeps providing them: burglary, B&E, drugs, disturbing the peace, drunk and disorderly.

Brandt's the cop; I'm not. He makes arrests; I don't. But even I can tell there's nothing in this Curwell's background that would indicate violent crimes against persons. And though Teddy has worked up some enthusiasm over the arrest, I can't. Curwell sounds like a property-crime type of felon. With no assaults in his background, what would cause a small-time thief with a drinking problem to turn into a violent and brutal murderer?

Teddy has no answer, but my observation dilutes his enthusiasm and Grumman's credulity a bit, and that makes me feel better.

"Anyway," Teddy says, "he saw me up the street, said you were looking for me. We got to talking."

"You and Karl Brandt? Got to talking?"

"And Curwell had just been nabbed. Coincidence I guess. It's already a press release."

"Happy coincidence I would say."

He's gloating a little too much for my liking.

"You know Teddy, I don't know where you were, but you had that thing at the high school you were supposed to...."

"On my way now," he says. "If I'd gone too early I couldn't have watched them in action. Maybe I'll bowl a string while I'm there."

He plops on his Bruins hat and he's out the door.

"He doesn't even root for the Bruins," I tell Grumman. "He's lying about that."

"Maybe," he says, "but the Curwell arrest is probably the better story. Why don't you get on that instead?"

"Even after what I said?"

"Then prove it's wrong. You can't just ignore it."

He returns to his office leaving me alone with Arlene who apparently knows I'm seething and doesn't pile on, just looks at me and shrugs.

"Tell Grumman I'm *on my way now*, just like Teddy," I tell her. God I hate going back to the police station—I either arrive angry or leave angry every time. But this Curwell arrest is bullshit and it's really important that everyone knows it. Even so, when I get there I try to start off on the right foot and thank Brandt for finding Teddy.

"Not much of a find," he says. "He was about ten steps from the office."

"He says you had a little chat."

"I guess."

"And you told him about the arrest."

"We already released the story. Everyone knew by then."

I didn't, but of course I was assessing the quality of granola and making unfriendly small talk with Joseph Lawrence—too busy for actual reporting.

"Are you angry?" he says.

"Confused. You don't even like Teddy."

"He was a missing person. I try to be nice to crime victims. Come on, what are you pissed off at?"

"Not pissed. Confused. Abigail Bennett wasn't robbed, and Melanie was running and didn't have any cash on her. For a guy like Curwell who commits crimes to score drugs, he really botched those jobs and then, what, decided on life in prison by killing the victims? Free room and board forever?"

"We have grand juries to make decisions like that. If they cut him, he walks. Wouldn't be the first time."

"But when he's in jail, maybe the real criminal is still out there."

"We're still following up, matching evidence to see what fits. We're not done. Teddy could have told you that."

"You must have had a long chat. Did you tell him about...us?"

"Us? There's an *us*?"

"You know what I mean. Having lunch."

"It may have come up," he says. "You say he isn't your boyfriend. If he is, tell me and I'll back off."

"I've told you—we work together. End of story."

"Because I know the look," he says. "I don't have to see it from you."

"What look is that?"

"The I-don't-want-to-be-with-you look. Linda and I have been practicing it for years, and hell, we even kinda like each other. Why don't we forget lunch for now—maybe try in a week or two when you get this settled."

"Get what settled?"

"Being seen in public with someone you're embarrassed to be seen in public with."

"I'm not embarrassed."

"Now there's a ringing endorsement. I'll have to update my résumé."

"Stop trying to trip me up. I'm not a witness."

"Look, I want this Curwell to be the one. I think you understand that."

And I do. I can't easily envision Karl Brandt agonizing over a lost love, but he is, and that's probably why he's convinced himself that some hapless multi-time loser has transformed himself into a serial killer simply to adjust for a downturn in the economy. And I take no pleasure in saying this, but a few days later when Brandt arrives for our Valentine's Day lunch, Curwell is already out, probably searching for the next unlocked window to crawl through.

He never killed Abby Bennett—never knew her—never intentionally had any contact with her. In fact, although at first he could find no one to verify his whereabouts on the night of her murder, that was primarily due to his own stupidity. He had been working at an oil change outfit, one which had closed early that day so that its employees could partake in a modest holiday party. By the time Abby Bennett arrived at her own home, Justin Curwell was too drunk to hold a beer bottle let alone a murder weapon of any kind, and completely incapable of stumbling the two miles between the lube joint and the Bennetts'. But unfortunately for him, he had stumbled one of those miles and been seen purchasing a gigantic soft drink at a convenience store where he gave the clerk a twenty and asked her to call him a taxi because it was snowing. The cabbie picked him up about a mile from the Bennetts', then dropped him off somewhere near the Common where, according to the cabbie, he planned to ride one of the swan boats before being convinced that they don't "float" on ice. Life is full of disappointments…and in Curwell's case, alibis.

As for lunch, I'm perfectly willing not to bring Curwell into our conversation. *I told you so* is never a good ice-breaker, and there is certainly ice, albeit not quite so thick as it may have been once. From the outset we focus on inoffensive small talk that steers clear of murder and investigation and suspects. And though harmlessness isn't really a basis for a relationship, the guy seems more personable away from his job and his desk and that creepy building and the attitude the position apparently demands. Apparently he wasn't lying about alcohol either: he orders a ginger ale. Not me. I'm not having a workday treat without wine.

"We're off the clock," I tell him, sipping at a Pinot Grigio. It's one of those whites that don't give me a headache, though it always seems so watery that I'm tempted to drink too much of it, after which, of course, I get a headache.

"I'm not much on wine," he says. "It's too much like work—sniffing and swishing and examining the cork."

"You can have a beer."

He frowns a little.

"My clock is different from yours. Maybe next time," he says, and though he has not meant the comment as an invitation of any kind, I let the suggestion go unchallenged. With others I might consider it a subtle come-on, but Brandt doesn't deal in subtlety; and despite his attempt at levity with Arlene in the office, he seems tired. Maybe he really did come in at 5:00 a.m., but more likely it's cases piling up—one case—the one that involves Melanie. But though we avoid that topic, we find one equally painful. His divorce.

"It's exhausting," he says. "You spend too much time talking to lawyers and aides and secretaries and you just want to kill yourself. Everyone wants a piece of something. Then because nobody wants to hear about it, it's just as exhausting keeping it to yourself."

"Couldn't you have done this without lawyers?"

He laughs. "You can do it online, for God's sake—download the forms, sign off, email the attachment. We're contesting so little. But Linda heard about a bad experience—some problem with filing fees—and she thought professionals would be better. And on we go. I can see why people stay married longer than they should. The alternative is a pain in the ass."

"You thought it might be wrapped up by today."

"I did. But the court doesn't like the idea of our amicable cohabitation."

"That doesn't make any sense."

"If we'd been less amicable—slapped each other around a little, fought over my service revolver and took some shots at each other—I'd be divorced now. Anyway, I did find a place to live and I figured I'd just slowly move out of the house. Linda is fine with that. She feels sorry for me. I feel sorry for her. If sympathy were love, we could live happily ever after."

"Sure you don't want that beer?"

"Wouldn't help. Now I've gotta hire a mover and...well, like I said: a pain in the ass. People on TV get divorced all the time. It looks easy. *Let's get divorced*—then they cut to another scene. Enough," he says and opens the menu. "Let's eat."

He asks me what I recommend, and I laugh. Their menu is about the same length as a Dickens novel and all I've ever had there is pizza. He says he doesn't do bread and sauce for lunch, but says he's never been to an Italian restaurant that doesn't make a good eggplant Parmigiano, so we order two. It's a good call; Teddy would be aghast.

The conversation is not so strained as I had feared, and after the little foray into divorce we return to the more bland—where I grew up in Maine and how I got into journalism. It's only later that I realize that, amid all my willingness to share my own autobiography, I never asked him why he became a cop. It would have been a good chance to learn something about Brandt—maybe something that would have disabused me of the opinions I'd settled upon. Well, he said something about next time. If there is one, I'll write out some questions—treat it more like an interview.

When he drops me off later I expect to see Arlene waiting up for me in the window, but she's spewing out layouts from the copier.

"How was lunch?"

"Went to Mattera's. It was fine."

She shakes her head.

"I wouldn't trust him," she says. She may have been busy with work, but she's been sitting on that analysis all the time I was gone.

"I don't think he tried to poison me, unless he was in cahoots with the waiter."

"I think you know what I mean."

"It was lunch. I'm not marrying the guy."

"Did you split the tab?"

"Really, Arlene?"

"I guess he can afford to pay. He makes good money at that dating service he calls the police department."

In some ways this is typical Arlene, of course, but there's a little more anger in her tone, a little more bitchiness.

"I wasn't gone that long. What happened here?"

"Joe Lawrence called. What happened yesterday?"

"I ran into him at Gretchen's."

"Well he's pissed at something. He withdrew the Chalmers ad for March. That's five issues where there'll be a quarter page with nothing on it."

"Did he give a reason?"

"Your name came up. Something about harassing him?"

"God, could that guy be a bigger asshole? I said maybe two words to him and he told me if I wrote about seeing him there, he'd pull the ad."

"Did you remind him he's a public figure—he couldn't do that?"

"No, but who would give a shit anyway? That's not a story...some self-important jerk-off has lunch somewhere?"

Arlene doesn't answer, but I know enough about her, and about her respect for journalism, to know that one thing she won't tell me to do is apologize. In fact she would be more likely to forbid me from ever dropping by Chalmers College again. She's mad. I'm mad. My pleasant lunch is already a distant memory, and then, as if to erase it entirely, Grumman calls. He won't be in for a few days—the cancer is flaring up and his oncologist needs to settle on a new protocol.

Curwell. Brandt. Lawrence. The perspective changes just like that. Arlene and I spend the rest of the afternoon in silence.

Chapter 17

A smartass might claim—and I've been that smartass several times—that the phrase "downtown Drayton" is an oxymoron: a few small variety stores and taverns, a hair dresser, a jeweler, a consignment shop, a struggling boutique that has a new name every six months (and was, for a short time, a pet grooming salon), and a smattering of the usual liquor stores, sandwich places, and most recently, a pawn shop. There's been talk of reopening a closed-down movie theater—the rumor that apparently surfaces annually. Then there's a children's clothing emporium that I root for as it struggles in the meretricious world of those hideous chain stores that insist on dressing kids like pimps and streetwalkers at a tastefully early age. I have some young cousins and I shop there when I can—but it has no chance of survival. And of course somewhere on the periphery of Joe Lawrence's imagination is a new Chalmers College extension of some sort. Apparently it's his little secret—and mine. Nobody else has heard anything about it.

Maybe the condition of our town is epitomized by the small black *Courier* sign that hangs slightly off kilter and squeaks whenever the breeze freshens. Most days I ignore it, but today with Arlene's assertion that Grumman's condition has worsened, I feel things should be made right when they can be. There's some kind of silicone spray in the closet—maybe I can blast away the rust and keep the sign as a souvenir when the paper shuts down. And it will. Without Grumman to oversee things, there will be no *Courier*, not unless someone steps in and buys it...and runs it...and probably brings in a new staff. Either way for me, at least, the job will vanish. We've been fighting an uphill battle anyway, so much so that even Grumman himself—rooted as he is in the world of print journalism—has mentioned the possibility of becoming a solely online entity. As if there isn't a glut of that already. And he knows, and I know, and maybe even Teddy with his one journalism course knows, that most of the crap online is just that: crap. There's no oversight, no interest in craftsmanship, no concerns about attribution and source integrity—just lasso an idle thought out of the air and blast it out to everyone. Fuck spelling and syntax and grammar and the skill of crafting an argument. Or even crafting a sentence. A struggling *Courier* might still need reporters for story writing, but an online entity needs only words—and if those words make sense, it's usually a bonus.

There's Arlene, of course, but she wouldn't take over; and if she did, who would want to work with her? When it came time to rein in Teddy, would she bother doing it or simply fire him? Arlene is not the answer. Nor is Teddy. And me? I'm not ready to run my own life, let alone a business on which others depend. No, without Grumman we're all out in the street.

And that's where I am—out on the street (or near it) idling under the squeaky sign like a lost tourist, when it occurs to me that there's a small stepladder in the closet. I could at least stop that infernal noise above my head. It's what my father would do, and he'd probably do it for the same reason: a little feeling of accomplishment. But as soon as I turn back toward the door, I see Jill Dennison crossing the street toward me.

She takes a cigarette out of her purse and lights it. "Where are you headed?"

"Just needed some air. Now I'm going back in."

"Walk around the block with me," Dennison says, touching my left arm. "I'll walk downwind—no smoke that way. My sister was the exercise freak so I learned how to keep it out of her face. I don't much go for that crap. How about you?"

"Go for what?"

"Exercise."

"I seldom have the time. Once in a while...."

"That's always the problem, isn't it? I hear there's a new fitness place opening up out on Route 9. That might be something we could do. I think it's a free trial membership. Of course once they hook you...."

I never actually hear much of the sentence past *we*. There is no *we* that includes Jill Dennison. I don't really want a confrontation, but this is the tea set all over again.

"You know," I say, motioning toward her cigarette, "they probably don't allow smoking in there."

"I didn't read the fine print," she says, and goes on about some that have bars where people can grab a beer after working out. That, to me, has all the logic of holding an AA meeting in a tavern.

"Anyway," she says, "I don't really smoke all that much—half a pack maybe."

"My boss used to smoke."

"He quit, huh? Everybody quits. That's the big new thing—new drugs to quit smoking. Patches and pills and electronic cigarettes. I don't want to quit. What's the story on Brandt? Is he still doing police work?"

"He's still working cases—far as I know."

"Hard to tell. Never any statements that mean anything."

She takes two long drags in succession, as if she's trying to fill every cavity of her body with smoke, then exhales quietly and tosses the butt into the street. "All scumbags. All those cops, don't you think?"

We're both silent for a moment, but it's an uncomfortable silence—one that she breaks as she zips open her bag for another cigarette.

"That guy he arrested—that Curwell?—a two-bit hustler. He was a bum in high school and he's still a bum. I actually knew him. Dipshit."

"He didn't kill anybody."

"Killed enough bottles, that's for sure. Cops should be ashamed...that whole force should be locked up. I'm gonna write a letter to your paper, register a formal complaint."

"It's your right of course."

We've gone down one side of a block and I tell her I need to get back to work. She seems wired, and people in that state just wear you out. We head back toward the the office—a refuge I hope Dennison won't violate. She moves closer and puts an arm around me, squeezing me roughly, smiling.

"Oh come on, Coop, I'm just having a little fun. I know you're dating the cop. I thought at least you'd defend him." She backs away a step and flicks open her lighter, sending a new trail of smoke curling into my face. Downwind had become upwind and I wave the smoke away.

"My private life..."

She doesn't let me finish. "Say no more. It's private. Of course it is."

She skirts to the other side, cognizant of the prevailing drift of wind. "But this is Drayton for Christ's sake. He took you to a nice restaurant on Valentine's Day. That's what lovers do. I just wondered how it was working out."

Now I'm beyond furious, and I don't even know why. If you have lunch with someone in a public place, you have to expect people to notice. I get that. But I don't want Jill Dennison noticing...anything. I mean when does noticing become stalking. Did she *notice* I was at the Johns house that night? *Notice* that people call me Coop? *Notice* what kind of car I drive? I force a smile and try to look like a young girl whose parents just learned she has a boyfriend—a little embarrassed, a little pleased.

"I guess you'll have to watch the restaurant surveillance tapes."

Jill stops puffing for a moment. Maybe the curtness of my response has caught her off balance: the lilting quality of her voice is gone, as is the Jill Dennison who gave me the facetious hug.

"I guess I'll have to. Did he mention my sister at all?"

"No."

"Because he could have in a number of ways, right?" she says, her tone darker. "I mean he was screwing her, so that's one way. Then if he murdered her, well I guess he wouldn't be confessing that. That might make you think you were next...for the murdering, I mean, not the other stuff. Or he might have talked about the case."

"None of the above," I tell her, leaving out the part where he told me he misses her. "It's chilly—I should be getting...."

"So what did you talk about then?"

"This and that."

"So it's a secret."

I'm forcing up the corners of my mouth and I know the result is some horrible grin. As awful as it may look, it's better than spitting—which is what I'd like to do.

"This wasn't an espionage mission. It was lunch. What do people talk about at lunch? The food. The service. The weather. The world. Listen, I have to get back to work. If you have something that relates to the *Courier*, a complaint, a suggestion...."

"Here's my suggestion," she says as we arrive under the sign I've vowed to fix. "I suggest you stop running away all the time. Do you ever not run away?"

"I'm not...."

"You are, right now, back into your little office where it's safe."

"And warm. And if you do have a complaint..." I continue as if she hasn't said anything, "...I suggest you come in right now and sit down with my staff and me so that we can address it."

"Your staff? This isn't the *Wall Street Journal*, honey. Staff? A sick guy and an old bat and some kid who lives with his parents? Now there's a Pulitzer waiting to happen. I think the committee sends out letters. I'd definitely keep an eye out."

"Is that all?"

"No. How come Chalmers fired my sister?"

"I don't know anything about that."

"But you know she was fired, right?"

"I know she used to teach there."

"And Joe Lawrence fired her. Well, he didn't, the academic dean did. A moral issue."

"From what I heard, it was money. She was an adjunct, a part-timer. People like that are let go all the time.""

"My sister was pretty discreet. How does a guy like Joe Lawrence, who has no contact with his staff, who wouldn't know an adjunct from an adjective, figure out that some woman who shows up once a week is having an affair? Beyond that, why would it matter to him?"

"Dealing with kids and all, you have to set an example maybe?"

"Kids? Have you been to that place? These kids are fucking each other in empty classrooms and selling drugs in the parking lot. They make my sister look like a goddamn nun."

"They're not all like that."

"That's some defense for Joe Lawrence letting this happen. I want to show you something in my office. Come on, whatever you *have* to do will wait."

Fix a squeaky sign? She's right. Besides, I've seen her angry and I've seen her sarcastic: I've never seen her earnest and it makes her more difficult to turn down. I follow her up to Jay-Van, where the Van half of the company is jabbering away on the phone and gives us a perfunctory wave as we pass by—a black woman in a maroon suit and a paisley scarf. Vanessa is clearly the stylish half of Jay-Van, and the more personable half too. Jill closes her office door and flicks on her desktop Mac. When she taps a few keys, the printer springs to life and we both watch as if it's the Second Coming. She hands me the printed sheet, an email, dated December 5.

"Two months ago," I say. "Slow delivery system, isn't it?"

She isn't amused. "Read it."

Jillian

Got shitcanned today from Chalmers. There goes the condo in Cancun I could have earned if I taught there another 25,000 yrs. The dean called me in but this was Lawrence's doing—cutbacks, attrition, the usual bullshit. Somebody knows something—well so do I. Haven't decided what to do yet, but I'm pissed. It's not the $, it's him, sanctimonious asshole. Let's see how he handles prison.

Mel

"So, what do you think?" she said.

"I never knew your name was Jillian."

"Really. I was hoping you might get something else out of that."

"That's not...what did your sister know?"

"That would make it easier, wouldn't it, if I knew?"

"Maybe she told her husband?"

"Marcus and I—we're not that close. Besides, she was with Brandt then—she'd have been more likely to tell him."

"Do the cops know about this email?"

"Who am I gonna show it to, your new boyfriend? He probably has his own set of emails he's busy hiding from his wife."

"Look, I came over here, so can you just get off that. He and I had lunch. Don't you have more important things to worry about?"

"So now you're mad," she says, as if the news is shocking in its suddenness.

"No, I was mad before. Listen, the turnover at Chalmers is ongoing—nobody bats an eye when someone leaves or comes on board. I'll bet a dozen people were let go at the same time."

"But they weren't all accused of impropriety, were they?"

"You don't know that."

She doesn't respond. She doesn't know. And she also doesn't know about Joe Lawrence's highfalutin expansion plans which, if they're true, would mean an increase in staff. Maybe those plans have washed out by now—the local rumor mill has been silent and the people I trust to tell me what's going on behind office doors know nothing. More Joseph Lawrence bullshit to pile on Jill Dennison bullshit. It's quite a pile I seem to keep stepping in.

I hand her back the email and she slips it into the shredder.

"I'm not ready for this to go public," she says.

"It's already public in one sense. An email has as much security as a postcard. Besides if she really does know something about him, wouldn't that be important? And jail? What's that about?"

"Don't know, but I do know what happens when you people get hold of something like this? You turn Melanie into a foul-mouthed and bitter young woman, just another person who lost a job she didn't even need because she already had a job. Then someone remembers high school and says *oh yeah, Mel Dennison—she got knocked up on prom night*. And suddenly Melanie isn't a murder victim anymore—she's just another lowlife who got her comeuppance."

I'd like to deny that, but I've seen it happen enough times—the victim winds up the villain and gets what she deserves.

"I understand what you're saying, but then why show me?"

"When I called you on Christmas, you have to understand, I was just frazzled. Now I'm calm and reasonable."

"But that night at your brother-in-law's when I…."

"I still thought the creep might have been celebrating. At the very least I wanted him to stay in mourning for a while. It was happenstance that you showed up."

"Are you staking out Joe Lawrence's house, too? And the dean that did the firing?"

"That's your job—you're the reporter."

"I did see Mr. Lawrence at that new natural food place."

"Vanessa calls it Retchin' Gretchen's—I guess she ate there a few times before the reincarnation. I doubt if it's better now. Why was Lawrence there?"

"I didn't ask. It looked like a business meeting. Two men in suits."

She shrugs: my so-called information is meaningless. "Okay, Coop," she says. "You should get back to work."

"That email…."

"Forget it. I'll post it on my Facebook page instead."

"Don't even joke. You have a business here—you don't want someone that vindictive on your bad side. I said the wrong thing to Lawrence the other day and he pulled the Chalmers advertising. Quarter page—that's a lot."

"Really. Well then increase ours. We have an eighth—go to a quarter. And I want his spot. Piss him off some more. Then try to find out why he singled out Melanie."

"He'll deny it."

"Let him. If he's a liar, let him lie. But he's an arrogant bastard too—he might just double down on your suspicions and tell you to go fuck yourself. And one more thing," she says, taking a cigarette from her desk drawer, "I have other siblings, and of course my folks. I don't want Melanie's name dragged through the mud. Believe me..." and she smiles faintly... "once Brandt gets a hold of a story, subtlety goes out the window."

"He would never do that, not where your sister is concerned."

"You have more faith in him than I do."

"You don't know me well enough to trust me on anything, but trust me on this."

She glares at me, but seconds later her face relaxes a little.

"And that ad," I remind her, "a quarter page? Were you serious?"

"I keep my word," she says, writes a check on the spot and has Vanessa sign it. It's a bizarre victory over Joe Lawrence in a war he doesn't even know he's fighting. But it makes me feel a little better. By the time I reach the antique elevator I'm on my cell talking with Marcie up at Chalmers. She says Joe Lawrence has some time the following week, but nothing until then.

"He's that busy? What's happening—his paperweight getting polished?"

Marcie doesn't laugh. "Meetings," she says, suddenly sounding more like a court reporter than the cynically acerbic receptionist. "Evaluations. Accreditation. Next Friday afternoon maybe. I'll pencil you in," she says, then asks if there's anything in particular I'm looking for. I could tell her I'm trying to get Jill Dennison off my back, but I don't think that'll fly. And besides, the stilted quality of her voice tells me that Joe Lawrence has given her new orders: I'm no longer the friendly young cutie from the local paper that Joe Lawrence wants to present with a job. Now I'm just some pain-in-the-ass reporter.

In a way I like it.

"Next Friday's good," I tell her. It's not, but I can always drop by without an appointment and poke around if I have to.

She doesn't question me, so I head back to the tension of the *Courier* office. I'm going to grab that silicone and spray the living shit out of everything in reach. When people grow nostalgic over the *Courier*, they'll remember more than a squeaky sign.

Chapter 18

My sign repair goes perfectly—I don't fall off the small stepladder and my aim with that little nozzle is true. I put the ladder away and go back outside to wait for the first breeze. It takes a minute or two: the sign still squeaks.

"Epic fail," Arlene says. "I always wondered what that meant."

"It's only epic if I fall off the ladder," I tell her. Since we have apparently arrived at some new détente, I tell her about Melanie and Chalmers and my plan to confront Joe Lawrence with my newfound information, maybe push him a little. She shakes her head.

"Joe has never enjoyed being pushed," she says. "I don't think he's going to start now."

"It doesn't matter what he likes."

"And that's fine—that's your job." she says. "It's good to see this aggressiveness, but listen, Joe Lawrence and I are, for want of a better term, contemporaries. Over the years I've heard things—they haven't always been complimentary."

"Any one in the public eye...."

"But he—I'm not sure how to put this—he enjoys the innuendo. It keeps his name out there. He may want to run for office again."

"Doesn't it usually go the other way—retired politicians get an honorary job as a college president?"

"Lawrence isn't typical," Arlene says. "Don't underestimate the guy. He can act like a harmless doof at times, but that's not the real Joe Lawrence. And what you said before—it doesn't matter what he likes. It does. Don't push him. He wouldn't mind playing the part of the beleaguered official hounded by some aggressive reporter.

"But you said it yourself—it's my job."

"It's gratifying to see that someone lit a fire under your ass—that's fine. You just don't want Joe Lawrence trying to put it out. Give it some thought. Too late this afternoon anyway."

She's right, but before I can actually call it a day, I have a retiree meeting. I grab a turkey sandwich at the deli down the street, hog one of the only three tables in the place, and call home. Maybe the word *retiree* has nudged me a little.

This time my father does answer.

"Breezy," he says—a nickname he had given me twenty years before and still uses when no one else is around. "Home from work?"

"No, just on my way to an assignment and thought I'd say hello. I take it Mom's out."

"Went into Boston with some friends. Lunch, shopping, like that. I can have her call you."

"That's okay. Just wanted to see how you were doing. We haven't talked for a while."

"How's that friend of yours, the one you brought over on Christmas?"

"Fine."

The clipped answer and surly tone don't escape him.

"Look, Breezy," he says, sounding conciliatory, "you know how Mom is about Christmas. It's family and only family."

"We're not the Corleones, Dad."

"I know that. If we were, your friend would have been shot dead in a revolving door."

And we're back to movies, recalling scenes from the *Godfather:* he still has the DVDs. Next time I'm home, he says, we'll pop one in. I agree that it would be fun, but it won't happen. My visits don't last long enough to watch a half-hour sitcom, let alone a three-hour movie. It's my mother, of course, who's keeping me away—or maybe it's me keeping myself away from her. I don't want to confess that to my father, so I blame work. It's something I don't have to explain in detail.

"I know, huh? It just beats you down. How long before you can retire?"

"Not long, thirty-five, forty years."

"We'll have a big party in the cemetery so I can be there. Tell Teddy he shouldn't judge our family by one visit."

"You remembered his name?"

"Seemed like a nice guy. Mom said so too."

"I doubt that."

"She did," he says. "Christmas Day was just a bad situation and nobody handled it well—including you. Am I right?"

I refuse to be the fall guy, but I can probably absorb some responsibility and admit that holidays never brought out the best in this family. I don't have to add the reason: Christmas long ago, Daniel in the other room, the tree unlit, the presents unopened.

"And I'm not preaching," he says, "but if you know that's the case, why push it?"

"I didn't think I did."

"Past history now," he says. "You be careful down there. I mean you don't live in the city but you've had those murders. They catch the son of a bitch yet?"

He's worried—cursing is often his way of expressing concern. I fabricate a little fiction about some leads I'm privy to, talk about the Curwell arrest while leaving out most of the truth, and talk about Jill Dennison as if she really is my new best friend, one from whom I'm never apart. Strength in numbers, he says. I could enhance the lie by telling him she owns a gun, but that would just make him nervous. If there's an opposite of a gun nut, he's it.

I remind him again that he doesn't have to tell Mom I called, but he will. He claims that relationships need constant mending, and jokes that if we all work together, the current grudge could end by next Christmas.

"Here's hoping," I say. "Just tell me this—was she always like that? Did I just not realize it when I was little?"

"I can't answer that. I mean you're on your own and doing things and they don't always jibe with what Mom expects you to do. I guess it's normal. I don't know if she was always that way. She always had expectations for you, but these days we don't talk much about things like that."

There's something about his tone and the phrasing that says their relationship is not going well, and though this may sound self-absorbed, I don't want to know. As much as I like to feel removed from the goings on at the Cooper household, I do want to believe that my folks are at least happy with each other, if not with me.

"I'm self-sufficient, Dad. I have a job. Did Mom ever work a day in her life?"

"No, but that's what we chose. Maybe that's what she wants for you. Leisure. Comfort. And she probably wants you to be more...I don't know...solicitous."

"The word is probably obsequious." I avoid the urge to tack on *like you*, but he senses the intent somehow."

"You know Mom loves you, right?"

"In what way?"

"In her way. No matter what you do or say—no matter how angry you get when Mom does something you don't like...you can't say that about anyone else."

"Anyone?"

"Anyone. Not friends. Not colleagues. Not even a spouse."

"I'd have to marry the right one."

"And I hope you do, but if you betrayed him somehow, he'd hate you for life. If you betrayed us, we'd be upset, disappointed, angry, but in the end you'd still be our daughter and we'd still love you. That doesn't mean we're special—that's just the way it is. Sorry, didn't mean to get so deep. Have a spouse in mind?"

"Not at all."

"That Teddy. He's...."

"Completely uninterested."

"Oh."

I can tell by his tone that he no longer wants to talk about it, but I don't want to leave it that way. Floundering, I reach into my bag of *non sequiturs*....

"I read that the Sea Dogs are raising ticket prices. Is that true?"

The Sea Dogs are some minor-league baseball team that plays in Portland and who, for some reason, my father has latched onto, often wearing one of their caps around the house.

"It's true," he says. "About ten percent."

He describes some recent enhancements to the stadium. He's newsy, but cordial.

"Next time you visit," he says, his innate optimism winning out, "I'll take you to a game. Bring Teddy—he's the sports guy."

"Sounds good."

It doesn't. And it won't happen. But sometimes it's a good idea to shut up and not compel those around you to share your misery. I don't want to sound like Albert Schweitzer—yes I looked him up—but our five-minute conversation may have done us both some good.

On the way to the retirement center I call Brandt on his cell—now that we're something like friends, I'm willing to run the risk that he's not fully dressed.

When he picks up I hear a lot of background chatter: he's at work and I ask him what he's doing at 9:00.

"Jesus, don't tell me Teddy's lost again!"

"Funny man. I need a...I need some advice, but I have a meeting first. Can you meet me at Deal's?"

"Deal's?" He pronounces it with two syllables, giving it a sophisticated cosmopolitan ring—how Target customers often use Tar-zhay. "That's sinking a little bit low, isn't it?"

"We can sit in the parking lot—that way we won't be seen inside."

"And what, smoke a joint with everyone else in the lot? Why not just come down here and we can talk in the office?"

"It's not that official. 9:00?"

"Your wish," he says. "Look for the unmarked car."

It's not that official—I should have phrased it differently. What is it if not official? Casual? Romantic. (Darling, I turned up some information.) One way or the other, Brandt is bound to read something into it. The thought of that is not quite so repulsive as it once was, but I could be just normalizing: my boss is probably going to die, my family is facing (or ignoring) some crisis, a woman I used to think was insane has confided in me, and my friend is dead. In this new world a date with a purported lecher in the parking lot of a greasy dive might almost be an upgrade.

Earlier I had told Jill Dennison I would hold off on sharing the information with the police, and I will. But I just want to let it slip that I'm talking with Joe Lawrence again, just so Brandt knows where I am. I'm not sure why, but Lawrence, whom I've always considered a blowhard and a buffoon, seems more problematic than before. Maybe that conversation with my father spooked me a little. I mean if he's worried that Drayton has become a more dangerous place, maybe maintaining a friendship with the police (is that like having a cop for a boyfriend?) is a good idea.

The meeting with the retirees turns out to be more enjoyable than I'd anticipated. They're not doddering golden-agers but instead a vibrant group of energetic activists. Unfortunately, they're shut up in a sterile, joyless, monochromatic building which may not have been designed specifically to break the human spirit, but probably does so quite efficiently. They want to talk politics and taxes, and they bring up several topics I know nothing about—like politics and taxes—and after a while I find myself listening, not so much for the sake of a feature, but because some of them are just interesting. One of the men, handsomely coiffed with a full head of only-slightly gray hair, brings up the murders. Safety issues, he calls them, but he's not worried for himself. Like most of the other residents he has relatives in the area, granddaughters and nieces, and he's worried for their safety. I assure them that the police are on top of things, that they're doing their job. I'm not sure how true it is, but I can tell they want to believe me. I leave the place with some optimism, suppressing the fact that the following week's calendar is darkened by Joe Lawrence.

When I get to Deal's there's an empty patrol car in the lot: Brandt's at the counter inside, his fork hovering over a piece of pie.

"My dinner," he says. "Not that bad."

"So I've heard," I say, and park myself next to him.

The guy in the baseball hat is on duty again and I order a tea, then wait for him to ask if I want pie. He does. I know his shtick by now, but I turn him down.

Brandt puts down his fork and leans back a little. "So what's up?"

"I have an interview next week with Joe Lawrence. Know him?"

"Know of him. He fired Melanie. Aside from that, not much."

"And he's the president of Chalmers College."

"And the owner. Did this information require a face-to-face? I mean it's always nice to see you, but..."

"Do you know why he fired her?"

He picks up his fork again.

"Cutbacks, declining enrollments. They're a private college—they can do whatever they want. Why do you ask?"

"I know that's the official explanation, but I guess I need to know what their bottom line looks like. Are they really that bad off or is it a smokescreen to get rid of people?"

"Good question," he says. "Let's get a table."

We pack up our edible belongings and move back a few feet to an empty booth. The waiter looks at us in wonderment, as if we've made a jumbo jet disappear, and for a moment I think he's going to order us back to our initial spot and ask us to do it again. He doesn't.

"I'm in the public sector," Brandt says. "Everything I do is out there—salary, benefits, personnel record, everything is public information. Corporations are different. If they release their employees and move overseas, are they strapped or just greedy? Maybe Chalmers' profits are down. I mean it's a business, isn't it? Aren't people in business to make money?"

"I understand he's involved in a divorce."

"I didn't know. Maybe he and I should get together and hang out."

"He's pretty much a blowhard. I don't think you'd like him much."

He smiles. "I'll take a compliment anyway I can. Now come on, you didn't ask me here to find out if I know Joe Lawrence. That's an email question. Or a text."

He's right. Maybe I can ease into the topic a little bit, maybe let Brandt finish my thoughts.

"While Melanie was teaching at Chalmers, did she ever mention a run-in with anyone? Another teacher? A student? An administrator?"

"Coop, really now. There are lots of intricacies in an investigation, but looking for a motive is not one of the more subtle ones. I'm sure you know we would."

"Did you talk about things like that with Melanie?"

"We talked about lots of things. Very often we kept our clothes on."

"I didn't mean that."

"Then why wouldn't we talk about things? Linda and I still talk—why would it be different with Melanie?"

"I'm sorry. I don't want to have another argument. I already had one with my father."

"And I had a sergeant tell me today that the established protocol was fine but he wanted to do things his own way."

"What did you do?"

"I wrote him up, showed him the letter, told him the next time he acted like an asshole I'd send it. So it was probably a bad day all around—we should have met at a bar."

"You don't drink."

"The ambiance would have helped."

"Let me start over," I tell him as my tea arrives. "Could some disgruntled student have complained about her and gotten her removed?"

"The way they run things up there, anything's possible. But very seldom does a student complaint get a teacher fired, unless that teacher is groping that student. I'd be shocked if Melanie had been involved in anything like that."

"Do you think if Joe Lawrence knew about you and Melanie, he would feel compelled to fire her?"

"A morals clause? Do you have something concrete you're not saying?"

Now I can go two ways here, but I decide that Jill Dennison, lunatic as she may be, deserves not to be compromised. So that's it. That's all I've got. And of course it looks as though I enticed him there for no good reason other than my desire to get him into bed...unless I can find a new topic.

"I talked with my Dad before."

"So you said. You don't get along that well, do you?"

"We do, but he's concerned about the murders of course."

"I can understand that."

"And I just came from a meeting with some seniors—they asked pretty much the same thing."

"I hope you defended your police force."

"I felt like your spokesperson for God's sake. Incidentally, one of the women there wants to buy a gun. What do you think?"

"I'm not an expert, of course," (and I know there's more irony to follow) but arming convalescent patients with assault rifles doesn't sound like the best idea of the day, or the week, or the...."

"I get it."

"Now as a method of reducing the number of Medicare recipients...is that what you had in mind?"

"Be serious. What about me? I was wondering if I should buy a gun."

"Of course," he says. "You can fill it with water and have hours of fun."

"A real gun."

"Squirt guns are real guns."

"I mean it. There are courses I could take and learn how to shoot."

"And they're all good, and you'll graduate as a responsible gun owner. And then somewhere down the road, someone less responsible will shoot you with that gun you're responsible for and make you dead."

"But if Abigail...."

"If your friend had had a gun, and if what happened to her went down the way we think, her weapon would not have saved her unless she was picking off squirrels at the time and had the thing in her hand. And Melanie—I doubt if she would have run with a weapon, even in the dark. And the girl in the parking garage...."

"Okay, I get it."

"I'm not anti-gun. I carry one. I always feel better when I know the other guy doesn't have one, but more and more often the other guy does. Or the other girl, like you. Now if you're serious I can help you make an informed choice, but...."

"So it's not a good idea."

"It's a fucking terrible idea. Then again I'm wrong about most...many things."

"Tell me about Melanie."

He laughs.

"Well there's a segue. She's not one of the things I was wrong about."

"I didn't mean that. Were you in love with her?"

He looks surprised that I asked, and I'm surprised that I had the nerve. Then I'm surprised again by the piece of blueberry pie in front of me.

"Last piece, it's free," the young man says. "We're only gonna toss it if it ain't eaten. Weren't you here the other night?"

I nod and mumble a thank you. Brandt is smiling.

"Life is full of decisions," he says. "Do I eat the pie? Do I then feel obligated to pay for it?"

Brandt has already had "dinner." I choose the pie, or at least a small triangle of it.

"Now where were we?" he says, but he knows and picks right up. "Melanie had this optimism—things had been bad, then they got good, they could only get better. As for your question—which I assume you're asking not as a reporter...?"

"If I'm eating pie I'm off the clock."

"I loved her," he says, "but we weren't together long enough for there to be any depth to it. I knew she would never leave Marcus. She told me that."

"Why?"

"He rescued her. She was fat and ugly, then she was pretty and thin—Marcus came along then and she equated her new self with his finding her."

"But she had to know…."

"She was loyal. I know what you're going to say—if she were loyal she wouldn't have been with me."

"Unless it was just sex."

"I don't know what it was. For her to get involved like that and know from the outset that it would never amount to anything—no, I don't think she was in love with me. Of course, Linda and I, well we were on our way out anyway, so I could easily envision a future with someone else, someone like Melanie. And maybe she'd seen some flaws in Marcus. Complicated, huh?"

"Yeah."

"But not tragic. Bottom line—it was wrong. I mean we weren't doomed lovers—we were doomed adulterers. That word takes away the romance of it all."

"But not the pain."

"No, not at all. Lately I've been thinking that if it turns out she's the last woman I ever kiss, I can live with it."

"You're pretty young to be shutting everything down."

"Things have a way of working themselves out I guess. Anyway," he says, "I think I could be comfortable saying I was in love with her. Still am."

He's qualified the disclosure with too many stipulations, but I get the point.

"Does Linda know?"

"You mean did she know then, or does she know now? Never mind, the answer is yes to both. I think she almost feels bad for me too. If afterwards she finds somebody and it works out, I'll be happy for her. Linda and I like each other—she's a terrific person. I've told you before—we're just not in love."

He signals for the check. "You take your time. I need to get back," he says. "And about that gun, if you're settled on getting one, at least let me teach you how not to get killed."

Like Melanie.

He doesn't say it but he doesn't have to, and I realize a new emotion has snuck up on me. I'm jealous of Melanie Johns. And in a way I'm even more curious about her. Who was this woman that the philandering Karl Brandt actually fell for? Is still falling for?

He lays some bills on the table and, since I don't want to be there alone, I gulp down the tea and follow him outside.

"Tell your dad I'll make sure you're looked in on once in a while, you know, especially at work. Will that bother you?"

"Will it be someone cute?"

"I don't know if Officer Randolph considers herself cute or not, but I do. Probably not your type. Sorry I bored you with my tale of woe, but you asked."

Standing by my car I shake his hand. It seems dopey, but so does everything else that's happened in the last half hour. And predictably, once he's is out of sight, I begin scanning the area, certain that Jill Dennison is sitting in her own car, chain-smoking in some remote corner of the parking lot and waiting to launch into another conversation. I've already spoken with her today—I don't need to do it again.

Two fives—that's what Brandt left on the table. So he paid for the free pie too.

One decision I didn't have to make.

Chapter 19

A week or so after my visit to the retirees, I'm sitting at home perusing my latest *Courier* piece for typos and misprints when a moose wanders into my kitchen. It's a female. My father sees it and asks when is a moose not a moose. I tell him I don't know. "When it's a cow," he says, and laughs. I tell him I don't understand, but he's begun moving furniture out of the apartment, then picks up a throw from the couch and uses it to shoo away the moose. This is much funnier than his lame joke and we're both laughing. The chaos all makes sense until the moose utters a few syllables in guttural tones and I realize she's talking to me. Even in Maine where I used to see these animals on a regular basis, their linguistic powers are minimal.

Just a senseless dream, of course, and I wake up staring at a blank computer screen—it's gone to sleep like me…again. As usual I promise myself to try to get more rest—an intention I'll summarily renounce the next time I'm "busy." I also trash what I've written thus far—if I can't stay awake to write it, who's going to stay awake to read it?

The weather has turned miserably cold again and an overnight dusting of snow makes the drive to Chalmers unpleasant, though the paved surfaces have been swept clean by a restless wind. It's early March and spring will officially begin in less than three weeks, but I've been forced back into layers and scarves, most of which I leave in the car before entering the administration building: I'd rather not look like an Iditarod contestant among the college kids to whom coats and sweaters have become anathema, irrespective of the weather.

Marcie continues her newfound chilliness and sends me right in without our usual banter, but everything is normal in Lawrence's domain—a spotlessly clean desk with him behind it.

"Twice in one month," he says. "Desperate times at the paper?"

"Not at all. I'm busy, so that's good. I noticed you pulled your ads this month. You must be doing well up here—don't have to advertise."

"Sometimes we cut back, or maybe use different avenues for PR. Don't worry, I'll bail you out before you go under."

The royal touch—in medieval England sick people would plead with the King to lay on his hands and cure them of whatever horrid illness they were carrying. Lawrence would have been expert at it—without any physical contact he's doing the same thing to me. He can cure the *Courier* of financial ruin, and will, as soon as I beg. I'm not doing that.

"Of course if you've come to sell me advertising, I'm sure I can...."

"I want to know more about your expansion. I've asked around. I can't find anyone who knows anything about a prospective building sale, transfer of ownership, even leasing. I wonder if you could provide some detail."

"Is that why you haven't written anything about it? You need details?"

"You said somewhere on Route 9...."

"I said *near* Route 9—the discussions are ongoing. You can't find anything because no one's going public yet. You can still say that Chalmers is expanding, even if you don't know exactly where."

And of course I would be providing free advertising for the dynamic and expanding Chalmers College at the same time the president of that college is withdrawing advertising from the paper. It pisses me off, but ethically I can't give any heed to disparate events. If he offered me a gift to report something, I'd dismiss the offer out of hand. The same is true if he withdraws a "gift." But I don't want to let this go.

"This expansion—last time you mentioned something about a dental program, maybe some culinary classes, something with the trades. Is that still in the offing?"

"You need the building first, but sure, all those things. Why not? Maybe we'll explore the possibility of a degree-granting program."

"You're talking about a four-year college. And this is on the record?"

"You're here and I'm here—of course it's on the record. Why should Harvard and MIT have all the fun?" he says. "We can provide a degree at a lower cost. Service more kids. Of course," he says with a wink, "that might be a little further down the road. What do you think?"

He doesn't really care what I think. If he did I'd tell him that there are over fifty institutions of higher learning in the greater Boston area, from Brandeis on the western perimeter, north and east to Tufts and south to Curry College. Then if you'd like, you can throw in Worcester and even Providence if you want to get the number over a hundred. There's absolutely no niche for a four-year Chalmers College, though obviously the other way of looking at it has merit: with so many, what's one more? Of course expansion on that magnitude would take place right here—not in Drayton center. Dorms, labs, food service, recreational facilities. Maybe I'm not a visionary—scratch the *maybe*—but I don't see it. Not here. Not with Joe Lawrence at the helm.

I let him blather on some more, and when I call him on topics like accreditation and staff, he glosses over it as if it were some minor detail, like where to order office supplies. It's a different kind of bullshit and I don't know exactly why. Usually he's playing the role of society's benefactor, but this is different. One thing is certain—I'm not filing anything about this until I can see something concrete.

"How about a figure?" I ask him. "Is this a million-dollar project? Ten million? Hundreds of millions? Do you have investors? Tuition certainly can't finance a project this big."

"Investors, loans, bond issues."

"Bake sales? Car washes?"

"Ms. Cooper, I'm giving you a big scoop here—you people still use that term? If you're not going to be serious...."

"I want to be, but I need something real, factual. If I say Chalmers is expanding, nobody will care. If I call it a fifty-million dollar expansion to a four-year school, then maybe I have something."

"Seventy-five million," he says.

"And that's what? Site development? Architects? Builders? Larger staff? Everything?"

"Seventy-five million, there's your figure."

"And you'll stand behind that."

"There are always cost overruns when you get near the end, but yes, that's the figure. And when have I *not* stood behind what I've said?"

Certainly $75 million is a headline grabber in a town like ours, but anybody can simply throw out big numbers. More prominent colleges have boards of trustees—people I could seek out for verification or comment—but Chalmers has Joe Lawrence. That's it. Of course I can't help remembering the last big building project I foisted on the publishing world—those wind turbines that still haven't materialized and never will. I want more but Joe Lawrence isn't offering any, least of all the names of the investors. He calls it the crucial development stage and it certainly sounds like a reasonable term. I'm about to leave—to leave in fact on slightly better terms than when he tried to intimidate me in Gretchen's, when I remember why I came.

"One more thing—can you tell me a little about your personnel practices, just in general."

"That seems pretty boring compared to what we've been discussing."

"It's part of a broader feature—area colleges, who gets hired, fired, retained, promoted."

"And I repeat," he says, "boring. Regardless you probably don't want me. Down the hall, three doors on the left, Joanne Patterson is our personnel chief. She looks over résumés and transcripts, background checks, previous employment records…she conducts interviews, interacts with payroll and academics, makes recommendations…."

"But she doesn't make the rules. If I write something like *according to Joanne Patterson at Chalmers,* who's going to care? People know your name, recognize it. If you say it, it means something."

"Okay, shoot."

"I'd like to know what specific qualities you look for in an instructor?"

"Well, we'd like them to be able to instruct, of course."

"Degrees? Experience?"

"Sure, degrees are nice, but you know one of our programs is cosmetology. We're just as likely to hire a good-looking woman with experience as a hairdresser or a clerk at a cosmetic counter—I mean if she knows how to take care of herself, she can probably instruct others on how to do the same. I'd hire you in a second. I guess that's sexist, huh?"

"No, just wrong. I don't like to wear a lot of make-up."

"My apologies, but we don't have a journalism program. We could always consider a course, a singleton. Maybe a full program somewhere down the road. Let me know if you're interested."

"But you're not hiring these days, you're firing."

"It's fluid—it always is."

"What about Melanie Johns? Everyone claims she was great teacher and yet you let her go."

"I told you. Money. Let me call Patterson. She can give you the nuts and bolts on every termination."

"You must know something about it. I'll bet the cops questioned you and probably never bothered with this Patterson woman."

"Well, let's see," he says, feigning a search into the deepest recesses of his memory. "If I recall correctly, we couldn't fill her class this semester. We have a ten-student minimum for all courses. We can't afford to open up a classroom and lose money in the deal."

"How many did she have last semester?"

"Students? I'd have to contact academics and get them to call up the numbers. As I said, someone in personnel...."

"Wouldn't it be someone in academics? Like a dean? Or you? Or even Marcie out there?"

He grimaces a little, tries to disguise it as a smile, and winds up contorting his features. He doesn't like to be contradicted, and for all his palaver about speaking up on social issues, he'd rather be heard than debated. I know he's wondering how a bitch like me snuck past security. Maybe because I didn't used to be a bitch like me, just a pushover for colorful charts and graphs.

He takes a second to reorganize his facial features.

"I suppose I can access the same information."

And just like that the other Joe Lawrence has returned—the same solicitous, can't-do-enough-for-you Joe Lawrence—but there's a little edge now, as if I'm an interfering parent infringing on his playtime. He punches in some codes on a nearby laptop—I expect some bats to fly out when he opens it, their diurnal rest period strangely disturbed—but instead the screen displays a seascape as the icons fill.

"Eighteen," he says after a few seconds, "Started with twenty—three drops, one add."

"A respectable number—is it unusual to go from eighteen to fewer than ten just like that?"

"Not at all, not in those computer courses. Let's say you're an older person entering college and you need to do word processing. So you buy Word and it's overwhelming. You take Ms. Johns's course to put your mind at ease. That doesn't happen as often during the second semester when you have more returning students than new ones."

"And the other course? Economics?"

"One semester."

He waits, as if to say *is that all you got?* And it is, but he apparently wants to rub it in a little.

"By the way," he says, pointing at the screen, "here's a list of her students. Of course as you can certainly imagine the cops have the list too, and as far as I know, they've interviewed all of them, you know, in case she pissed somebody off."

I glance at the list from a distance—I sure as hell don't need the individual names, not if Brandt has been running them down in vain for a few months.

"Couldn't you have given her a different course? I mean if she was that competent."

"And fire someone else? No. Besides, these kids aren't stupid. Sometimes they like the instructors who let them off easy, the ones they can bullshit and get away with it. You can't always go by what the students say in terms of quality."

"But don't you have the kids do evaluations?"

"Of course," he says, with that expansive smile, "but you know how it is. Some dope who can't spell his name can't very well evaluate a teacher."

"You have students here who can't spell their names?"

"I have spoken."

"Come on now, wouldn't you try to retain the teacher who taught them how to spell their names?"

"Try, yes. That's all we can do."

Joe Lawrence has this thing he does with his voice, dropping everything a register at the end of a thought to let you know that his previous statement was the final one, incontrovertible and binding. Most days that works, but today I won't let it.

"So when someone gets fired, what's the process? I mean do you call them in and tell them, or do they get a termination notice? How does it work?"

"They usually get a letter."

"Who signs the letter?"

"Technically they all go through me, but I don't always sign them. Marcie has a stamp, you know, in case I'm not in the office."

"I don't mean a stamp—I mean actual authorization."

"That can be anybody."

"Anybody? Can Marcie authorize a job termination?"

"Any administrator. Any dean."

"So it's just capricious."

"Not at all," he says. This time he doesn't drop his voice. He knows I'm not quitting. Melanie Johns has become so real that there's a part of me that believes we were, in fact, lifelong friends. And though I wish it were Abigail's murder driving me onward here, I know it's those prickly conversations with Jill Dennison.

"One more question. Let's say somebody's a really good teacher. Would you find a spot for her and maybe let someone else go?"

"I already told you. No."

"Never? I don't mean tenured instructors—just part-timers."

"We call them adjuncts."

"I know what they're called. I want to know if there are any circumstances—any at all—under which you might have kept her."

"I've never done that, but I suppose it's possible."

"Because from what I've heard, she was the kind you'd want to keep."

"You should take notes, or use that recorder," he says, a little more acerbic now. "We've already been through this. I told you, sometimes it's just numbers."

"And you maintain that she might not have been good...that her students were wrong."

"That was hypothetical."

"Sowing the seed of doubt."

"I resent that. All I said was that, in general, students...."

"...act like students. But as far as you personally know, personally now, she did her job well."

"Yes," he answers, his features harder and his tone no longer pleasant. Then he adds another redundancy, just to maintain what he has left of control, "As far as I know."

Clipped responses and frowns—it's a little like going a few rounds with my mother. Those bouts usually end in tears, but not today. Not yet anyway.

"What about other reasons for firing someone? Would you let someone go on moral issues, I mean if she were sleeping with a student, selling drugs...."

"You said one more question. You already asked it."

"I suppose I can ask another administrator...."

"Those are different scenarios—the first probably involves consenting adults; the second is a crime."

"So the first one, then, moral issues. Aside from distributing pornography or appearing on the Internet with her ass in the air—pardon the expression—morality doesn't enter into it?"

"It can."

"Because, and this is just hearsay, some people think she was let go for misconduct."

"Some people? This is probably where you tell me you can't reveal your source and therefore I don't have a chance to defend myself. Melanie Johns was not let go for misconduct."

"It's only a rumor."

"I answer questions," he says, "not rumors."

"In general then. Misconduct. What would happen?"

"Misconduct with a student?"

"No, outside of school."

Lawrence looks dubious but pleased. It's a softball question.

"Not my business unless it becomes public."

"What about the spring semester?"

"This *is* the spring semester."

"I mean last spring. Any problems? Anyone infatuated with her, harassing her, stalking her, dating her?"

"Dating her? I believe Ms. Johns was married."

"That isn't always a deterrent."

"If that was going on," he says, "I wasn't aware of it. Besides, there was quite a lapse between those students last spring and her murder."

"Not for some sicko with an obsession."

I don't have any real reason for wanting to see that older list except for his hesitancy, so I figure I might as well be a real pain in the ass. If Jill Dennison can do it and not give a shit....

"Never mind," I tell him. "I'm sure I can get that list from Marcie."

For a moment Lawrence says nothing. I'll bet he wishes he kept a few items on his desk aside from that ghastly paperweight. It would give him something to do with his hands while I'm scribbling notes instead of just sitting there breathing louder.

"Anything else, Ms. Cooper?"

The script says to thank him and leave, but I don't feel like following it.

"How about complaints and threats? Even the best teachers...."

"You know, Ms. Cooper, we have students making complaints about instructors all the time. *He's too hard* or *She doesn't explain things* or *He talks too fast*—we don't document every complaint, but we try to rectify them by switching the student into another class. In Melanie's case, her section was the only one. Now it's possible that a student sat seething in her class, then waited six months to cool down, couldn't, then murdered her. That's hardly the fault of the college."

My pulse is racing but steady. And my eyes are still dry. Maybe I can get used to this pushy reporter stuff, maybe be better at my job—provided I can hold it together a bit longer. But—and this is the problem when I step outside myself—I'm so intent on maintaining my equanimity that I lose sight of specifics.

"So," he says, "who else are you interviewing?"

"What do you mean?"

"You said you were interested in personnel policies. Just ours or others'?"

Oh yes, my original contrived premise.

"Policies in general."

"Well, like where? B.C.? Northeastern? Wellesley? Where're you off to next in this campaign?"

Funny thing about lies, even little white ones. Sometimes they require followup, and I don't have any. I glance everywhere but toward him, then announce that nothing he said today will be in print without his authorization—whatever that means. I'm stammering now, avoiding the question, and that newly acquired bravado is gone. He could bail me out with some of his usual small talk, but he's going to let me hang.

"We're just starting," I mumble. "Eventually we'll get a good cross-section."

"How many colleges?"

"What do you mean?"

"How many would constitute a good cross-section?"

"I don't know, we haven't actually counted, or decided...."

I make a motion toward the door. He's still sitting, his condescension obvious.

"So this isn't so much an investigative piece as it is a fishing expedition. Is that about right?"

He could probably stand up and look menacing, but he doesn't have to. I'm already on the defensive...and it happened so quickly.

"An ongoing exposé, huh? Selling papers," he says. "I guess that's what it's about."

"We don't charge for the *Courier*."

"You sell ad space. Without that you couldn't run the thing, and if no one reads it and your advertisers learn that, then they stop buying and you're out of business. The only reason I point that out is this: I can't think of any topic less interesting to readers than the personnel policies of...of anyone, not just Chalmers. I mean unless some scandal occurred and you were following up, who would possibly care? Unless this is only about Melanie Johns, in which case, you should have said so."

It's a threat obviously, his way of saying that a few well-placed criticisms might reduce our already paltry readership and poison other advertisers. I've already conceded that the *Courier* isn't going to survive Grumman's departure, so I paste on a smile, gather my things, make sure my eyes aren't beginning to moisten, and thank him for his time. A hint of rancor remains as he stops me at the door.

"I know why you're here—I'll make it easy for you." He goes back to his laptop, punches a few keys, and the printer near Marcie's desk spews out a dozen or so sheets.

"Every student Melanie Johns ever taught at Chalmers. Alphabetized. Enjoy the list. And remember, when someone else beats you to the story on expansion while you're screwing around with police work, don't wonder why you work where you do."

It's an insult, but I know why I work where I do. I'm just not that good.

*****

When I finally escape, the March sunshine has won out and the outdoors seems almost pleasant. On my way to the car I pass a few students heading to classes—probably a few instructors too—and I wonder how many of them know about the Chalmers dismissal policy, and how many of them could possibly give a damn.

Just as I unlock my door I hear a voice from the next car over.

Drayton High?"

"Me? No."

"You didn't go to Drayton?"

I shake my head. She looks familiar, kind of exotic, the kind of face I would remember if I'd actually met her.

"I had exhibit there," she says, as a gust of wind lifts her scarf like a pennant. "I think a friend introduced us, but I'm bad with the names."

But I'm not—I can even remember long ones like Yasmin Maskhadova.

"Are you still the best Chechen painter in Boston?"

"I am on my website," she says, smiling. "I've forgotten...you're a reporter...."

"Brianna Cooper," I tell her. "Do you have something going on here? An exhibit?"

"Learning to get rid of my accent. An ESL course. You?"

"Working. You went to Drayton High?"

"Two years when I first come to America. Night school."

"I didn't know."

"Melanie Johns," she says, out of nowhere, as if I'd fed her the line. "You wrote about her. Her husband."

"I've written about the murders."

"They will catch the man who did it?"

"I hope so. Was she your teacher, Yasmin?"

"One night, but we were friends. Did you know her at all?"

I shake my head and wait for the inevitable next line—you'd have liked her—but instead the she launches into an impromptu tribute: nice woman, patient, taught her smooth conversation, better than her actual instructor. Conversations in the library, out for drinks once or twice, that sort of thing. Yasmin's words seem every bit as powerful and heartfelt as those I prepared for Abigail's eulogy. She may have an accent, but her facility with the language doesn't restrain her at all.

"I was in the paper," she says. "Did you see my name?"

"The accident, the Talbot kid. You weren't hurt?"

"A cut. He has called me a few times."

"He's cute. Very handsome."

"He asks me out, but I'm afraid to ride with him," she says. "He tells me he will pick me up in cab if I don't trust him driving."

"What did you tell him?"

"Cab drivers in your city scare me even more. Eventually I will say yes."

"You're playing hard to get."

"Hard to get?"

"That means—you would like to be with him but you don't want him to know that, so you make believe you don't want to be with him."

She smiles. "Hard to get. We have same customs…I just need to know how you Americans say it. You do this too with someone?"

"I should have done it many times. I think I'm doing it now."

She laughs, then looks up at the clock tower.

"I will be late," she blurts out, and I notice for the first time she's carrying what appears to be a small suitcase.

"Going on a trip?"

"This is telescope. I have to make presentation for my speaking class."

"You know Melanie had one too."

"Yes, a gift from her husband. He is nice man to buy her gifts like that."

I tell her she's right, and maybe she is. Maybe Melanie was at the end of that long rough patch and on her way to living happily ever after.

"She liked astronomy," Mashkadova says, "just like me. We were going to be friends."

She bites her lower lip so hard I think it's going to bleed.

You know," she says, her expression darkening, "I'm sad but I'm angry too. Is that normal?"

"It's normal."

"Melanie was angry when she lost the job. But funny too. She said she would hit Joseph Lawrence with telescope but she was afraid it would break and her husband would not buy her a new one."

We both laugh at the thought of it, and in a moment the young woman is hurrying to class. How unusual for me—a pleasant conversation—where one of us was practicing her language skills and the other was glad to be talking to anyone not named Joseph Lawrence.

Chapter 20

I guess my recording app is losing its charm—I don't use it quite so much any more. Maybe I'll go back to some primitive form of keeping track—like a digital recorder. But since I have the thing running...I was thinking about Yasmin. That woman must be able to chart her life on some graph where the y-axis steadily climbs. Or maybe that's the x? "X to the left, Y to the sky." I guess that little mnemonic hasn't helped me quite so much as "i before e except...."

Just to clarify, there's something ennobling about Yasmin's struggle and I think I do more bitching than struggling. And with Grumman being sick and all, I should be planning how to keep this paper in business after he's gone, not trying to figure out my next job when it shuts down.

And I thought of how little my mother is like Yasmin, though I do wonder if they ever looked toward their lives in similar ways before their paths diverged.

*****

Grumman's SUV, in all its massive grayness, sits in the parking lot behind the *Courier*. Given Arlene's gloomy predictions from a few hours before, I have no idea why, unless his wife has come by to retrieve his personals. As difficult as phoning Grumman might have been, facing his distraught wife will be worse. Of course I can just turn around and leave and no one would know I'd been there, but I can't keep avoiding the office—I'm supposed to have a job there.

So I steel myself for hysteria or sadness or anger, open the door, and find Grumman in my chair, alone, rhythmically tapping on the desktop, the way someone might if he were wondering where the hell you'd been or what the hell you'd done. I'm wrong on both counts.

"How long have you had a metal desk?"

"I don't know. Since I started here. All the desks are metal."

"You should have oak," he says, tapping the surface with his fingernails. "It would be more like a real desk. This rattles when you pull out a drawer. That's not the sound a desk should make. A desk shouldn't make any sound."

I know we shouldn't be talking about desks, though I don't exactly know what we should be talking about. Mortality maybe.

He shakes the desk again. "Didn't expect to see me, huh?"

"Uh, no...I don't know. Arlene thought you were ill yesterday."

"Ill. I like that word. It's better than sick. Psychopaths are sick, and child molesters, and animal torturers. It's a good newspaper word. But people like me, we're ill."

"I never thought of it that way."

"Of course you have, Bree. You're a writer—you're always making word choices. But yes, I'm ill. Did Arlene think I was on the way out?"

I try to look surprised, apparently the attempt is not very effective.

"Don't ever play poker," Grumman says with a wink. "Is that what Arlene said?"

"She thought you looked more ill than before."

"More ill. Worse—that's the comparative form of ill. You can use that word—it doesn't offend me. And you can have your place back now."

He pulls another chair over and sits across from me.

"They found another spot on my right lung about a week ago. Then they did some tests I can't even pronounce, took some fluid, checked my lymph nodes—it's like one of those oil change places—they do everything while you wait and they keep telling you more things that are wrong until you finally say yes, you can put in the air filter if you just promise to go away."

"I've never been to one of those places."

"Change your oil once in a while."

I force a smile, but I'm sure it looks artificial. He isn't paying attention anyway and I don't blame him.

"Today I have a date with a pulmonary specialist. Four o'clock. That almost has to be fun, don't you think? I didn't know those guys worked that late."

I finally manage to get my coat unbuttoned. "What about treatment?"

"That's the oncologist. Gotta keep those specialists straight, speaking of which, I learned all sorts of stuff about cancer recently, stuff I had no interest in knowing, Small-cell. Non small-cell. You know if they had said to me, would you like small-cell or non small-cell cancer, I'd have gone with the small. Non-small means big and who in his right mind wants a big cancer? Smaller the better, right?"

"I really don't know."

"But I do. I have the small—it's the way to go, if you want to go faster."

"Mr. Grumman..."

"I know, gallows humor is offensive. But what the hell, it's my gallows. Hold on a minute."

He walks into his office, comes back with a pint of bourbon, and stands it on my desk.

"They think chemo will have some effect," he says, "but I'm planning to self-medicate. Using it right now, administered it just before you got here—medication from Kentucky. Don't worry—I'm not driving. Elise dropped me off—she's around town somewhere. She gave me an hour—I hope the doctors give me more than that. What do you think?"

I'm not sure what kind of answer makes sense, but he doesn't require one.

"Anyway," he says, not offering me any liquor and sounding not so much resigned as philosophical, "they have more treatment options than a diner menu. I like the chemo idea. Kill everything—it even works sometimes. For now you're in charge."

The sudden shift brings me up short.

"What do you mean? In charge of what?"

"You run this place until I'm settled."

"I'm not ready to do something like that."

"You're not running an airline. This is a weekly with four employees, five if you count Arlene's nephew. You don't have to manage yourself and I'm—what's that word?—oh yes, ill. That leaves Arlene and Teddy. So it's you until I'm settled."

He can probably see the terror on my face.

"Don't get all weepy—I don't mean settled into the ground. They're going to find me a treatment option or two and have a go at it. I looked it up online—there's a pretty good chance I can even work another year or two. Quality of life—that's the term. Next couple of days, though, I don't know where I'll be and when. You're in charge. Call my cell if...ooh, there's that word again."

I'm supposed to laugh, but my attempt produces nothing but another weird facial contortion.

"Not as funny as I thought," he says. "Okay, you call me if you have a problem, or text, or email. Now I think I'll go sit at my nice oak desk and do some work."

He stops at his door and turns around.

"Thanks for not crying," he says, and he seems grateful. "Elise didn't cry either. I thought that was pretty neat. It'll give her something to do at the wake. Now go online and find an oak desk."

"You mean like an office supply store?"

"It's furniture, Bree, not a staple remover. Look around. Find one you like. I'll order it."

"Furniture is expensive. Real furniture."

"Try Crate and Barrel. Elise likes their things."

"A desk from there—that may be $1,000!"

"I saw one for $1,499, but don't settle. Like I said, my wife buys stuff there—I don't expect to get away cheap."

For a few moments afterwards, I handle all the pedestrian activities I'm accustomed to—log on, check email, and return some calls—including one from Gretchen thanking me for stopping by. She's fishing for a preview of what I said, and though I wouldn't do it for Joe Lawrence, I don't mind sharing a few phrases. It's a favorable review, mainly because I'm skewing it toward the patrons' enthusiasm and away from specific menu items. It's not so much damning with faint praise, but it's close. The busywork does the trick for a while, but I know myself well enough to sense trouble just beneath the façade, so I drag myself into the bathroom before the tears start. A few moments of controlled breathing transmute smoothly into a short period of face repair, and pretty soon I'm settled in again at my metal desk. When my composure has returned, I figure I can share with Grumman my morning at Chalmers.

I don't receive the response I anticipated—maybe it's the bourbon but he finds it amusing. Grumman has always had a good handle on Joe Lawrence, and he's about to assure me that I will too after a few more similar experiences—until I feed him the punch line: Yasmin Maskhadova. Then his expression changes.

"The girl in the accident? What was she doing there?"

"Polishing her English. She sends out lots of letters and emails, wants to be able to write, as she puts it, more American."

Grumman smiles. "She should set the bar higher. The mediocrity of 'American' is within everyone's grasp. It's English that's unattainable."

"She's pretty ambitious and she's trying to sell her work. She figures any advantage...."

"This is where I should ask who her instructor was, but I don't have to, right?"

"Only once. But Maskhadova has an interest in astronomy. I guess she was at Melanie's house a few times."

"Okay. Now I've had a few pops here and I must have missed a sentence. How the hell does that come up in conversation?"

"It's easy when you're carrying a telescope. She was making a presentation on tele-, teles-..."

"Second syllable. Telescopy. Just say astronomy and save yourself the trouble."

"Whatever it is, she and Melanie got to talking once, found they had a similar interest. They led pretty different lives—but they went out for drinks a few times. Apparently that's when Melanie told her she would no longer be teaching at Chalmers."

"Did she tell her why?"

"Cutbacks, that's what she said...or that's what Maskhadova says she said. I don't think she enjoyed talking about it. I didn't get all the details—we were both in a hurry. Melanie was plenty pissed, I got that much out of it."

Grumman runs his palm over his face as if he were feeling the results of a bad shave.

"Do the police know this? Did they question her?"

"I don't know. I freaked a little when I saw her."

"Because of the stranger in the garage that day. You have to ask Brandt. If he doesn't have this information, we can't just sit on it."

"I guess it wouldn't be ethical."

"Hell it wouldn't be legal—withholding evidence in a capital case? I could be arrested, and I'd deserve it. Can you find out?"

"I think so."

"I'm not asking you to be coy. Tell him what you know."

Grumman ought to realize by now that I don't do coy, so I phone Brandt and ask him flat out. Turns out he does know. He's not happy that I do and he doesn't express any real enthusiasm over my "clues" in an ongoing investigation turning up in the *Courier*, but he is aware of the women's impromptu post-exam party and has a list of everyone who attended. Some men too, though they appear to have left early—all questioned, all cleared. Now two of the five women are dead. Brandt doesn't know, however, that Melanie and Yasmin were the last two there. That seems to perk him up a little. Maybe, alone, and with a few drinks behind them, they opened up more. "Of course," he says, "it's just as likely that they got silly and started throwing tortilla chips around."

"Doesn't sound like Maskhadova," I tell him.

"Not Melanie either," he says. He sounds wistful. They were already apart by then, and though he doesn't say as much, I know it's eating away at him that if he could have held on to her a little longer, she might still be alive. How he would have been able to guarantee that, I have no idea—the idea is as irrational as Maskhadova's, but he misses her and he's having no success hiding it. Maybe solving this crime has become more personal than professional. I remember Grumman warning me about the same risk and I feel comfortable enough to broach the topic that maybe he and I both are too close to this case.

Silence. Either I've struck a nerve or he's daydreaming. I let a few seconds pass before speaking again.

"Karl?"

"I heard you," he says, "and I know what you mean. I'd love to arrest a murderer, but this *is* personal. Even so, I would never withhold evidence just to get revenge."

"Sorry. I had to ask. This artist, Maskhadova, is her life in danger? That incident in the parking garage...."

"She's over in Brighton, but the cops there have eyes on her—within their budgetary limits. But if that was a botched attempt on her life, I doubt if whoever did it will try it again. I mean people saw him."

"I hope you're right. If I hear from her again, I'll let you know."

"And if you don't hear from her?"

"You can still call me anytime."

You can call me anytime? That had all the subtlety of a lap dancer in a gentleman's club. Whatever happened to good-bye, or see ya? Jesus, a few weeks ago Karl Brandt embodied everything I hated about males—not just males, mankind in general. Now here I am making myself available in the most obvious terms. Yasmin wouldn't like that—it's not playing, how you say, *hard to get*. But here's something I didn't know: there's an advantage to working alone in an office—you can laugh out loud and nobody accuses you of having lost your mind. I exercise that option for a moment or two, then find respite and sanity on the Crate and Barrel web site.

Grumman's recommended desk is teak and rattan, small drawers and limited space, almost useless in an office like this. It's not $1,499, but only $1,399. A steal...until I see the matching chair. No height or back adjustment, no swiveling, the antithesis of multi-functional office apparatus. $575.

Quite lovely, though, and how much function do I need? I'm always on the road traveling from interview to opening to fire to arrest: as long as my car upholstery is comfortable, why do I need to swivel in the office? Maybe a desk is becoming a quaint throwback. Nowadays a desk is anywhere you can lay your laptop, including your lap. A pencil, pen, stapler, tape, paper clips, scissors—all the things that desks kept organized are all available in virtual—but usable—form on the laptop. And for those who find even a laptop unwieldy, there's the tablet. And though I haven't done so, I know of reports having been filed from a smartphone.

So no one needs a desk, but this one in the catalog is a beauty. I jot down the item numbers and bring them into Grumman's office. He doesn't question a thing, just picks up the phone and, glass of bourbon by his side, slurs the order; then probably because he was prompted to, repeats it. Before the conversation can come to an end, I hear someone calling my name from the outer office. It's Jill's business partner Vanessa.

"I'm sorry to bother you," she says, "but I can't get in touch with Jill. A year ago if she hadn't shown up for work I wouldn't bat an eye, but lately she's been...pretty good."

"About showing up."

"About everything. I think her sister's death did a number on her. I'm not saying people with problems can be shocked out of them, but her focus is better. That's why I was just wondering if she'd come by here at all."

"Last time I saw her I saw you—in the office that day."

"I don't want to call her parents. They're not doing well and I don't want to make things worse."

"Do you have any idea where she'd go?"

"She's been in some...places. Institutions. I wouldn't be amazed if, after Melanie and all, she checked herself in. But I think she would have said something first, I mean even if she lied to me and said she was going to spend some time with her folks, that would make sense."

"Are you two close?"

"Nobody's ever really close to Jill. We're business partners—I can count on one hand the times I've seen her outside of work."

"Does she have a boyfriend? Girlfriend?"

"She's had some boyfriends over the years. No one special, no one who's ever come by the office. I think they were men who satisfied needs for a certain period of time and then moved on—or she moved them on. Unless she's found a new one, I can't imagine her staying with one of them. If you do hear from her, tell her to give me a holler."

"You do the same," I tell her. It's not that I want to develop our friendship, but if anyone knows what's happening in Drayton real estate, it's Jill Dennison. And even though she often seems nonchalant—or maybe just lackadaisical—when it comes to work, she'd know if a multimillion dollar real estate deal were in the wind.

As soon as Vanessa leaves I try Jill's cell. Another long shot that doesn't pay off. The thought occurs to me that I should tell Brandt, but I'm sure he's heard all about Jill through Melanie, and though a sister would be kind, a lover might be truthful: Brandt certainly knows that there's an imbalance in Jill that may have suddenly and spontaneously arisen. He'll tell me to forget it—and I can do that for a few moments, busy as I am devising places for my belongings—the ones that will suddenly be homeless when my new desk arrives.

On top of the last pile I toss Joe Lawrence's list, then pick it up and browse through it. Then I do it again—and a third time. Yasmin Maskhadova's name is not on it. I'm not surprised.

Chapter 21

When I first moved here from Maine I used to drive all the time, just start the car and ride somewhere. I hadn't done much of that at home, but here I was independent, unfettered...at least until my job became full time and began to interfere. But today I have a minute or two and I take Old Drayton Road past some of the family farms still extant and a few factories in small business parks, then finally down a road that appears no more developed than a logging trail, ending up on a tract of land called Site C. I don't know what the C stands for. Maybe it was to throw people off. Only "C" they might say: it can't be as important as A or B.

It's still winter on the calendar. The trees show no hint of the season to come, and not even a spate of warmer afternoons has nudged any life from the branches, though it has turned the road sloppy and thick with melted snow. I can smell the mud, the decaying vegetation from the autumn leaf drop. I follow the tire tracks as they wind deeper into the wood, then on a whim, flip on my GPS. Meadow Road it says, and if I stay on it long enough I'll end up where it ends up—within a wooded mile of Route 9.

This is where the wind turbines were supposed to have risen. Maybe by now construction would have been proceeding and the rest of the trees would have been cleared. Development: paved roads, power lines, maybe a convenience store or two for the workers to grab lunch. Instead—nothing. Just woods and mud. I've probably saved more trees through my slipshod reporting than any eco-terrorists with their hammers and spikes. I hope the environment is grateful.

*****

Every once in a while my past catches up with me. It's not like descending from the altar on my wedding day and heading for the exit with my new husband, only to find a former lover reaching out to remind me I solemnly promised in a bar some night that I would marry him. (That really happened to a classmate back in Portland—I have witnesses. Eventually the police came and rescinded the promise.) Even that's not as dramatic as the somewhat threadbare movie plot where a child shows up at your door and says, *Hi, Mom, I'm your son* and merriment ensues. As for me it seldom goes beyond running into some guy I slept with who for some reason (dim lighting? alcohol? wanton desire? all three?) seemed a lot more attractive when we did the deed. Embarrassment. Little more than that. The fact is I never really thought I had much of a past, but I guess Grumman disagrees.

The next afternoon it's just the two of us at work and I'm typing out and punching up interviews I did that morning with some parents who claimed their son was being bullied at school and that the teachers weren't doing anything about it. With all that's been occurring on that front the past few years, a school deliberately turning a blind eye seemed unconscionable, let alone foolish. Turns out the official paperwork, at least what the principal could share, was in order. And something else, and I don't enjoy saying this, I didn't like the so-called victim—there was something in his expression, a kind of sneer, that said "write something good or I'll kick your ass." I could envision him bullying everybody himself—his parents, other students, teachers, maybe even the building principal. But I wanted to paint this boy in at least a glimmer of positive light, and I'd been picking Grumman's brain most of the afternoon.

He'd been helpful, but he seemed distracted. Illness, mortality, I thought, that was usually the case. Something undoubtedly lay ahead, a new regimen of pills or potions or IV drips, and he was understandably distressed. It seemed as if he wanted to talk about it with me, but he seldom liked to talk about it at all, so I let it go. I figured, when he's ready....

Late in the afternoon the front door opens and a guy in jeans and an overcoat walks in. He's wearing those photosensitive glasses so at first I don't have a good look at his eyes, but he doesn't seem at all suspicious, and when Grumman rushes over and extends a hand, I figured we're good.

"Eric Wilcox," he says, leading him over to my desk, "this is Brianna Cooper."

He looks too young to be some friend of Grumman's, but a publisher gets to know a lot of people so I don't register any surprise, just half stand and shake the man's hand. When his overcoat falls open a little I get a good look at a somewhat crumpled white shirt and an almost comically outdated tie that hangs too short—it makes him look like a chubby little kid whose stomach got in the way of his clothing. But he was neither—not chubby, not a kid, older than I but not by much.

A fix-up, so that's it. No more putting Teddy and me together. Grumman is branching out to strangers. On my mental calendar I immediately start checking off dates when I can't possibly go out with this person. Of course the easier solution would be "I'm already seeing somebody," but that admission is fraught with its own set of difficulties. So I say nothing. And I wait.

"I've read your work," the man says to me. "Even used some of your articles in my classes."

"You're up at Chalmers too?"

"Oh no," he says, smiling. "I'm at the high school. I teach journalism, advise the school paper, that sort of thing. I'll have to admit, I haven't been in a real newspaper office since college."

He looks around, but there is little of nostalgia or reminiscence in his face—this undoubtedly is not the newspaper office of his dreams. Of course I don't know what to say other than what the hell are you doing here? which would be inappropriate at best. I could suggest he look around, but he isn't my guest and this isn't my paper. I settle back into my chair and make as if to get back to work when Grumman interrupts me.

"Eric's going to be helping you out for a while."

Now I have to tell you, Grumman—who seldom speaks without perfect clarity—softly mumbles that entire sentence, the way you would mumble bad news to your parents when you brought home a crumpled heap that used to be the family sedan and hoped they'd miss the confession—some sentence with wreck and police in it, but which might not be heard because of the mumbling. But this time Grumman doesn't mumble quite enough for me to miss it, or to miss the word *you* as opposed to *us*.

Now I think I've mentioned that Arlene has a nephew who helps out on occasion, and there was a time we hired a stringer for the summer, a junior named Cecilia Murray from Simmons in Boston. She was terrific—a good worker and a great colleague. Lots of fun. Everyone loved her but she left in August and never came back. Even now I Google her name once in a while just to see where she ended up—another form of self-torture where I agonize over the accomplishments of others. But for the most part, it's the four of us and I didn't think we were hiring—or that I, not we, needed help.

"Helping me?"

"Just once in a while—a few assignments here and there."

"Really? I didn't know we were that backed up."

I guess my question sounds somewhat accusatory because Eric looks more uncomfortable than I feel.

"Geez Dan, I thought we were all on the same page." My new friend Eric turns to me and apologizes. Nice. But he didn't do anything wrong. So I wait. More mumbles.

"Yeah, well," Grumman says, "a lot going on around here...forgot to mention it."

Now I'm scouring the room for eye contact. Not happening. So I wait. We all wait. Someone really has to speak or an hour from now we'll be closing up the office and all be stuck inside, frozen in time, through eternity. I'll give this Eric credit—even though I'm sure he's there to take my job, he speaks up when he has to, sans mumbles.

"Tell you what," he says to Grumman. "You two work this out, then let me know what you decide."

He's cordial enough: it's hard to dislike him but I make the effort and don't even mumble a goodbye. Grumman rolls a chair next to me as soon as the door closes.

"I should have told you earlier," he says. It isn't an apology, just an admission of forgetfulness.

"I didn't know you were firing me. Does he get the new desk?"

"Of course not. And you're not fired."

"We don't need another reporter unless we're going daily."

"We don't want to put the *Globe* out of business."

Ordinarily a funny reply—I'm not laughing.

"So what the hell, boss? Who's Eric Wilcox and why do we need his help? I mean why do I need it?"

"He's a teacher over at…."

"The high school. That part I get."

"Well," Grumman says, "it's like this. I'm hearing things about some plan to redevelop the old Fenton factory building out near 128. Apparently some specs have been turned in—rudimentary I guess—but it'll be a big deal if it goes through. Lots of little businesses looking to open up."

And if this project can be fucked up, I'm the one to do it.

I don't say that: I want Grumman to say it because I know goddamn well why Eric Wilcox was here—that guy never sabotaged a deal that would have brought all those jobs and all that money to the Drayton area. I accomplished that, did it all by myself in one drunken night in some guy's bed in a Portland hotel. I wish it weren't true, and I wish I didn't have to pay for it for the rest of my natural life, but I did it—pure and simple—I did it. I just want Grumman to say it.

Of course he knows that I know, and instead of the previous three-person stalemate, we're down to two. There's no way I win this, but I can still go into my newly acquired attack mode.

"So I can't be trusted."

"I didn't say that. Wilcox has a good reputation and he's a good guy."

"Maybe Eric and I can hook up—that would be a bonus, wouldn't it?"

"He's married."

"I've dated married men."

He bristles at the admission, but he forges ahead.

"This isn't about character—I'm concerned about leaking a story and having a lot of people's lives affected. We never know the extent of our mistakes, where they end up, who suffers. Eric's bright and experienced—he could have worked anywhere but he wanted to teach. I don't get it but he does."

"Then let him teach. Let me report."

"One time—you go with him. Take the camera and say you need a few photos. And listen to him, pay attention, let him write the article."

"Because he'll know what not to say."

"You know, Bree, you can be as offended as you want. The fact is you screwed up and I was partly responsible. Now you pay by playing intern for the day and I pay by feeling bad because I hurt your feelings."

"I'm not hurt; I'm pissed."

"Even better. Now I don't have to feel bad. Tomorrow, 4:00, Holiday Inn on Route 9, the Marlborough Room, you, Wilcox, and a dozen investors. Can you do that?"

"Are you asking me?"

"No."

"And if I do well as an observer, maybe I get to cover something other than a restaurant opening?"

"Bree, you fucked up. When people fuck up, they're expected to fuck up some more. We even have a name for these people which I don't have to repeat. I don't necessarily think you're in that category, but if you refuse to watch somebody do something right because you're too proud to learn, then how could you not fuck up again? That's rhetorical—I'm adding this to your calendar. I'll fix things with Wilcox."

He rolls the chair back where it came from.

"Let me know if you refuse. I can always send Teddy."

With his one journalism course—it's the perfect insult, but the thought of it is so outlandish that I have to smile, and I will once Grumman's door is closed. I remember Jill accusing me of running away from things. I guess I sort of stood up for myself this time, even though I had very little to stand up for. I wonder what someone like Jill would have done. Quit? Storm out? Collect unemployment? Take off her robe and stand naked? On the other hand, for someone who wants people to take responsibility for their lives, she seems to have fled without a forwarding address. Maybe I'll hear from her next Christmas—a kind of annual event.

I spend the rest of the afternoon and most of the evening contriving smarmy little comments to make to Eric, but it turns out that Grumman is right: Eric Wilcox is a good guy, perfectly comfortable among the reps from other papers, as well as all the movers and shakers from the area. I recognize some of them—some dean of something or other from Chalmers is there. Tyler—don't know his first name—but I'm sure any development plans in the area would have an impact on the college, even if it's only part-time jobs for students.

There's time for some questions afterwards. I'll confess, sometimes mine sound like an elementary journalism assignment—Eric could pass for a moderator on *Meet the Press*. He could take over my job in a second and never miss a beat. But what Grumman said about him is true—he loves teaching, and his wife is a teacher too, elementary. (He showed me her picture—she's cute the way an elementary teacher always seems to be.) They're going on vacation to Cancun next February, and thinking of buying a home in Waltham, and considering children maybe five years down the road. Whenever I think there aren't any good guys out there, I meet someone like this. Of course I meet them too late.

When I get back from learning about the plans for that factory building, I approach Grumman.

"Eric will write it up and send it in."

"Good, you edit," he says.

I will, but what you said yesterday about my character, how you're not concerned with it. My character is okay. I just wanted you to know."

"So you made a stupid comment and it bothered you, didn't it? Good. Believe me, if you had no character, you sure as hell wouldn't be working for me. And by the way, I fired Eric…who was actually grateful. He likes you—said you were a good student. Not so good a photographer."

"I was a pretend photographer."

"Even pretend photographers remove the lens cap…unless it's a pretend lens cap.

"He told you that?"

"He may have mentioned it in passing, said you missed a photo or two. So you aren't much of a photographer: stick to what you do.…"

"…Best?"

"I was going to go as far as *well*. Anyone there we know?"

"Someone from Chalmers—Tyler."

"Not quite a mover and shaker. Did he say anything?"

"Just sat and listened."

"Little get-togethers like that are probably beneath the dignity of Joe Lawrence."

"There was pastry from that new Italian bakery over on Vance."

"There's your next food review."

His grin is so full of self-satisfaction that he deserves to be flipped the bird: I think he's waiting for it. But the new Brianna Cooper, aggressive and feisty but still needing a job, gives him a thumbs up. I think he understands.

Chapter 22

For no particular reason other than maybe a shared mortality, Grumman's illness makes me think about Andrew Bennett. It's been months since I've visited or called, and because I have some knowledge of human nature, I can surmise that most others—with the exception of close family—have distanced themselves also. When I ask him if I might drop by, there's a coolness in his acceptance; and when I get there and he says "haven't seen you since the holidays," it's indictment more than chronology: the holidays will always be little more than a euphemism for Abby's murder.

I produce a litany of work-related and family-related excuses, but they're only excuses, hardly reasons. I ask about his son. He's away...again...this time with Abby's folks up on the North Shore.

"Some nights he's scared to be here," Andrew says, "afraid the murderer will come back. For all I know, he will. Nobody seems to be trying too hard to catch the guy."

"They did make that arrest."

"Of a petty thief. I'm sure they were disappointed my story checked out. Then of course there was the murder in the park. Luckily I had an alibi for that one too."

I don't want to be suckered into this lambasting of the cops, not now that Brandt and I are "buds," so I try to shift the emphasis.

"How often does Nicholas stay with your in-laws?"

He shoots an odd glance my way, as if to ask where that question came from, but I think he knows. This is not a house where a child lives. It's not dirty or dusty or messy with toys—just grim. We sit in the living room and the light from the two lamps is sufficient, but I can see other doorways and they're dark—again—not a place where a child scampers from room to room.

"He's away fairly often." Andrew says. "And at times with my parents. One of the counselors thinks he'll be better when the weather gets warmer and he can play outside. He'll feel more comfortable again being...here. I do see him every day," he says. "I changed my work hours so I could pick him up from school. Sometimes I take him out to eat; sometimes we all eat at my folks'."

"It doesn't seem...fair," I tell him. It's a pretty obvious observation.

"Or healthy, but too late for that. He needs time to adjust and that I can give him. Luckily he likes his grandparents and they like him. Maybe they spoil him a little, but that's what grandparents do, isn't it?"

"He's a nice boy. If you ever need a babysitter...."

"I won't," he says, a little too quickly, but I understand why—he wants me to know he's not going anywhere, that he doesn't leave the house unless he's required to. Translation: no one has taken Abby's place. When he asks how things are going at the paper, I provide my usual noncommittal shrug. There's no sense going into detail. The workaday issues and trivialities pale by comparison to what he and his son are enduring, and even Grumman's illness would mean little in that context: just another set of cancer statistics and just another name afflicted. Besides, lung cancer victims invariably get blamed, often becoming the basis for some diatribe on smoking. I don't want to have that discussion.

He rubs his hands together. "Can I get you something? A drink? Coffee?"

"Thanks, no. I just wanted to see how you were doing."

He stands up and walks over to the hall closet.

"I just remembered—there's something here for you," he says, rummaging. "Abigail had bought some presents before the holidays and I still have some."

"I couldn't."

"She'd want you to have it, and I don't need the reminder. Besides, it's not wrapped: you won't confuse it with something festive. Save it for your birthday."

He returns with a brightly colored box, a teapot emblazoned on the side. I'm not sure what facial expression the gift engenders, but whatever it is, it's obvious.

"Uh oh," he says, "you already have one."

"I have lots of them—I'm a tea drinker," I say, once again envisioning my headstone, more certain than ever how it will look: my name, a teapot, born, died, *tea-drinker*.

I feign excitement and tear open the box—please don't let it be the same as Jill's. But I know it isn't—it's plastic or some kind of carbonate with a tinted infuser. No faux Asian writing anywhere—this one's all-American, and made in China.

"Very cool."

"So you don't have one like that."

"I have lots of them, but not this one."

It's a convenient half-truth. This is the antithesis of Jill Dennison's ceramic piece of art. It's purely utilitarian—something to take to work, leave lying around unwashed—drop, topple, and otherwise abuse for the next millennium.

"Abby never got a chance to wrap things this year, but I gave away most of the gifts she bought. I thought it was an insult to her memory to throw them out, and I wasn't going to stare at them."

It's Jill Dennison's speech redux and not the speech anyone wants to hear when she's receiving a gift—twice: *here—I can't bear to look at it—you take it.* He laughs when I share my frivolous concern that history will mark my appearance on earth as nothing other than a tea drinker. It's the first genuine cheeriness of the evening, and after that the visit becomes a little more comfortable.

I know he's lonely—that's a given. But there's more. He wants to keep the house, but the mortgage is tough with only one paycheck, especially since he's cut back his hours to fit into Nicholas's life. He doesn't want his son to grow up in an apartment, leaving the somewhat distasteful option of moving in with his folks, or hers. Beyond all those critical decisions lie a million little tasks that constitute the life of a man whose family has been ripped apart. How does he even look at a paper or watch the television news when, day after day, the murder goes first unsolved, and then unmentioned?

"I'm going to just go along for a while," he says, "then re-examine things in the summer."

"Maybe you'll have a clearer picture by then."

It seems like the thing to say, though I don't know what could possibly happen between now and then to make things better, not even an arrest. What's he going to do, sue his wife's murderer—no doubt some monstrous degenerate—and live off the settlement?

"You need to come over again," he says. "I'll get Nicholas and we can order Chinese or something. He asks about you sometimes. It's odd how he's split his life into before and after. You're one of the people from before."

"I'll come back...let him see me in the now. Maybe it'll seem more normal to him."

"Normal," he says. "That doesn't come easy. There's mail for Abigail every day—catalogues, offers, magazines. Anyone significant knows she's gone, but still, seeing her name like that. Today she got some adjustment to her grade—another joke."

"Grade?"

"From Chalmers. She originally got an A, changed to an A-. Someone converted the numbers incorrectly. Don't they even watch the news up there?"

My father advised me once never to play poker—Grumman repeated the suggestion earlier today— advice designed for situations like these when I'm speechless and all the color has drained off somewhere. He leans closer.

"Are you okay?"

I say I am, but I'm not. I ask him who taught the course, but it isn't Melanie Johns; it's a professor with an Italian name. Vincenti, Vincenzi—he offers to look it up, but he doesn't have to. I can't say I feel relieved, but the panic over what might have been diminishes. And it made no sense anyway: I'd already seen the rosters from her class. Abby's name would not have slipped by unnoticed. Then again, Maskhadova's name wasn't listed at all. I ask him again, to be doubly sure.

"It wasn't an introductory course in computers, right?"

"That's the last thing she needed. Are you sure you're okay. Want some water or something?"

I assure him again that I'm fine but I need to get home. He offers to walk me to my car and I'm about to tell him it won't be necessary when I realize that it will be. This is the neighborhood and the time of day when his wife, safe and secure at her door, was murdered—a pleasant residential scene where nothing can possibly go wrong but everything did. In the time it takes us to traverse the distance from the front door to the street and exchange some parting words, not a single car drives by. It's the perfect place for some hoodlum to lie in wait. Involuntarily I scan the area, and I even sneak a glance at the backseat of my car before I enter it and drive off.

I want to call Brandt immediately and tell him the whole convoluted set of relationships—Abby, Melanie, the artist—but Brandt must know this—he's under no obligation to share details with me. Mostly I'm annoyed that I didn't know as much about Abby as I always claimed, yet called her a best friend. I shouldn't laugh at Teddy when he lays the same designation on me.

Once I get behind the wheel and out of that neighborhood, I relax a little. It's difficult, though, to excise the picture of Abby's house. How sad she would be to see its current condition—the mausoleum silence, the funereal gloom. I guess I am a pessimist at times (or is that one of those permanent conditions?) but either way I don't think of death that often, and I seldom consider the minutiae associated with it. When my grandmother died my folks were pretty busy tending to what she left behind, selling a house, divvying up belongings, a myriad of necessary tasks that needed completing. But who would ever think about anything as trivial as undelivered Christmas gifts—I mean someone buys things and dies, or the recipient dies. In the grand fabric of life it's of absolutely no consequence—the items can probably be returned. But now I've seen it firsthand—twice, and it makes me wonder how many other elements of survivors' daily lives I have no concept of. What else is Jill Dennison dealing with, or Andrew, or Marcus Johns, or yes, Karl Brandt? Some wag once said only the dead survive death. I think I'm beginning to understand what he meant.

.....

No more than a few blocks from the Bennetts', I turn onto Route 9, heavily traveled even at night, its landscape crammed with gas stations and auto dealers and electronics outfits and donut shops and every imaginable chain restaurant. Four lanes, no divider, an open invitation to try that risky left turn across oncoming traffic—one reason why the road provides a constant and varying panoply of police cruisers and ambulances hastening from one wreck to the next. The myriad of turning lanes and restrictions makes for aggressive driving, unsignaled turns, and emergency braking; worst of all, in recent years smartphone dependency has multiplied the danger exponentially. It's nirvana for tow-truck operators. I generally avoid the stretch, but as a short cut home, it's hard to pass up, especially on a night when I don't want to be traveling alone. There's no alone on Route 9.

There's also no dearth of tailgaters, and tonight I've acquired one. I'm going my usual 50-plus in the 45 mph zone, but that doesn't matter to someone who wants to go 60 and finds both lanes occupied in front of him. I endure it for maybe half a mile, uttering the occasional obscenity, then turn down a less congested street. I wait for the car to scream by me on the right—the aggressive drivers' way of saying fuck you—but he doesn't: the headlights remain fixed in my mirror.

Three months earlier I'd have called it an annoyance and ignored it, especially a mere two miles from my well lit apartment parking area and its blanket of security cameras. But this time I add myself to the list of distracteds and reach for my cell phone. For once I'm not terribly concerned that Brandt might be naked.

"It's Bree, I'm in my car—I think I'm being followed."

"Are you sure?"

"No. Not at all. But someone turned off Route-9 after I did. He's right on my tail and I'm not going slow."

"Where are you now?"

"Davis Drive."

"Heading which way?"

"Toward my apartment."

"And which way might that be?"

"I'm heading...uh...south I guess."

I don't know why I thought he should know where I live, but I did, and the impatience shows in my voice.

"South on Davis. I know your car—I'm calling this in on another line. You stay on Davis—if you can't, tell me if you have to make a turn. How long have you been on that street?"

"A minute or two. I'm a few miles from home."

"I need your license plate number."

"I'm not sure of the beginning. It ends with 123—is that any help?"

"If you can learn your social security number, you can learn your license plate."

"I don't know my social security number."

"Jesus Christ!"

His little epithet is followed by a few seconds of silence.

"Karl?"

"Hang on."

So I do, feeling essentially naked in my well-illuminated interior.

"Sorry about that," he says. "The person behind you, can he see you talking?"

"It's like daylight in here."

"Just drive normally. Speed limit."

"What if he shoots me?"

"He's not going to shoot you. Keep driving."

"Should I pull over?"

"That would make it a lot easier to shoot you."

"This isn't funny, Karl…."

"When you get to Birch, take a right."

"Where does it go?"

"It doesn't," he says. "Dead end. A patrol car is coming from the opposite direction. Cop named Trumbull."

"Already?"

"Already. There's a circle at the end of Birch. Just slowly drive around it and head back out. Trumbull will block the street after you're gone. Got that?"

"Then what?"

"Then the night is yours—knock yourself out."

Stupid question. I check around but see only the lights illuminating my interior…and there's Birch Drive.

"Are you sure about that patrol car? I don't see anything."

"Sometimes the siren and lights ruin the surprise," he says. "Just stay on the line until you're clear, then go right home…or wherever you're going."

"What if the guy has a gun?"

"He doesn't."

"How do you know that?"

"Trumbull is imaging that car. If there were a gun in it, he'd know."

"He can do that?"

"Of course. Now make that turn when you come to it."

"Can you come and see me afterwards?"

"Trumbull is very competent. He'll be able…."

"I meant to my place. I can tell you where it is."

The words are spilling out faster than I can edit them. Inviting Brandt over for protection has the same inherent wisdom as inviting a leopard over to babysit an antelope. But I think it's his impatient but organized calmness juxtaposed with my complete trepidation that does it—his voice registers unequivocally that this will all be taken care of in short order, and mine says I'm screwed. Karl Brandt may be too brash and arrogant to allow himself to show any fear—such emotions would be an insult to his manhood—but tonight that bravado works, and maybe I want to be around that for a while.

"You're scared," he says.

"What?"

"Your invitation. Let's get past this first. Are you at Birch?"

"But what I said..."

"I heard you. Are you at Birch?"

I am. I take the corner. The car with the high beams goes straight and speeds off. And just like that, before I can exhale, it's over, and I'm parked on some cul-de-sac trying to keep my heart from jumping out of my ribcage and choking me.

"He's gone."

"Somebody in a hurry." Brandt says. "You were in his way. It happens."

"Now I feel stupid." The phone is still crushed against my ear.

"Your voice is shaking. Take a few deep breaths. Do you have water?"

"I think so."

I feel around the floor in back and find one that isn't empty. He tells me to drink something, that my voice sounds like that of a chain smoker. He waits.

"I'm okay," I tell him. My voice sounds normal again.

"Could have been just kids screwing around," he says. "They wanted to scare you or annoy you. When you turned down your street, they figured you were home and they lost interest or panicked."

"That wasn't my street."

He laughs. "They didn't know that. Now listen, you're going to calm down really fast when you get inside your apartment and lock your door. By the time I arrived you'd be wondering what the hell I'm doing there. Trust me on this."

I figure he's with someone—after all, we may have had a pleasant lunch but he's still Karl Brandt. Regardless, I can always drive to the police station tomorrow and file a report—a very meaningless one about someone who might have been following me but never did anything threatening. One thing is certain—I'm not going home, not yet.

"I'm going to drive for a while, Karl. Thanks for getting that cop here."

"He's parked at the end of the street. Pull over and give him a statement. And don't tell him you know about that imaging for the gun. It's supposed to be confidential—a pilot program."

That somehow makes sense to me—probably another indication of my mental state. As soon as I get near the patrol car, the strobes I had wondered about spring to life, bathing the neighborhood in blue and red and white and filling the darkness behind them. A uniformed officer comes over.

"Are you still on the line with Detective Brandt?"

"Yes, sir."

"You can loosen that grip on the steering wheel a bit. You don't want to cramp up."

I take his advice and try to relax, maybe just breathe while Trumbull assesses my state and tells Brandt I should probably not drive.

"I'm okay," I tell him. "I'm better now."

It's a weak, ineffectual protest, one that Brandt picks up on.

"Coop, leave the car and have Officer Trumbull take you home," he says. "I'll meet you there."

"I don't want to leave my car."

"Oh yeah," Brandt says laughing. "That Maserati you drive."

He convinces Trumbull to follow me home.

"Colony Apartments," I tell them both. "Not very far."

Trumbull says he doesn't need a statement, that there's been no crime or threat of a crime, but he assures me he'll sit in his car until I'm ready to drive. Brandt is still on the line.

"Listen," he says, after a brief silence, "put the phone away, take a breath, and drive slow. You get a ticket from Trumbull, I'm not going to fix it for you when I get there."

So he's coming after all. The knowledge that I won't be alone lowers my pulse noticeably and I realize that I'm breathing like a normal human being. I know why: I want to be shielded from all the bad shit that's out there—from the assaults and the murders and the cancers and widowers and the mothers who have no qualms about fucking up their daughter's lives. Add to that asshole drivers who scare people and speed off into the night. Brandt can be that shield, even temporarily, and if my willingness sends the wrong message, well then, maybe it isn't the wrong message after all.

"I'm in building three. Apartment 227."

I toss the phone into my bag, and this time—though my hands are shaking—it finds the mark.

Chapter 23

It's like handing off a prisoner—Trumbull waits until Brandt arrives to take custody of me, then drives off. Only one of them looks like a cop and it isn't Brandt in his preppy throwback outfit—khakis and a wrinkled pale blue oxford shirt. And he's wearing a tie that seems predominantly orange but whose pattern approximates a paisley that someone started but then lost interest in. And black sneakers. If I had invited a Harvard undergrad to my birthday party when I was six, he'd probably have looked like this.

"I didn't expect you to get all dressed up."

"Business casual," he says, scanning the parking lot. "Never actually seen this place. Drove by a few times. Looks nice enough."

"Not a high crime area—so far. Thank you for doing this."

"You sounded a little frazzled before. Better now?"

"A little. Come on up."

I unlock the apartment but he stops me in the doorway and enters first. He wants to see the place, to make sure there are no surprise visitors lurking in the shower or closet. The idea that there might be does very little for my peace of mind, but he knows why he's there. When he finally motions me in, I do feel a lot more confident.

He's still scanning, but this time for other reasons.

"Gotta start looking around when I move out. What's the rent in a place like this?"

"More than I can afford. Can I get you something?"

He says no, but when I ask him to sit down he picks out the chair I use when I'm alone, leaving me the couch all to myself. Perfect…if I have ebola, which I don't. I hand him one of my Colony Apartments brochures that provides some rental prices, even though I'm not sure if I want to share an address with him, the advantage of a cop-on-premises notwithstanding. When he recoils a bit at the rent estimates, I figure he'll be looking for something that maybe doesn't look "nice enough."

We talk about what happened and I admit I may have overreacted, especially since my pursuer had no gun.

"You never know," he says.

"But the scanner—you said that, you know, there was no gun."

His face contorts weirdly. That's probably what happens when someone is trying really hard not to laugh..

"So that was a joke, right? There's no such thing?"

"Technology is moving at an incredibly rapid pace." he says. "There may very well be, right now, a scientist...."

"That wasn't fair."

"Probably not, but what were you going to do differently if the guy had been armed? Drive lying down? You did the right thing—why risk aggravating someone with road rage? Just drive normally and wait for him to lose interest."

"Or shoot me."

"Unless you did something specific to piss him off...."

"I didn't."

"And he didn't shoot you. He lost interest. Or they. Bunch of kids with a few beers in them."

"You think that's all it was?"

He shrugs—he has no idea. How could he? But he tells me not to worry about it and the next minute I decide maybe he's right and that a glass of wine would hasten my recovery. He declines the offer to join me—maybe big bad cops don't enjoy a glass of chilled white chardonnay—and I find myself in the kitchen rummaging through a cabinet filled with liquor bottles. I seldom know what's in there, though the bottles themselves provide a history of my dating over the past few years—a Scotch drinker, a gin and tonic fan, and some guy named Dirk who liked peach brandy. Actually what he "liked" was licking it off specific body parts—mine—a plan I agreed to until a few drops ran into my armpit and felt like, well like I had used molasses as a deodorant. I wound up in the shower— alone. I subsequently explained to Dirk that many people use a glass from which to drink their peach brandy, after which he stopped calling

"What's going on out there?" Brandt asks. The clanging of bottles is hard to ignore.

"I have vodka."

"Not for me," he says. "Just water, no ice will be fine."

When I come back in I put his glass on the end table.

"Sit over here so I don't have to yell across to you," I tell him, then modify the invitation by strategically placing a few throw pillows next to me. It's a perfectly adequate physical barricade and I don't feel like some pariah relegated to the other side of the room.

"Did you get a look at the car at all?" he says. "The one that was tailing you?"

"Just headlights in the mirror."

"Trumbull couldn't get a plate—would have if the guy had turned when you turned. What kind of headlights? Were they bluish?"

"Bluish?"

"High intensity...xenon, something unusual?"

"They were normal brights. No drinking on a school night, huh detective? I didn't think you were that...I don't know...steadfast."

"I have work tomorrow. Besides, if anyone needs a drink, it's you."

"Trying to get me drunk?"

"Trying to get you normal."

I lift the wine glass, meaning to sip it. Two minutes and a few gulps later the wine is gone. He doesn't seem to notice, though: his eyes wander about the place. He points to the slider, obscured by a heavy beige curtain.

"Nice view?"

"Woods."

"How much open space between the deck and the trees?"

"You really are here on business, aren't you?"

"If you're worried about security...."

"I don't think there's an animal alive that could make that jump."

"What about a human with a rope. Could he swing that far? Or a guy with a ladder? Do you have a flashlight?"

I do. He rolls back the curtains and peers outside, then nods.

"The security lights help and it is a good distance, but I'd keep this locked all the time."

"I do."

"There's an abandoned Christmas tree in the woods. Yours?"

"Guessing or detective-ing?"

"Shortest distance between two points—it's either you or the folks downstairs. Tell me about tonight."

Now I'm on my second glass of wine and I feel vaguely disappointed that he's treating me like any other complainant instead of a young not completely unattractive woman whom he's taken to lunch and confided in and managed to find himself alone with in an unchaperoned apartment. And with his reputation for not being choosy—well, maybe he doesn't want to take advantage. Maybe he knows that my recent escape from...whatever...is working like an aphrodisiac, and if he gave the slightest inkling, I'd be bathing in brandy without complaint.

He hasn't even loosened his tie.

"While things are fresh in your mind," he says, then repeats the request.

"I was at the Bennetts', Abigail's house. I hadn't been there for a while. I don't think Andrew is doing so well. His son is living with his grandparents."

"I know. Too soon for either of them to be okay, but give them time."

"You knew that? You still consider him a suspect?"

"Not at all, but I've been there a few times to check in—the kid is never home."

"Check in? Officially?"

"More or less. Sometimes victims remember things after a while, things they consider trivial. Something she might have said days before that didn't seem to mean anything but really did. I don't exactly grill him: we talk, I leave. Five minutes. I'll tell you though, until that guy remarries...."

"Isn't that premature?"

"Right now? Yes. But the sooner he gets to the point where maybe dinner with a woman seems feasible, the sooner his life will seem more bearable."

"So he needs a marriage to make his life bearable. That's an odd take on the world from someone like you."

"Someone like me? I'm not anti-marriage just because mine didn't work out. His did. Maybe if I remarry I'll find out it's me queering the deal, but Andrew Bennett—he got it right. He was a success at being a husband. He can always be a success again."

There's a certain fatalism in that argument that really does define him, and undoubtedly he has used it to justify all sorts of bad behavior. Tonight, though, I think he's clarifying some sort of wistful personal philosophy—one that was gained at a price. And then, just like that, he's back on the job.

"So you left there, then what? You said you were driving on Route 9. That's practically a convention for bad drivers. Did it happen as soon as you got on?"

"That's when I first noticed it."

"But the car could have been behind you from the time you left Bennetts'?"

That possibility, that someone was waiting for me, heightens the anxiety again. Maybe if I had refused Andrew's offer to walk me to my car, I'd be lying there dead now. I immediately gulp down half of my second glass. When I ask him again if he wants something other than tepid water, his answer is the same.

"Okay," I tell him, "I'll just drink alone."

"I used to do that all the time. Don't get me wrong, it's not a complaint. I met some clever bartenders, customers, we had interesting conversations."

"So it's good then—opens up the realm of possibilities?"

"In a roundabout way, yes."

"But you don't want to reopen that realm tonight?"

If my father ever heard me say that, he'd be disappointed. Not because I sound like a slut—though that would not exactly please him—but because after all the good movies we've watched together, I uttered a line straight from a B-movie, C—if there is such a thing. Of course I can blame the alcohol, but when I make eye contact again, his expression has not changed at all: apparently he doesn't know that my *realm of possibility* implies a lot of clothes tossed about at random and two sweaty bodies rubbing together in the next room. Or maybe he does—maybe he hears so much stupidity during his day-to-day dealings with miscreants and creeps and fuck-ups that he's inured to it. Whatever the reason, his answer is straightforward...again.

"It's not that I couldn't have a drink—it doesn't work that way. I just know that booze keeps me from sleeping. Occasionally I need to sleep."

"But in the bar that time we saw you..."

"At Mattera's, you and Clousseau. Club soda, though maybe I had one. Anyway, I wasn't going to be sleeping that night."

"Because of the...murder. Well, I think maybe I'm feeling better."

"That's the alcohol deadening you."

I laugh, but I'm about to finish the bottle—maybe half a glass left—and I think maybe I can redeem myself.

"When Melanie died...I'll bet...."

I'm not sure how I want to phrase this, but he seems to be waiting patiently enough so I take some time to choose the words.

"What I mean is, a death usually brings sympathy, condolences. You didn't get those, did you?"

"Didn't expect to…didn't have the right."

"I'm sorry that happened to you—losing someone and not being able to grieve is awful."

"I grieved before she died," he says. "I grieved when I couldn't see her anymore. It got worse when I had to treat her like just another crime victim, but there are rules and I broke them."

"You both did."

"But she paid. My life goes on. That's not self-pity, believe me. I may not always do the right thing, but I own up."

"Do a lot of owning up?"

He reaches across the great pillow barrier and taps my hand.

"I do my share of it. Thanks."

"For what?"

"For not judging too much. And for that great come-on line about opening your realm. Watch a lot of adult films when you're not reporting?"

So yes I want him. I'm not sure why. That sounds incredibly disingenuous—it's only sex and alcohol for God's sake. But I've been drunk with other men and not felt this tingling. How many times have Teddy and I sat around slurping beer and never once did I want to feel his hands touching my face. Even that late night when I wondered what that would be like and baited him with conversation about hidden tattoos, there was no real desire. Just ego. Vanity. Curiosity. With Brandt it's different. It may not be right, or good, or love—whatever that is—but it's different.

And I'm not trying to compete with Melanie—I want him because I do, because there's more to him than his public image, and unfortunately maybe less to me. That's not easy to admit, not when I'm examining my life this way, but sometimes all this examining and philosophizing and moralizing—sometimes I think it covers up our own emptiness. Happy, well-adjusted people just live. I don't mean they mindlessly welcome each new dawn with a lilting tune and a smile, but they live and accept and move on. Of course, speaking as an unhappy maladjusted person, I may not be an expert. But I think I might be right this time.

So I'm sitting here philosophizing as my skin, which knows nothing of examined lives but does enjoy the sensation of other skin touching it, begins to warm and moisten. It's nowhere near an unpleasant feeling, but my brain jumps ahead a few squares to Dirk and the peach brandy rolling down my breast into my armpit and I wonder if my deodorant is still working. The situation and the hour and the wine have conspired to make me a mass of disconnected absurdities while Karl Brandt sits calmly, adjusting the knot in his tie. After that little touch of his hand he pulled away quickly and we both sat back in the couch, like two teenagers whose parents just walked in on them before that first item of clothing hit the floor.

It's getting late. I'd like to regain some control of myself before he leaves.

"Your wife—she's probably used to your leaving all hours of the day and night. I'm just curious—does she know where you are?"

"Does it matter?"

"I think so."

"Even though I got all dressed up and made it look like business?"

I smile, but I do want an answer. "Yeah, even though."

"Linda knows where I am."

"But you wouldn't do this for just anybody."

"No, I'd send a few uniforms over to secure the perimeter. You probably wouldn't even notice them. I would have done that tonight...."

"But I asked for you personally. Your wife, I mean she's a cop's wife. She knows this isn't normal."

"Linda's great—she really is—but those intimate aspects of marriage—the perks," he says with a grin, "those don't come my way anymore."

"With your wife."

He shakes his head. "My reputation is somewhat overblown. I'm certainly not celibate, but I know celibates who get more action."

"Celibates don't have any...."

"I was using poetic license—like a journalist. Anyway, it was no big deal leaving the house tonight, but I am expected to come back, if only for appearances. Otherwise, if I didn't turn up for a week, it would be no big deal. Not that I..." he seems suddenly flustered, "I don't mean I want to stay here for a week."

"Do you?"

"If you can't afford the rent, how could I?"

"You didn't answer my question."

"Of course a detective's salary is probably higher than a beat reporter."

"I don't have a beat, and you still didn't answer my question."

"About staying the week? That'd be a commitment. As you well know, I'm not good at that."

Not many straight answers, but I like the fact that he is at least trying to be funny, to make me laugh. Of course I'm not asking many straight questions, influenced still by the accumulation of events. Panic is a weird emotion. Once, in the fifth grade, a teacher yelled at me for talking in class and wrote a note for me to take home, sealing it in an envelope. My parents weren't there when I arrived and I spent the next hour staring at the window, one hand squeezing the evidence; the other pressed between my legs. It wasn't the most romantic of first orgasms—I didn't even remove my clothes and I didn't have any idea what was happening—but I remember that, after I'd reclaimed my normal breathing pattern, the envelope didn't seem quite so terrifying. Tonight is probably not the time to share that anecdote with Brandt, though if he leaves me in this state, I'll be reenacting that afternoon for sure—without the note or the clothing.

He's playing on my well-documented aversion to him, poking fun at me and himself. It's a side of Karl Brandt I haven't seen—not a sneer or dismissive comment since he arrived. It could be, of course, that it truly is just business and he's simply trying to calm a shaky crime victim. Or maybe it's an act—a little comedy where he plays the role of the apathetic lead who in actuality wants only to get the heroine's clothes off, and I play the part of—well that's just it—I don't know my part, but I'd like to...perhaps the heroine who wants to take her clothes off?

I lean toward him with one hand on a throw-pillow.

"You did a nice thing for Teddy the other day, and you saved my life tonight."

"I don't think I saved...."

"You seem to do a lot of good things for people you don't necessarily get along with."

"You mean people who don't like me."

"No, I mean..."

"Listen, Coop," he says, then stops and looks away again. I don't know if I've ever seen anyone that uncomfortable. I'm pretty sure he isn't going to finish the sentence, but I listen anyway. And listen. And wait. The silence exacerbates his discomfort and without warning he's standing near the couch, straightening his tie. He's leaving, and goddamn it I do want him to stay...with me...not for the week but at least for the night. Yes it's a fucking tailgater and half a bottle of wine talking, but I don't care. I want him to kiss me, or at least want to kiss me and beg off on some moral grounds. I don't want to spend the rest of my drunken stupor in some fantasy that leaves me refreshed but alone.

So I don't stand.

"I'll just sit here. I'm a little woozy."

"No you're not," he says, and he sits again, maybe an inch or two closer. "I'll tell you something. A couple years ago Linda was in an accident. Some guy in a van sideswiped her car, then crossed the median and hit a dump truck head-on. Guy in the van died. Linda was fine but shaken up—more so when she found out the other driver died."

"She was lucky."

He nods. "That night we had sex. We had pretty much stopped by then, but that night was different. Linda was one of those, I don't know, modest? women who would never let me see her naked. Except that night—that night was like she was releasing all the sexual energy she never knew she had."

"Because of the accident."

"Right."

Well, that renders my little tale of the envelope and the orgasm pretty mundane, especially with a death added in for a kicker. I guess my singular experience, the one I've guiltily dragged around all these years, isn't so singular after all, and every woman has had that envelope moment.

"Do you think that's me? I'm scared so I'm coming on to you?"

"So much for subtlety."

"I'm over twenty-one, Karl. If I want to take my clothes off for a man, I have that right."

"I don't think I can arrest you in your own home, but if you pull that nonsense on the street...."

He smiles and taps his chest where his shoulder holster might be under ordinary conditions.

"You'd shoot me?"

He doesn't answer because I've broken through my improvised pillow barrier and begun kissing him. It's more attack than seduction, but he's a willing victim and puts a hand on the back of my neck to hold me there. When I pull away, I don't go far. I figure I'll just bury my head in his shoulder and hide, but he won't allow that. It's eye contact, very close.

"You have to understand something," he says. "I'd like you to take those clothes off, but not because you had a scary experience. Otherwise tomorrow morning when you're not scared anymore, you're going to loop a rope over the nearest beam and hang yourself."

"I have no beams."

"There's that big tree out back."

"Lots of women kill themselves after you've had sex with them?"

"I have my suspicions."

"I'm too drunk to tie a knot."

"Are you sure?"

"Yes. Do you always use a questionnaire beforehand?"

"And there's an evaluation afterwards. Be kind when you fill it out."

He leans back on the couch and smiles and I'm practically on top of him—laid out almost sideways in an awkward entanglement of limbs and pillows.

"It's the tie," he says. "It ruins the mood." He throws it on the armchair, but before he can get comfortable again, I stand and lead him away from the couch.

He hesitates. Or I do. We slink toward the bedroom like burglars.

He still hasn't kissed me again, and the thought occurs to me that maybe he doesn't want to. If he just wants to fuck—even horny as I am—it's not going to be okay tonight. The wine would get me through, even allow me to justify it the next morning, but it's still not going to be enough. I'm not that far from thirty, and I'd like to start looking ahead a bit, find something more permanent. I lay my head on his shoulder as we walk, and he kisses the top of my head. Better. I pull back the comforter from the bed and let it fall to the floor. Usually I can't stand the thought of entering those cold sheets without it, but then most nights I'm alone.

Brandt unlaces his sneakers, then takes my hand and places it on his heart. It's pounding harder than mine.

"I should have asked the doctor if this thing is healthy enough for sex."

"Only one way to find out."

"Kind of a tough way," he says.

"If worse comes to worse I'll use your cop phone to call 9-1-1."

"Cop phone?"

He takes out his cell and lays it on the table, then reaches behind me under my sweater to unhook my bra. I feel it give, then slide slowly off each breast. It's not one of my nicer bras—then again I wasn't choosing my frilliest and most sensual undergarments when I left for work that morning. The feeling as it slides past my nipples is more irritating than erotic, and I know there's a momentary grimace—one that vanishes just as quickly when his fingers touch them. I cooperate by lifting the sweater over my head, allowing it and the bra to fall away somewhere.

I want to tell him I hadn't planned this, that circumstances had conspired in a jumbled sequence of abstract coincidences—whatever the hell that means. But then we're lying down and everything is speeding up and my brain is trying to remember when I poured the second glass of wine and if I had the third and if I'm drunk at all. And that envelope from my teacher? My parents hardly even yelled at me. I was scared for nothing. And tonight? What if I'm scared for nothing again?

Before I can compose an answer I won't like, I pull off the rest of my clothes and lie back.

"I guess I undressed in front of you."

"Still kind of dark in here," he says. "I'll feel my way around if that's okay." Both his hands are on my face now. Finally he kisses me again and it's good. It's really good.

No, I didn't plan this, not in any real sense. That saying about life being what happens to us while we're busy making other plans—I always thought that was dumb. Maybe not.

Chapter 24

In the dark—seconds, minutes, hours later? I have no idea—I hear him rustling through his clothes.

"I'm awake," I tell him. "You can turn on the light."

"I'm fine," he says. "I just need to get going."

I flip on the lamp next to the bed. So far he's found only his shirt, hopelessly wrinkled.

"Next time I'll hang up my clothes," he says, then comes over and sits on the edge of the bed next to me. "Can't stay—one of those things."

"But if Linda doesn't care...."

"Nobody cares. But until everything officially ends...legally ends...we've agreed not to rub each other's noses in it. If I pull in at 3:30 and some neighbor is up taking a leak, I'm on a case or I've been closing some bar. But if I pull in at 7:00...."

"You've spent the night with somebody."

"Something like that. Look, Coop, this is a hard conversation to have without pants."

"You can get back into bed. You don't need pants in here."

"That won't solve the problem."

"It would solve one."

He leans down and strokes the side of my face, then kisses me. It's not foreplay—it's afterplay if there's such a word: preparing me for his departure.

"I'm off tonight," he says. "Let's have dinner or something."

I tug at his shirt tails. "Can I iron this for you? You can't go out in public this way."

"No one is going to see me this time of night. What about dinner?"

"I can cook for you."

"We won't be eating any dinner if I come here. I know myself well enough to know that. I'll call you at work."

He's almost out the door when I remember how the evening started, the conversation with Andrew Bennett, the mail from Chalmers.

"Andrew Bennett said Abby was taking courses at Chalmers."

"Really?"

Brandt may have several talents, a few of which I have recently experienced, but feigning surprise isn't one of them.

"So you knew that, right?"

He's fiddling with that tie and looking pretty much everywhere but at me.

"I'm not sure if that ever came up. So many people take a class there—probably a coincidence. I'm sure someone checked it out."

"So you did know."

"In a case like this with so much evidence that turns out to be nothing...I'll have to check but probably yes, why?"

I'm standing at the door in only a t-shirt—hardly the proper outfit for a serious discussion. I don't feel self-conscious, of course, because Brandt is studiously avoiding eye contact, and not just with my eyes. When I remind him that even if he doesn't look at me, he can still hear me, he guides me back inside.

"We don't make everything public, but we don't sit on information that would endanger someone. By the way, you should have a talk with Teddy."

"What does Teddy have to do with this?"

"He's working the case."

"What do you mean, online with his geeky detective group?"

"For pay."

I laugh, of course, because the idea is preposterous. And illegal, I think.

"Don't you have to be certified?"

"Licensed. The first thing you do when you hire a PI is call the licensing bureau and make sure his paperwork is up to date. That's after you physically look at his license. Then you check the directory for that state, maybe get references. There's lots of stuff you should do...unless of course you know the guy and he's working on the sly."

"You think I hired Teddy to look into Abigail's murder! I would never put him in that kind of situation."

"Not you."

"But if someone else did it, Teddy would have told me. He tells me everything. I'm his...he says I'm his best friend."

"He couldn't tell you—unauthorized disclosure—it's unethical."

"He's a sports reporter!"

I'm softly shrieking, if that's possible, the only permissible method of yelling at 3:00 a.m., especially with the door ajar. I slam it shut before he answers—and probably awaken as many neighbors as my shrieking would have. Funny how a person's moods can shift when his clothes are back on.

"If someone hired Teddy," he says, "and let's leave it hypothetical. If someone did, it would have to be a person who didn't care about legality that much...someone who trusted Teddy to do the job because he or she knew him."

"Like me."

"You said it isn't you. You don't have that big a stake in it."

"So who?"

"It would have to be someone who's angry, who's probably given up on the police ever solving the crime."

Given up...as soon as he says that, I know who it is. Desperate irrationality is pretty much Jill Dennison's approach to everything. She can handle the harassment and stalking pretty well on her own, but someone to help her fill in the remaining tasks would be invaluable.

"Melanie's sister."

"You didn't hear that from me. The problem is—and there are many problems—a real PI is bonded and insured. If Teddy gets hurt in this little charade...if your health insurance carrier at the paper were ever to learn that he's out investigating crimes, your boss would be looking for a new plan, and a new sportswriter, and maybe a new career."

"What about Dennison?"

"If she indeed hired an unlicensed professional..."

"If?"

"Yes, if she did, she can be held accountable for any damage he does while in her employ. Not to mention that if a licensed PI surveils you, it's surveillance. If Teddy does it, it's voyeurism, or stalking."

"Can you stop him?"

"I laid off because he's your friend," he says. "I guess I can arrest him for false representation, but you wouldn't want that."

"If it kept him safe...."

"I thought arresting Curwell would keep him safe—call off his little adventure."

"So that's why he knew before everyone else. But you never thought Curwell was the one."

"I don't think he bought it either. You know, he's not bad at this. That day we spoke he had this Chalmers College connection all figured out. You didn't know your friend was taking a course?"

"I don't know if we were as close as I used to think. She sure didn't tell me everything she did. That doesn't mean there was anything seedy going on in her life."

"I know. She's clean. Are you taking any courses up there?"

"No, but I'm there often enough. Tonight, that car following me...."

"If I wanted to do someone harm, I'd want to be subtle, not crawl up your ass on Route 9. And you're safe here. You don't have a lot of people buzzing people up without checking, do you?"

"We have video ID. And you have to go," I remind him, though I'm hoping he'll change his mind: Linda doesn't need a protector as much as I do.

At the door he loops his hands around my neck and pulls me closer to him.

"If you want to broach this with Teddy, go ahead," he says. "You probably don't want to embarrass him. He's your friend; it's your call. And maybe a word or two in Dennison's ear would be effective."

"She's not around."

"I don't mean right now."

"I mean she's not around. Her business partner came by the other day asking me if I'd seen her."

"I guess she's not as cured as…as her sister thought. If you hear from her…."

He kisses me again, and it's tender and meaningful and all those other things a good kiss should be, but it's also goodbye.

With Brandt gone, I do manage to get some sleep, but none of any long duration. After a few more frustrating intervals of semi-wakefulness, I drag myself into the shower where the hot spray revitalizes me and I go directly from lethargic to jumpy: I don't know if it's due to the little problem on the road or to making love to someone who, until recently, has been little more than a necessary evil. Then there's that little thing about Karl Brandt's still being married.

That whole idea of sex and morality has always been problematic. When I was thirteen I let an older boy—he was a grade ahead—unhook my bra and touch my breasts, one at a time. I remember thinking in my catechism-fevered brain that if he touched both of them at once it would be a more mortal sin and I somehow prevented that with a series of intricate movements. The experience was completely devoid of eroticism, at least for me—not only had the boy treated each nipple like a dial in need of precision tuning, but the whole experience took place in a swampy area behind a crummy strip mall on a chilly afternoon the day before Thanksgiving. At home that night I worried more about my shoes being ruined than any loss of innocence or privacy, but all the next day—even after my shoes had dried and seemed all right—I felt jumpy. Some significant moral principle had been breached, and repairing it was no longer possible. My breasts could never again be unseen, untouched.

Brandt, too, was an "older boy," but he had been gentler, less awkward, more solicitous; and I'm pretty sure that, at one point, he touched both breasts simultaneously—thereby endangering his immortal soul and mine. But though the eroticism had been overpowering, the jumpiness that followed was the same. And I can't keep an old conversation with my mother from crowding its way into my mind—something about the sinfulness of going to bed with someone and waking up without him. I think the conversation involved the word whore, but that's a given with my mother. She would be gratified to know that Brandt and I did wake up together…before he went home.

His request that I not go into work early—he wants others around me—allows me time to look as if I did not spend the night in a drunken debauch. When I saunter in at 8:00, I find Teddy and Arlene chuckling about something—I can't imagine what, in light of how we left things yesterday, at least as far as Grumman was concerned—but the boss is there too, hovering near them. It's like a bizarre reunion, maybe even a resurrection. Teddy's greeting is pretty much expected.

"Did you sleep last night? You just look whipped."

Arlene laughs. "Good call, Teddy. I see the passage of time hasn't done you any real harm."

He looks surprised. "Oh, no, I was just..."

"Don't ever get murdered," Arlene says. "There'd be too many suspects…most of them right here."

"It's all right, Arlene," I tell her. "Truth is I didn't sleep much last night."

"Change of season," Grumman says. He's been quiet, taking things in, coughing occasionally, quietly. "Happens a lot. Your detective friend called this morning."

"Teddy's my detective friend."

Arlene arches an eyebrow and smiles. My response was too quick. Too glib. Arlene doesn't fall for bullshit like that. I doubt if Grumman does either.

"I meant Brandt. He wanted to know if you were at your desk. Kind of early, isn't it?"

"He was probably up early."

"Or out late."

"You know him, boss—probably still drunk."

I look at Teddy, just to see if there's a reaction. If it's true he's been in contact with the guy, maybe he'll show it. Nothing. Then I figure, what the hell, might as well tell them what happened, or part of it.

"There was a little incident last night. I had to call for backup."

Teddy has been quietly recovering from Arlene's insults, but he perks up at the sound of something police-related.

"Backup? Like the cops?"

"One cop, probably," Arlene says, then begins tapping at her keyboard as if it doesn't matter. But she's still listening. Everyone is.

"I was followed. About halfway between the Bennett house and my place. I stopped to visit her husband and when I left, this car kept tailing me. I called Brandt."

"Wow," Teddy says. "Brandt scared him away? Did he shoot the guy?"

"Actually another cop in the area showed up, but whoever was following me just took off."

"Did the other cop shoot him?"

Grumman knows how to say "shut up" using several different approaches: this time it's "Teddy, ask that again, and I'll shoot you."

"So," Arlene says, "once again, or should I say for once, the Drayton PD actually earned their paycheck. That's reassuring."

"You should file a report," Teddy says. "If it happens again and they catch the guy, they can add stalking, harassment....did you get a look at him?"

"I'm not even sure it was a guy. I couldn't tell. It was probably just kids," I say. "More stupid than malicious. Besides, one man's stalking is another man's surveillance."

I just throw that out there, hoping it will stick to the erstwhile private investigator. Before it can, Grumman breaks in.

"From now on you should take Teddy with you on assignments. Two people together can be a deterrent," he says.

"Boss," I tell him—we've had a similar conversation before, "you have two reporters and a couple high school stringers who check in about once a millennium. You're going to send us out together and basically cut your staff in two? I talked to Brandt about it. He said..."

"I thought another cop handled it."

"He did, but I called Brandt first—he just wasn't available. I talked to him after. He's the one who thought it might have been kids screwing around. I turned down a side street and the car kept going—probably lost interest."

I can tell he's unhappy with the explanation, but I'm fine with it; of course I'd feel better if he attached some credence to it also, you know, so it doesn't look as though I'm fooling myself.

At noon Arlene takes off. It's Saturday after all, and there's little for her to do. Grumman is holed up in his office, but Teddy lags behind, says he wants to talk to me about something. This is aberrant behavior at its best—Teddy wants to talk only about sports or pizza. Unless...it's the big confession—bless me, Brianna, for I have kept something from you. But with all those wonderful options available to him, he sets off in a new direction.

"Something is going on up at the college."

At first it sounds like an event we're supposed to cover, but he looks too serious to be suggesting an assignment, and doling out the work is not his department. He pulls a chair up to my soon-to-be-retired metal desk and checks to make sure Grumman's door is closed. It all looks very cloak-and-dagger, and if I hadn't been so terrified the night before, I might have found it amusing.

"This is between you and me," he says.

"This is you being a PI?"

"No, it's me being a gambler."

"You gamble?"

"I put a few shekels down now and again."

"Shekels?"

"Yeah, that's just a slang term...."

"I know what it means. Your vocabulary doesn't usually include a lot of Yiddish words."

His eyebrows rise dramatically.

"I thought it was Chinese: one of those expressions my father always uses. Anyway, I'll bet fifty now and then—a hundred on the Super Bowl. I lost."

"And now I'm lost."

"Sorry," he says. "My book—my father's book actually...."

"Book?"

"Bookie, you know. The guy is a friend of the family. My father went to school with him. Small time, but he hears things and passes them on. No one could care less about who owes what and who's in trouble than my father, but sometimes I hear pieces of conversation, find out who has whose chits."

"From now on, Teddy, English please."

"Little IOUs. Couple weeks ago my dad mentioned something about Chalmers—I don't remember if you were on your way to interview Joe Lawrence and the name came up, but my father said something like *now there's a guy in really deep*."

"Why?"

"Joe Lawrence doesn't bet with my book. He's way beyond that. To me fifty bucks is a big bet; a hundred is daring. To Joe Lawrence that's a poker bump or a blackjack turn."

"So he has a gambling problem?"

"It's only a problem when you don't win. So yes, he has a problem."

"And he owes money?"

"My father says at least a half million dollars."

"Jesus, are you certain?"

"I don't know how much is true, but my father doesn't usually exaggerate. Upwards of five-hundred thousand dollars—I say upwards because this conversation happened a few weeks ago—I doubt if he quit cold turkey."

"Maybe he's been winning."

"Joe Lawrence doesn't win. There are gamblers and there are losers and the bookmakers always know who's who. People like Lawrence keep them in business with hunches and feelings—the book will pay off once in a while, but the house always comes out ahead."

I'm trying to remember Lawrence's salary. I know he's well paid, but he's not making half a mil. It's a private college so his earnings are not a matter of public record, but other community college presidents are in the $120-$140K range. I figure Lawrence is there too. Of course with Teddy around, I needn't have bothered figuring it out.

"He makes $132,000," he says. "Overpaid but typical. He gets a few perks, too, but the bottom line: he owes three times his salary."

"I don't know much about bookies, can you pay these chits in installments?"

Teddy smiles. Maybe someone else would have laughed and asked me what kind of idiot I really am, but he just beams that best-friend look.

"Yes you can, but there's interest. And bookies aren't governed by any legislation that limits rates. Thirty percent is common. In other words, if Joe Lawrence owes 500 grand, pays off 100 grand next year, he'll owe *more than* 500 grand afterwards. Of course the other interest collected can come in the form of physical pain and suffering. I'm sure you know that. That's why he's selling."

"Who's selling? What?"

"Joe Lawrence. Chalmers is on the market."

"Are you sure?"

"No. But two years ago the place was in the red and nobody wanted it. Now it's making money and there's a strong rumor that Castleton Academics is interested. They run a string of colleges on the west coast, L.A. to Seattle. Last year they bought a failing business school near Cleveland. That was their easternmost property, until Chalmers. They're also looking at a business school up near your territory, Portland. I guess they want Chalmers too."

"I never heard of selling a college before. What does someone pay for a college?"

"Harvard would probably set you back three or four billion—of course that's a guess—but Chalmers, maybe ten mil?"

"And how does it work? I mean does someone write a check to Joe Lawrence for ten million dollars and then he gives them the key?"

"They take over the accounts, the operating expenses, the salaries, and of course the income. That sale price is all accounted for. Castleton will make its money when the college thrives. It's more of an investment. That's the financial end—the academic changes would probably come along with it."

"And how does Joe Lawrence make his money?"

"Same way any seller does—you have to sell the product for more than it's worth. Act as the agent, maybe cut some side deals, who knows?"

"But five hundred thousand more?"

"If that's what he needs."

I know how businesses make money: lower operating expenses, cut staff, pray that the finished product doesn't suffer too much. Melanie Johns and a few others were let go. Classes eliminated. Supplies not reordered. There were lots of ways a business could retrench and come back from failure. Still, there's only so much that can be done by reducing staff and cutting back on paper clips.

"Anyway," Teddy says, "I kept it under wraps. I didn't want you storming off and confronting a man about his gambling debts."

"I wouldn't do that. But what about his profits—you said they were out of proportion to what was going on in other institutions. How is that happening?"

"It's probably not sound business principles. I'm meeting someone this afternoon and we're going to talk about it. A friend of a friend. I'll call you if she tells me anything."

"And if you were selling a college, would you add on beforehand?"

"What do you mean?"

"Well, would you expand, maybe put up some new buildings or convert an older one?'

Teddy shakes his head. "You do that when you're investing in the place—when you hope to recoup those expenses—have more students, more income. To do it now—it would be like adding a room to your house before you sell it. Why bother? If the purchaser wants a new room, let *him* add it on."

"I guess. This friend of a friend, have you spoken to her lately?"

"Three or four days."

"Is it Jill Dennison?"

"Even if it were, I couldn't…."

"She's gone."

"Gone? She's dead?"

"God, Teddy! She's just missing. Vanessa doesn't know where she is. This friend, is it Jill?"

He shrugs. "Even if it were...."

"When you see her, tell her that people are worried about her."

"Who's worried?"

"People. You, for one. Just tell her. And you have to ask her something. Ask her if she knows of any buildings in Drayton that are, let's say, desirable for conversion to maybe classroom space."

"Why that in particular?"

I'm not sure how much Teddy needs to know, or when he asks Jill, how much she needs to know; but Teddy isn't much of a rumormonger so I come fairly clean with him about the Chalmers expansion project. It was probably right to tell him—he gets a good laugh out of it.

"So you were serious about that expansion," he says. "Don't be. Unless there's a lot more going on here than we think, you have a very simple situation of a guy who needs money and is going to find the easiest way to get it. You might have a tag sale—he's selling the college."

"Then why would he feed me this line about new buildings and new programs and a four-year university?"

"You're asking me?" he says. "I had that one journalism course—everything else is hands-on. But," and he smiles because he's the expert and I'm not, "I do know that people use the newspapers to get stories out there—to publicize ideas that may or may not be true. Maybe Lawrence needs that information available to the public so that somewhere along the way, the value of the college rises and he asks for a higher selling price.."

And I'd be the jerk who broke the story that wasn't a story. And of course he knew I'd do it because I'd done it before. If Teddy's theory has any merit, then Brandt was right: Teddy's pretty good.

Chapter 25

Teddy won't tell Brandt about Lawrence's gambling woes. He says it's a family matter. Private. He means his family—his father. He says word would get back eventually and then Mr. McClendon would be in trouble. The big guys always get away, Teddy complains, while some guy making penny-ante football bets ends up in court.

I'm already past the gambling: some say it's a disease and should evince some sympathy. But embezzlement or misappropriation seems like a no-brainer, and that means trouble for Drayton which, despite its shortcomings, is a college town. It may not have the same relationship as Harvard to Cambridge or Yale to New Haven, but businesses—fast food outlets, small night clubs, strip malls out on Route 9, even that funky Gretchen's with its gravelly granola—derive a good deal of business from all those day students. Anything that interferes with the success of Chalmers has a negative effect on Drayton, and if Joseph Lawrence is going down and taking the college with him, the ripple effect will be extensive. This Castleton Academics outfit that Teddy mentioned—who's to say they'll keep Chalmers as it is, or tend to it at all when it's merely one of their many properties?

Joe Lawrence's personal debt pales next to a pair of murders and a subsequent three-month-old investigation. But does it matter—as Grumman likes to ask? Yes. Of course so do Teddy's friendship and the security of his family. I drop him off—no further mention of Jill Dennison along the way—then head back to the *Courier*.

I do actually work there. I mean I may give the impression that I have nothing better to do than gather snippets of disconnected information on those murders, share the occasional pizza with Teddy, indulge in some sporadic late-night sex, and fight with my mother. In the past few weeks I've covered a local park beautification project, a couple arrested for illegal puppy breeding, and a local Methodist church struggling to keep its food pantry open. I'm also responsible for little life-style features ("Hey! It's…" and then insert your own season, or month, or holiday.) Not momentous, any of it, but they're the kinds of stories that make us relevant—that keep us from becoming merely a conduit for national items to snip off the wire and reprint. And the ones that come out well I add to my résumé, which is out there floating from one newspaper personnel office to the next, apparently gathering neither interest nor dust.

The Chalmers story has legs, but it borders on a "gotcha." Grumman never wanted the *Courier* to descend to that level and neither do I. Damn it, though, it's tantalizing, and on the off chance I might be able to pursue the story somehow, I Google some articles on gambling. Brandt would not be happy that I'm in the office alone. Neither am I, and I'm distracted by every shadow from a passerby and every car that slows down. When I leave I do a little more street scanning than usual and, once inside my car, narrowly avoid two accidents because my eyes are in the rearview mirror more than on the road.

I cruise by Marcus Johns' place. His wife after all was fired by Lawrence and the husband might know something he doesn't even know he knows—maybe something Melanie let slip along the way. Skittish as I am after last night, it is after all daylight and I've already been there and can already visualize an escape route. It turns out that his place looks better than mine would—and the only residue of negligence is a coffee cup on the floor in the living room. My father used to do that—sit a few inches from the TV at night so that the sound wouldn't disturb anybody, then leave his empty coffee cup right there.

It's obvious Johns doesn't know why I'm there, so I need to establish right away that I'm not trawling for Melanie's old lovers. That sounds vulgar, but the coincidence does occur to me after sharing my bed with Karl Brandt not even twelve hours earlier.

"This is about Melanie," I tell him, before I even get through the front door, "if you have a few minutes."

"I don't suppose there's anything new."

"Not that I know of. I just wanted to ask—when Melanie was let go at the college, was she angry?"

"Well she did say she was going to burn the place down and castrate Joe Lawrence. Does that qualify as anger? Come in."

On this second visit I feel a lot more comfortable, but I think that ease might be a result of my simmering anger for the man Melanie hated also.

"Of course," Johns says, "she also said that Chalmers would fail on its own—that the place was going downhill and Lawrence would wind up—if you'll pardon the expression—fucking up the school and himself."

"Because of open admissions?"

"It's not that easy to condemn. Melanie used to brag about the serious students there, but she had the most fun with those non-students, a lot of them who just needed a chance. She was good at it—patient, understanding, and she knew what she was talking about. Not the kind of teacher you get rid of. It's not the policy, it's how the policy is effected and that comes down from the top.

"But she thought the place was in trouble?"

"When you throw open your campus to anyone, you really need to monitor what's going on and whom you allow to be part of the college. There was an element on campus—it wasn't so much that they were non-students—it was more that they were criminals."

"Real criminals?"

"I'm not sure how you distinguish a real criminal from some other kind, but Melanie called them criminals, and she was a pretty charitable person."

"With open enrollments you can't always exclude people like that."

"That isn't exactly true—it's a private college—you can exclude anybody you want as long as someone draws the line. But the criminals kept getting second chances, and third and fourth ones too. It was frustrating for the instructors, but it was money for Chalmers."

"What kind of money are we talking about?"

"Look at it this way," he says. "Chalmers is up around a thousand students, give or take. Let's say you add fifty that have no chance of gaining any certificate or diploma, but they pay the $20,000 a year tuition. That's a million dollars. Now it's obviously not all profit—more use of facilities, more instructors, supplies, operating expenses. But a lot of these kids won't show up anyway. It's win-win. You get money to provide a service, but the people you're supposed to help seldom avail themselves of that service. And if they wash out and someone new takes their place...double the fun."

"No way that can be legal."

"I'm sure Lawrence has received sound legal advice, and if he's living on the edge of the law, then he hasn't fallen off yet."

"But how can the kids afford it?"

"The kids? You make them sound like toddlers with their little Sponge Bob lunch boxes. They're not kids, and they can't afford it. But there are plenty of federally-funded programs that provide aid for people who want to advance themselves. I suppose dealing drugs on campus, planning burglaries between classes, stealing cars—those are all forms of advancement. Meanwhile, the reputation of the school diminishes."

"But if the school goes up for sale, and that's the rumor, what are the new owners going to do with a failing business?"

"That's for them to deal with. Joe Lawrence gives the buyers a balance sheet that underscores the profits, then he gets out and everyone else can fend for themselves. Maybe the new owners will revamp the application process, clean house. Or maybe they'll hire guards instead of instructors. All you need is leadership without an idiot in charge. Maybe in the long run it's a good thing— Joe Lawrence shouldn't be running an educational institution any more than a crack dealer should be running a halfway house."

"Did the faculty ever raise this issue—these alleged criminals on campus?"

"All the time. Lawrence was always cordial and receptive and agreeable to looking into the matter—even hired an extra security officer to hang out in the classroom buildings—but nobody wants to butcher a cash cow, so the basic enrollment never changed much."

"The cops don't seem to be zeroing in on the school as the source of the...murders."

"Or they are and we don't know it. I'm hoping there's a lot going on behind the scenes. Are you going to use this?"

I give Johns some equivocal response, but the truth is I'd sure as hell like to. I'd like to see that blowhard Lawrence account for everything he's done or hasn't done. And I'd like to hear his response when I confront him with an opinion— though wild and unproven—that some of these characters he's chosen to "rehabilitate" may be the same ones guilty of two murders. I won't go public with that just yet: I do retain a fairly accurate definition of libel, and implying that Joseph Lawrence willingly admitted criminals to Chalmers and knowingly let them roam free on and off campus might fall nicely within that area, especially with both murder victims having some tangential ties to the college.

Lawrence won't be there on a Saturday, but I head for the college anyway. Halfway there I get a call from Brandt—he wants to know if I'm comfortable driving after the previous night's incident. I am, though my rearview mirror is getting a pretty good workout. He still wants to have dinner, and I'm agreeable of course. A place and a time, I tell him. He'll get back to me.

"I'll be at Chalmers," I tell him, for no other reason than I feel like talking to him. I want to know how *he* feels after last night's incident—our incident—but he's not much for small talk and probably isn't that eager to discuss our new relationship over the phone. Neither am I—I have no idea what this new relationship actually is and even less of an idea where it will end up.

Chalmers is bustling. For some colleges weekends mean quiet and inactivity. But Chalmers prides itself on offering an abundance of Saturday classes and today everything is going full force. I don't even get my usual parking spot in the first row. Is this is what Marcus Johns meant about turning a profit?

The administrative offices are quiet—no Lawrence, no Marcie—but when I leave them I find one of the deans, something-or-other Tyler, standing by a concrete bench in a little common area, a clipboard in his right hand and a cigarette in his left.

"Dean Tyler? Brianna Cooper, from the *Courier*."

"My bad," he says, and hurriedly grinds out his cigarette as I approach. "We're pushing for a non-smoking campus."

"You're setting a bad example."

"Nasty habit."

I want to respond that so is saying "my bad" when you're older than twelve, but one issue at a time.

"I'm not sure if you remember me. We met…."

"I've seen you around. How are you?"

"I'm well. Busy day, huh?"

"Typical Saturday. You probably want Joe—he never comes in on weekends."

"I didn't think so. Maybe you can help me, though."

"If you want to sign up for something, I can get you in. A little late for spring, but the summer is wide open. We've added a few courses."

Tyler is about forty, good looking with perfectly coiffed near-blond hair that's just starting to recede. I don't know if he has an eye for the ladies, but he certainly has one for me this particular morning. Maybe he's homing in on a hint of recent orgasms in my expression, something akin to the aurora borealis—few people in this latitude have ever seen it. Whatever his motives, a course at Chalmers is well below the bottom of my priority list.

"My plate's pretty full these days," I answer. "Actually I talked to Joe Lawrence a few days back. I just wanted to see the campus in full vigor."

Full vigor—it's a Dickens phrase and I don't know why it came to me at that moment—but it just seemed appropriate.

"Full vigor," Tyler repeats. He likes it too. Ten to one it turns up in a catalog some day, next to a photo of fully vigorous students. "Well," he says, pointing toward the quad, "Saturday's the day, and the real learners are here, not the hangers-on."

"Explain?"

"The weekend students need a course for advancement, or a raise, or promotion. They're intent and focused. This isn't the college experience for them—it's a fuckin' pain in the ass after a week of work, if you'll pardon my French."

And of course I do because he's every bit as big an asshole as Joe Lawrence, maybe bigger and stupider and more classless. But I'm sure he thinks we hip young folks modify every noun, adjective, adverb, and maybe the odd exclamation with some vulgarity or other, and now he's one of us. Except nobody has said pardon my French in about a thousand years. He's not one of us, or one of anybody, and when I don't slap him a high-five or give him a fist bump for his insights, he desists from his leering and backs away a step or two.

"I really have to get to a classroom," he says. "One of the instructors called in late and I have to cover. Nice seeing you again."

"Just...before you go...what's happening with college expansion. I understand there'll be a satellite college closer to town. Any ideas when?"

He looks as though I just asked him to explain dark matter, then quickly recovers, fumbling over phrases like *early stages* and *preliminary discussions* and some other nonsense that tells me he has no clue. Then he claims he really has to run and I let him. He and Joe will have something to talk about.

My bad...as Tyler might say.

I head back toward the parking lot when I see an oddly familiar face, though the name doesn't immediately come along with it. Mid-twenties, scruffy, some satanic black t-shirt exposing his equally satanic tattoos. No coat, of course, despite the wind and cold. I have a bad feeling about him, but I'm supposed to—that's why he's dressed that way. Two generations back my grandparents would have had a similar response to a long-haired freak with beads and a headband. Maybe I'm not as liberal or enlightened as I like to think, but while I'm assessing my prejudices I remember the name. It's Deron Hillis, all-around creep and convicted criminal. The head is shaved and there's a mustache, plus he's lost weight and looks like a refugee from a country where the wars never end, but it's him. My prejudice was well placed after all.

He carries no books, no notebook, no indication that he's a student there except a Chalmers ID around his neck on a blue lanyard. Melanie Johns' words echo—Chalmers will fail without outside help. Sure enough, here's one reason why: Deron Hillis—supposedly in prison for another year or two—is loose and roaming about the campus.

He passes within five feet of me and we make brief eye contact. It's possible he remembers me from the courtroom—I did show up at his trial a few times—but it's more likely I'm just someone he'd like to assault and batter, or maybe rob. I've already punched in Brandt's' number.

One thing I have that my grandparents didn't is a cell phone with a built-in camera, and I'm about to do something absolutely out of character. I'm going to take his picture. Of course there was a time when you held the camera to your eye and everyone within shouting distance knew what you were doing; but today's cell phones make it easy to make believe you're talking when, in fact, you could be doing anything—checking email, playing a game, or in my case, taking a picture. It's really important though, when you want to be secretive, to make sure the flash doesn't go off. Maybe this is why I don't work undercover.

Hillis responds to the flash of course, and walks over to me, looks at the phone, then glares at me.

"Did you just take my picture?"

He isn't smiling. He isn't…anything. Trying to glean some emotion from his face is futile.

"Selfie, I must have hit the flash when I was turning the camera."

"So you took a picture of me?"

"I think I got trees and sky."

"Let me see."

Please would have been too much to expect, but I can't be too critical since I just took his picture without asking if I could. And he's a convicted felon. Of course there are enough people around so that I can be pretty sure he won't attack me, and to any disinterested observer we probably look like two students comparing notes before class…and I intend to keep it that way. I touch the icon and the most recent photo comes up—his: half of his face and his impressively tattooed right shoulder, and then as I had said and hoped, trees and sky.

"I don't like having my picture taken. Delete that," he says, and then adds "please." He struggles with the word as if it's from a foreign language containing letters he doesn't comprehend.

"Sure," I tell him—no big deal. He watches me drag the thumbnail to the garbage can icon and we both watch it disappear.

"Now empty the trash."

"What?"

"The picture is in the trash. It's not gone. Empty the trash."

"I didn't know you could. I don't know how."

He reaches into his back pocket and I'm just about to scream for the cops when, instead of a knife or a gun, he pulls out a cell and takes *my* picture.

"Now we're even," he says, then looks at the photo. "Cute, maybe I'll call you sometime."

I've always been programmed—maybe pre-programmed—to utter one of several responses when a guy says that. *I'm married. I have a boyfriend. I'm in a relationship.* But with someone like Hillis I'm afraid he might kill the other guy—or find out I'm lying and kill me—so I shrug and say nothing.

"That picture," he says, "the one you can't find. Did you send it anywhere?"

"You mean did I post it? I don't do that."

He holds out his hand and I immediately know my options: hand him the phone or watch it sail across the quadrangle into the side of a building.

"I have some pictures there I want to keep," I tell him. Photos from Christmas before my angry departure—relatives, a few friends.

"I don't want your photos," he says, makes a few movements with his fingers, then returns the phone. "Make sure it's okay."

I do. My pictures are there: his is gone. He promises to delete mine, then leaves for the administration building without another word and I'm left mostly embarrassed. But by the time I get to my car, I'm shaking so much I misdial Brandt's cell the first time and have to start over.

"I'm up at Chalmers," I tell him when I finally manage the use of my thumbs. "I just had a conversation with Deron Hillis."

Chapter 26

During the trial, the prosecutor referred to Deron Hillis as the most dangerous sociopath he'd ever seen. Sociopath ought to be damning enough without an adjective to qualify it, but simple hyperbole just doesn't cut it in the twenty-first century where we've witnessed the Newtown murders and Aurora, Colorado, and Columbine. We're no longer overwhelmed by a misfit like Deron Hillis, though we're all happy to know he's behind bars. But when people like that are roaming about the community, when they're attending classes at our local institute of higher learning, then we're not quite so happy.

Now I know that despite what we sometimes see on television, a cop doesn't follow the "careers" of people he's busted. Once these criminals are hustled off to prison, they're forgotten. They have to be: some new low-life understudies are waiting in the wings to take their place. But if there's another Hillis out there, he'll have to wait for the original to vacate the premises, and that's not happening.

"He got out just after the first of the year," he says when I call him on my phone with Deron Hillis's prints. "Happy New Year."

"How could they do that?"

"He was either a model prisoner or a snitch. Take your pick."

"And you knew."

"Departments hear things. We get notified when it's close to home. Bree...."

He's ready to apologize but I don't give him the chance.

"Did you know he's up here at Chalmers?"

"We don't have a tail on him, but we know he's around. Did you talk to him?"

"Yeah, we're gonna hang out."

"I mean did he recognize you?"

"I don't think I'd ever met him. I just remembered the face...and the ink."

"How did you happen to see him?"

"Karl, how do you happen to see anyone? I don't know—I was walking to my car, he was in the parking lot. I took his picture."

"You what? Why in the world would you do that?"

"I wanted to show it to you—make sure it was him."

"I could have gotten you one," he says. "We call them mug shots—maybe you've heard the term—and we have plenty."

Brandt sounds concerned, or angry—hard to tell which, though I hope it's the latter because if he's concerned, then I should be too, and more so. The whole story, replete with the inadvertent flash, doesn't improve his attitude.

"You know, for undercover people, you and Teddy are good journalists."

"We're not undercover people."

"I noticed that."

I wish I had a snappy reply ready for him—he's still to blame for not telling me that this *most dangerous sociopath* was roaming about the community. And of course I could mention the seeming lack of progress in the murder cases; then again the police don't share every speck of new information with the public. Bottom line: taking that photo was idiotic, and instead of coming up with a more idiotic excuse, I just admit it. He's right.

"Okay listen," he says, "somewhere on that campus we have a black-and-white. If you feel the least bit uncertain."

"I'm fine," I tell him, but scan the campus anyway and locate the black-and-white, which in Drayton is navy blue. "I see it."

"Good. Get in your car and drive over here first."

I drive past the cop—he's parked near the entrance—and he waves. I'll give Brandt one thing—he's thorough. An uneventful ride later I'm in the quiet police station. Of course it's a Saturday and the cops are probably seven, eight hours away from the first brawl at Salerno's or some other titty bar on Route 9, and then there'll be the usual skein of DUI's and drunk-and-disorderlies that won't end until the sun comes up on Sunday morning—if then. I certainly don't begrudge them their temporary tranquility.

Brandt opens a cabinet and pulls out a folder but doesn't open it.

"Reporters can get in trouble you know."

"Already been there."

"That's not what I mean, Coop. I'm not talking about your boss yelling at you for a late deadline or a misspelled name. I mean a bad guy beats you up for calling him a bad guy."

"Like Hillis."

"Yes. You need to be careful. Deron Hillis didn't kill those women, but he's not above beating the crap out of a reporter."

"I'm not even interested in him. He happened to be on campus."

"Where you're waging war against Joseph Lawrence. Admirable, I'll admit. But Hillis is right there, and so are others just like him. They don't know your intentions: it's no shame pulling back a little."

"I think it is. I actually feel like a reporter these days, like I'm accomplishing something."

"Such as?"

"Fact-checking, following up, all the things I used to ignore. I'm not afraid of Deron Hillis."

"Why?"

"What kind of question is that?"

"Obviously the kind you can't answer. So until you have a reason *not* to be afraid—like he's moved to Australia—you probably should be."

"Okay, I won't take his picture anymore."

"I'm not joking, Coop."

"I get that, but I—I'll be more careful."

"Not careful—conscious."

He opens the folder he's been using as a pointer.

"Deron Hillis," he reads, "born 1988, Lamoine, Maine. Moved down the road to Ellsworth in 1993 and attended local schools. Three suspensions between 2001 and 2003. First arrest: 2002, stealing liquor from a parked vehicle—juvenile probation. 2003, stole his father's car and he and some buddies drove to Bangor where they tried to find prostitutes. Instead they found a vice cop and a few more juvie agents. Same year, beat up his father and cut him with a broken liquor bottle. No charges. Same year..."

"I get it, but this is all nickel-and-dime."

"Until 2006—he and two associates rob four gas stations in a two-hour period. One owner doesn't cooperate and they beat him. He winds up in the hospital for emergency surgery. He was 68 years old. Still nickel-and-dime?"

"Did they serve time?"

"Ten months for Hillis—the state couldn't prove he was the one that beat the victim, and in these robberies no weapons were used. The defense made the case that they were goofy kids, probably high, too stupid to even know that they needed guns to rob people. They conceded it got out of hand with that one vic, but the jury saw it their way. Hillis was still 17.”

“How did he get here?”

“Picked up a girl one night and she turned out to be his soulmate. God I love that term, maybe because it sounds a lot like cellmate and often turns out to be about the same thing."

"Karl."

"Sorry, my cynical side. Anyway he followed her to East Boston and convinced her family to let him live with them in a spare room. Even paid rent. He worked for a delivery service for a while, then in a sandwich shop, then as a clerk in a convenience store, then as a custodian in an industrial complex. That’s where he met Len Cochran.”

“Don't know him."

"You should—he’s a Chalmers guy. Joe Lawrence’s recruiter-in-chief. And he was interested in people like Hillis. See there’s a program where someone with a criminal record who has been clean for one full year can have his college tuition paid.”

“Clean? He was in prison!”

“Best behavior. Plus he had a job on the inside. And he had a family to vouch for him. And he knew about the program. But of course you have to be able to get into the college. M.I.T. and Harvard might be a bit of a stretch.”

“But Chalmers?”

“Just proof of a high school diploma—Hillis had that. And the best thing for Chalmers is that the tuition payment is guaranteed. If the kid drops out after one week, or shows up but never does a lick of work, same thing.”

“So it’s a fundraiser for the school.”

“Ongoing.”

He sifts through the file and comes up with another sheet of paper.

“Here’s a list—kids with criminal records enrolled at Chalmers. Now to be fair, some of them have done well.”

“Hillis?”

“Not one of the success stories.”

“Because he’s a criminal. How did he get out of jail?”

"Official story? Good behavior. My theory? Snitch. I know what you're thinking—here's a guy capable of murdering two women. Fact is he was released after the first of the year. Besides, I can envision him attacking a woman on the spur of the moment and robbing her, but lying in wait for just the right moment, in just the right place—that doesn't seem like Deron Hillis."

"Do you think one of Lawrence's so-called posse—these convicts—chased me last night?"

"There'd be no reason to, but we're keeping an eye on them when we can. Hillis too."

So there we are, Karl and I, just chatting in the ambience of the run-down police station. It seems a bizarre sequel to the previous evening's intimacy.

"I should be getting back to the office," I tell him, though I don't feel like leaving.

"Are we on for tonight?"

I'm just about to say yes when I remember my conversation with Teddy. He didn't swear me to secrecy, though I know his intent was for me not to divulge anything. But Jesus, I can't go anywhere anymore without a police escort, and if Lawrence has issues that the police should know about, well then I should let them know.

"Joe Lawrence has a gambling problem."

"Why do you say that?"

"I just know."

"Let me rephrase that: why does Teddy say that?"

"You don't know I got the information from him."

"Mr. McClendon lays down a few bets here and there and probably knows who's doing the same. Don't worry, Teddy's not going to lose the private eye license he doesn't have."

Brandt listens quietly as I tell him what Teddy told me, trying like crazy to avoid references to his father.

"Having debts like that," he says when I finish. "That changes a person."

"Half a million dollars. Teddy claims that bookies aren't very understanding."

Brandt smiles. "Teddy may not know much about investigative work, but he has that whole understatement thing down pat. What about tonight?"

"So that wasn't so important then?"

"Maybe. We don't have a gambling task force, and the big players are pretty well protected. Plus with online gambling, it's even harder to keep things under control. But we can look into it. And listen, Teddy's dad is safe. Seven?"

"What?"

"Tonight. Seven a good time?"

Seven is fine. Again he reminds me to be careful I tell him to pick a restaurant. I don't feel like going through a catalog of local eateries—I just want to get back to the office, which should be empty and therefore conducive to an afternoon of some catching up. The thought of doing research on this prison-to-college plan sounds appealing, especially since the results of this boondoggle have ruined my peace of mind. But as soon as I get to my car, the cell phone chirps. Jill Dennison. Unlike the Christmas Eve intrusion or its followup a day later, this one comes as a relief.

"Where have you been?"

"Sometimes I have to get away. What's going on?"

"That's it? That's your explanation?"

"I was away. If you'd like I could make something up."

"People are worried about you."

"How many?"

"I don't know. Vanessa, your folks."

"You?"

"Well, yes, me."

"Okay that's four," she says. "Barely enough for a game of canasta. You'd think that someone who disappears after three decades on this planet would cause a little more concern. Anyway, I called my folks and left a message for Van. And you make four."

"Are you in the office?"

"No."

"Will you be?"

"Not for a while. I'll let you know. Remember that email I showed you? The one Melanie sent me? Show it to your boyfriend."

"He's not...."

"Show it to Brandt."

"I don't have it."

"Yes you do."

She clicks off before I have the chance to question her about Teddy. I consider calling Karl back and telling him I've heard from Jill Dennison, but she isn't a missing person and the knowledge would be meaningless. I check my email—nothing. If I have that letter, I don't know where it is.

There's a vein of dishonesty and secretiveness, maybe reticence, that runs through Jill Dennison. Now, though, she needs help and doesn't really know how to obtain it, to open up so that someone like me can feel some empathy without qualifying it with that overarching feeling that she's always holding back. She doesn't tell lies, only offers clever prevarications: she doesn't believe in hiring a PI, but that doesn't mean she didn't take on an amateur doing the same thing. Maybe I'm no better: even in that truncated conversation I could have snuck in a question about Teddy instead of answering her little math problem of how many were worried about her.

I return to an office that isn't empty after all. Teddy is pecking away at the keyboard.

"Spring sports preview," he says. Apparently every coach will win every game. Very promising. We'll check the results in May."

He waits for me to commiserate, but I'm not in the mood. Instead I check my mail and there it is—an envelope with my name: no address, no stamp, just Coop.

"How did this get here?"

"How did what get where?"

I hold up the envelope. He squints, as if seeing it more clearly will somehow explain it.

"No idea," he says.

"Teddy, I know."

"About the envelope?"

"About everything. You and Jill Dennison—I know you're working for her."

He looks like a child who's just been told that his suspicions were right after all—the tooth fairy actually is a fabrication. The silence goes on a little too long for me.

"Well?"

"There's a code of privacy," he says. He sounds very serious.

"You're a not a *licensed* PI. Not only that, but you're probably violating a number of statutes by pretending to be one. So let's back up a bit. I know about you and Jill Dennison."

"She sent me the envelope."

"There's no stamp."

"It came in a larger envelope. I was supposed to give it to you. I'm just doing my job."

There's no sense reminding him again that the job doesn't exist, but I can't in good conscience let him keep taking these risks.

"Teddy, listen. I'm not asking you to betray any confidences, but you have to stop this little charade."

"I'm only asking questions. I'm not tailing anyone or surveilling. I'm just...."

"...running the risk of getting the shit kicked out of you."

"Just doing someone a favor. Are you mad because I didn't tell you?"

"A little, yes. But I'm angrier that you're putting yourself in jeopardy."

"I haven't kept secrets—I've told Brandt what I found out."

"And he's warned you, hasn't he?"

Teddy nods.

"It's kind of embarrassing," he says. "I mean you're going out with Brandt but he was, you know, involved with a victim."

Involved with a victim is Teddy-speak for cheating on his wife. I know he wants to ask me how I can be with a man like that. I'm glad he doesn't because I don't know the answer. The fact that Brandt really loved Melanie, that he misses her, that he's suffering over her death—it all sounds pretty tawdry considering he made a legal commitment to someone else, their impending break-up notwithstanding. And if Melanie hadn't been killed, would Brandt still be hanging around, trying to break up her marriage just as his own was crumbling? And that professed love for Melanie Johns—I doubt if he was thinking much about that earlier this morning when he was gathering his clothes in my bedroom.

It was mere weeks ago that I considered Brandt to be one of those guys who would—as one of my college friends was wont to say—screw a snake if he could figure out where to hold onto it. Then, practically overnight he evolved into this sensitive victim of a lost love, grieving alone for someone he had no rights to. So now I don't know—but we're having dinner this evening—I doubt if that's going to clarify much.

As for Teddy, if he's actually annoyed with me, he doesn't show it. And anyway, by tomorrow this conversation will be forgotten. I never had that gift: I dwell much more easily than I forget. It's a sure path to misery—any fool knows that—but many aspects of my life seem to lie outside my will to change, this among them. I give it a try though when I hand him his windbreaker.

"A little breezy out," I tell him.

"It'll be spring one of these days," he says. Ten seconds of dwelling was about his limit.

He leaves for God knows where—an assignment? a meeting with his "client"? I need to get out of here too, but I have work I can't take home because if I did, I'd open a Chardonnay and never get it done. Then Brandt would arrive to take me to dinner and sometime around three in the morning—if the past is any indication—would be putting on his clothes and heading out to save his wife any embarrassment.

You know, I have friends who are married and who have kids and who live in nice homes and who probably don't spend most of their waking hours figuring out why they're acting the way they do…because they're not. Instead they're raising children and planning vacations and going out to a movie and figuring what lies within and outside their budget. I wonder if I'll ever be like that. And I wonder if I'll even like it. The life Abby had—it was stolen from her but it was a life. What lies ahead for me? Another night when I audition for the role once performed by Melanie Johns. Maybe in the dark she and I felt the same, sounded the same, smelled the same, tasted the same. Maybe I'm still in the running.

My cell chirps again. Chalmers College. I'm not in the mood to talk to anyone.

I wonder when my wood desk will arrive.

Chapter 27

The Jail to Yale Program (my term for it—clever but not for publication) is actually a pretty good deal, but it can be and has been exploited—so much so that another watchdog group has been formed to monitor it. (Your tax dollars at work—and mine.) By late afternoon I have about five-hundred words down. With revision and editing, it will make a good feature. Then it'll just be a question of whom I pissed off...in addition to Joe Lawrence, that is.

Before I escape for the weekend—I call it that even though I work on Saturdays—I check the wire. Grumman hates papers cribbing too many stories from the national sources, but if we can make a tie-in, why not? The unemployment statistics aren't good, but some small machine shop just off our downtown area has begun hiring. So that's one of those "hooray for Drayton features" which won't help the workers collecting unemployment, but will make everyone else feel that we're on our way back—whatever that means. I've met the owner so I call him. Five new workers, that's what he's taken on, and it looks like maybe five more come June. I try a few more places and learn that, despite the prevailing belief that America is floundering, most of the reductions in staff have stopped and there may be a recovery after all. I throw together the shell of a feature —to be polished later. It's not much, but I need to have some moments when I feel like a journalist and not some middle-schooler trying to figure out who likes me.

I'm sure that the logistics involved in running a machine shop differ markedly from those involved in running a college, but I figure what the hell—I can get Melanie's name back into circulation by tying in the seeming boom at Chalmers. Besides, if someone from there took the time to call me on a Saturday, the least I can do is return that call.

No one answers. Payback. Now I really am ready for a drink or two. A chilled Chardonnay is waiting to be uncorked (it's a screw-top but *uncorked* sounds classier) and sucked down, and I'm the one to do it—or some of it. Maybe a little wine on a Saturday afternoon will give me a truer perspective of where I am and where I'm going...*in vino veritas* and all that shit.

I pull into the apartment complex where I have my pick of parking spots. Maybe people living in condos feel less confined than apartment dwellers, but on

Saturdays residents treat the Colony like a prison farm where the guards have left and forgotten to lock the gate. Gone by breakfast, my fellow inmates don't wander back to their cellblocks until late afternoon or early evening—those that come back at all. Others are up in New Hampshire skiing or over in the North End queued up at some ristoranti. I can actually park a few yards from the door—I should be this lucky some day when the sleet is bouncing off my forehead.

I wish I could say that something looked amiss, that I had some kind of presentiment, that I just knew—but I didn't. Everything seemed perfectly normal when I carded myself in, eschewed the elevator for the stairs, dug out my apartment key and opened the door. I remember trying to figure out if I should hit the wine first, take a shower first, or perhaps combine the two. I was still weighing the possibilities when I saw movement, a shadow. When you live alone you don't see shadows or anything else in your house. Everything is always the way you left it—even the maintenance crew gives us a week's warning now before they come in to paint or patch or even change a lightbulb. But I saw something and then, in an instant, I was jolted—it was like an elevator coming to an abrupt stop. After that everything became blurred—snippets of sounds, images, conversations, pain.

—A siren.

—Teddy's voice maybe and, what the hell, Jill Dennison? Why would she be here? Who would let her in?

—Another voice—"We're losing her," someone else says, the sound right there in my right ear, like some Bluetooth device. I try to remove it but I can't find it.

I can taste blood the way I used to with my former overly enthusiastic hygienist. But she's not there—the person near my face now is a stranger, a man, my age, black, shaved head, expressionless. "You're going to be fine," he says, then repeats it. I have no idea what he's talking about. I'm already fine except for the taste of blood and the fact that some stranger has gotten into my apartment. Many strangers—other voices fill the background.

And then everything goes dark again and I hear Brandt yelling at someone to get away from the fucking door. I look for him. He isn't there.

The taste of blood becomes stronger and I feel as if I'm going to choke on it. Then my mother says she'll buy me new things and my father agrees with her as he tosses coats, sweaters, shoes, off the deck to the ground below. There's blood on everything and the Willises downstairs are toasting with Margaritas and laughing as the clothes fly past their deck. Everything will have to be dragged to the woods and covered with snow. If Daniel were here he would do that for me and the family would be all together. I keep asking about him but nobody answers. The man with the shaved head tells me he'll call Daniel as soon as he gets me ready. Ready for what? He doesn't answer.

On my bed the blood runs everywhere.

And then it's Sunday. I know that because I ask one of the duty nurses leaning over me.

I'm in a hospital bed.

It isn't until the next day that I learn that Joseph Lawrence is in the morgue. Shot dead.

*****

In the grand scheme of things, Chalmers College is a sapling in the forest of prestigious higher learning institutions that blanket eastern Massachusetts. But since none of us knows the grand scheme of things, we can still concede that, theoretically at least, a college ought to stand for something more than dubious accounting procedures and the exploitation of felons to maintain its survival. Given that premise, the revealed malfeasance of Joseph Lawrence, former public servant and college president, astonishes most people. There's immediate talk that Chalmers will shut down, that an accrediting organization will close the doors and send everyone—students and instructors—packing.

If that were to happen, the town would suffer, as would most of its businesses— the *Courier* for instance. But nobody would suffer quite so much as the legitimate students who would be, in a sense, tossed out on the street having paid their fees for nothing.

I suppose I should give a damn, but your perspective and priorities change when you're lying in a hospital bed feeling as though you belong there, so I don't give a damn. And maybe I should care more about why Joseph Lawrence decided to take a break from his gambling habit to break into my apartment and try to murder me. But my own damage inventory will keep me busy for the foreseeable future. I'm not paralyzed—that's the cheery part. All that tingling I felt when I first came to—Teddy says it's like a stinger in football, as if that's supposed to clarify it somehow. And speaking of terms I have no use for, I'm going to require something called maxillofacial reconstruction to knit together some broken bones near my left eye: afterwards I'll be 99.9% human and, according to my surgeon, one-tenth of one percent titanium with a face that might chill down a little faster in the winter. It does anyway, but he assures me that this will make it worse. Nice.

My broken nose is trivial by comparison—already repaired. Nothing to do now but wait for the inkiness to drain from my face. And then there's the swelling: they can't do the surgery until that diminishes. One of the nurses says it'll probably be a week, but another claims Thursday will be time enough. The conjecture is all very interesting, but I don't give a fuck what they say. Something about being hospitalized—you can easily work *fuck* into every sentence. I did promise Grumman, however—who has a strong sense for the way young ladies should speak— to stop as soon as they release me. Maybe I'm channeling my dead friend Abby, who was wont to unleash her share of obscenities when anything went the slightest bit awry, or maybe I just want someone to come by and tell me I can go home. Fuck knows when that will be. Best estimate: surgery Friday morning, home by Saturday at noon. Unfortunately my health care provider has decided that my rainbow-hued body should await the completion of the cycle in the comfort of my own place. And so on Tuesday I wind up hitching a ride home with Teddy's lock-picking niece Suzanne (filling in for Teddy—I no longer ask what new indiscretion has rescinded his right to drive) and find Brandt in my apartment, picking up the pieces—something he already did days before when he and his colleagues gathered evidence. I have a vague recollection of his comings and goings—the problem is I can't remember whether he's visited me in the hospital after the assault or if I remember them from before and can't tell the difference. It's all a little clearer when I'm less medicated—and one of the doctors has claimed that all the haziness will disappear in a couple days. For the most part, though, I prefer the haziness of the Vicodin to the clarity of the non-narcotic world. And I know the drugs are working because, under ordinary circumstances, I'd never allow someone to straighten my place without my supervision.

As I'm waiting to become well enough to become sick again after corrective surgery, I begin to realize that my face isn't the only damaged part of me. I have ligature marks around my neck, and my right knee won't take any weight. It's not that I'm planning any long-distance runs, but I feel as though I need a cane to get around. Brandt assures me it's merely a sprain, that he's done it a hundred times and I'll be better in a day or two. But I remember a high school friend with a similarly sore knee, incurred during the last 100 of an 800-meter event in some invitational meet. She finished the race, and finished her track season so that she could begin her arthroscopic one. I wonder if my maxillofacial guy does knees. I mean, while he has the anesthesiologist hanging around and all....

He doesn't...do knees that is, but just short of a week after the attack I'm in surgery. The procedure lasts nearly three hours, but that's only important to the people with the scalpels and the gas. I spend the time drifting about in some dreamless nether world where clocks either haven't been invented or their use has not yet been discovered. The operation goes well, and by that I mean I awaken from it with a face more swollen and the discoloration more general; but I do awaken, and that's always one of the surgeon's goals. And my knee feels better too. No surgery, just rest.

But rest, I find, is merely a euphemism for throwing up constantly in a variety of directions and locations. One of my nurses, a dour but efficient redhead named Vera assures me that it's just my body purging the anesthesia. Well, okay. If she doesn't mind mopping it up, I don't mind spraying it around. But as active as that particular orifice is, another one is stubbornly quiet. I can't be released until I pee, and I can't pee until I take in enough liquids to make me puke some more. The body certainly is a miraculously annoying mechanism, though these medical personnel somehow have a handle on it.

Finally I force down a few drops of apple juice and dribble out a thimbleful of like-colored urine, enough to satisfy some minimum requirement, and an orderly wheels me out of the place for the second time in a week, this time, I hope, for good. I think even Vera is happy to see me rolling down the hall with my police escort—there's a limit to how much vomit even the most solicitous nurse can abide.

This time Brandt, off duty, drives me home where the mental calisthenics begin. I insist on staying on the couch. I refuse even to look in the bedroom where a cleaning service has boiled practically everything and Bedding Bonanza—they of the annoying TV ads featuring that repulsive sloth—has deposited a new mattress and box spring. Brandt assures me that insurance will cover it, not that it matters—I could never put my face close to that blood-fouled mattress again.

Brandt spends that whole first day with me—at least I think he does. I doze through most of it and moan through the rest, including the part where, I'm pretty sure, Teddy came by with a pizza and I ate some and threw up, but Brandt says neither event occurred. Teddy was there though, that much I know because whenever they laughed, I laughed, and I think that made them laugh more. It was all very silly and I was more or less part of it, but mostly not.

My name didn't make the papers, but the story did, even back home. My Dad called to tell me he knew they shot the guy—that I could rest easier now that Joe Lawrence was dead. He was shocked that someone that prominent could be a murderer, but he was relieved. Mom too, he said. An afterthought but no doubt true. I didn't tell him the Vicodin was helping me rest even easier and that I had been scheduled to be the final victim. I'll sanitize the story and tell them someday, but our family is practiced in the art of secrecy. This one's a no-brainer.

All together I've lost ten days now since I wandered blithely into my apartment and almost died. This afternoon Brandt and I talked—actually talked—a conversation that extended beyond the narrow confines of my health and recovery. The apartment looked strange—I mean it looked too normal, as if nothing bad had happened, and the normality spooked me. And then for the first time I asked the question I should have asked days before.

He shakes his head—I wasn't raped.

And then, as if everything else had been painless and traumaless and too pedestrian to worry about, I start to cry. Between spasms I beg him not to leave and he keeps saying he won't. When the crying eases off a bit, he holds up a brand new toothbrush, still wrapped.

"I'll stay as long as you want," he says, and there's a momentary warm feeling when I realize he's planned that much in advance: later I would learn it was just one of my new backups he had found in the bathroom cabinet. Even so, if he had wanted to make love, I'd have done it then and there. I think though he was taking some satisfaction in nursing me back to health, and he probably thought tossing in an orgasm or two might sully the magnanimity of the act, let alone undo my sutures.

So now he's sitting at the table with a magazine on his lap and his eyes closed. I feel more or less safe. If there are other Joe Lawrences out there ready to kill me, I want them to see Brandt first so that they can watch him put a round or two between their eyes. With Brandt nearby I feel comfortable enough to sleep in my own bedroom, to utilize the new mattress. He says he ordered the same model but of course it's been discontinued and the salesperson found an equivalent style—said I wouldn't be able to tell the difference."

"Is the old one evidence?"

"Evidence?"

"You know, for DNA, something like that."

"As far as I know they took it to the dump and disposed of it."

I shrug as if it doesn't make any difference, and it probably doesn't. But wouldn't anything in that apartment be valuable in a criminal case, even a hearing when they decide if Lawrence's being shot was justified? Brandt disagrees.

"Joe Lawrence is dead, killed by the police in the commission of an assault."

"Killed by what police?"

"It was a good kill. There'll be a hearing of course."

That's all I'm going to get. Cops don't generally like to regale civilians with tales of taking people's lives.

"So it was you then."

"It was a good kill. That's all you need to know."

Chapter 28

As much as my pride makes it difficult to concede the point, I will: a good police report is a lot like a good newspaper article. The 5 W's and the H, the old bromide we first learned in high school journalism (or in Teddy's case, only in high school journalism) constitute the first rule of police-report writing also. And though it may not be as elegant as something we read in the *Globe* or the *Times* or even the *Courier*, the same rules obtain.

So after I sit there imprisoned in my apartment pestering Brandt for bits of information, he logs on to the back door of the Drayton PD website and accesses the official report on the death of Joe Lawrence. I think it's the first police report in which I've ever had a featured role: I played the part of the white female—something I'd been prepping for all my life I suppose, though the other W's and the H were added later.

As for the other players, Brandt was dispatched with another cop named Cahill to the threat of violence at the Colony Apartments in Drayton and upon arrival heard loud noises coming from inside apartment 208. Finding the door locked and fearful that "grave bodily harm" might befall said white female, he kicked in the door and found an assault in progress and a white male who was using an article of the woman's underwear to strangle the victim. I didn't like the perversion implicit in that particular detail, but I wasn't going to contest the truth of it. I still had the abrasions on my neck to prove it. The bra itself was in a landfill somewhere—somewhere near the mattress and far away. Apparently I was fully clothed, so either he found one hanging in the bathroom or raided one of the drawers. It doesn't matter—I'm burning everything that appears to have been moved.

The rest was pretty standard I guess, if a shooting in one's apartment can be considered standard—an order to stop and surrender, an attempt to assault the arresting officer, the discharge of a service weapon, the assailant falling to the floor wounded, an immediate request for medical help and rescue.

After that I went from *white female* to racial- and gender-neutral *victim*, and found that I had been advised on a number of particulars—I don't remember any of them. One of them was to remain fairly still until the EMT's arrived to minister to my injuries. Another was to keep a cold compress on the bridge of my nose. Almost everything in the report is new to me—as if someone wrote an unauthorized biography but I couldn't contest it because I was suffering from some sort of amnesia.

In the end Rescue Team Three arrived—I never knew there was even a Two—and treated the victim (still me) who required transport to a medical facility. The officer on scene could not determine for sure if there had been a sexual assault and advised the emergency workers of that fact. They found no evidence of such an assault. The victim was transported by ambulance to the hospital where she was admitted.

Thorough. Detailed. Done.

I tell him that I know Cahill and ask him if they work together often.

"No, never. He was in the area, heard the call."

"Who called this in?"

"Called what in?"

"Who heard what was going on? Somebody dialed 9-1-1."

"There were a few, I guess. Neighbors of yours who heard the racket."

"Because the report doesn't mention that, and on Saturdays this place is mostly deserted."

"I do my best to keep non-involved people out of things; otherwise reporters—not you of course" he says with a wink, "but others—they'll be harassing those neighbors who did nothing other than their civic duty."

"But if I wanted to thank them...."

"I can get you the names."

I look at the screen again.

"He was shot once in the chest when he came after you. One shot?"

"One."

"You're that good?"

"I can shoot."

"But one shot?"

"Do you want me to shoot him again? I can dig him up."

"One shot. Dead."

"Listen, someone comes after a cop like that, people get hurt. I had my shot and took it."

"Cahill didn't shoot?"

He shakes his head. "He lucked out. Look, Coop, it was the proper response. Not the proper response because it was you, just the proper response. You understand what I'm saying, don't you?"

"I just didn't know."

"Is there a problem?"

"Someone was killed in my apartment—I guess that's a problem."

"But it wasn't you—so that's a good thing. Believe me," he says, "if there had been another way, I'd have taken it. Nobody wants a week of desk duty and endless sessions with the shrink, but that's the deal. And I can't let those prospects interfere with my judgment."

"Is that all it will be? I mean with what's happening with police shootings? Is there going to be, you know, an indictment?"

"We interrupted the commission of an assault and you're the victim. That's it."

"I understand."

"It doesn't seem that way."

He logs off and closes the laptop.

"Of course I do," I tell him, but he knows I'm lying.

"Not really," he says. "I can tell. I almost feel like you want me to apologize for it. Believe me, I'm sorry it happened, but given that situation again—him or me, him or you—I'd pull the trigger again. Now I've had one psych sit-down already and I've got more scheduled. I have a formal meeting with the suits coming up and I can expect a number of letters to a number of editors—maybe to your boss too—on excessive force by a trigger-happy cop. All that's going to happen. I'd still do it again."

I'm listening, but somewhere in the middle of his defense my typically queasy stomach begins to churn. New mattress, new box spring—they're a nice beginning, but that's all: I find myself scanning the place for signs of blood, even though I know the evidence has been gathered and the place has been professionally scrubbed. I'm glad of that, but it's not going to make me comfortable any faster.

"I never heard the gunshot."

"You did. You screamed."

"I thought maybe I was out."

"You were, at least for a short time. When you came around, you were disoriented and strapped to a gurney on your way to The Brigham."

"The report doesn't say that—that I was unconscious."

"You were hysterical and distressed. You want me to add those two words to the report—for the sake of accuracy—I can do that."

"I don't like the word *hysterical*—it's sexist."

He shakes his head. "I know that. I didn't use it. I don't want to argue over something I didn't do."

"Listen, Karl, I'm sorry you have to go through all that bullshit now—the shrink, all that."

"It was a good shoot and everybody knows it. It's only protocol now. I'll be fine."

"And I don't mean to be cross-examining you—it's just that I feel it happened to someone else and I was there half-witnessing it. It's surreal."

"You should feel fortunate. You won't have horrible images popping up for the rest of your life."

"I think I will anyway. Who repaired the door?"

"What?"

"The door. If you had to kick it in, who repaired it?"

I'm not even sure why I ask, but I covered a burglary where some guy kicked in a door. There was all this splintered wood around the jamb and the knob was hanging loose at some amusing angle. My door looks fine.

"Maintenance, I guess," he says. "You pay for that, you know. If you do get the bill, you'll have to notify your insurance."

"It's the same door."

"And if you break a window, the replacement will be the same. There must be 500 units in this complex—of course there are going to be spares and inventory. They had it fixed by evening."

"Why so fast?"

"We have to secure a crime scene. The door wasn't evidence."

He has an answer for everything, and every answer seems right, but there are snatches of images I remember that keep getting in the way.

"It's already been in the news, right?"

"Yes."

"My name?"

"No. An assault of a possibly sexual nature on an unnamed victim, an assailant that refused to surrender, a justified police response."

"What about the *Courier*?"

"What about it?"

"Was the story in there?"

"Your boss wrote something about women feeling safer now that the murderer had been stopped. Of course he couldn't mention any tie-in with the paper, with you."

"So everyone is settled on the fact that Joe Lawrence killed the other two women?"

"There was evidence at each scene that we couldn't link to anyone, but once his name became a possibility, everything fell into place. So yes, he did the crimes, came after you, probably planned to murder that artist if he got the chance."

"But why? I mean he and Melanie had differences, but murder? And he couldn't have known Abby."

"The bank where Abby worked—they turned him down for a loan that same day. She was part of the lending committee."

"But we're talking about murders here. Two of them. Over a teaching assignment and a loan? These are motives?"

"Bree," he said, his voice low and almost secretive, "you're never going to know all the answers. The man is dead and you're alive. No trial. Done. It's good for all of us."

Good for all of us. I don't have to undergo a trial and Andrew Bennett doesn't have to relive Abigail's murder. Marcus Johns doesn't have to hear murmurs about his wife sleeping with another man. And Brandt, that other man, won't be linked to Melanie, because if some shrewd attorney discovered an affair between them—wouldn't that impugn Melanie's motives? Sure she was a victim and didn't deserve to be killed, but if her immorality allowed her to break the marriage vows, wouldn't it also allow her to blackmail Joe Lawrence, to threaten to expose the seamy side of Chalmers College unless Lawrence agreed to pay her off somehow? Maybe she wanted her job back, but maybe that became a minimum requirement once she discovered Lawrence's scheme. Then of course there's Brandt pulling the trigger on the man who killed the woman he loved, the adulterous relationship notwithstanding. A trial would be a mess beyond imagining and nobody would come out of it unscathed.

Brandt is right: good for all of us.

Except he's lying. He just is. Maybe some of his account is true, maybe most of it. But in that jumble of images competing for space inside my mind, none of them involves a forced entry and a cop in the doorway. And then there's Teddy, and there's Jill. I keep thinking they were there. Then again, I missed a gunshot. How out of it was I? How much was I imagining? Did I really see them or was I linking them together because I knew she had hired him?

I have the peace of mind of knowing that Joe Lawrence can't hurt me anymore, or hurt anyone else. The fine details—maybe they'll sift down in time. Plus, Teddy is the world's worst liar: if there's more to it, and if he knows it, there's little chance that I won't eventually know it too.

"Maybe you should get some rest now," Brandt says.

"Just...one thing...where was Lawrence shot? I mean was he on my bed?"

"He came at me as soon as I got in."

"And where did he die?"

"He was DOA at the Brigham."

"One shot to the chest. Of all the cops that could have shown up...."

"It's appropriate force."

"What?"

"What I did. Shooting him. Given the circumstances my use of force was within department guidelines."

"Even though he wasn't armed."

He nods. "The threat to you, the intent of his attack, my belief that he would do more bodily harm were he to escape—all that justifies my action."

"I'm not questioning what you did—I just mean it's lucky it was you and not someone who wasn't that good a shot."

"Are you done?"

"What do you mean?"

"You're here," he says, his voice as calm as I've ever heard from him. "And you're alive. No one is practicing a eulogy for you and I'm not assuring your parents that we'll find the guy who did this. Because it didn't happen. Do you understand that?"

"Of course I do. I just..."

"Why don't you just express some gratitude that you're alive—that you're a little bruised up instead of dead—or isn't that something worthy of appreciation?"

"I wasn't trying to make you angry...."

"Then stop talking," he says. "And get some rest."

*****

The surgeon who rebuilt my face wants me to wear some sort of plastic mask when I sleep. It's hideous almost beyond description and I'd just as soon not have Brandt see me in it, not if I ever want him to find me desirable again. Out of his sight and in the dark I slip it on. If he hears the Velcro that holds it together, he doesn't respond. As he suggested—commanded I suppose—I'll get some rest.

At 2:17 in the morning I get up to pee—at least one of my bodily functions has rebounded. I glance into the living room and Brandt is asleep on the couch, his clothes well on their way to being unsalvageable. He stirs when I take another step, and when I come out of the bathroom, he's sitting up. I get a glimpse of him on my way to the bedroom.

"You all right?" he says.

"I'm fine. You should maybe get home, you know, for Linda's sake."

"I don't have to anymore," he says. "I'll keep the TV low."

It's late and he's tired—I can dismiss his lack of interest easily, but we're not going to sleep together anymore. Not ever. I think we both know that much.

My thoughts keep trampolining from one idea to the next, and as if that's not bad enough, there's something else trying to work its way out from the inside, something that I should be considering—but I don't know what it is. As secure as I should feel, my first thought when I close my eyes—my only thought—is Joe Lawrence choking me. But then it's Lawrence himself—the man we all thought we knew. Unless you live in Drayton, you can't possibly grasp the impact of his crime. It's not that he was merely someone with a clean record—every criminal commits his first offense. But Lawrence had led a life of public service, self-aggrandizing or not. If he had been indicted for embezzlement, fraud, some sort of misappropriation of funds, even sleeping with a student, I'd have nodded and recalled all my negative notions of the guy and simply moved on. But murder? I still can't draw a mental picture of Joe Lawrence standing outside the Bennett house in the snow, waiting for Abigail to arrive so that he could bludgeon her to death—or waiting in Silvermine for Melanie to reach a spot on the trail where he could cut her throat. Lawrence was a big guy, probably strong, and maybe like most of us capable of some pretty awful things. But murder? How do you take the life from a person and just walk away? I'd prefer to lay that sort of thing at the feet of Deron Hillis, but I can't: that creep was still in jail back then.

Sleep does not return easily—a combination of bumps, bruises and intermittent flashes from the other room that remind me that Brandt remains awake. Old habits, I guess: all the times he and Linda were estranged and he'd fall asleep watching TV—now he's at it again. Maybe if I were a better person I'd go out there and try to be some company, but I pushed him too far before and I'm afraid we no longer have much common ground.

Fatigue finally renders my thoughts less frenetic, and as soon as I'm able to sort them, I remember a conversation with Teddy when he said that bookies never murder their marks. If they do, he said, the money is deceased too. With Joe Lawrence dead someone is holding a lot of useless…chits Teddy called them, that's the word.

So someone somewhere is lamenting the death of Joe Lawrence. That's one more person than I'd have hoped for.

Chapter 29

It's an odd thing, being sick like that. You think you'll never get better and then you just do. Within days of Brandt's playing nursemaid and treating me like the invalid I was, we're taking walks around the apartment complex or he's driving my car and buying me ice cream. I'm still not sure what our relationship is, but I no longer sense imminent death and, maybe for that reason, I don't need to know. Time will settle it and I have time.

I still ponder the motives but I don't obsess over them. And I haven't had any contact with Andrew Bennett or Marcus Johns. Its not that I don't care, it's just that for one thing the death of Joseph Lawrence is not going to return their wives to them so I can't imagine their feeling any joy. But also, if they're curious about the motives and I'm curious also, the chemistry would not be good. Nicholas Bennett's birthday is the Fourth of July. I'll send a card and maybe a gift or some money and let things go from there. As of now those people have to heal too.

My involvement in this whole sorry mess could have ended right there—right with Brandt telling me to shut up and go to sleep. But one day, out of nowhere, Joe Lawrence's wife sends me an email through my *Courier* address and asks if we can meet for coffee. My first impulse is to refuse—if she's going to put some spin on her husband's murderous behavior, I'm not going to be able to feign acceptance. But she's been quiet in the aftermath—no public statements—and I can't claim to be a journalist and turn this down just because I'm not comfortable with it. I agree to meet her at Deal's and, when I arrive, find her alone in the last booth, facing the door. I approach her tentatively—I've only seen her face in pictures—but it's her and I slide into the booth so that I'm facing her.

"I'm glad you were able to come," she says. "Are you recovering from what happened?"

She's not supposed to know what happened, or at least my role in it.

"I'm not sure I know what you mean," I tell her.

She nods. "Don't worry, I'll respect your privacy. I guess I know more than most about this...this whole thing. I was just wondering about you."

"I'm better," I tell her, and that's all. I don't want to go into detail about how her husband smashed my face, choked me, and came close to killing me. I'm pretty sure she doesn't want to hear it either. Her phrase, *what happened*, will suffice.

A waitress—I guess the guy in the baseball cap works only in the evening—brings two coffees. "I ordered one for you," Mrs. Lawrence says. "I hope that's okay."

"It's fine, thank you, Mrs. Lawrence." I remember my little feuds with Jill Dennison over hot beverages. So meaningless. I hope those days are gone.

"Please call me Virginia," she says. "I just wanted you to know a few things. I'm not asking you to forgive him and I'm not trying to excuse what he did."

"I understand."

"Joe was...he was an ambitious man when I married him. I think he thought he'd be governor some day, not just a local politician. But he had a way about him that sometimes just, you know, put people off."

"Politics is tough."

"Then the college came along and made him the offer. It was politics again, but different. So he took it. Chalmers did well with Joe in charge."

I want to tell her that Chalmers did well because he was practically subsidized by the state and the Feds while he populated the place with creeps and felons. Maybe she knows. Certainly it no longer matters.

"That's true," I tell her. "The college made money."

"And he did too. But enough was never enough. He was always looking for a business deal—something he could invest in with a high return. The casino they're building over in Springfield, he was so angry to have missed out on that. He said it was a gold mine but he was too late. When he did find something and made the investment, the new project collapsed and we lost everything. He had always gambled for fun," she says, and looks almost nostalgic. "He told me once he loved the sound of the cards, the moment of tension as they were turned up, the vulnerable omnipotence of the dealer, the joy of watching others' systems fail. But when he was almost broke he started gambling to survive. He wasn't good at that."

I remember what Teddy said about gambling debts and the means used to collect them, but before I can respond, she continues.

"I tried to get him involved in Gamblers Anonymous. He said he didn't have a problem."

"I understand denial," I tell her. Our family thrives on it.

"For a long time," she says, her tone more contemplative, "I didn't really understand how bad it all was. We always had money—not extravagance, but comfort. Then we didn't. He never used to care what I bought; then he began questioning everything. I don't want you to feel sorry for me because I had to return a dress or two—that's nothing compared to what you went through—to what he did to those other girls."

She shakes her head. Regret? Disbelief? I don't know. I'm pretty sure, though, I won't be able to help her—be able to pull someone out those depths of disappointment and loneliness.

"How are you getting on, Mrs. Lawrence?"

"I'm getting on. Joe had a life insurance policy through the college so I won't lose the house. I do have some friends who haven't abandoned me, and my face is not so well known that I can't walk through the grocery store or go to the gas station. Other than that, I mostly stay around the house."

I tell her that things will get better over time—it's something to say and I do partially believe it. I've been sipping at the coffee throughout, hoping that an empty cup will signal an end to this conversation. It doesn't.

"Then the trouble at the college began."

"What trouble?"

"Kids. He had some bad actors there and some of the local cops had it in for them. They started making arrests and the reputation of the school began to drop. People stayed away. Enrollment is way off this semester, and the summer session wasn't filling up the way it used to. Then some of the staff got on his case."

"Do you know who?"

"He never told me—one of them was that girl that was killed around Christmas. He seemed so broken up about that. I don't want to believe he was responsible, but I guess there's evidence."

"Melanie Johns," I tell her. "I know her sister."

"Terrible thing, but I refuse to live in denial. Everything seemed to go to hell after his loan application was denied."

"I did hear something about that."

"I guess the word is out there. Still, is that a reason to kill someone? To do something that awful. That Bennett woman had a kid. The women themselves were just kids."

Virginia Lawrence has been holding it together pretty well, but she takes a tissue from her purse and dabs her eyes. No sense mentioning Nicholas's name or the fact that Abby and I were friends.

"Sorry," she says. "It's easier to live in denial."

I'm sure it is, but her refusal to accept the motives is no different from mine. I insisted to Brandt that nobody commits murder over such trivial matters, but here's Virginia Lawrence uttering the same denial and unwillingly accepting the same motives. I remember that logical fallacy from a writing course—*post hoc ergo propter hoc*—just because something happens after something else doesn't mean it happened because of it. But in this case I'm not so sure. Maybe the causes and effects multiplied, became larger than themselves, and the tragedies spilled out of monstrous errors in judgment.

She's finished the coffee taken out her wallet.

"I can still afford coffee," she says with a half-smile.

"In this place, so can I. It's on me."

She thanks me for coming and I follow her out to her car, a small blue sedan that Joe Lawrence would certainly never have been seen in. A second car—now probably the only car. We've cleared the air, Virginia Lawrence and I, and she's ready to go home. There's no reason in the world for me to hold her back, but every once in a while I still display the instincts of a reporter and feel obliged to follow them. This time it's something in her story that didn't sit right.

"The investment that he made, Virginia, the one that fell through. What was it?"

She's already in the car with the motor running. Some mystical power is urging her to leave and urging me to let her go, but goddamn it all, we both ignore it.

"Crazy stuff," she says, shaking her head. "For someone as conservative as Joe. Just crazy."

"How crazy?"

I keep asking the questions, but I already know the answer; and even though I don't want her to say it, there's some malevolent force, some perverse power— no, that's bullshit—it's me wanting to hear it.

"How crazy?"

"Wind turbines," she says. "Can you imagine? Wind turbines."

Chapter 30

Remember that old concept of a butterfly flapping its wings in South America and a resultant hurricane developing in the Caribbean? Chaos theory. I know it was part of a math course in college, but either I was high that day, or the professor was high, or the stuff was so abstruse that we might as well have all been high. But now, just like everything else I declared bullshit in my younger days, it's coming back to bite me in the ass.

So who killed Abigail Bennett and Melanie Johns and planned to kill that artist?

Yes, Joe Lawrence. But I set everything into motion—started the wheels turning when I decided that sleeping with an old classmate just for fun was a good idea. And if that was a good idea, how much better would it be to convert the little tidbits of information I picked up while we were both drunk, and form them into an article that would prove what a sterling addition I was to the Courier *staff? Once I did that, lying to my boss was easy. And afterward when I had to eat some crow, well, no harm done. No wind turbines in Drayton: as my friend Abby might have said, who fucking cares?*

But now I know the answer. Joe Lawrence did.

But even that's only one part of the answer. What I don't know is the effect on others, not so much other investors, because my dad told me more than once never to invest money I couldn't afford to lose. But there would have been a multitude of jobs that came with it—construction of course, but all the ancillary work too: transportation, clerical, even maintenance after the fact—all gone because I felt like getting naked with somebody.

I can't say any of this out loud. It's a pity-party in full bloom, and it's nothing compared to what Andrew Bennett faces daily, trying to raise a scared kid as a single parent—or Marcus Johns passing by that telescope he bought Melanie and afraid to move it because it's become a shrine to the woman he married. And Jill who lost a sister...and Abigail's folks...someone should have netted that butterfly in South America before it decided to move that current of air.

*****

A WEEK AFTER THE installation of my new face, I return to work. The discoloration has diminished greatly, and though I feel a little puffy, to the rest of the world I probably look like just another sleep-deprived worker bee. Grumman sends out for sandwiches from across the street—he does that occasionally—and we're all sitting at our own desks, Grumman at a work table. Asking him about his cancer puts him in a foul mood, so even though I feel as if I've lost contact with everything, the fact that he's there and socializing and looks pretty much the same as he has for the past six months will have to suffice as the answer to the question I'm not supposed to ask.

Teddy called a few times while I was laid up but I didn't really want visitors—now he's solicitous to an extreme and practically catapults himself out of his chair whenever I need anything. His over-attentiveness today provides almost constant amusement for Arlene, who baits him by wondering aloud if I need another tissue or would like more iced tea or if I need help getting to the bathroom. Dirty looks only encourage her.

After lunch Teddy is off on another pedestrian assignment at a middle school, and Arlene and I talk occasionally about nothing in particular. The afternoon reminds me of many similar ones in the days before Christmas, before the murders, before every scintilla of normality seemed strained. It's gratifying to be able to go back, but still it's different. Not only can you not go home again—you can't go anywhere again. When I let Grumman in on my fairly commonplace epiphany, he sloughs it off.

"This wasn't your fault," he says, and motions me into the chair near his desk.

"A lot of it was."

"My job," he says, "and it's still my job regardless of having a headache or the flu or lung cancer—my job is to make sure you do yours. And when you don't, I'm supposed to make you pay. I didn't do that—I gave you a little slap on the wrist and told you to be more careful. I should have suspended you—two weeks without pay, maybe more—and I should have told you that if it ever happened again you were gone."

"I'm glad you didn't."

"Yeah. But minimizing harm—I didn't do that. And once you violate the ethics code in any way, you've violated all of it. I'd like to think that isn't true, but it is. There are no exceptions, no immunities. I sit here and rail against all the crap on the Internet—how none of it is vetted, most of it is illiterate. But I can't go criticizing it if I'm no better. So before you go carrying your cross all over eastern Massachusetts, try to remember that this is shared responsibility."

"Thanks, but I still know what I did."

"Hell, everyone knows what you did. I'm just telling you not to do it again. You want to beat yourself up, be my guest. Just try to keep straight in your head where remorse becomes ego."

"I don't understand."

"That project could have died at a hundred different turns along the way—it just so happened to die at yours. Maybe. But maybe some investors were dying to get out and used your little indiscretion as an excuse. Believing it was you who exercised all that power? That's just ego, nothing more. God, Bree, not everything is about you."

"I know that."

"Then act like it."

"I will, but I can undo some harm, maybe," I tell him. "I'll be out of the office for a while."

"Half hour," he says. "That should be enough time to fix everything."

It's enough time to start maybe, and all I have to do is cross the street. Jay-Van's outer door is locked, but through the frosted glass there appears to be at least a glimmer—a desk lamp maybe, a computer screen? My knock produces nothing. I try again. Same response. I have the Jay-Van number on my cell, so I try that, and though I can hear a phone ringing beyond the door, nobody picks up. This isn't terribly suspicious. I mean if the dentist's office door had been locked, that would have been weird—all his work is done on site, so to speak. But real estate only exists outside the office, and though there may be no lack of paperwork going on behind the scenes, it can hardly be considered unusual for both women to be showing a house somewhere, or attending a closing, or checking on a title or deed or any other legal aspect of their business.

More out of frustration than expectation, I knock again.

The beam of artificial light I thought I saw is obstructed for a moment. Someone is in there. I figure I'll take a guess.

"Vanessa?"

Calling out Miss something-or-other would probably sound more professional, but I've forgotten her last name, or I never knew it, so I try again. Nothing.

"Miss Dennison?"

Now I know what solicitors feel like when they approach a house they know is filled with people, yet no one will answer the door, or some officer of the court with a subpoena is trying to serve someone who refuses to be seen. My knocking rises a level or two—it isn't quite pounding, but it's close. I do it again and I see a shadow approaching the glass and hear the lock slide open. The door opens and there's a stranger staring at me. Jeans, sweatshirt, running shoes—she looks as though she's been moving furniture all morning.

"Yes?"

"I came to see Jill Dennison."

"She isn't here."

"How about Vanessa?"

"The office is closed."

The woman looks familiar though I don't think I've ever met her. She doesn't seem at all interested in conversation or explanation—that much is obvious—but she seems more annoyed than secretive. Either way, I don't want her to close the door yet.

"Do you work here with Jill and Vanessa?"

"Do I look like I work in a professional office? If you've come on business, call first and I'll arrange for you to speak with someone."

I shake my head and the woman starts to close the door.

"I'm Brianna Cooper from across the way."

"Across what way?"

"From the *Courier*, the paper. I haven't seen Jill since...for a while. I was just wondering how she was doing."

"The reporter, I know who you are," she says and tilts her head at some odd angle. I've seen this look before and heard this voice and suffered the glare of similar eyes. It took me a moment, but I know who this is.

"You're Jill's sister."

"And you're the one who was supposed to help her. You were going to make things right."

"I never said...."

"You told her that the first time she called. She has a lot of foibles, but she doesn't lie."

I guess I did tell her that, or something pretty close to that, and I probably said it on Christmas when I wanted her to leave me alone.

"I have tried to help, but I'm not a cop, just a reporter."

"How come you people are 'just reporters' until you uncover something like Watergate or Madoff or Guantanamo? Then you're our national conscience? Why don't all of us deserve that same tenacity?"

She's Jill's sister all right in sloppy dress—but nice hair, good makeup, nothing overdone the way Jill sometimes is. The outfit may be casual but she's a pro: this is not the time for some condescending explanation on the differing roles of investigative and beat reporters.

"When Jill first contacted me, she came on pretty strong."

"Melanie had just been murdered."

"And I had just come from my best friend's funeral. Maybe I could have been in a better frame of mind, but I wasn't and I can't go back and change that. I did what I could."

"What was that exactly? Aside from dating the man we thought murdered our sister?"

"You know he didn't do it."

"I know it now. I find it convenient that he killed the alleged murderer and that he no longer faces scrutiny, but that's neither here nor there."

"Joseph Lawrence was guilty."

"Maybe so, but there'll never be a trial so there'll never be a judgment or a confession. But like you said, you're just a reporter. Is there anything else I can do for you?"

"I guess...no...I just wondered how Jill was doing."

"Jill is fine."

She snaps off the response, curt, dismissive. Reporters get the kiss-off all the time, but this one seems too unfair for me to just tuck in my tail and leave.

"Tell her I was asking for her."

"I'll leave a note with Vanessa."

"Can you just have Jill call me?"

"I'll see," she says. I know she won't.

"I don't even know your name."

"Some reporter you are," she says, a little less icily. "Melanie's's obituary listed her siblings."

"Do I have to go back and read it?"

"I'm Faith. Please don't use me as a source."

"I'm not...this is not official. I'm truly sorry about Melanie. If I could have done more, I would have, but I never knew who she was until after."

"It's ancient history already," she says, her tone a little less harsh. "People die and we realize that nobody is indispensable. Isn't that true? Isn't Melanie old news?"

"Jill told me so much about her—always said I would have liked her."

"Everybody liked her. Look, I really have to get back to work."

"So you do work here."

"I don't live in this office so if I'm here I must be working."

"Jill and I—just so you know—we talked plenty of times, and I think we pissed each other off plenty of times, but we always left the door open in our own weird ways. And even when Melanie's death was fresh and immediate, she was usually cordial."

"Jill isn't a phony so I doubt if she was cordial."

"Honest, then."

She smiles at the understatement. The sister is pretty, like Jill, but I'd bet she works harder at it. Jill is a little more slapdash.

"Anyway," she says. "Jill's not around."

"Is she in trouble?"

I don't even know why I asked that question. Some past conversation with Teddy—I think it was Teddy—and a reference to psychological problems in college. Faith shows no emotion, just the same pique in a modified version.

"If she were, what kind of assistance could you offer? Are you an attorney?"

"I told you, I'm...."

"A reporter, I know."

"I didn't come here as a reporter."

"Well if you came here as a friend, then what took you so long?"

"I was laid up for a while. This was my first chance to get over here."

I point to my face which still hasn't returned to normal.

"I can see that. You couldn't call?"

I don't want to tell her I was Joseph Lawrence's last victim, even though that would probably assuage some of her anger. Even if it garnered me some sympathy, I'm still alive and facing a minimum of short term inconveniences. Melanie wasn't that fortunate.

"We're off to a bad start here," I say, then stop. And smile. She looks puzzled.

"Something funny?"

"Sort of. I'm pretty sure Jill made the exact same statement to me a few months back. You and I, Jill and I—bad starts."

"I can hear my sister saying that. Nobody gets off to bad starts better than Jill."

"Honestly, Faith, I'm not looking for a story. I really just wanted to say hello. I haven't seen her lately and I just wondered if she felt better...or maybe relieved, you know, with Lawrence dead."

"It doesn't undo the harm, but it's the end of the episode. Now we move on. All of us. That includes you, Ms. Cooper. You and Jill aren't friends—you're merely two people who lost someone close. Now that chapter is finished and that relationship is over."

"I don't agree. I think we were friends." Her sister frowns, but within the denial there's at least a hint of uncertainty. No sense letting it pass. "Please have Jill call me. She has my cell."

"If she wants to call you, it's up to her. I'll tell her we spoke."

She maintains a neutral expression—it certainly isn't a smile but it's not a scowl either—then gently pushes the door closed. I hear the lock snap shut and watch a shadow move away. I listen for a minute or two, half convinced that Jill is in there. But the only sounds I hear emanate from an office down the hall where a UPS man is dropping off a package and bantering with someone I can't see.

I'm pretty sure Jay-Van is closed, and even more sure that, for the Jay half of it, it's permanent.

Chapter 31

It's Memorial Day and we've decided against a big American flag above the fold. Arlene agreed that we should play up something local and Teddy didn't care one way or the other. Eric Wilcox, that high school teacher who was supposed to keep an eye on me back before all hell broke loose—before Joe Lawrence came after me three months ago—sees nothing wrong with our decision, just reminds us that citizens in towns like ours have expectations, and something construed as unpatriotic could have ramifications. We're all agonizing over seemingly simple decisions like this now that Dan Grumman is gone.

I've stopped pouring my emotions into my recording app too. Maybe the unexamined life is not worth living, but I'm not that sure about the over-examined life either. I've been obsessed with Joe Lawrence for months—not only his utter depravity, but the ease with which I became a victim—then Dan Grumman enters the hospital for a routine procedure and never comes out. What difference did my obsession make? Or my reporting? Or my observations spilled out like tiles in some mah-jongg game nobody cares to win.

*****

Maintenance, Grumman called it in mid-April, something about draining fluid from his lungs. It didn't even require general anesthesia, he said, so he'd be able to watch the whole creepy affair if he wanted to. He even threatened to take pictures. Then there'd be an overnight stay, maybe two, home for a while, then back to the *Courier*. After an over-long winter, early spring had been almost dazzling, and despite the usual instability of profits and losses, the paper was doing okay and so, it seemed, was Grumman. But it was his wife who phoned the following morning, and while Teddy and I watched, Arlene kept the phone pressed to her ear and kept turning her face farther and farther away from us. As soon as I heard her call Elise by name, I knew. So did Teddy. Both of us sat there and waited for the conversation to end, both of us hoping it wouldn't.

"When?" I asked, as soon as she hung up. She had expressed her sympathy so many times that there was little doubt about what happened.

"Just before one this morning," she said in that way she has of making all news, good or bad, simply news. "His heart stopped sometime after midnight and they couldn't start it again."

"The procedure," I said.

"Went off without a hitch," Arlene said. "Elise left around nine."

"But his heart was fine," I said. Of course I had no idea whether his heart was fine or beset by some virulent condition that was waiting for the slightest trauma—like draining his lungs—to just shut down. He'd been a smoker—he wasn't much for staying in shape—there could have been a myriad of reasons why a man in his sixties just dies, but instead of admitting that, I decided to deny Arlene's statement, as if she exercised full control over living and dying, recovery and death. Teddy said nothing at first, just sat and stared, then had another one of those moments that surprise us.

"Cancer takes its toll," he said, "in ways we can't imagine."

I didn't push him on it—he must have known someone who went the same way. I thought of my father, Grumman's wife, this job—and I'm not sure of the order. I'd like to think it was Elise first—someone roughly my mother's age who will now have to go it alone. That analogy doesn't work for me though: my mother has opted to go it alone for years and I'm pretty sure my father's death would be a momentary impediment around which she'd be able to step quite deftly and move on. That may sound callous, but it's no less true for that. And in fact my father is like Grumman in many ways, once you take away the nicotine addiction. He's been a sporadic exerciser and a sporadic healthy eater, but work keeps him busy and his wife keeps him on edge—and I'm never sure how much that distant son weighs on him, or on both of them.

As for my job and the *Courier*—how long do they last without Dan Grumman? No one is indispensable—no one is irreplaceable—we all learn hard truths like that by the time we get out of our teens, but if there are exceptions, I thought I might be about to suffer one of them.

As the initial paralysis began to dissipate, Arlene started ticking off what needs to be done initially—flowers, she said, and statements.

"We're going to be interviewed," she said. "This is a big deal in Drayton, and other papers will be on it. These days there is no competition between papers—they're all in this together—and if the *Courier* goes under, it hurts everyone."

If the *Courier* goes under—Arlene was the first to verbalize what Teddy and I were thinking, but she made it sound as though it was not a done deal, so we never even commented—just let her continue.

"And there'll be TV news too—we're a business people rely on. Expect to be interviewed. Know what you're going to say. Some of these TV people have no shame: they'll ask you questions that either have no answers or that already include the answers. They don't want your opinion—they simply want you to corroborate theirs while some videographer records the whole sorry mess."

She was angry—I had heard her lambaste field reporters before but never with quite so much vitriol. And she wasn't done.

"Be ready to take over the interview," she said. "Redirect questions. Have an agenda and get it out there. They want to look pretty on camera? Fine. Make sure they look stupid too."

Her eyes were glassy but she was holding her sorrow in check by channeling it into anger. We were silent for a moment, then Teddy cleared his throat, looked round the office, and said with some hesitancy, "So we're not all in this together."

I laughed, and so did Arlene, and we shunted away our concerns for job security, at least for a while, and prepared for the onslaught. Arlene was right. Papers from as far away as Hartford wanted more than the press release we gave them, and over the next day or two, I spoke with several correspondents by phone—spoke to people who asked good questions and allowed me to respond comfortably. Only the *Globe* sent an actual person to the office, a young man who looked (but could not have been) younger than Teddy. At times he seemed almost manic, as if his thoughts raced ahead of him so fast that he couldn't keep up. But through it all his questions were measured and he never hurried our responses. Even better, he knew how to elicit answers without asking asinine questions—a concept a local TV reporter should have practiced before he asked me to "talk to him" about how much the *Courier* was going to miss Daniel Grumman.

I thought of Arlene and said, "talk to you? Isn't that what I'm doing now?"

That particular exchange did not make the 6:00 news. Maybe I should have asked him what kind of asshole wants me to quantify the loss of a human being, but instead I waited silently. To his credit he was able to rephrase the question in such a way that I could list all the functions that Dan Grumman fulfilled on the paper. I even managed to work in the quote he had framed on his office wall, the one about absolute truth; and even though the reporter dismissed it, I thought I owed that much to Grumman. Arlene said to make them look stupid. I tried for a while—even succeeded momentarily—but even on his worst day Grumman would have been courteous to colleagues and provided a story: I couldn't do any less.

The wake was well attended, the funeral too. The burial took place in a small cemetery I never knew existed, a treeless expanse that provided no relief from the unseasonable heat that had everyone murmuring about a boiling summer. But nobody fainted, and then it was over. As Teddy, Arlene, and I left the graveside, Arlene said "we can get Eric to help us, maybe some of his students. He's always talking about a baby someday—he can use the money." And that was that—the *Courier* would continue to publish. No one is indispensable—no one is irreplaceable. At night though, home and alone, I cried a lot, most times unable to distinguish between tears I shed for Grumman and his wife, and the ones I shed for myself. I tried to remember if, on that day when Grumman admitted he should have suspended me or worse, I ever thanked him for not doing it. I can't remember.

*****

Memorial Day and I'm driving on the Mass Pike. I'm headed west, restoring balance to the state—everyone else has already gone east to the ocean. Alone in the car with some 90's hits to remind me of middle school, I keep thinking of feature ideas—like observing how many mental health facilities have trees in their names. There's Birch Hill over near Worcester and Maple Acres up on the north shore. Growing up outside Portland, kids were always threatened with a spell over at Three Oaks when they misbehaved, and I had an uncle who spent time in Shading Elms. I guess just the sound of a name that includes trees has some restorative value—they flourish, fade, come back every spring good as new.

Jill Dennison is at Five Willows. Even without any real help from her sister Faith, figuring that out wasn't difficult—she's been there before and she made the mistake of telling Teddy without adding that he shouldn't share the information. Five Willows occupies a beautiful piece of property in the Berkshires just north and west of Pittsfield, not far from the New York border. It's a two-hour ride on a chaotic turnpike which, after Springfield, becomes a leisurely and scenic excursion all the way out to Lenox. But Five Willows, despite its evocative title, looks pretty much like what it is—an asylum. It reminds me of a college administration building, all brick with white trim and a bell tower in the middle rising up above all else. Three stories tall and longitudinal as a barn on an egg farm, it's meticulously landscaped with stone and cinder blocks and what must be truckloads of that red mulch that looks like colored tortilla chips.

An American flag droops on a flagpole near the circle in front, and I drive around it and park in the nearly empty visitor's area next to one of the ubiquitous willows. (Whoever named the place may have stopped counting at five, but he could have gone much higher.) It's the weekend and I expect there'd be more families there to visit the, well what do we call them, inmates? tenants? clients? Whatever we call them, they're not being disturbed by visitors.

"Jill Dennison," I say to the receptionist who provides no greeting but simply nods. Has she confused me with one of the residents who has gone off for a morning's shopping?

"Are you expected?"

"I called yesterday, said I'd be here at noon."

She looks at the wall where an enormous clock clicks away the seconds. 11:10.

"Light traffic. I made good time." I hold up two coffee cups. "I even stopped at Dunkin'."

"We don't allow our patients to have outside food."

"Then it's yours if you'd like it."

Her face finally shows something other than annoyance. She reminds me a little bit of Marcie, Joe Lawrence's secretary who, incidentally, is still working at Chalmers for the interim president; but unlike Marcie who smiles and jokes but whose face always seems plastic, this woman's eyes really do twinkle when she allows them to. It's too bad—there probably isn't much demand for twinkling at Five Willows. And they're called patients, so that's good to know.

"I just had one, but thank you." She pulls a cup from behind the counter and waves it. Proof I guess. "I can't let you see Miss Dennison until noon. She needs to be prepared."

"Prepared?"

"Bathed, cleaned, taken to the bathroom—typical morning routine."

"Really? Jill can't do those things herself?"

"Actually she can, but some days she chooses not to."

"From way back," I say, remembering Teddy's college story. "Is there any place I can wait for the next...wow...45 minutes?"

She points to a small room off the lobby.

"I'll do my best to hurry things along" and she consults her schedule before adding, "Ms. Cooper."

I thank the woman—Deborah Saunders it says on her deskplate which I finally notice—and head off toward the waiting room. The chairs are comfortable and the magazines are varied, but the ambient light befits a place where sensitive historical documents are kept under protective glass. I put both coffee cups on an end table and check my phone messages. Two of them need follow-up, but not immediately, so I pick up a copy of *Good Housekeeping* for the first time since I was, oh, maybe three and showing off to my parents how well I could read. Now I'm more interested in pictures—a chocolate cake recipe that looks appealing. Five layers—two has always been my limit, and one is my normal output. I won't be baking that little item. Then it occurs to me that I'm unprepared for this visit and rush back to Ms. Saunders.

"Do you have any pamphlets?"

"Do you wish to refer someone?"

"Me, probably, but not right now."

She smiles—how many times has someone said that to her?

"I was wondering if you have some advice on how to talk to...someone...who has been committed here."

"Not like that," she says, the smile broader now. "They know why they're here and they know why you're here. Euphemisms don't work very well. I do have some pamphlets, but basically, just be understanding."

"That's it?"

"It isn't that easy. You're living in a rational world full of causes and effects, where actions cause predictable reactions. Our patients, most of them anyway, are tangentially aware of that world but can't seem to stay inside it. Sometimes it makes them angry."

"So what do I say?"

"That there's a place for them, that it takes time. If they have that goal, then it has to be broken down into small steps—meeting with counselors, using medication, getting regular exercise, making individual decisions. But don't list them—lists are daunting. Pick one."

"I can do that."

"And talk in general terms about what she'll be doing when she's better. Be positive, even if she's not."

Deborah consults a chart she's pulled up on her computer.

"It says here she worked in real estate. You can maybe feel her out—see if she wants to go back to that—make it appear to be a reasonable goal."

"It's not?"

"That's for the professional staff to decide—and Jill herself. If things she says make you uncomfortable, just listen. Don't judge. Do you still want the pamphlet?"

"You are the pamphlet, Ms. Saunders. Thanks."

"You can call me Deborah. Wait here. And it's probably safe to give Miss Dennison that coffee."

She punches some numbers on a phone console. Moments later an orderly brings Jill Dennison to the lobby where we exchange nods of recognition— nothing more. Maybe this wasn't such a good idea after all. The orderly—a man in his sixties I'd bet—leads us to an enclosed sunporch where we sit on some wrought-iron summer furniture as the sun permeates the walls of glass. I wouldn't want to be here in July.

Jill's appearance hasn't changed much—shorter hair, a little less color in her face. It's not that I expected some metamorphosis: wild-eyed lunatics have no place at Five Willows; instead it's populated by young women who might just as believably be on their way to some job as a legal secretary or company exec. A pair of them passed by me earlier while I was waiting, both of them smiling my way, welcoming me to their world which (and they know this) is no less crazy than mine. Jill smiles the same smile and removes her ubiquitous wool sweater, exposing the remainder of a chenille floor-length bathrobe, a hideous shade of royal blue. She tosses the sweater on another chair.

"Remember when orderlies were cute college kids?" she says, motioning toward the one who has barely left the room. "Jimmy there finished college before I was born."

"Maybe they don't want you being tempted by handsome young men."

"No chance of that with Jimmy," she says. "I'm so glad you came."

I don't even miss a beat: I start crying right away.

Not bawling or weeping—I'm under control—but my cheeks are wet and my vision is blurred and Jill Dennison is quickly traipsing around looking for Kleenex.

"Here," she says, handing me the box. "Didn't Saunders give you a pamphlet to read?"

Now I'm crying and laughing at the same time and struggling for control. I try to muffle my sounds and I keep my back (and my heaving shoulders) to the lobby so that Ms. Saunders doesn't arrive to find out she wasted her time trying to educate a non-educable.

A fistful of tissues sufficiently dries my face and a nonchalant stroll to the ladies' room helps repair the collateral damage. When I come back Jill is drinking the tepid coffee and perusing a pamphlet.

"Listen," she says waving a pale green pamphlet as I sit down, "And I quote," she says, "*try to lower the stress level for your loved one*—that's me. And also...*everyday stresses that most of us are accustomed to can set back the recovery of a Five Willows resident*—that's also me. And I should tell you this, since you're probably never going to read it, if a resident should mention suicide, you should notify a professional. That's especially true with you, Coop. You're not the one to talk someone out of it. Rather the opposite."

"I'm okay now."

"You're supposed to be okay—that's why *you* are visiting *me*. I like the coffee. Still trying to convince me you don't like tea?"

"Did it work?"

"No. And it's such a long drive just to prove a point anyway. How long did it take you?"

"To buy the coffee? Maybe ten minutes."

A half-smile from Jill. "You know what I mean."

"About two hours."

"Lots of traffic?"

I shake my head, but I'm trying to steer the conversation in another direction.

"I didn't come here to talk about traffic."

"Do I have to read to you again—because there is a section about listening attentively and being receptive."

"Is there one on smoking?"

"Not in the building—there's an area where it's allowed. Want to see it?"

"That's all right, I believe you. And I don't know if you're dressed for outside."

"Dressing the way I want is just proof that I'm in charge."

"Are you?"

"Not at all. So tell me how you've been."

I'm not sure if my medical condition is permissible conversation, but I chance it and tell her about my surgery and recovery. She winces a few times, looks sympathetic, asks how much residual pain I have, wants to know if there are a lot of follow-up visits; in short, she wants details, not out of any morbid rationale, but because, seemingly, she needs some contact, dialogue, some connection. I haven't seen her since the incident, and for that matter, not many times in the weeks before. We weren't exactly buddies and I never felt I should keep in touch, even though I realize that she did, on occasion, reach out.

"My folks came out here Sunday." she says. "They said they'll drive out twice a month, though I don't think I'll be here that long, not at these prices. Faith came with them. You met Faith, huh?"

"We had a little chat in your office."

"She told me. She can be a screaming bitch when she wants to be. Hard to believe we're related, isn't it?"

"Mystifying," I tell her. "There wasn't any screaming though."

"So I was only half right. And she told you I was here. I'm surprised."

"It took some research."

"Oh, then Teddy told you. He'll never be confused with the man who put the P in PI."

"I think he felt sorry for me—I was jumping through so many hoops to find you that he just gave in. So I called your sister back and I guess she figured out I meant no harm.…sometimes I get a little too emotional."

"I never noticed that," she says, rolling her eyes practically out of their sockets.

The sun has hit just the right spot so that, no matter where in the room someone sits, it's blinding. "Come on," Jill says, and leads me outside where an awning provides some respite. "I meant what I said before—and don't get all weepy again—but I'm glad you came. And I'm glad you looked for me."

"But why are you here? Does the pamphlet allow me to ask that?"

"Comfortable surroundings—I like it."

"That's what Faith said, but why this time? Why now?"

"Mental illness is a funny thing—you're never really cured."

"That pamphlet must be awfully grim."

She smiles. "Actually it says just the opposite, but what the hell, you didn't read it anyway. How are things at the paper?"

"Good. The same."

"And Teddy? He's still not your boyfriend?"

"Right."

"I heard about your boss. I never knew him, but when someone has a reputation that solid, it's usually for a reason. How is his wife taking it?"

"They were married a long time—it's a tough adjustment."

"Do you visit?"

"I do. We all do."

"And your mother, do you visit her?"

"I'm not ready."

"Everyone's ready when the time requires it. You should reconcile with your mother first—that kind of baggage weighs you down."

"How do you know about that?"

"Poorly kept secret. You should take some time off—spend it with your folks."

"When that happens we can room together here."

"It's baggage—I'm telling you. Get rid of it. Will the paper survive?"

"We're okay for now. None of us wants to be in charge and we're afraid if we look for someone from the outside, we won't like him."

"Change is scary, speaking of which, I would be insensitive if I didn't inquire about your boyfriend. If what I know about the police is correct, he's seeing a shrink, too. How is that going?"

"He finished all that. He's back to work."

"I saw on the news that he took a lot of shit from the review board, but public opinion probably helped. You shoot someone who murdered young women, no one's going to complain too loudly. Shoot a college president, though…."

"Someone said he should have used a taser."

"Some asshole who probably never faced danger in his life. Were you at the hearing?"

"It was closed."

She nods.

"Figured that much. You know, for a long time it bothered me that he and I were mourning the same loss. I guess I'm over that. He's back on duty and working and all?"

"Yep, still on the job."

"And you two. Where's that headed?"

"It's not. You may not want to hear this, but I don't think he ever got over Melanie."

"I would think you're the one who doesn't want to hear that. Just proves that the heart doesn't know right from wrong. People always say trust your feelings, but you're also supposed to follow your conscience. They're never the same. I'm sure in his heart he still loves my sister, but that doesn't mean he shouldn't have known better."

"I guess that's one way to think of it."

"Around here after you count the willow trees, there's not much else to do but think of things like that. So, you're not seeing each other, you and Brandt?"

"I think we're giving it a rest for a while."

"Hmm."

"Hmm? What does that mean?"

"It usually takes couples a little longer than that to decide they need to reassess, reevaluate. You reached that point fast."

"We did, or I did. His shooting of Joe Lawrence—I mean he was absolved and all, and he certainly eradicated a creep from all our lives—but I could never get past that notion that he was avenging Melanie's death."

"But at that moment," Jill said, "did he even know that Lawrence had committed the two other murders?"

"I think he did. They had evidence that seemed scattered and messy, but once Joe Lawrence became part of the story, he fit in nicely."

"Maybe. But I think there's something else too as far as you and Brandt. You can't compete with a dead woman."

I'm surprised she said that, but it's true. Melanie can never again lose her temper, say something stupid, wreck the car, wear the wrong shade of lipstick, burn the muffins, or have her period when she and her husband have flown off for a romantic weekend. She can never succumb to time. To Karl Brandt she will always be a lovely twenty-something while I just get older and older.

"I don't think I ever could have competed."

Jill's eyes become enormous.

"Wow, I can't believe you admitted that. That had to be hard."

"It is, and I know it sounds like self-pity. It's not. It's just the way it is."

She's quiet for a moment, then smiles. "I don't think Melanie would have taken any pleasure in winning a competition with you, but you know how I always said you would have liked her? Maybe she would have liked you too."

"Maybe."

"Well, Coop—you don't mind if I call you that, do you? You used to get all pissed off."

"I was different then."

"I don't want you to make a mistake here—lose a chance at a normal life and a decent relationship because you misconstrue motives."

"With Karl Brandt?"

"With anyone."

"You never even liked Karl Brandt."

"I still don't. But you do, so he must have some redeeming value that I'm not aware of. Let me assure you. The shooting of Joe Lawrence was definitely revenge."

"But you just said...."

"Karl Brandt didn't shoot Joe Lawrence. I did. And I'd do it again."

Chapter 32

When I leave Five Willows I keep replaying Jill's confession, all of which was delivered with a disconcerting sangfroid, as if she were giving me a recipe over the phone, step by tedious step—add the milk, fold in the egg, quarter cup of sugar, point the gun, shoot the son of a bitch. Her account was so precise and explicit—it's hard to imagine she made it up. Besides, it was pretty much in keeping with her standard operating procedure: she spied on people, followed them, became a general nuisance. This time her annoying peccadilloes probably saved my life.

She was at Chalmers that day, then in town at Jay-Van. She saw me leave and followed me home. Or I should say she simply followed me. Just like the night I interviewed Marcus Johns, Jill seldom knew the destination—she just followed people. And in my case, she told me later, she thought I might someday be another victim. (It's probably just as well she never told me that before.)

But because she loves to eavesdrop and surveil, she knew Joseph Lawrence's car and license, and she saw it parked halfway down the second row of places. She investigated, found it was empty and she called Brandt.

"But you let me go into the apartment," I said.

"I blew it. I never thought for a minute he could get inside. I was expecting him to ring the bell."

"I wouldn't have let him in."

"Maybe not, but some people don't care. And I've seen plenty of times when a person who doesn't live someplace gets let in anyway with a smile or a wink or two bags of groceries and no free hand. It happens. Anyway, it was only after you went in that I acted."

"And how did *you* get in?"

"Real estate people have a pretty strict ethical code when it comes to access to homes. I may not be able to work in that field anymore."

She didn't admit to having a key, only claiming she had always been suspicious of Joseph Lawrence but couldn't see a firing or some harsh words as any reason to murder someone.

"He was broke," I said. "Desperate."

"So he was going to rob you and get back on his feet? It still doesn't make sense. There was more, but it's over and done with, and what's done cannot be undone," she said. "That's from *Macbeth*."

I'll assume it is. And as for there being more, that's something she can assume. I'm not ready to share my role in Joseph Lawrence's desperation.

But Jill is accurate to a fault, and her details are impeccable, except for the new ending.

"I just shot him," she says. "That's it."

Everything afterwards she isn't sharing, but that could explain her new residence—some reaction to the shock of having killed a man. When I leave that day and check out with Miss Saunders, she hints that Jill spends time at Five Willows on a more or less continuing basis.

"Sometimes people just need a rest," she says. "A little bit of rejuvenation."

"As long as she has visitors, I guess it's all right."

She looks sheepish. "Oh she never has visitors—you're the first."

"Her parents haven't been here? Not last Sunday?"

"I'm not here every minute, but—maybe I shouldn't do this. I can check the log."

"Would you?"

She does. No one has signed in to see Jill Dennison. Her parents live at the other end of the state practically in the Atlantic—I can't imagine their driving four hours to visit their daughter who, in almost every respect, is perfectly fine. So she lied to me, probably to avoid my pity. As Grumman might have said, absolute truth is a very rare and dangerous commodity—at least that's what the plaque on his wall said—says—it's still there.

So I leave feeling worse—at one point I'm tempted to race back in, à la *The Graduate*, convince Jill to come with me back to Drayton, then race away to the Mass Pike and points east. (My father would be gratified to know that all those movies we enjoyed had produced at least one positive effect.) Then again I don't have friends on the Pittsfield police force, and they might not appreciate the humor of my proposed abduction. But Jesus, to be stuck in the hills alone like that—I should have just been completely irresponsible and brought her a carton of cigarettes. Why not? She's a big girl, certainly capable of reading and comprehending the Surgeon General's warnings; besides, what disease could be worse than disappearing into that anonymous Berskshire landscape, forgotten forever.

On the way home Karl calls my cell—just to talk, something he's done a few times since my recovery. His marriage having been officially terminated, he moved into an apartment near the police station. Drayton doesn't have any really run-down, high-crime areas, but he's found one that comes close—a tenement with an off-site landlord who has accumulated more code violations than any other property owner in town and finds it cheaper to pay the fines than rectify the problems. Having a cop living there will change this guy's perspective—at least that's what Brandt told me with a satisfyingly evil tone. I haven't yet shared Jill's confession with him—I think I want to hold onto the idea that he didn't lie to me, even though he did. And if he did it to protect Jill, while he took the heat for it, well, it's hard to fault him for that.

Deron Hillis is in jail after all. He's not a murderer or a rapist, just the same idiot who moved out of my home state and unwittingly followed me to Drayton. Somedays I think it was he who got Lawrence into my apartment, B&E expert that he is, but with Lawrence himself dead, I'll never know. With the college itself under renewed scrutiny and Hillis's conduit to a campus full of potential victims terminated, he decided to return to his former occupation: robber. He pistol-whipped a local convenience store owner who, sadly for Hillis, had recently emigrated from Bosnia. A simple robbery became a hate crime—it doesn't appear that Deron Hillis will be matriculating anytime soon. I don't doubt for one second his willingness to take a human life under the right circumstances—but it was Joe Lawrence who killed my friend, and Joe Lawrence who left Melanie Johns to die on that frozen trail. Hillis may belong in jail, but Joseph Lawrence belongs right where he is.

The other day I went back and checked my files on the wind turbine story and you know, I did a pretty thorough job—references to property purchases, sightline disruptions, noise factors—it's all there—and with it is the actual *Courier* from that week alongside the issue with the retraction. It didn't identify the original source as a former classmate whose eyes seldom rose above my chest in a Portland bar that night, and whose hands behaved in a similar manner later. Anyway, yes, a pretty thorough job. But I remember Grumman's admonition about being *pretty* careful—it isn't good enough. Then again he also reminded me that lots of things can go wrong in a project like that, and that maybe I'm not solely to blame. "It's not always about you," he said. I hope he's right.

*****

It's every journalist's dream to break the big story, but I'd be lying if I overplayed my magnanimity. I'm still no Albert Schweitzer (Grumman would enjoy hearing me say that) but I'm not some immoral hack either. When I was still in high school a reporter in Bangor uncovered a child pornography ring working out of the Capitol in Augusta. Then came the now-commonplace seizing of computers and high-profile arrests—standard fare—except one of the accused was a single mother, and if that wasn't sick enough, she had been padding the user groups with photos of her own son and daughter. While awaiting trial she took her estranged husband's hunting rifle and shot both children and then herself. She survived, as did her daughter. Her eight-year-old son did not. The reporter who broke the story spent the next few months seeing a grief counselor on a weekly basis, convinced that he was responsible for the death of that child.

Nobody talks much about journalistic responsibility these days, not when a reputation can be ruined by an impulsive tweet or an irresponsible blog entry or a well placed leak, but it still exists; and I'm coming to terms with the fact that my wind turbine story, as professional sounding as it may have been, served no purpose but mine.

This afternoon in work I got a call from Officer Trumbull, the one who guided me home the night I was followed. The police are running some youth basketball tournament and they're hoping for free publicity, maybe a photo or two. Arlene's nephew is decent with a camera, she can Photoshop away most of his worst glitches, and Teddy can do the rest. I told him we'd do it. It's the kind of request Karl Brandt would ordinarily make, but he seems to be weaning himself off the *Courier* and its employees—at least one of them. I ask Trumbull if Detective Brandt is available.

"He's at a meeting with county detectives and won't be back at his desk until 5:00."

Trumbull does such a poor reading of his lines that I feel bad for him, forced to lie for a colleague. I let the poor guy off the hook and drive to the station. Brandt is, of course, at his desk, almost hidden behind a scattering of papers that has somehow grown deeper.

"How was your detective's meeting?"

"We got out early."

"Nothing to detect?"

"Not as much as you might think. What's up?"

"I just wanted you to know I visited Jill Dennison a few days ago."

He nods but says nothing.

"You don't want to know how she is?"

He shrugs. "I know she left town. So how is she?"

"Terrible."

He seems surprised.

"I thought she was just, you know, resting."

"She told me a story. Want to hear it?"

"I've heard it."

"And?"

"She's been in Five Willows numerous times, and she's been there for a reason. I think that speaks to her credibility."

"I believed her."

"I don't have a problem with that."

"Is it true?"

"Is what true?"

"Karl, please. Did she shoot Joe Lawrence?"

He reaches into his desk, pulls out a sheath of photocopies, and tosses them on the desk.

"This is the result of my need to fire a weapon. Do you think I'd fill these out for fun?"

"You didn't answer my question."

"You didn't answer mine."

I thought maybe we had gone beyond the old Brandt, but he's back and just as pissy as ever. But it's a different me. And though it's hard to have a private conversation in that station house, I'm resolved to try.

"Listen, Karl." I lower my voice to a whisper. "We slept together, remember? And we were going to dinner that night—that very night. Now none of that means fuck-all anymore now that you have your cool new life in your cool new apartment, but at least you can treat me like a human being when I come in here with a simple question."

"Fuck-all? I'm not familiar with that term."

He's smiling.

"It's not funny," I tell him. Except it is, I don't know what it means either—it was merely a return to my glorious days of continuous cursing when my friend Abigail was mentoring me. But I won't laugh, or return the smile.

"You win, detective. I'll send Teddy over with a camera."

I stand up to leave but he stops me.

"Let me ask you a question, Coop. Let's say Jill Dennison, nutcase that she is, that everybody knows she is...let's say this time she is telling the truth. Then what?"

"Then we'll know the truth."

"And then do I arrest her? I mean I could pile up weapons charges on top of weapons charges on top of trespassing and assault, maybe even B&E—we could lock her up for a long time. She'd certainly lose her real estate license. Is that what you want?"

"You know it's not. I just think people need to know the facts so that they can make a judgment."

"Let me put this in your terms: fuck the people and their judgment. Jill Dennison isn't running for President. She's just a person who got caught up in some bad shit, some of it my doing and some of it yours and some of it her sister's and none of it hers. Why does everyone have to know?"

"So it's true then."

"I'll tell you what's true: for some reason, and believe me I don't know why, she thinks enough of you to share her version of what happened. I don't think she trusts many people."

"And she trusts you."

"A little, at least enough to know I'll do right by her. Now why don't you do the same?"

"It's going to come out eventually, isn't it? You'll lose your job."

"I can't see Jill publicly contradicting my story, and I can't see people believing her if she does. And let's face it, the tale of a trigger-happy cop is more commonplace than that of a person with a gun defending a friend. And the commonplace is good."

"No it isn't."

He smiles. "I may not have Teddy's extensive semester of journalism training, but even I know that much. You put that vigilante story out there and the war begins: why does someone like Jill Dennison have a gun? vs. thank God Jill Dennison had that gun. And the whole Second Amendment debate begins and meanwhile your friend and my friend are still dead. You think you know what happened? Okay, let that be what happened. You have a newspaper—run with it."

"But an investigation…."

"A full-scale investigation will prove that the weapon that killed Joe Lawrence belongs to Jill. It'll also probably find hair and clothing samples that put her in that room and certainly prove that I fired my weapon two hours later in the woods behind my house—my former house—before I turned it in. These forensics people—they're incredible, don't miss a trick. But currently forensics is telling the story of a cop who fired on a violent man intent on doing grave bodily harm and removed him from society."

"So you colluded."

"Oh, man, yes, we colluded. The only debate is whether I'm a murderer or a hero, but nobody thinks I'm lying. Why not leave it that way?"

"They're protecting you."

"No, they're just not borrowing trouble," he says. "You can't restore the world to balance—you know that—but at least you can keep it spinning smoothly on some new axis."

"What? Karl, that's not you talking, is it?"

"No."

"It's Melanie, right?"

"Yes, when she said she couldn't see me anymore. She was talking about herself, about what it would be like to go back and make a go of it with her husband. It was the right thing to do. So on this new axis a murderer is dead and a bad guy is back in jail and you're alive and well. Why fuck it up?"

"…As I might put it."

"Exactly."

"I suppose now I have to thank you for being honest."

"I know everything is on the record with you…."

"That isn't true."

"So if you want to track that Pulitzer and launch a ten-part article on who killed Joseph Lawrence, I can't stop you. It'll sell papers and maybe land you a better job."

"And cost you yours."

He scans the heap of papers at his desk, the paint chipping from the walls, the watermarks on the ceiling.

"I can probably live with that."

"No you couldn't. Besides, absolute truth is a very rare and dangerous commodity."

He looks impressed. "Your new philosophy?"

"It probably should be."

We part with no agreement to meet anytime soon, no promise to keep in touch, nothing to indicate we'd ever been more than casual acquaintances. And maybe that's the way it should be: he didn't protect Jill because she's my friend: he did it because she's Melanie's sister.

Brandt's a good cop and a decent friend, but he's still in mourning. I could add that he's a patient and gentle lover who made me feel special that one night, but until he comes to terms with Melanie's death, I'll have to go back to feeling pretty plain. I don't know if I can ever admit to him my role in this whole sorry mess. I don't want to—and Grumman wouldn't either if he were alive. For him there were always too many butterflies flapping too many wings in an endlessly chaotic world: there was never a simple reason for anything.

Chapter 33

Last weekend in Cambridge Yasmin Maskhadova organized an art exhibit with maybe a half-dozen local painters. After Lawrence's death when his picture was everywhere, I phoned her to see if he had been the one in the garage that day at the museum. The police had already done that. She said she wasn't sure, that everything had happened so fast that day, but she invited me to the exhibit. When I arrived I found her talking to a slightly disheveled but awfully good-looking young man standing behind a makeshift bar pouring wine for the guests. He didn't wear a name tag, but I knew him: the senator's kid, crazy driver. Did I mention he was awfully good-looking?

I walked around a little, checked out a few of her paintings, then when she was alone went over to say hello. I'm still not enamored of her work, but she was beaming: there was a red dot next to one of her oils—her rent would be paid for at least another month or two.

"The dude pouring drinks," I said. "I thought you…"

She didn't let me finish.

"Ben drives better now, or I don't ride in his car. Want to meet him?"

"He looks pretty busy."

"You have boyfriend, don't you?"

"Kind of, but not really."

"That is funny answer. Ben has friends, nice men. You will call me if you are, what is it, unattached?"

I told her I would, though I don't see how anyone could be more unattached than I am. I left anyway. If I'd stayed I would have slid my reporter's cap back on and questioned Ben Talbot about the man in the garage. And really, at this point why bother? He had Yasmin and she had him and some creep intending to do her harm was the furthest thing from their minds.

Teddy, who occasionally used to accompany me to events like this, now has a girlfriend. I guess it was bound to happen eventually, and actually he's cooler about it than I thought he might be—no starry-eyed looks or blushing when he mentions her name: Caroline, a local kid who works as an assistant manager at a credit union. I guess he went to school with her, lost touch, regained it. He seems happy enough, and I'm losing weight by consuming less pizza, though as a regular-by-proxy at Mattera's, I do drop by on occasion. I'm not jealous of this Caroline—Teddy was never the one for me despite all these dumb stories about the one you love being right under your nose. If he were, I'd have known it. I wish I were as settled as he suddenly seems, but that's as far as my envy extends.

We don't talk about Lawrence's murder very much, and I hardly ever mention Teddy's online investigation cadre. Maybe he was too close to the seamy side of life to find that profession attractive anymore, or maybe he's keeping a low profile because he knows I feel that way.

Somehow the *Courier* retained its advertisers—no one left us, not even Chalmers College. Irony doesn't have to be funny, and with all the pain and heartache, this is one of those times. The three of us all mucking in together did leave a leadership vacuum, so Arlene has agreed to "run things" on an interim basis—two years, tops—provided we can utilize our journalism teacher/reporter, Wilcox, from the high school. He's stretched thin, but he's pretty energetic so it may work out. He's also informally providing Teddy with his second journalism course within the casual conversations the two of them sometimes have. Things are holding together.

*****

I checked some travel app on my cell this morning—I wanted to see how much closer my parents were to me than Jill was. Thirty miles. Immediately I felt guilty, called home, and set the timer on my laptop. Five minutes of friendly conversation with my mother. It wasn't that difficult, but sure enough we began drifting toward the Joe Lawrence murder and became typically uncommunicative. Or maybe I did. Before she could ascribe it to anything other than what it was—our usual strained relationship—I told her I had an interviewee walk in and I had to hang up. Interviewees don't walk in, of course—something she might know if she had any interest in what I do. Fixing things at home is going to take a long time and I'm not sure I have the time or the energy...or (and I understand this too) the desire. Baggage, Jill called it. I'll be jettisoning it slowly.

I do feel lonely at times. I have some friends back in Maine and we keep up with each other on Facebook, but my postings are so far removed from the realities of my life—of the world—that I derive little joy from seeing someone's cat typing on a laptop or a fancy dessert in some upscale restaurant. They don't know about Lawrence, about Grumman, about Brandt, about the blunder I made that set everything in motion. And they won't know. I won't let them.

I didn't have a steady boyfriend before Brandt, and I guess not during Brandt either, so it isn't that. I can't even say I miss Teddy as a friend, not since he and Caroline—not once but twice—have asked me over to her place for a drink. So I have Teddy and I have his girlfriend; in other words, I feel lonely. There are those who would say that Grumman would have died a happy man if he could have married me off, that I was like a daughter to this man who had not fathered any children. Let me just say this: Grumman had no intention of dying either a happy man or otherwise, and I'll never get over the belief that someone in that hospital fucked up—someone who was supposed to be monitoring him went off for a smoke or traipsed down to the cafeteria for a coffee and missed the fact that his heart stopped beating. Arlene keeps telling me to let it go, that first off I'm not an investigative journalist, and second, if I were to undertake such an investigation, the time commitment would kill every other assignment on my schedule for months. One day I pushed her too far..

"So let's say you investigate," she yelled. "And in the end, what would it prove? Negligence? Not likely. The man had lung cancer, Bree. He died of lung cancer. His death certificate says lung cancer. Was there negligence? Yes. He shouldn't have smoked."

A few minutes later she apologized for yelling, but she was right. I never brought it up again.

It's been a half year but I miss Abby. I don't visit her husband anymore—he's getting better and doesn't need me to remind him of his previous life. I did bump into Marcus Johns at the mall in Natick one day and we talked for a moment, but he didn't invite me by to reminisce either. Both he and Andrew need to get on with things—to settle in on some new axis. So my world consists of the *Courier*, an occasional Margarita festival with the Willises downstairs (Betsy had her baby—a girl—and they're looking for a house so they'll be moving away soon enough), and diminishing numbers of nightmares about the time Joseph Lawrence tried to murder me.

Things are beginning to work out for people, but they're all people who have been through unimaginable loss. Me? I suffered a few moments of terror one afternoon and had some surgery. I lost nothing—not by comparison. And I am, after all, alive. As for the loneliness, that's on me, and I can either keep bitching about it or do something. I'm going to do something.

Last week the *Courier* started running an ad for that exercise chain on Route 9—the one Jill mentioned when she presumed we were going to be friends and I told her we weren't. The place is running a trial program cheap, and before I even leave for work today I'm on the phone to Five Willows. Deborah Saunders remembers me and puts me through to Jill who immediately assumes somebody died.

"Everything is fine," I tell her, opting not to bring up my discussion with Brandt or my recent failed attempt at family rapprochement. "When are you getting out of there?"

"We go into town tomorrow, then the following...."

"I mean for good. When?"

"That's up to me. Why do you want to know? Are you hiring?"

"You already have a job."

"O yeah, Van Real Estate, formerly Jay-Van."

"It's still Jay-Van. I just spoke with Vanessa. She's waiting for you to come back."

"Yeah, well..."

"Listen, that fitness place out on Route 9, remember you mentioned it once?"

"You wanted nothing to do with it," she says.

"That's not true. I just...I'm putting on some weight."

"You can't lie to me if we're going to be friends. You wanted nothing to do with it."

"You're right."

"And it's funny," she said, "'cause it's not like you're in such great shape."

"Let's not push the honesty thing, Ms. pack-a-day."

"Point taken. So what about this fitness place?"

"I was thinking, if you can go without a cigarette long enough to ride a stationary bike, there's a good introductory offer. I can sign us up."

She says nothing for a second or two, and when she finally speaks, her voice sounds softer.

"My rubber room is paid up through the end of this week."

"That's fine—maybe next week."

"Money isn't an issue. It's just that…."

She seems hesitant. I know that there are people who find sanctuary and stability in places like Five Willows and I don't want to rob her of that.

"If you feel you aren't ready…."

"Hell no, I'm ready. But it's Wednesday. We have prime rib on Wednesdays—can you believe in a place like this they….. "

"Are you serious? You'd stay locked up for a slab of beef?"

"I'm here for a reason, remember? Crazy? Do I have to read you those pamphlets?"

I know she's laughing, and I have this image of the entire staff and every patient at Five Willows gathered around Jill (who probably has me on speaker) waiting to hear what she'll say next. And if that's true, good for her.

"The pamphlets won't help. How about tomorrow, after the prime rib?"

"Sure? I can't think of any real reason to stay after that."

"What do you do when you want to leave? Just put in your notice?"

"I don't have to. I have keys for everything. Of course I'm going to need a ride, and that means we'd be stuck in the car together for two hours—are you ready for that?"

"We can take smoking breaks if you need to."

"That's not what I meant, Coop—you don't mind if I call you Coop, do you?"

"No."

"Remember what I said about lying?"

"I used to mind."

"That's better —now what about that long ride?"

It won't bother me. I actually want to understand her—I don't know if I've ever done that with anyone. I have the feeling that I'll come to understand Melanie too—Melanie, who seems more persuasive and influential in death than I've ever been in life. It's not that I want to figure her out in order to win over Brandt—things like that are beyond my control—but I just want to know her. She struggled and fought and overcame things—I tend to sit around and rail about my job and my family life and the fact that I have no friends.

And as for that long ride, actually I have a longer one in mind sometime in the near future. North, past where I grew up. Past Bangor, not far from the Canadian border where, though it's nearly June, traces of snow probably remain in the deeper woods and, in one place at least, and for one person, there is no passage of time. Up beyond 95, beyond the Maine Turnpike, where secondary roads carry drivers north past Caribou, stands the Thomas Lipscomb Institute. It sounds like a degree-granting college, but it isn't. It's the place where my brother Daniel watches intervals of darkness and light meld into some semblance of time. I don't know if I'll ever be able to go there with my parents, but maybe I can practice alone first. And though I know Jill Dennison hardly at all, and though our initial dealings were mostly tense and combative, I know she'd come with me. But first I have to transport her back to where she belongs, back to Drayton and Vanessa and Jay-Van and the life that she's convinced is driving her crazy and I'm convinced is keeping her sane .

"I'll fill the gas tank and be there tomorrow," I say, "unless it's all-you-can-eat lobster lunch day."

"Tomorrow? If it is, these bastards haven't told me. Tell you what, even if it is, I'll tag along with you. Give me a time."

She doesn't sound reticent: she sounds excited—if that word can apply to her.

"It'll have to be late afternoon."

"After tea. Too bad—you drink tea, don't you?"

And she laughs—an actual laugh devoid of cynicism and anger. I don't think she's been "cured" of all her issues by spending a month or two in the Berkshires; if they performed those kinds of miracles, I'd give it a try. Even so, I can sense a difference. The man who murdered her sister is dead, and though layers of anger may still reside in her psyche—many of them going back decades—at least one of them has been stripped away.

"Late afternoon," she says. "I can wait."

So tomorrow then. I'm going to break somebody out of an asylum, just like McMurphy in *Cuckoo's Nest*. My dad would like that—it's one of our movies—though he'd be concerned because it's not the kind of thing a young woman should do alone. If I asked Teddy, he'd accompany me of course, but he and Jill had a business relationship and she might feel uncomfortable. And Brandt who probably saved her from prosecution may not feel like socializing, especially since the whole affair cost him. So it's me...and one other passenger.

"Arlene," I say to her when she has a mouthful of coffee so that she can't reflexively say no. "Want to take a ride tomorrow?"

"With?"

"Me. After work."

"To?"

"Pittsfield."

"That's on the other side of the state," she says. "What's in Pittsfield?"

"I have to pick up a friend."

"I thought Teddy was your friend. You couldn't possibly have more than one."

"Don't you even want to know who the friend is?"

"I don't want to interfere...."

"I know what happened."

If someone said that to me—even if nothing had happened—I'd be inclined to think something did, but Arlene has had many years to develop that cool detachment.

"Could you be more specific?"

"In my apartment that day when Joe Lawrence was killed. I know how it went down."

"Went down? You're starting to sound like Teddy."

"Don't change the subject."

"Tell me what the subject actually is and I won't change it."

"Okay," I said. I wasn't angry. "We don't have to talk about it now or ever, but I know...and I'll have a talk with Teddy when the time is right."

"And you'll warn him about all this detective crap? As a friend, not a co-worker."

I tell her I will. She understands office politics and discretion and minding one's own business. I can't hold that against her because, if Teddy screws up as a journalist, Arlene will be all over him; but his personal life is still his.

"And this odyssey to Pittsfield," she says, "what's that all about?"

"Jill Dennison is there. As you know."

"I may have heard that. Finally going to pay her back for the teapot?"

"I am. I'm going to break her out of the asylum."

"It's not the kind of gift I'd select, but I'm not a hip, young person like you."

"Hip enough."

"Why do you need me there?"

"Moral support."

"Do we need masks? Do I dress in all black?"

"Masks can put people off. You look good in black?"

"I look pretty good in anything. Do we leave at dawn?"

I remind her that we both have jobs—in the same office, actually—and that we cannot blow off a day of work any more, not if we wish to maintain future days of work.

"Late afternoon," I tell her.

"Listen, this little caper of yours—Jill is okay with it? She wants out?"

"She doesn't belong there."

Arlene sits back and folds her arms.

"If I could just point something out," she says. "There are several areas in which your knowledge is limited—I can't believe mental health isn't one of them."

"She doesn't belong there, Arlene, and yes, she's okay with it. She would have left earlier but it's prime rib day."

"See," Arlene says, "that's the kind of statement that makes me think maybe neither one of you is ready to come home. Then again I'm far too well-balanced to comprehend mental illness—I only wish I could."

"Maybe riding in a car with Jill and me will expand your consciousness...help you empathize with the rest of us. When it comes to mental issues, I think we all have our share."

I'm thinking of my mother when I say that, unfair as that may be. Is she the one I should be rescuing, does she even want to be rescued, is there a pamphlet for her?

"Well I'll go with you," she says, "if only to keep you out of trouble."

Teddy's arrival with Caroline suspends our discussion—he doesn't need to hear about some caper or he'll put on his PI hat again—it's a hat that would only, eventually, get him killed. And speaking of hats, he still wears that Bruins cap, dishonestly ingratiating himself to the locals and maybe to Caroline. I should really have that talk with him, and sooner than later.

But not now—I have enough of my own baggage to jettison first, and I've hardly begun.

www.ingramcontent.com/pod-product-compliance
Lightning Source LLC
Chambersburg PA
CBHW030352120726
47901CB00007B/1995